A RAKE'S PROPOSAL

"I am a wealthy man now, Harriet. Marry me and spend it as you will," he suggested quietly.

Harriet clutched at the side of the carriage. She swallowed. Hard. Oh, she *must* keep this light, as teasing toward him as he must mean to be with her. "Is that a proposal, Sir Frederick?" she questioned, a lilt forced into her voice and a smile to her lips.

A flush spread across Sir Frederick's cheekbones. "As gauche and awkward a proposal as a woman ever received, I fear, but yes. I'm quite seriously asking you to marry me."

Her hand tightened over the wood at the side of the carriage. He *couldn't* be serious. "I cannot believe this."

"That I wish to wed you?"

"But *why*? Why *me?*"

Harriet worked hard to control her feelings. How *could* he do this to her? Or had he somehow guessed at those ridiculous emotions she couldn't quite control whenever he was near? Had he decided she'd be easy prey? Did he think to lure her into his web with a pretended engagement? Undoubtedly, for one reason or another, an engagement which was to be kept a secret between themselves? Knowing she wouldn't be easy game, he'd very likely realized he'd need some stratagem to get her into his bed, and if she were to succumb? He'd only throw her aside when something better came on the scene . . . except that, surely, better game *was* available?

Oh, if only she understood the man!

ELEGANT LOVE STILL FLOURISHES —
Wrap yourself in a Zebra Regency Romance.

A MATCHMAKER'S MATCH   (3783, $3.50/$4.50)
by Nina Porter

To save herself from a loveless marriage, Lady Psyche Veringham pretends to be a bluestocking. Resigned to spinsterhood at twenty-three, Psyche sets her keen mind to snaring a husband for her young charge, Amanda. She sets her cap for long-time bachelor, Justin St. James. This man of the world has had his fill of frothy-headed debutantes and turns the tables on Psyche. Can a bluestocking and a man about town find true love?

FIRES IN THE SNOW   (3809, $3.99/$4.99)
by Janis Laden

Because of an unhappy occurrence, Diana Ruskin knew that a secure marriage was not in her future. She was content to assist her physician father and follow in his footsteps . . . until now. After meeting Adam, Duke of Marchmaine, Diana's precise world is shattered. She would simply have to avoid the temptation of his gentle touch and stunning physique—and by doing so break her own heart!

FIRST SEASON   (3810, $3.50/$4.50)
by Anne Baldwin

When country heiress Laetitia Biddle arrives in London for the Season, she harbors dreams of triumph and applause. Instead, she becomes the laughingstock of drawing rooms and ballrooms, alike. This headstrong miss blames the rakish Lord Wakeford for her miserable debut, and she vows to rise above her many faux pas. Vowing to become an Original, Letty proves that she's more than a match for this eligible, seasoned Lord.

AN UNCOMMON INTRIGUE   (3701, $3.99/$4.99)
by Georgina Devon

Miss Mary Elizabeth Sinclair was rather startled when the British Home Office employed her as a spy. Posing as "Tasha," an exotic fortune-teller, she expected to encounter unforeseen dangers. However, nothing could have prepared her for Lord Eric Stewart, her dashing and infuriating partner. Giving her heart to this haughty rogue would be the most reckless hazard of all.

A MADDENING MINX   (3702, $3.50/$4.50)
by Mary Kingsley

After a curricle accident, Miss Sarah Chadwick is literally thrust into the arms of Philip Thornton. While other women shy away from Thornton's eyepatch and aloof exterior, Sarah finds herself drawn to discover why this man is physically and emotionally scarred.

Available wherever paperbacks are sold, or order direct from the Publisher. Send cover price plus 50¢ per copy for mailing and handling to Penguin USA, P.O. Box 999, c/o Dept. 17109, Bergenfield, NJ 07621. Residents of New York and Tennessee must include sales tax. DO NOT SEND CASH.

A Reformed Rake

Jeanne Savery

ZEBRA BOOKS
KENSINGTON PUBLISHING CORP.

ZEBRA BOOKS are published by

Kensington Publishing Corp.
475 Park Avenue South
New York, NY 10016

First Printing: March, 1994

Printed in the United States of America

Special thanks to Annick for her patience. Merci, Annick.

For simply being themselves, this book is dedicated to Willa and Margot.

Prologue

Hortense de St. Onge, Comtesse de Beaupré stared down her aristocratic nose at Miss Harriet Cole, her granddaughter's companion and music teacher. Harriet stared back in a composed way. The silence stretched.

"I cannot believe you suggested that. Not *seriously*, Harri." The old woman chuckled. "Not that it would *hurt* our young lady to retire to a convent for a repairing lease! Is that correct, repairing lease?"

"Quite correct, Madame, assuming you mean a period of time during which one recovers from a hectic social season, rather than the meaning which implies an escape from one's creditors until the dibs are in tune again—dibs, Madame," she continued with a perfectly straight face, "is cant for money and if they are in tune, then one has some."

"Thank you," said Madame la Comtesse in an amused tone.

Harriet Cole grinned. "But Madame, if Françoise were at the convent, the comte could not continue to harass her! Or us, of course." A thoughtful look crossed Harriet's face. "Perhaps I *was* serious!"

"But, my dear, can you not imagine the poor Sisters'

7

state of mind after Françoise had been there several days? No, no, it would never do. The poor dears would never recover from the responsibility of caring for our Frani!"

The two women laughed comfortably. One was well up in years, having survived the French Revolution and Madame Guillotine and since, in exile, the years of war. Gradually, exile had changed from a temporary retreat to something which was truly home. Madame's palazzo on Lake Como was both elegant and comfortable, and she loved it.

The other lady seated on the terrace overlooking the water was a youngish woman, in her middle twenties and, in the eyes of the world, no more than a hired companion and music teacher for the old woman's granddaughter. Yet they understood each other very well and each found amusement in the company of the other.

After a long moment, Harriet asked, "Do you have a plan, Madame?"

Madame la Comtesse nodded, a sad expression blurring the strong lines of her face. Again the silence stretched, but Harriet waited patiently. She'd lived five years in the de Beaupré household and knew that Madame would explain eventually. At a minimum she would tell Harriet what was needed and, from that, Harriet would extrapolate the rest. Or as much as possible.

"I exaggerated when I said I had a plan," began Madame. "What I have decided is that our Frani needs a male guardian. As much as you and I love her, Harriet, we are women and the comte discounts our ability to guard her."

"But you have said there are none—outside of third and fourth cousins, few of whom you know and none of whom have the necessary authority."

"That is on our side of the family, Harriet. What I have not discussed is her mother's."

Harriet faced another high-nosed stare. This one she thought contained a question. "Her mother?" prodded Harriet, wondering where the conversation would now lead.

Madame dipped her chin, nodding in a stately way. "My daughter-in-law," she said.

Harriet nodded in much the same manner, suppressing an imminent smile. Of course Frani's mother was Madame's daughter-in-law! But that, she knew was not the point. Madame was finding it difficult to discuss the woman.

"You wish to laugh at my lack of explanation," said that perceptive lady. "It is because I do not know where to begin or how to ask the questions I wish to ask that I cannot yet explain."

"Madame, you are insulting," said Harriet, mildly scolding. "Do you not know me well enough, after all these years, to know I am discreet and will be as honest with you as I can?" Somehow she needed to help the old woman relax and confide in her. If there were a way they might prevent the persecution the comte visited on their small household, they should immediately set it in motion.

"You are right. But it is embarrassing to admit a father disinherited his daughter merely for marrying into one's family."

"Into *your* family? But it is one of the oldest lines in France! And you managed to extricate most of the family fortune from France before the Terror came. How could anyone object to such a marriage?" Harriet shook her head. "I do not believe it," she said in a no-nonsense manner.

9

"Nevertheless, that is what Frani's grandfather did. Would he, one wonders, visit his anger on his granddaughter? Or would he take her in hand and protect her from that villain?"

"Since I've no clue as to whom her grandfather is, how may I answer you? For that matter, how may I be of help in any case? I am unfamiliar with most of the French aristocracy."

"But he is *not* French. I thought you knew."

"Not French?"

"He is English."

"Ah. Well, I do know a few amongst the English *ton*. We proceed."

"I am aware you spent nearly the whole of your life at various embassies, but you will have heard the gossip and you will have learned the relationships amongst the English *ton*." Madame fell silent again.

"I erred," Harriet said lightly. "We don't proceed at all. Madame, would you be pleased to inform me of the name of the British aristocrat so proud he would deny your family's right to marry into his?"

"Have I not?" A faint color touched Madame's cheeks. "Oh dear. I am not usually such a flutter-brain. That is right? Flutter-brain?"

"Or skitter-witted or addle-pated," said Harriet absently. She leaned forward and grasped the old woman's trembling hand. "Madame, is it so hard to say his name?"

After a moment Madame spate out, "Lord Crawford."

Harriet jerked back, her sleepy grey eyes widening. "Crawford! But Madame, that is impossible. His daughter died in . . ." Harriet did some quick calculations. "Why, it was the year before our Frani was born! I was only five."

"She didn't die. She married my son in the year before

Françoise was born." Wise old eyes caught and held Harriet's. "I told you. His lordship disinherited her. Why did you think her dead?"

Harriet's lips firmed, anger growing within her. "Madame, she and my mother were in school together. Even though I was very young when the news came, I remember Mother's tears and how she mourned. They were friends as well as cousins, you see."

Madame la Comtesse reared back in shock. "Your *cousin. Mon Dieu!* For five years I have treated a connection of the family as a servant!"

Harriet chuckled. "Madame, if you were to treat all your servants as you and Frani do myself, then we would be one big happy family, would we not? The relationship to Crawford is not close. In one way or another most of the British *ton* is related. But that doesn't answer the question of whether his lordship would protect his granddaughter." Harriet frowned. "Madame, if we could give him a story which he could give the *ton,* I believe he would do so. He has a reputation of being quick-tempered—which would easily explain his disinheriting his daughter—but also he is thought to be an intelligent man. I suspect he regretted that rash moment." Harri paused for thought. "What," she said, in a dreamy way, "if, on her deathbed, your daughter-in-law regained her memory?"

"Regained her memory?" Madame la Comtesse might have been said to gape at the notion, except, of course, she was far too aristocratic to do any such thing. "Harri, dear," she said politely, "my daughter-in-law never *lost* her memory."

"Oh, I'm sure she must have. After almost drowning—did I say that, according to her father, she drowned in a Channel crossing? Anyway, I think your son rescued her

11

from a watery grave, and they fell in love—but she never remembered who she was or where she'd come from. They married, lived happily, had Frani and then . . . the accident! At very nearly the moment of her death, your daughter-in-law told you the story of her life and, of course, who she was. You, loving Frani, came to what must be admitted was a rather selfish decision. You did not inform Lord Crawford of his daughter's death. After all, he'd thought her dead for a very long time—why add the pain of knowing he might have had more years with her when he no longer could?"

"How is that selfish, Harri?" asked Madame, picking up on the one point Harriet had hoped she'd miss.

"Why, in not telling the man of his daughter's life, you have avoided telling him of his granddaughter as well."

"Hmm. But now, when I need him to protect her, I come crawling to him and ask his forgiveness?"

The high-nosed stare didn't discommode Harriet, who chuckled. "Come down off your high horse, Madame. This is a game. And, as a game, it may be modified. Perhaps we could sacrifice my distant cousin, your daughter-in-law? Recently you found a diary in which she admits to regaining her memory, but remembers that her father told her that if she married her own true love he'd disinherit her, and she decided she would not contact him."

"Hmm. But wouldn't he wish to see the diary?"

"You burned it, of course. There was much in it you would not want your granddaughter to read."

Hortense de St. Onge, Comtesse de Beaupré was silent for a very long time. "How fortuitous," she said, at last, "that I chanced upon that diary."

One

Two men rode up out of Italy and into an Alpine valley. On all sides the musical rushing of falling melt sang a song of approaching summer. The steep green hillsides were dotted with the pale hides of brown milch cows, the clitter and clang of cowbells sounding now and again as the herd moved slowly from one patch of flower-starred growth to the next. Above all, the peaks, an eye-blinding white, were covered with eternal snow and ice.

One of the two travelers was somewhat older than the other. His broad shoulders were set off by a well-tailored coat and, as he scanned the heights with eyes protected by heavy lids, he brushed thumb and fore-finger across the moustache he affected although such was not in style. Then he brushed back wind-ruffled wings of white at his temples and resettled his hat. His eyes passed over the gentle scene, and he sighed, a sound denoting contentment.

Last autumn he'd been right to leave Paris and move on to Italy. Now, after months in Italy he was returning to England and this incredible scenery was what his soul craved. Clear air was mountain cool and clean vistas

13

soothing where Italy had merely amused and, last fall, the frantic pace of Parisian society had exacerbated the ache in his battered heart. *This* would surely finish his healing!

Ah, the wounds Eros inflicted on one! He had predicted that dark Roman beauties or those of Florence would provide the final cure, but they had not. Not entirely. Not that he ached as he had last summer. No, the wounds were thoroughly covered with scar tissue. They hurt now only when the tilt of a pert head or a friendly wide-eyed smile would remind him of the woman he'd left in England—in the arms of his best friend.

Love, decided Sir Frederick Carrington, was not at all what he'd assumed it to be during the nearly twenty years he'd played at it and teased it, but hadn't really believed in it. When it came, pain came, too. The pain was deepened by the finality of his selfless decision to put his lady's happiness before his own: He'd given her up to the man she loved. He sighed again, but this time with a touch of irritation.

Forcing the past from his thoughts, he allowed the awesome terrain to fill his mind, his very soul, with a peace he craved. The two men rode gently, not pushing their mounts as their way rose northward, and ever higher, toward the Simplon Pass. Sharp curves in the road built at Napoleon's orders, when he required a better route into Italy, carried them back and forth, and gradually, nearer the top. There was no hurry—the small carriage provided for their luggage and the comfort of their valets would necessarily fall behind on the grades. Tall trees surrounded them now, but the mountainside was so steep they often looked through the tops of gently swaying branches, even, occasionally, over their tops.

"You are a silent companion today, Frederick."

" 'Tis like a cathedral, Yves, have you not noticed? The mountains demand silence of me."

"I was not aware you loved the Church so well, my friend." Yves' dry humor was accompanied by twinkling eyes. In answer Frederick flicked a smile toward the young man.

Some months earlier Frederick had rescued Monsieur Yves de Bartigues from a pair of cutthroats in a narrow Paris street. Yves had won heavily that evening. When the young man left the card party, Frederick, too, had been collecting his cloak, hat, and the antique sword stick he'd begun carrying when he'd been a counter-spy in British service. Acquaintances, but hardly friends, the two men strolled along the boulevard, their way the same for some distance. Then, stopping only for brief farewells, they'd taken different routes.

Moments later Sir Frederick heard an outcry, and returning, found Yves defending his person and his purse from a pretty pair of ruffians. The villains were sent fleeing and a bond formed between the young Frenchman of twenty-three and Frederick, who had recently passed his thirty-seventh birthday. The odd friendship grew to the extent that Yves insisted he accompany Frederick when, tired of Paris, the latter decided to continue his exploration of a Europe freed from all threat of Napoleon's ambition—a Europe which was finally at peace after more than twenty years of war.

"Do you think we'll run into bandits, Frederick? The innkeeper was so very insistent that they are a constant menace."

The thought jarred, and Frederick winced. "Do not, pray, sound as though the adventure were one to be desired, Yves. I feel much too pleasant to exert myself so. Don't you think that, if our host had had his way, we'd have waited, perhaps for days, to join a large party—spending our coin freely at his inn while we did so?"

"You are a cynic, Frederick. But if you truly believe the landlord was telling tales to frighten children, then why are we prepared to defend ourselves from desperate men?" Yves held up one of the pistols which, primed and ready, rested in a saddle holster. "Ah, I rather wish we would meet up with such! It is just the sort of invigorating day in which I could enjoy ridding the world of one or two desperados."

Frederick hoped it would *not* be necessary. It was much too peaceful. Overwhelmingly peaceful. Beautifully peaceful. Frederick badly needed that sense of peace.

Minutes later the peace was shattered by the sound of a pistol shot and a second. A horse neighed and rough voices, the words indistinguishable, intruded. The sound came from above, around the next curve or perhaps the next. Frederick grimaced. His eyes met Yves' and his mouth turned down at the excitement he saw, the anticipation of adventure. He shrugged and gently lifted his pistol from its saddle holster. He heeled his mount and set it to a faster pace, Yves half a moment before him. They rounded the curve. Three rough-looking men held up a carriage; a fourth, mounted on a showy black gelding and, by his better dress, their leader, waited nearby.

One more shot sounded, followed by the piercing squeal of a wounded animal. The black gelding bucked, nearly unseated his foppishly dressed rider, and broke into a run. Frederick moved his mount to one side as the masked leader tore by. The man leaned into his mount's mane as he grabbed at a dropped rein. For an instant their eyes met, and Frederick shivered: Wild eyes, hating eyes. Eyes glittering with madness? He hoped he never again

16

met those eyes—particularly not in a dark alley some misty night!

He looked ahead to where Yves helped the coachman control a nervous team, glanced around, but found the other villains had melted into the wooded hillside. Pocketing his pistol, he joined Yves and helped settle the sweating horses. Only then did the two men separate, riding back on either side of the carriage. A very fine carriage, noted Sir Frederick, the high wheels picked out in crimson and the varnished panels decorated with gilded wreaths of flowers. There was, as well, an ornate coat of arms painted on the door—French, he thought.

And, from an open window, gleamed the long muzzle of a dueling pistol, the tip shaking ever so slightly.

"Good day, Madame," said Frederick, speaking French to the dim figure holding the pistol. "If that thing is loaded I pray you point it elsewhere."

"Who are you?"

Before he could respond, the woman leaned closer to the window, fine grey eyes narrowed, sharpened. Recognition gleamed in them. He bowed over his saddle, his eyes never leaving the oval face framed by a grey scarf which covered a neat little hat and then wound around her neck. One end moved gently, fluttering against the young woman's slim shoulder. "Sir Frederick Carrington at your service," he said.

A faint gasp parted well-shaped lips. "I couldn't believe my eyes." The pistol steadied, again aiming for his heart, and straight brown-blond eyebrows pulled in to form a vee over wide-open eyes which matched the color of the scarf. The woman went on in English. "You are a friend of Henri," she stated. "You'd best follow after and rescue him." Scorn iced her words. "As you must know, he isn't much of a horseman and . . ." A sob from within

17

the coach interrupted what threatened to be a blistering tirade. "Oh do be still, Frani. I'll not allow Sir Frederick to run off with you."

"You mistake." Frederick allowed only the faintest chill to enter his voice. "I know of no Henri and have no desire to run off with your . . . sister? Put up the pistol now, do, and comfort the poor frightened child."

His gaze slipped beyond the speaker in the window and drifted over a girl who looked to be about seventeen, perhaps eighteen. Dusky curls escaped the close brim of a traveling bonnet, touched the cheeks of a pert little face down which crystalline teardrops rolled one after another. A pretty child, he thought.

"Please cease crying, Mademoiselle," said Frederick with a gentleness which would, once, have been foreign to his nature. "All danger is past. My friend and I will see you safe to your destination."

"Me, I do not cry because we were attacked," said a sweet voice with only the faintest of French accents. The girl's tears ceased abruptly. "I cry because Harriet shot the horse, poor thing, when she meant to kill Henri for me."

"Who is this Henri?"

"Henri de Vauton-Cheviot, Comte de Cheviot. Monsieur le Comte wishes to marry me, and me, I do not wish it at all. He is a horrible man. He wants my fortune and also that our marriage will justify his holding estates in France which were once my family's. He thinks because my father is dead he can force me . . . Oh, Harri, do stop shushing me!" Cherry red lips pouted, an endearing frown creasing the young brow. "Grand-mère, do tell Harri she is not to scold so."

Sir Frederick became aware of the third woman tucked into the far corner of the carriage and felt a strong sense

18

of relief that the two young and attractive women were not traveling alone. "Your servant." Again he bowed over his saddle. "May I offer our protection?"

"Monsieur de Bartigues has done so. We would be pleased to accept." The old woman nodded regally, her English also carrying a faint accent. Despite the situation, she had not lost a jot of the aristocratic bearing bred into her. Whimsically, Frederick thought he could almost see a battalion of ancestors ranked behind the stern-visaged, hawk-faced woman, supporting her and protecting her.

"No, Madame," the one called Harri, whispered loudly—this time in Italian. "You must not. It would be to jump from the pan into the fire . . ."

"Silence, Harriet. I know this young man." One gnarled hand gestured toward the window where Yves bent low over his horse's neck, the better to see into the carriage. A grim smile warped the old mouth. "At least I know his family, which is more than can be said for the comte. One *never* knows with the new aristocracy. They themselves rarely have the least idea. Monsieur de Bartigues and his friend, Sir Frederick, have offered to see us on our way. We will not refuse their offer."

"You do not understand . . ."

Grey eyes, thought Frederick, should never be so cold, a perfectly oval face so severe. The dueling pistol was still pointed directly at his chest, but at least she'd laid her finger along the barrel instead of on what was without doubt a hair trigger! He glanced back to the aged and aristocratic profile; one vein-heavy, age-spotted hand rested easily on her open window. The other was crimped tightly around the top of a cane. That last was the only sign of nerves Frederick could detect. Yves was making headway with the old woman so Frederick returned his attention to the antagonistic face of the one called Harri.

He smiled. If anything, the cool expression iced still more.

The younger girl leaned closer, eyes dry now, but still sparkling with a natural good humor that lit the pert face. "We should introduce ourselves, should we not?" she asked. Dimples showed beside the girl's flashing smile, reminding Frederick painfully of the English love he'd handed, by his own decision, to his friend and rival. "Sir Frederick Carrington—" She gave the rrr's a slight roll that was very attractive. "—that is Grand-mère, Hortense de St. Onge, Comtesse de Beaupré, and be pleased to know my companion, Miss Harriet Cole." Harriet nodded, a stiff forbidding movement that lowered her chin barely an inch, her condemning gaze never leaving his. "And I," said the girl, pointing to herself, "am Mademoiselle Françoise de Beaupré, daughter of Philippe de Reignan, Comte de Beaupré."

"I believe, Mademoiselle, that I am already known, by repute, to Miss Cole." There was wry self-derisive humor in Frederick's tone. "Let it be stated quite clearly, Miss Cole, I am no danger to you or yours. Monsieur de Bartigues and I wish only to be of service." He met her gaze firmly and hers wavered, dropped, and rose to meet his more fiercely than ever. Magnificent, he thought. Proud and courageous and magnificent. "Excuse me," he said, wondering at the strong impression she'd made on him. "I must confer with my friend."

Yves met him at the back of the carriage, his eyes wide with shock. " 'Tis a pretty story, Frederick."

" 'Tis a common story," answered Sir Frederick, thinking of his own attempt to wrest happiness by force. But the abduction he'd plotted and carried out had been based in an honorable emotion. There had been love in his heart which, when he discovered that the object of his affections had given hers elsewhere, thought first of her. The expression he'd seen in the eyes of today's villain had, he felt sure, nothing whatever to do with love. "What is today's destination?"

"Today to Madame's cousin who owns a mountain chalet not far beyond the pass, but on to England by easy stages." Yves indicated the direction of travel. "Frederick, do you know whom we have rescued?"

"*We* rescued?" Frederick flicked open his snuff box, pretended to take a pinch. "I believe Miss Cole had already achieved their rescue. The youngest is a surprisingly bloodthirsty young lady: She is unhappy Miss Cole hit the horse instead of the man!"

Yves laughed. "We ride with them?"

"Yes. I believe we must."

Several hours later Frederick lolled in a hip bath placed conveniently near the fireplace in the room assigned him. A fire had been laid, for, at this altitude at most any time of year, the rooms were slightly chilly. His eyes rested on the windows which framed an unparalleled view of the Aletschhorn and, beyond and to one side, the Jungfrau. Incredible.

He lifted his hand and watched the drops drip from the ends of his fingers as his thoughts drifted to the scene of their arrival at the Swiss chalet. That had been the first surprise, of course. The family might call it a mere chalet, but, by its size and furnishing, it was more of a French château. The second surprise was the warmth of the welcome extended himself and Yves. Miss Cole's expression of horror when he and Yves were invited to break their journey and visit for a few days had been classic. She would never forgive him for accepting. And why had he when he knew he was not wanted—at least, not by one of the party? Oh those expressive eyes!

Ah, his question could be easily answered, could it not? For instance, the accommodations were far better than those he'd expected for this night—their original destination being a flea-ridden hostel on the south side of the mountain, just before one made the final climb to the pass. But, to reach the chalet, they'd already come through the pass. It would be absurd to go back.

And, as Yves reiterated more often than necessary, there was the fact they had no schedule, no definite plans. So why should they not rest a few days in this delightful chalet? There would be trails to explore, perhaps a day's climbing with the husband of the de Beaupré Swiss cousin. Gerard Vaudray was, after all, a noted mountaineer.

So, why should they not? Frederick asked himself again and chuckled as he again remembered the look on Miss Cole's face when the invitation was tendered. He'd like to change that look to quite another, he thought—and then pushed the salacious notion from his mind. Miss Cole might have been reduced to earning her living, but she was still very much a lady. Oh, but those eyes!

No, he would not tamper with her as he might well have done a year or so earlier. It was good he no longer felt the need to avenge himself on every woman he felt the least attraction to. He was a free man—a *reformed* man. Frederick, the Reformed Rake, he thought and chuckled, seeing, in his mind's eye, a vision of himself dressed in badly tarnished armor!

So, if not for Miss Cole, then why else should he agree to stay? There was Madame's granddaughter, of course, who was, quite simply, an imp. Frederick wondered why he felt no particular attraction to the child, who was very much the same type as the love he'd left in England months earlier. This girl aroused no feeling in him except a gentle sense of amusement.

No, not for the child. Much to his surprise, stern straight brows and an oval face were surprisingly intriguing. Miss Cole had a rare type of beauty . . . but he'd only confirm her opinion of him if he were to pursue that thought and then to act upon it!

Cole. Where had he heard that name? He dismissed the question, allowing his mind to wander to more pleasant visions of a Harriet Cole who had put aside her distrust, becoming more agreeable. . . . Frederick chuckled ruefully. What a fickle soul he must have. Or was it simply his long period of abstemious self-denial that led to such delightfully prurient daydreams?

Frederick's long-suffering valet opened the dressing room door and entered silently. He carried a coat of grey superfine and pantaloons in a lighter shade of grey, which he lay neatly on the bed beside his clothes, a pile of cravats, and a pristinely white shirt. He chose a vest of stiffly lined piqué and added it to the collection before turning to where a towel, draped over a low screen near the fire, warmed itself. He straightened it, then waited for his master to finish his bath and rise from the water.

"Your accommodations satisfactory, Cob?" Frederick asked.

"Somewhat better than might be expected in foreign parts, Sir Fred." The words were said grudgingly and the sentence was finished with a sniff, denoting the English valet's opinion of all things foreign.

"You may put up a trundle bed in the dressing room if you prefer. I won't mind."

"No, Sir Fred. Not in this establishment, Sir Fred."

"Ah. You approve."

23

"It is quite a proper establishment." Again the words were grudging. Those following were more hopeful. "Will we be staying, Sir Fred?"

"For a few days, I think."

Cob eyed the master he'd served since, as a lad, the future baronet had first needed a valet. His voice was tinged with a question when he spoke again. "The young miss looks a proper chit."

"Hold your tongue, Cob." Frederick moved restlessly, sloshing water onto the hand-painted tiles fronting the fireplace. "I am a reformed character these days."

"Hurrah, hurrah." There was sarcasm and skepticism in the tone.

"Don't mumble. And don't look down your long nose either, my old friend." Sir Frederick's eyes warmed and a wry smile curved his lips. "You might come down off your high horse and stop 'Sir Fred-ing' me while you're at it," he teased.

"Yes, Sir Fred."

Frederick's chest rose and fell. "Cob, you know why we've come to the continent. Why I travel."

"For so many months, Sir Fred? I do wish we might get back to a civilized world. I don't much like foreigners."

"I can send you home."

"And then who would do for you?" A huge paw crumpled the towel, relaxed and smoothed it. "No. If you must travel, I must, too."

"Paris was enjoyable, was it not?" coaxed the master. "And I know you liked Florence." Their eyes met, both with a vision of a pert little maid in their minds. Cob actually blushed. "Now," added Frederick quickly, looking away from Cob's embarrassment, "we are in the most scenic portion of the entire world and—"

"Oh, scenery." Cob sniffed. "Scotland has scenery if 'tis scenery you want."

"The last time we were in Scotland you sulked the whole of our visit."

Cob sniffed again. "Would you like more hot water, Sir Fred?"

Frederick shifted, the water lapping against his chest. He decided he'd soaked more than enough and reached for the pine scented soap. Anticipating the move, Cob reached it first, laying it in his master's hand. The man tested the water in the remaining cans, lifted the first preparatory to rinsing off the soap and poured part of it over Frederick's head when his master indicated he wished it. The rest Cob sloshed over his back, down long well-muscled flanks and, setting the last can aside, he lifted the towel. Frederick stepped out of the hip bath and took the long piece of soft linen, drying himself.

Yes, decided Frederick, they would remain a few days in this well-managed château if for no other reason than the hope that Cob's temper might improve!

Harriet found the days crawling from one slow moment to the next treacle slow moment. She could not be satisfied. If Sir Frederick and his friend were within sight and sound, she feared for Françoise. If they were gone out with their host, Gerard Vaudray, it was worse. She hated the rampaging emotions roused by her bête noire and even more the jealousy she felt for petite dark-haired Françoise. It was wrong to feel either attraction to the rakish Frederick or jealousy for the charming child—but how did one control one's feelings? How did one hide from the one that he made her heart beat faster and from the other ones stupidity in wishing one were other that one was?

Harriet stared out the château's window toward the snow-covered peaks and told herself she could do no better than to remain cool toward Sir Frederick and calm and watchful where her charge was concerned. Surely it was a case where familiarity bred contempt. After all, wasn't that all one *should* feel for a man such as Sir Frederick?

"Miss Cole, there you are. We have been looking for you," said Yves de Bartigues, coming into the big front room. "Frederick believes it would be wise if you were to learn the oddities of your father's pistols. That way, if you were ever required to use them again, perhaps you would not shoot the horse?" He chuckled.

Both unwilling to hurt this lively and happy young man and finding his teasing amusing, Harriet turned, a smile lighting her expression. It faded when she saw that Sir Frederick had silently followed his friend into the room.

"Do come," coaxed the younger man. "Monsieur Vaudray has given permission to test your pistols at the back of the garden."

He offered his arm and somewhat against her better judgment, Harriet went. After all, she justified herself, Sir Frederick was correct in one respect: she should know how to properly use her father's guns.

"Here we are," said Yves. "You see? Vaudray has put up the targets against that low cliff and has had that table brought out for your powder and shot." Yves looked around. "Do you need anything else, Frederick? No? Then we are off."

"We?" asked Harriet quickly.

"Mademoiselle de Beaupré has accepted an invitation to join some local young people for a picnic. Do not worry. We will be well chaperoned, and I promise you we'll not leave the group even for a moment. Mademoiselle will be perfectly safe, I assure you," he said earnestly.

"Madame has given her permission," added Frederick. "They will be within the neighbor's grounds and Vaudray is sending armed servants to watch unobtrusively."

"If Madame has said she may go," said Harriet, frowning, "then I can have no objections."

"Even if you do," said Frederick softly.

She flicked a look his way only to wish she had not. He was too charming, too knowing. It wasn't fair, she thought. Another thought rose to the surface of her mind. If de Bartigues was off with Françoise then she could not, as she'd almost decided to do, tell Sir Frederick she would try the guns another day. If she were to do that, then he might decide to join the picnic party. No, it would be best to pretend an interest in the pistols and keep him here and away from Frani.

Yves made his adieu and left as Harriet turned to stare at Sir Frederick. He was observing her thoughtfully, and a blush rose up her throat. She put a hand to it. "What do we do?" she asked, gesturing toward the table.

"First I would like to see you load one."

Harriet threw him a look of dislike and moved to the table. Carefully she went through the routine she'd been taught and, with extra gentleness, laid the pistol back on the table. She had discovered the pistols did not have what was called a hair trigger, but they did fire easily, and she had great respect for them. Finished, she looked again at Sir Frederick. He nodded. "My father taught me," she said.

"I assumed he did. I merely wished to assure myself

that you'd not forgotten how much powder, for instance. Now, will you try that target?" He pointed to the nearest.

Harriet lifted the gun and extended her arm. She sighted as she'd been taught and carefully squeezed the trigger. The gun jerked.

"You did that well," said Frederick.

Despite herself, Harriet felt a glow at the praise. She turned to reload the gun and found he'd readied the second pistol.

"Try this one on the second target. We must see if there is a particular pattern after several test shots."

"Pattern?"

"You'll see."

Despite herself, Harriet became interested. She fired each gun several times at the designated target, and then Sir Frederick urged her along the path toward the cliff.

A touch of chagrin filled her when she neared them. In neither case had she, as she'd thought she'd do, come near the middle. In one case the shots were clustered toward the right side and in the other in the lower right quadrant. "I must truly be out of practice. I was certain I'd done just as Father taught me!"

"You did. See how closely patterned these holes are. What that indicates is that the gun is at fault not the shooter. If you were to aim it here—"He pointed to left of center. "—then I suspect you'd hit the target *here*." Again he pointed, this time at the bull's eye. "Will you try?"

"I'm to aim for this part of the target?"

"Yes."

Harriet studied the other one. "And with this pistol, I must aim about *here*." This time she pointed.

"Exactly." He grinned as if she were a prize student.

Her voice sharp she said, "I am not stupid, Sir Frederick."

"No. Most certainly," he said softly, "you are not stupid."

For a moment tension seemed to grow between them. With great effort Harriet pulled her gaze from his and turned back up the path. She must *not* allow her feelings to soften. She must *not* forget the sort of man he was.

Harriet picked up the gun and turned toward the targets. Again she raised her arm. Carefully she sighted toward the left. She shot—and nothing happened. She pulled the trigger again. She sighed. With a faintly rueful look at Sir Frederick, she muttered, "And I just said I am not stupid!"

He chuckled. Soon Harriet laughed as well. He took the gun from her. Harriet watched his hands as he deftly loaded it. Such long-fingered, strong-looking hands. *He'd make a pianist,* she thought. She glanced at her own long-fingered hands and suddenly yearned for a piano on which to play out the emotions she could seem to control no other way. The piano had been her salvation when her parents died. Now she needed it again, but for very different emotions.

Too bad, she thought, *that the Vaudrays did not own one!*

Two

The few days at the château extended to very nearly two weeks. The men had a day's excellent if careful climbing—spring not the season for such activity—and rode along trails to hidden mountain lakes and falls made incredibly beautiful by the spring thaws. They spent lazy evenings listening to the family's string trio or to Françoise play on the harpsichord. The music was surprisingly good.

Frani told Frederick that Miss Cole was her music teacher and that Harri was truly excellent, but no amount of coaxing would make her teacher play before company. It was, asserted the child, frowning prettily, most vexing of her. A quick smile had taken the sting from the words, and Harri's indulgent grin met by Frani's wry smile implied it was an old argument between the two.

Even as they played and rested and enjoyed their stay, the men were consulting with Gerard Vaudray concerning the ladies' journey.

"I'd have thought they'd have had armed guards if that devil has harassed them half so much as the little mademoiselle says," complained Yves.

"The ladies thought to disappear from Italy with no

30

one the wiser—especially not the unwanted suitor, of course," answered Gerard. "If they'd gone off with a large entourage, it would have been a proclamation of their intentions. They put it about that they were visiting friends in Varese for a few days."

"The ploy didn't work. One assumes there is a reason it didn't work," suggested Frederick, his brows arced questioningly.

"My thought, as well," said Gerard, nodding slowly in a manner which, on an older man, Frederick might have stigmatized as pompous. "We've questioned Madame la Comtesse's servants. A young maid will travel no farther. She is infatuated with the comte's valet, you see," he finished dryly and proceeded to the complicated project of lighting his long-stemmed clay pipe.

"One does see, of course," said Sir Frederick. "Have you been very careful about the guards you've hired for when they continue on? One would not wish to find some among them subverted by love of another sort."

Gerard frowned and tipped his head. "Love? For the *valet?*"

Frederick chuckled. "I referred to love for money. Greed."

"Ah. It is an English jest. You mean bribes." Gerard drew in a deep breath, his smile fading. "One is as careful as one may be." The Swiss looked Frederick in the eye. "I wish I were free to go with them. They need a man in authority, someone to show the world they are not alone and unprotected." He continued to hold Frederick's gaze.

Frederick didn't pretend to misunderstand. "You wish Yves and myself to travel with them."

"I do. Madame has asked that I request that you escort them. She understands that you, too, go now to England?

31

It would not be taking you from your own plans to help them carry out theirs?" he asked with more diffidence than he'd shown in the original request.

Frederick turned away, walked to the window, and stared out at the Aletschhorn, barely visible within a cloud. "I would be happy to oblige Madame, but there is something of which she should be aware. My reputation in England is not good. On this side of the Channel that will be no problem, but once across the water—" He turned back. "No. It would not do."

"Miss Cole has said something . . ." Again a touch of the man's diffidence could be heard.

"I doubt very much if she could say anything worse than the truth," said Frederick with a certain dryness.

Gerard looked him straight in the eye. "Miss Cole does not trust you."

"Ah. That is a different kettle of fish entirely. I may certainly be trusted with the protection of Madame la Comtesse and the young women. I have no desire to seduce young Françoise," he finished bluntly, "which is, I believe, Miss Cole's primary concern?"

Gerard chuckled. "Madame said there was nothing in it. She is a very wise old woman and rarely does anyone put wool in her ears." He frowned. "Is that correct?"

"Pull the wool over her eyes," said Frederick carefully. Gerard had evinced a strong interest in English sayings and English cant, but he often got them wrong. Frederick had learned not to laugh, correcting him gently.

Gerard nodded, repeating the phrase under his breath. "May I tell Madame you've agreed to escort them?" he asked.

Frederick paused. "Tell Madame I will be pleased to escort them as far as Calais. There we must discuss the situation further. I would not wish to besmirch innocent reputations by my mere presence; and traveling in England with me would, at the very least, do them no good."

"Madame will be pleased even though you add the caveat." Gerard nodded in the formal way he had and left the room.

"We go on to England, then, with Madame's party?" asked Yves.

"I think we must. The man we saw on the mountain will not stop with one attempt."

"Ah. We must be ever alert to protect the little one, then," said the young man fervently. "She is so beautiful, Frederick. So intelligent and talented. She is perfection itself. Can it really be true you have no designs on her virtue?"

Frederick raised his eyes heavenward. "Believe me, I've no interest in that child. I think, Yves, I must be getting old. I freely admit that at one time I would likely have pursued her to the ends of our mutual pleasure. Now?" He shrugged, thinking of grey eyes and how amazingly expressive they could be. "Now I've no interest in Mademoiselle Françoise." If there was a very faint emphasis on the name, Yves did not notice. Frederick added, "No. None whatsoever."

"That is good, I think," said Yves very seriously. "You see, Frederick, I would have disliked it very much if I'd been forced to . . . to *reprimand* you for too warm attentions to Mademoiselle."

Frederick grinned. "Puppy! Do you think you *could,* er, reprimand me?"

"I would try."

They looked at each other, Yves solemn and Frederick bemused. "Ah," said the latter. "I see." He grinned at the revelation. "*You* have become intrigued by our young miss, is that not so?"

"And if I have? I know I am not enough eleve—ele-vated do you say?—to wipe her feet. I know I have no chance of ever achieving bliss with her. I also know I will give my life to protect her."

Frederick groaned. "Lord protect me from the idealis-tic passions of the young! Give over, Yves. I've no interest in your Françoise and I, too, wish to protect the women." This time it was Frederick's turn to catch and hold Yves' gaze. *"All the women, Yves, not the youngest and prettiest only."*

Yves had the grace to blush.

In another part of the château Frani flounced from Har-riet's room and slammed the door. Harriet winced and turned to stare out the window at the soothing view of mountains ranged one behind the other. *I did that all wrong,* she thought, rue filling her. *How could I have been so stupid? Madame will certainly have words to say to me if little Frani takes it into her head to challenge the rake for no other reason than that I warned her she mustn't! Oh dear . . .*

Others had done so, she recalled, challenged him, and they had found themselves humbled, their pride if not their reputations in shreds. *Why,* she wondered, *did the young find a man of Sir Frederick's stamp a gauntlet to be picked up? Why must they risk all just to teach him a lesson? How could any woman think she would be the exception to a long established rule!* Not that Frani had suggested an interest in teaching him anything.

Harriet frowned. Frani insisted Frederick had never put a foot wrong, that he had never once done more than lightly tease her as a man might his younger sister. And Frani was not unused to flirtation—the minx. She would

34

know. In fact she had giggled and admitted that if anyone were flirting with her it was de Bartigues. Which meant what? That Frederick knew the chit was carefully guarded and bided his time? Harriet would not believe he had no interest in Frani. How could he *not* have an interest?

Harriet looked down her length and lamented that she, too, was not petite perfection. Would Sir Frederick look at her as she'd seen him do to others, if she were tiny and pert and not a great lummox of a woman with hair so pale it faded to non-existence next to Frani's black locks?

Realizing where her thoughts tended, Harriet bit her lip. She must not allow herself to think of drawing Sir Frederick's attention—not even in her dreams. She must never forget that the only possession of value she still retained was her good name. She must do nothing which would lose her that as well as all else—as had happened at her parent's death.

She drew in a deep breath. Tomorrow they would leave the château. For many long miles they would travel across France. They would cross the Channel to England. Days and days of association with the one man in the world who had ever tempted her. A man who still tempted her. A man dangerous to her peace of mind at every level. . . . A *man who must not be trusted to stay away from Frani.* Well, she would be strong and she would not, *not for a moment,* forget her duty to Madame: She would protect Françoise from Sir Frederick however much her own heart might ache, however hurt she felt.

Harriet, thinking of Frederick's wicked brown eyes, feared she might be very badly hurt.

Travel was difficult at any time. Traveling with three carriages and grooms and postillions and the teams to

35

pull them, with riding horses for eight, with luggage and four personal servants, and with six hired guards was, sometimes, very nearly impossible. Madame had planned her journey with easy stages from one friend or relative to the next—but it was not always possible to visit in a private home.

Sometimes the stages—as between Lausanne and Champagnole, where Madame had a friend—were too long, and a break had to be made at an hostelry. That particular stop had been peaceful and without incident. Tonight was another such a night, and Frederick hoped it too would prove quiet—but had his doubts.

It was too bad they had to stop at all. Tomorrow would see them in Paris and at the home of Madame's goddaughter. The woman, long married, had returned with her family to her hôtel on place des Vosges soon after Waterloo. Visiting there would make a pleasant break for Madame. But tonight they could go no further.

Madame la Comtesse never complained, but Frederick could see how tired and worn she'd become. Long hours over jolting roads, new faces every few days, the worry about her granddaughter, and the ever present tension, wondering when the comte would strike again . . . it was no wonder Madame felt her age! Assuming accommodations were as good in Paris at the goddaughter's hôtel as he expected, Frederick thought perhaps the women should remain there a few extra days. Madame needed time to recover before they made the last effort to reach England and the child's English grandfather.

Frederick turned from where the grooms saw to the comfort of the horses in the rather poor quarters available. He watched Yves pick a dainty way through the mud—and worse—making the inn's yard nearly impassable for a man on foot. "Have the women retired?" asked Frederick.

"They will rest while dinner is prepared. I cannot like this place, Frederick. I don't understand why you insisted we stop."

"I didn't insist. In fact, I'd have preferred to go on, but Madame could go no further today. Have you taken a good look at Hortense de St. Onge, Yves?"

Spots of red appeared on Yves' cheeks. "She is tired, but will she rest well here?"

Frederick shrugged. "She refuses to go farther tonight, so we've no choice but to chance it." He turned back to have a word with his coachman before joining Yves for the return to the inn. He too had had second thoughts about the wisdom of stopping here, but the relief Madame hadn't tried to conceal as she'd been helped from her coach had decided him. He sighed. Perhaps it would be best if he and Yves were to take turns standing guard tonight along with their valets and the hired guards. It would take at least three of them to cover the different approaches to the bedroom floor in the rambling old structure. Perhaps they should reconnoiter . . .

An hour later Yves escorted the women to the private parlor, where their evening meal would be served. The landlord arrived soon after, a bottle of fine brandy in his hand. Yves inspected it with interest. Frederick, however, knew better than to drink when expecting a long night of duty. Alcohol and responsibility did not mix. He wanted nothing to cloud his mind. So, although he accepted a glass from the inn keeper, when the man left he set his aside and, after Yves had a few sips suggested, quietly, that perhaps it would be best to stay completely sober. Yves agreed.

A few minutes later the younger man yawned, a huge gaping yawn which surprised him as much as it did the company. Frederick was immediately alert—especially when a second yawn followed on the first. When the landlord again entered the parlor—this time followed by several maids with trays, Frederick pretended to yawn. He noted the expression of satisfaction on the landlord's face. The meal was laid out, and they took their seats, Yves again yawning widely.

"I don't know what is wrong with me," he said a bit petulantly. "Only minutes ago I felt fine. Now I can barely keep my eyes open."

Frederick didn't respond. He was watching the service of the meal, especially that given Françoise and Harriet who would sleep in the same room. As soon as the food had been passed once, he relaxed slightly and told the landlord and his maids to go. They would help themselves to anything else they required.

The landlord casually picked up a tureen of steaming soup and walked out the door, followed by the maids. Immediately Sir Frederick scanned the table to see who had accepted a serving from that dish. Only Madame. Even as he watched, she lifted another spoonful to her lips. Standing, Sir Frederick reached across the table and knocked the spoon away, the broth flying out to spatter over Françoise.

"Sir Frederick!" wailed the girl. "My gown!"

"Why did you do that?" asked Harriet, standing. "What is it? What has happened?"

Frederick ignored both young women. "Madame, I fear an opiate. Perhaps worse. Will you please empty your stomach of what you have eaten? I think Yves has been

38

drugged by the brandy which I was also expected to drink and now you are the only one to eat of that soup, which I recall the landlord saying had been especially prepared for your delectation. Please, will you do as I ask and empty your stomach?"

Madame stood up. "Come Harriet. You must help me." She crossed the room. Suddenly she doubled over, clutching her middle. She groaned. The spasm passed and she looked fiercely at Frederick. "Not an opiate, Sir Frederick. If I die, promise me you'll see my granddaughter to safety."

"I promise," said Sir Frederick already at her side. "But do not concern yourself with such morbid thoughts. You ate very little. However little it was, you'll now have to accept some embarrassment," he added grimly when she again bent with the pain. He helped her to lean down and put his finger into her mouth, forcing it back until he achieved a gag reflex. The next few minutes were not pleasant, but were, he believed, necessary. Harriet worked in concert with him. Madame did not object, already suffering pain more intense than any she'd ever endured.

When they had cleared her stomach twice more, making her drink from the common coffeepot in between induced vomiting, Sir Frederick picked the weak and very sick old woman up in his arms. He carried her from the room and looked sardonically around at the wide-eyed servants clustered in the hall. "You may tell your master," said Sir Frederick, "that he requires a new cook. The food has not agreed with our lady's system—as you will see." He forced a path through the crowd, found the landlord hovering near the stairs and stared at him for a long moment before carrying Madame on up to her room. Behind came Harriet and Françoise.

Monsieur de Bartigues brought up the rear carrying

the basket of rolls. He had a notion they might all require something to eat before the night was ended, and the bread seemed to him the safest item on the table!

Madame's maids and Harriet settled Madame into her bed. Once leaning back on her pillows, the old woman insisted she must see Sir Frederick. To quiet her, Harriet reluctantly called him in. "You have saved me, I think," said Madame in a whispery voice.

"I certainly hope we have. But it was Miss Cole who knew what should be done. I merely helped her."

"It was you who guessed there was something wrong. I cannot remember if you promised me you'd see my granddaughter safely on to England . . ."

"I did."

"Good. We will see how I do in the morning. But for this night? She will be safe?"

"Monsieur de Bartigues and I had already laid plans for your protection, Madame. We have set up a rota of guards and have found the positions where they will stand. They will be armed and alert. You may be calm, Madame. Although we rid you of much of the poison, some will have gotten into your system. You must rest now."

"Yes. Now I will rest." She closed her eyes.

Harriet accompanied Sir Frederick to the door. "Is there no more we may do for her?"

"I know of nothing."

"Shouldn't we send for a doctor?"

"I fear we'll be unable to trust any doctor we might find in the immediate neighborhood."

Harriet bit her lip. "I'd not thought of that. She looks so terribly pale. She's so weak."

"I believe she will recover, Miss Cole," Sir Frederick reassured her. "We'll see how she does in the morning.

If she is well enough to travel we will take her to her goddaughter. If she is not . . ."

Harriet chuckled although there was the slightest touch of hysteria in it. "If we must stay here, then I'll review what I know of cookery. I can boil water. And, therefore, I can, I believe, boil eggs. We will use the tea from Madame's private stock and perhaps we will not starve utterly before we may leave here."

"You are a very brave woman, Miss Cole."

"One does what one must, that is all. Inside I shake like a blancmange."

"But that is exactly what bravery is all about. One does what one must even in the face of a not unreasonable fear." He reached for her hand, squeezed it gently. "You will do, my dear." He turned and walked away, fearing he'd do something outrageous if he were to stay in her presence much longer. Perhaps something as simple as raising that long-fingered hand to his lips. Or perhaps more. He might pull her into his embrace and, once he'd gentled her, tip up her face and kiss her and then . . .

Sir Frederick growled deep in his throat. This was no time for daydreams of what he'd very much enjoy doing with and to Miss Harriet Cole! He looked down the hall to where Yves stalked toward him, a frown on his face. Daydreams fled on the instant. "What has gone wrong now?" he asked, fearing the worst.

"The men are sleeping soundly. All of them!"

"As we were meant to be." Sir Frederick sighed. "Well, Yves, we've a rather large responsibility this night. Can you do it? Or did you drink too much of that drugged brandy?"

"I'm a bit woozy, but it will pass. What do we do?"

They laid new plans and took up positions near the women's rooms. They waited. The wait was not so long as might have been expected. About one in the morning a door along the corridor opened. A head poked out and looked in both directions.

When the man sighted Yves and Sir Frederick, the head jerked back out of sight. Carefully, it showed itself again. Sir Frederick had very good hearing. The soft gutter French flowing from the room and down the hall brought a grin to his face! The door shut with a snap.

The rest of the night passed without incident.

Three

Nearly a week passed before Harriet gave in to Madame's urging that they go on. A carriage was converted for the use of the invalid who was still far from well. A makeshift bed was well padded with featherbeds in the hope the jouncing would be eased. Cushions were put in. In fact, everything the party could think to do for her comfort was done. They proceeded slowly toward Paris and Madame's goddaughter's where the women were made welcome and pampered and coddled.

After assuring themselves the women were protected by old retainers long known to be loyal, Sir Frederick and Yves continued on to stay with Monsieur de Bartigues' uncle until Madame was well enough to travel on.

Sir Frederick began to chafe at the delay. At the time of their first adventure with the comte, he'd been returning to England. It was already weeks beyond the date on which he'd rather expected to cross the Channel. If Madame were slow to recover her strength, it might be still more weeks before they moved on. Frederick wanted to go home, but, hiding his impatience, he sent still another note to warn his friend in England that he'd been delayed

43

and would, when he knew it, send information concerning his new arrival date.

Sir Frederick's impatience was based in the fact that, for the first time in his life, he had the wealth necessary to carry through his dreams of renewing his wasted estate. His father had begun the rot. He'd mortgaged the land heavily and had no interest in his tenants or in modern agricultural methods. Inheriting debts rather than money, Frederick had been unable to do anything upon becoming baronet, but he'd planned what he would do if he ever had the means by which to do it—and now he did. Unexpectedly and from a surprising source, he'd inherited a fortune!

While in Florence, he and Yves had quite literally stumbled over a sick old woman dressed in rusty black. She'd been on the steps to one of the city's many churches, hunched into herself and coughing terribly. Something about the woman had roused compassion in Frederick and, although he was rather short of funds at that moment, he'd taken the creature in, called a doctor, and had seen she was cared for. Once she was well again and gone, he'd forgotten her. Barely a month later, he was accosted by a lawyer who informed him he was heir to the woman's fortune.

Frederick's moment of compassion had unknowingly been made to one of the city's eccentrics, an ancient miser who had outlived both family and friends and who, upon recovering from the chest ailment she'd had when Frederick found her, had changed her will to her rescuer's advantage. Changing her will was something the old lady did with great regularity. This time she died before the next revision could be made, and Frederick was now a very rich man.

As a result, Frederick wished to get himself home and

put in motion the first of the plans for improving his land and making it, once again, as productive as it was in his grandfather's day. On the other hand, Frederick was reluctant to take himself too far from the intriguing Miss Cole. He found himself dreaming of big grey eyes night after night and, during the days, making excuses to visit Madame for the purpose of spending a few moments with the disapproving Harriet.

"How is Madame today," he asked on one of those visits.

"As well as can be expected," said Miss Cole, her voice cool. "Frani, I believe it is the time you were to read to your grandmother. You had best go now."

"Harri!"

"Françoise."

"Yes, Harriet."

But as the young girl said goodbye to Sir Frederick, Harriet was certain she saw the minx wink at him. It was too bad of her. She would have to have another talk with her charge.

"Now tell me that you are not overdoing," demanded her unwanted guest when they were alone.

"I am not over-doing," she repeated, seemingly dutiful. Harriet eyed him. He didn't *seem* disturbed that Françoise had gone. If anything he seemed more relaxed than before. If only she understood him! She watched him studying her features thoughtfully and blushed, lowering her eyes.

"I think you tell a lie, Miss Cole. Your face has fined down to the bones and your eyes look as if they haven't known what sleep is, ever."

"In other words," she said stiffly, "I look a hag."

"To the contrary. You look ethereal and as if a breeze would waft you away. Since I know you are not at all fragile, I can only assume you are taking too much onto those slim shoulders." He sighed when she refused to rise to the bait. "Miss Cole, it will not do if you too were to fall ill."

Harriet bit her lip, quickly stopped the revealing action when his gaze slid to her mouth and something beneath the skin of his face seemed to intensify, tighten . . . "As you say, I am not the type to succumb to a little hard work."

"That is not what I said at all."

A rueful look in his eyes, an almost smile, made Harriet want to smile in response. She forced herself to scowl lightly instead.

"You deliberately do all you can to misunderstand me, do you not?" he asked gently. "I wish I knew what I had done to make you dislike me so."

"One cannot like everyone one meets."

"No. That isn't it, I think. Well, never mind. Someday I will figure it out. But for now I must go." He rose. "Good day, Miss Cole. You may now tell that little baggage in your charge that she may come out from behind the door and no longer need listen at keyholes." He raised his voice slightly. "Good day, Mademoiselle."

To Harriet's distress a faint giggle was heard in response. Françoise came through the door to the adjoining salon immediately Sir Frederick left by the door to the hall. "He is such a funny one, Harriet. I cannot see why you do not like him. Especially when it is so obvious *he* likes *you.*"

"Nonsense. He comes in pursuit of you, Françoise. It is too bad of you to encourage him as you do."

"Encourage him! I am not allowed to say a word to him."

Harriet frowned. "You are aware of what I mean, Frani.

It is for your own good that I scold you. He is a dangerous man, my dear. If only we had other support for this journey, I would gladly see the back of him." A faint pain settled in her temples and Harriet knew she lied. She would not be glad to see him go. "Oh, if only I understood him," she exclaimed.

As the days passed Miss Cole made it quite obvious she had no trust in Sir Frederick. She hovered, thin-lipped, near Françoise whenever the girl would speak with him. It became a game, almost, Sir Frederick teasing Frani and Harriet thinking up chores for the girl which would take her away from his contaminating presence—and with Françoise gone, he could enjoy some quiet moments with the object of his visit, although he was too experienced and too wary to allow Harriet to know his aim.

Harriet Cole didn't understand him. She said so. Often. Well, with luck, perhaps one day she would.

At last they were on their final stage to Calais. Sir Frederick wrapped his fur-lined traveling cloak closer and set one well-shod foot against the opposite seat, bracing himself into the corner of the rocking carriage. He smiled as his companion did much the same in the opposite corner. "Ten months since I came to the continent. I can barely believe that, at last, we near Calais and the last stop before England. I can barely comprehend it, Yves— so much has happened. What has *not* happened," he added as another jounce shifted him in his seat, "is an improvement in the Paris to Calais road."

Yves de Bartigues shrugged. "No, it does not improve itself. But roads do *not* improve by themselves, do they, my friend? And who is there, in my battered land, to waste time on the road work?"

Silence followed the exchange. At a particularly nasty lurch each reached for a strap hung from the frame for just such occurrences. Sir Frederick hoped Madame was not so uncomfortable as he was. She had not regained her strength to the degree he'd wished, but she'd insisted they must continue, that she could not rest until Françoise was in the hands of her grandfather. So they planned short stages between Paris and Calais and today was, Frederick hoped, their last day on French soil.

As the men looked out the sides of the carriage over a sodden French countryside rapidly disappearing in a chilling evening mist, Monsieur de Bartigues wondered if he had made the right decision to continue his travels with his English friend.

Sir Frederick mused as well: now that it was almost upon him, he wondered if he were, in truth, ready to face old friends and, most particularly, look again on the face of the young woman who, by now, was many months married to his closest friend. *Odd,* he thought. *If I'd not saved his life on that Sussex beach he'd not have won from me the one woman I've ever loved . . . But would I wish him dead? Certainly not,* he decided—and meant it.

Over the months, particularly those spent in Italy, Elizabeth's features had blurred. Since meeting Madame la Comtesse and her party, more often than not, grey eyes had a place in his dreams rather than laughing blue. Serious grey eyes, which looked out of an oval face topped by pale yellow hair that glinted red gold in certain lights. He was, he decided, ruefully, merely fickle.

The chilly air developed a hint of salty tang. Calais couldn't be far, now and Sir Frederick was impatient for the day's journey to end. A particularly bad rut caught an off wheel just then, jerked the carriage to one side, and, with a crack like a rifle shot, something broke. The carriage settled abruptly toward one corner, throwing the men together.

Untangling themselves, they forced a way from the tilted chaise and climbed onto the road. Sir Frederick ran to the heads of the plunging team and jumped to reach the bit of the wild-eyed leader. The rearing animal was obviously about to tangle itself in the traces and would hurt himself and perhaps his teammates. Once the animals settled, Sir Frederick looked around. Yves knelt over the prone figure of the postillion. A groom leaned woozily against the frame of the carriage. Assuring himself the horses would harm neither themselves nor anyone else, he went to the groom.

"What happened?"

"Don't know. Don't understand it," muttered the man.

A sudden suspicion filled Frederick's breast. He looked down the road toward Calais, but the women's coach had disappeared. He turned to the damaged wheel but, in the bad light of the fading day, could not be certain there had been tampering . . . but the accident was too pat, too providential, followed too soon after their last stop for rest and refreshment—and they must not take chances on the women's safety. He moved to the horses and began unbuckling harness. "Yves, we must go on. Quickly now."

"You think . . . ?" asked the younger man, turning to look at Frederick.

"I do. Will that man survive?"

"Yes. He's in pain from a broken rib or two as well as a clean break in his left arm, but he'll survive."

"We'll send help as soon as we may. Do you understand me?" He spoke in French to the groom as he worked, frantically, to free a horse. The groom grunted. "You watch over the postillion. We aren't far from Calais

49

so help shouldn't be long coming." As he talked, the first horse was loose. "Light the lamps so no one will run into the wreck . . . Goodbye," he added, pulling himself onto the broad back of the carriage horse.

Yves was not far behind him, and the men urged their animals to make their best effort. Soon they started down the hill into Calais. It lay below, open to their view, lights flickering from a few small windows along the darker streets.

"You think it is a plot on the part of the comte?" called Yves, his horse somewhat to the rear.

"I'm almost certain of it," responded Frederick, urging on his awkward mount.

Again silence fell except for the clippity-clop of hooves on cobbled streets as they proceeded quickly through narrow ways to the chosen hostelry near the sea front. Frederick caught a glimpse of the choppy waters of the Channel. If the weather didn't change overnight, it would be a rough crossing. The windy, cloud-studded sky was unfavorable to a gentle passage. They could wait, he supposed, for better conditions. Many travelers did so.

He and Yves ducked as they rode under the arched entry to the inn yard. The fat landlord bobbed and smirked, but looked around himself a trifle uneasily.

Frederick, in perfectly idiomatic, but languid French, asked if Madame's carriage had arrived. He was informed it had and that Madame had gone up to the room ordered for her. Frederick's breath whooshed out, his relief intense that his suspicions concerning the women's safety had been wrong. "Then we require the rooms ordered ready for the two of us, stabling for the horses and, *tout de suite,* a meal in a private parlor." The host bowed over his hands, which he rubbed and rubbed in an irritating manner and again Sir Frederick had a feeling the man was overly nervous.

Suddenly a commotion arose off to one side of the yard and, idly, Frederick glanced that way. A stray beam of torchlight lit pale golden hair, and he peered more closely. With a word which shocked his friend, he touched Yves' arm.

"History, it seems," said Sir Frederick to Yves, "repeats itself!" He raised his voice as he strode forward. "Monsieur le Comte, a word, if you please."

The melee stopped on the instant. The struggling women stilled in the arms of their rough captors and de Vauton-Cheviot, who had been directing the kidnapping, turned on his heel.

"You!" he snarled.

"We meet again. Good day, Miss Cole. May we be of service?"

A response muffled by the dirty hand covering her mouth indicated yes, and probably, thought Frederick, in language unsuited to her sex and station. Her companion, the lovely Françoise, stared over the grubby hand of another ruffian, her eyes wide with fright.

"You . . . you . . ."

"You repeat yourself. Release the women."

"They are mine," howled the comte.

"They are not," asserted Frederick sternly.

A crowd gathered as the cloudy sky turned blood red under the setting of the sun. The French fop glanced around, a hunted expression on his face. He stared at Frederick, didn't like the Englishman's composure or his height or the strength of the arm holding a bared sword stick casually at rest.

"You interfere once too often," snarled the would-be villain. "I will not forget." He made an abrupt movement

51

and, so quickly were they freed, the ladies staggered, would have fallen, had Yves not reached steadying hands their way. The comte clambered into his carriage, shouting orders to his men. In moments the coach, faced to move from the yard as soon as he had the women aboard, left without the ladies.

"You have made a dreadful enemy, my lord." Françoise's eyes filled with admiration.

"How did that evil man manage to capture you this time?" Yves asked and led Frani toward the inn.

Miss Cole, hesitating only a moment, placed her fingertips on Frederick's offered arm. "We sink deeper and deeper into your debt, Sir Frederick." She glanced at the carriage horse from which he'd dismounted. "Did something happen to your chaise?"

"Yes." He told her of the accident and was reminded to send help. Once he'd arranged for the rescue, he probed for information. "I'm as interested as Yves in how the comte managed this latest outrage."

Harriet sighed. "I don't *know* how he could have entered our rooms and captured us. As you well know, Sir Frederick, we've been closely guarded ever since you met us in Switzerland. The only thing possible is that he managed to bribe Madame's servants. Somehow."

It turned out she was wrong. Madame's servants were discovered just then by a serving-wench who set up a screech. They'd been bound and gagged and stuffed into a storage room at the back of the inn and were beginning to recover from some drug. A new babble of voices exclaiming and disclaiming roused the inn all over again.

Sir Frederick watched as Harriet soothed the servants and sent them to their various beds. "Is that wise, Miss Cole? You need their protection."

"We needed it before, and they did not provide it. Not

52

that I blame them. Why should they fear wine offered in my name? I've ordered it for them in the past after a long stage—not that this one was long, of course. The comte must have had us watched carefully to know my habits."

"And now?"

"Frani and I will retire to our room and stay there. With the door barred."

A new commotion erupted at the top of the stairs. "I *will* go down. I *will* know what has happened."

The arrogant French voice was unmistakable. Fran-çoise, who had been breathlessly relating the whole to Yves, swung toward the sound. Lifting her skirts slightly, the girl ran up the narrow stairs. "Grand-mère, you should not have left your bed. You know you should not."

Sir Frederick eyed the nervous landlord, noted shifty eyes sunk in plump cheeks and debated with himself how deeply mired the man was in the plot to capture Françoise. He turned to Miss Cole and speaking in clear French, loudly enough the landlord had to overhear, he said, "Monsieur de Bartigues and I will order *our* men to guard your rooms. *They* will not be tricked, I assure you. You may sleep in peace. I think it best if you retire now and stay closely protected in your rooms."

"Thank you, Sir Frederick." Harriet held out her hand. "We are indeed in your debt."

"And," he said, deep crinkles slashing a pattern at the corners of his eyes, "you wish it were not so. Do not think of it, Miss Cole. Any man would have come to your rescue." He thought of that scene in the yard where many milled around the struggling women but not one had lifted a finger. He knew she was thinking the same thing. "We will see you in the morning," he added, "and discuss our next move in this, our own personal odyssey."

"Madame is unwell," Harriet said with a frown. "The

53

journey has tired her, and she should not attempt a crossing in this weather. "However that may be, I have no way of stopping her if she decides to do so." She noticed he still held her hand and, blushing, jerked it from his loose grip. "Good evening, Sir Frederick." He watched as she too disappeared up the stairs, her movements quick and graceful—and revealing now and again a trim little ankle!

The silence was broken by Yves. "Well!"

"Is it well, Yves?"

"No it is not. How can that man continue to frighten that shy little bird so badly? How can he behave in such a dastardly fashion to such a sweet child?"

"Shy? Sweet? You refer to Mademoiselle de Beaupré?" Sir Frederick ignored the glower his friend turned on him and, throwing back his head, laughed heartily.

Yves' expression didn't lighten. If anything his anger deepened. "She was frightened."

Sir Frederick sobered. "Both women were frightened. Badly frightened. Yves, we must see our valets guard them well. Too, I believe we must keep an eye on that plaguey landlord. He played some part in all this, I think."

Yves looked much struck by the notion. "He *must* have. There were too many inn servants out there ignoring the situation and only his orders to turn a blind eye to a kidnapping could have had it that way."

"My thought exactly."

Yves and Sir Frederick spoke with their men, who arrived just then with the last carriage and the luggage. After refreshing their travel weary bodies with a glass of brandy—Sir Frederick's private stock which had made a timely arrival with the baggage coach and *not* that provided by the inn—they returned to the ground floor and followed their host to where a meal was laid out for them.

"Now, mine host—" Sir Frederick spoke languidly, his

eyes on the cold meats and sauce boats, the thick soup and bread, "—you will sit down and taste each and every item on that table."

The man blanched, backed toward the door.

"But I insist!" Sir Frederick forced the tubby little man into a chair and served him from each bowl, sauce boat and platter on the table. "Eat."

Sweat spouted in tiny beads on the man's forehead. "My lord, you cannot make me."

"Eat."

The landlord eyed the small pistol which had suddenly appeared in the large tanned hand, and the sweat ran down one side of his fat face. "I did not wish to do it."

"It?"

"I was ordered . . . I had to obey . . ."

"The comte *ordered* you to, umm, add special seasoning to our food?"

"He is powerful. He is terrible. He insisted . . ."

"Just when did this powerful terrible comte insist?"

"He . . . He . . ."

"He returned to the inn?"

"He returned, my lord." The pistol nudged pudgy flesh. "He returned and made me . . ."

"Or paid thee?" The man blanched. "You are a greedy blackguard. Eat."

"No. No, I *cannot.*"

"Yves, I think you must feed him."

"No. No, no, no."

"But you would have had us eat." A thought crossed his mind, and Frederick's pistol pushed, not gently, against the side of the man's head. "What of the food sent up to the women?"

"It is all right . . ." the man's voice rose to a thin screech, his skin so grey Frederick thought him near to fainting. "I would not poison women. No, no. I would not."

"But will it, perhaps, put them into a deep sleep?"

"No. Nothing. I swear it."

Sir Frederick let his pistol hand fall to his side. "Clear this away and see it is a danger to no one." Then he smiled. It wasn't a *nice* smile. "Perhaps," he said slowly, "I've a better notion. Serve it to *mon ami, le comte.*"

"I *couldn't.*"

"I think," said Frederick gently, "that you could. If you do not, you will, mine host, eat it yourself."

"He will ruin me."

"Ruin or death. Which do you prefer?"

"It will not kill me. I did not," he seemed to be trying to convince himself, "put in enough to kill." The man looked at the food, reached hesitantly for a spoon.

Yves stared. "You would rather suffer agony from whatever poison you added to our food, than serve it to the man who ordered it and deserves to suffer?"

"I would. He is evil. You do not understand what he would do to me."

"That's enough," Sir Frederick said when the man raised the first trembling bite to his mouth. *"I am not evil."*

The man seemed to disintegrate. He slipped from the chair and groveled at Frederick's feet. "I will serve you properly. The comte need not know you ate. He will think you fasted, not trusting the food . . . or that you absently fed a bite to the dog there," he pointed to where a small pooch lay before the fire unnoticed, "and were warned when the animal became ill. Yes, that is what I will say. He will believe me." The man was babbling. In disgust Sir Frederick walked away. Slowly the innkeeper climbed to his feet, pasty-faced, and wavered toward the door. "I

56

will serve you myself, m'lord. And I will taste what I bring so you may trust me." He backed, still babbling out the door, closing it behind his exit.

That night Frederick slept with a pistol under his pillow, but he'd no need of it. He'd finished shaving when, early the next morning, he received a message that the comtesse wished to speak with him. Not bothering with breakfast, he dressed quickly. About to leave for the assignation with Madame, Frederick turned back and shook Yves awake. "Madame requires words with me. I will return shortly, but stay awake, my friend. I do not trust our acquaintance, le comte."

Sir Frederick bowed when brought into Madame's presence by a tall, thin, grim looking maid, one of the pair of sisters who had been in Madame's service for many years. "Madame?"

"Sir Frederick. Again we are in your debt."

He waved a hand. "Please. It was nothing. I would know how I may serve you now." His eyes noted the palsied shaking of the hand gripping the ever present cane. Her face, which had worn age-wrinkled but healthy looking skin on first meeting, seemed shrunken, the skin tightening around the magnificent bones of her skull. It had a faintly yellow tinge to it, too, which he did not like. He knew she was holding herself stiffly erect by willpower alone and moved toward her, seating himself after receiving permission. He laid his hand over the one on the cane. "Madame, please. Do not exert yourself so."

She relaxed enough the back of the chair helped support her, but kept her chin raised. She stared at him for long moments before stating, "You mean my Frani no harm."

"I mean her no harm. My only wish is to help all of you."

57

"Yet Miss Cole reads your reputation as such that you will wish to seduce my granddaughter."

Frederick chuckled. "What it is to have a reputation. At one time, I certainly might have done so. She is just the sort of lively minx that appealed to my grass-time. That has passed, Madame. I swear to you I have no evil designs on her person or reputation." He frowned. "But the very reputation which bothers our Miss Cole will make it difficult for me to help once we've crossed the Channel."

Shrewd eyes held his, the steady look disconcerting even to one as strong-minded as Frederick. "I see, I think. If you escort my granddaughter to her English grandfather, he would not believe you had not touched her."

"You speak bluntly, Madame. You also speak truth."

"But you *would* help?"

"I would help in any way you can conceive."

"You *will* escort us." He didn't speak. "Yes, you will escort us, and you will pretend to be enamored of Miss Cole. If that proud old man sees you are after the other, he will believe my Françoise safe."

"And Miss Cole's reputation?" A bleak expression chilled his features. "What of that, Madame?"

She shrugged. "Miss Cole is a sensible woman who loves our Françoise almost as much as I do. She has been a true friend to the child. Once this is over I will set up an annuity for her support, and she need never go into service again."

"Yes." Frederick held the old woman's eyes, his voice stern. "She can live quite out of the way, never meeting those of her own station and, thanks to loneliness or a need for love, actually become what you would make her, in reputation, thanks to me!" He waved a hand, a sharp dismissive gesture. "I think not, Madame. Another plan, please."

Those shrewd eyes narrowed. "You are rather vehement in Miss Cole's defense, Sir Frederick."

"Is that a crime?"

She chuckled, a chuckle which turned into a cough. When the spasm passed, she looked still more exhausted. "You are, behind that sardonic mask you wear so well, a good man, are you not, Sir Frederick," she suggested.

"I doubt it," he responded. His casual denial of humanity was spoiled when he added, "You must rest, Madame. We will speak when you are less tired."

"Yes. On the packet. Or when we reach Dover."

"You are determined to sail today?"

"The sooner we leave French soil, the sooner my granddaughter will be safe."

Frederick didn't attempt to argue with the determination he read in her words and expression—although it was his belief the comte wouldn't let the English Channel interfere in his pursuit. "Monsieur de Bartigues and I will see to tickets for the packet, Madame." Frederick rose and bowed, feeling great admiration for the proud old woman who would endanger her life to protect her grandchild. "Might I suggest that you pretend you are removing to another inn, not trusting the landlord at this one, but that you will wait elsewhere for a better crossing? That way, perhaps, if it is well-timed, you can be on the packet and away before the comte realizes you have escaped?"

"An excellent notion, Sir Frederick. You are not only a good man, you are a wise one as well.

Ignoring her compliment he said, "I'll reserve staterooms for your party." He bowed again and let in the maid who stood guard at the door to Madame's room. Speaking to her in soft French, he said, "Take care of

59

your mistress. She is tired and not well." The maid lifted her demurely lowered head, the look in her eyes scathing. He smiled. "I apologize. You know better than I her condition, but I cannot help worrying about her." There was a slight softening in the hard features under the tight braid forming a high crown on the woman's head. The maid nodded, and passed on to go to Madame. Frederick went to find Yves.

After a brief conference the two strolled down to the main taproom. They studied the men lounging there. Choosing one they believed they'd seen in the comte's train, they took seats nearby. "I could not convince her to leave on today's packet, Yves. And truly, she is too unwell to attempt it. But she will remove with Miss Cole and Mademoiselle to another inn. I wonder if we, too, should stay."

"Her servants are warned. They will not be tricked again, I think."

"I am needed at home. We delayed in Paris too long for added delay now."

"Yes." Yves scowled at his friend. "That express you received indicated speed was of the essence, but you *would* wait for the last of your order from the tailor there."

Sir Frederick chuckled at his friend's accusing tone. Yves must have taken part in amateur theatricals at some time in his young life, that he was able to deliver the falsehood with such believable vehemence! "I was much in need," he said, his voice caressing, "of a new wardrobe. And it had been a very long time since I could afford one. Do you blame me, Yves?"

"Yes," was the blunt response. Again the younger man took on a scolding tone. "If *I* had received such a summons . . ."

Sir Frederick, fearing Yves would over-do his play-acting, interrupted. "Madame and her charges are safe, I think, and I only promised that we'd see them to Calais. We will, as planned, leave for Dover on the evening packet."

The two men finished their wine and strolled out into the bright day, the whipping clouds not yet thick enough to obscure the sun. Passage would be quick, the winds blowing, for once, in the right direction. Assuming, of course, that, fickle as such winds were, they continued to blow toward England. It would not, however, be an easy passage. Great swells rolled in, splashing up over the quay and wetting anyone unwary enough to get too near.

"That went well, I think," said Yves, noting that the suspected man followed and was watching as they walked toward the packet office. "Will he come in and actually check that we take passage?"

"I think not. Especially if we hold tickets in our hand as we leave, only putting them away as we return to the inn. I will hide the tickets for Madame's party and be very careful I'm not seen delivering them."

"It's as good a plan as we've time for," said Yves with a shrug. "Once aboard we may relax for a time."

"How wrong you are, Yves! We must watch ourselves while at sea. The comte will very likely send along a well-paid cutthroat to push us overboard if the chance arises."

"That," said a wide-eyed Yves, "would not have occurred to me."

"You haven't the mind for such deviousness."

"You do?"

"What do you think?"

"It always surprises me when that side of you appears,

61

Frederick," said the young man, his tone completely serious. "It doesn't often, but when it does, you are always right about the evils in the human soul or the folly to be found in those we meet. Where did you learn to see so clearly and act so quickly?"

"I had need of the twists and turns of an inventive mind when I worked against Napoleon during the war."

"That, I think, surprised me most of all," said Yves. "I discovered the languid self-centered man you pretend to be hid a strong patriotism and the ability to play the dangerous games involved in spy and counterspy."

Frederick flushed slightly, wishing he'd not drunk so much the night he'd told Yves tales of his war experiences. "I was thought a coward by my countrymen. Why else, it was said, would I avoid joining the army in defense of my homeland? The canard was, of course, spread deliberately by the war office. After all," a tiny smile played around Frederick's mouth, "who would believe a coward to be a counterspy?"

"It was never revealed, the part you played?"

"No. I didn't wish to be whitewashed by compliments to my bravery when my original reputation was built on another sin entirely."

"It would have stilled the gossip you were a coward and proven you a patriot."

"Nothing could be said while the war continued. Then the war was over. I was what I was, a gamester and a known seducer of women. Patriotism," he added, his cynicism surfacing, as it did so often, "is only revered when a country is in danger."

"And your sudden wealth, what will be said about that?"

"Not the truth. That I selflessly helped a destitute old woman who turned out to be a wealthy woman and that

62

shortly thereafter her heart gave out and she'd left it all to me? No. That is a fairy tale. There will be rumors ranging from marked cards and duellos in the dim light of dawn to outright murder and mayhem."

"I can't believe you are indifferent to what others will think!"

"Long ago I learned the shallow twisted nature of too many of those who comprise the *ton*. I am truly indifferent to what such as they think of me."

"Your reputation in England is so truly black?"

A self-deriding smile twisted Frederick's mouth. "Truly black." He turned his head, and looked out over the cloud-shadowed water toward England. "You'd best desert me now and return to Paris, my friend. At my side you will not be well-received by the English *ton.*"

"You are not received?"

"Oh yes," said Sir Frederick, carelessly, "By all but the highest of sticklers. And I'm perfectly welcome in the clubs and other haunts of men. But cautious mamas hide their daughters behind their skirts and, in mixed company, husbands and fathers keep a wary eye on me. You are more in the petticoat line than I, Yves," he teased. "Associating with me will make the most innocent pursuit difficult for you. Perhaps," he went on thoughtfully, "I could give you an introduction or two before it is known you arrived from France in my company. My friends will see you are given the entrée."

"But I would be required to cut you in the street?" Yves scowled. "No. You know better, Frederick. I could not do it."

"Ah well," suggested Frederick, bored with the subject, "when you become restless, you may always return to Paris."

"I will," said Yves fervently, his hands moving in a

very French manner, "never understand you. Never." He entered the packet office in Frederick's wake, shaking his head in disgust.

Harriet Cole was unknowingly echoing Yves' words. "I do not understand him. I only met the man once during my season. But during those weeks in London I observed his behavior often. He is everything black. Truly."

"That was," said Madame, "eight years ago. Men may change, Harri." The old woman lying in the big feather bed spoke firmly although her voice was weak.

"Not *that* much."

"You can have no idea what happened to change him. The war, for instance, changed many men."

"He played no part in the war. He bore the label coward because he took no part in it."

"But he is not a coward," spoke Françoise from the chair by the window. "He has, twice, come to my rescue. Me, I think that is not the behavior of a coward. You cannot say it is."

"I *cannot* believe he is helping us with no ulterior motive. He *must* be after you, Frani, whatever he says. You must be on guard always."

A weak chuckle from the bed turned to a body-wracking cough. When Françoise and Harriet had Madame quiet again and when, once again, she'd overruled their insistence they not leave that day for England, the old woman smiled at Harriet. "I suggested to your rake, my dear, that in order to protect Françoise from taint of his reputation, he pretend to be after you. He refused and was angry I'd suggest such a thing. Very angry. It was a test, you see. He passed it."

"Oh, no, he did not. I am not the sort he favors. Frani

64

is. If he pretended to be angry, it was to fool you, Madame."

Wise old eyes stared up into Harriet's and Harriet felt an inner confusion. Why was she so vehement? Did she give away those hidden and forbidden longings and desires which had touched her young heart during her aborted London season? And why had she been so foolish, then, to feel such yearnings for a heartless rake who couldn't even remember her name for the duration of a dance? Did Madame guess those idiotic emotions had been rekindled all over again during those lazy days in Switzerland—that they had grown stronger while in Paris?

Wishing to avoid Madame's perceptive gaze, Harriet said, "I'm tired. I did not sleep well last night. If we are to leave on the evening packet, I will nap now. If you'll excuse me?" She looked at Madame who smiled at her and nodded. She glanced at Françoise who picked up her book and sat down with it near the window. "Frani," said Harriet, "you'll not leave your grandmother, will you?"

"I'll be good. I do not *wish* to be kidnapped by Henri de Vauton-Cheviot."

"Excellent. Call me if I'm needed." Harriet opened the door connecting with the second bedroom and pulled it wide. Before entering, she looked around carefully to see that no one was there. She had, she thought, learned caution too late, given it was from this room she and Françoise had been taken the preceding evening; but she had, she hoped, learned the lesson now. Harriet removed her dress and pulled a robe around her slim form. She sat before the fire Madame ordered, as always, to be lit in their rooms.

Staring into the flames, Harriet's mind wandering back over the years to the season she'd not wanted, but which had been thrust upon her by loving parents. There had been sad farewells at the Lisbon dock, the captain hovering in the background anxious to set sail. How unhappy she'd been when she'd left Portugal for London, the captain's wife her chaperon until she reached that mecca for the marriage minded. Tall—too tall—and occasionally awkward with the extra inches she'd not quite learned to handle, Harriet had felt out of place, had sensed the disappointment in the distant relative hired to present her to the *ton*.

Not surprising, thought Harriet bitterly, that the poor creature should feel disappointment. The fashion had been for petite blonds and although Harriet's hair qualified, there was, in certain lights, a hint of despised red tinging it, an odd and unsuitable color. Nor was she petite by anyone's definition!

They'd been a penance, those weeks in London. She'd hated nearly every moment of it, her awkwardness increased by the insistence she rid herself of the odd sophistication she'd gained by being reared in foreign diplomatic circles. Although it was an education-based sophistication, her mentor swore it would be misinterpreted in one so young: Harriet would be labeled as coming, as far too forward, and perhaps worse. Horror of horrors, she might find herself labeled *fast*.

Those despised inches had made Harriet taller than too many of the young men introduced to her. Besides, she'd scorned most of them as wastrels and fops. There'd been a very few men, older men, she'd admired, but she'd had no way of bringing herself to their attention. She had no title. She had no friends among the highest in the land. The daughter of a diplomat, a fifth son who'd had to make his own way in the world, there wasn't even the lure of money to bring those men her way.

Harriet's eyes closed tightly, trying to banish memories of the ball where she'd been formally introduced to Sir Frederick. She'd seen him early in her stay while walking with her chaperon in the park. He'd ridden a magnificent stallion, one Harriet would have died to own, an animal she later learned he'd won in a wager. She'd been warned, of course. The baronet was dangerous and must be avoided and, besides, he lived from win to win, his estate badly depleted and heavily mortgaged. He was not eligible.

Knowing all that didn't help when she saw his height, a well-developed form enhanced by excellent tailoring and then there was that drift of premature white at his temples, frosting the blue black of his hair. But, why, when she'd known he was a rake . . . Or perhaps, in her immaturity, that very danger had been . . . ?

Harriet's eyes opened, but she didn't see the room in which she sat as she compared, mentally, the man she'd met in the wilds of Switzerland with the one she'd not been able to ignore eight years earlier. More white at the temples, of course. But the same healthy bronze to his skin, the same intelligence in those dark eyes. Or was it the same? Intelligence shined from his face, yes, but not the boredom or the arrogance. Nor did he seem to hold one at a distance as he'd done in the past.

Nor, she thought, a smile twitching at her mouth, was he totally preoccupied with another woman as had been the case at that London ball . . .

"Miss, er, Cole?" The hard featured matron, her hostess for the evening, had swept up to where the eighteen-year-old Harriet sat. Harriet, as usual, had been bored nearly to tears by the ball going on around her, a wallflower sitting amongst the chaperons and other unlucky

67

young maidens who, for one reason or another, had not *taken.*

Her hostess had a distracted Sir Frederick in tow and made the introduction. He bowed over the hand Harriet hesitantly presented. She saw that his eyes were directed elsewhere, however. "Your servant," he said and asked, as forced to do by convention. "May I have the honor of this dance?" He still hadn't truly looked at her.

Harriet hadn't known what to do. She'd been warned to have nothing to do with Sir Frederick, but wouldn't it be wrong to refuse when her hostess had made the presentation? She glanced at her stony-visaged chaperon who glared at their hostess, but that well-padded matron was oblivious to everyone and everything but her duty to see that all the young ladies had partners.

"Excellent. Very good," muttered the hostess, already searching for other prey to introduce elsewhere. "Enjoy yourselves."

Still hesitating, Harriet rose to her feet. She almost laughed, biting her lip hard to repress it, when Sir Frederick found himself facing a young woman only a few inches shorter than himself. He blinked, offered his arm and they joined a set—not the set nearest where Harriet had sat, but one farther down the room. Even so, as soon became apparent, it was not the set Sir Frederick had wished to join. The faint scowl he'd worn deepened as he stared at a couple in the set beyond theirs.

Harriet sighed. It would obviously be another miserable half-hour. She stood waiting for the music to begin, not quite knowing what to do with her hands. Sir Frederick was no help. He stared beyond her shoulder to where brittle laughter assaulted Harriet's ears. But conversation was expected—or so it had been drilled into Harriet. She cleared her throat. "The weather has been unusually mild this winter, would you not agree?" she asked.

"Hmm? Oh, yes. Of course."

"But spring seems delayed. I look forward to the flowers in the park."

"As you say, Miss, er, Collins?" He glanced at her, his gaze resting just below her chin, which startled him. He raised his eyes to meet hers.

Harriet lowered her lids, seemingly demure, but really to hide a twinkle. Poor man. He so obviously wished to be elsewhere. But conversation. What could possibly interest the man? "What do you hear concerning the war in the Peninsula, Sir Frederick?"

"War?" Again his eyes flicked, impatiently, toward her; again they lifted to meet hers.

It was, she thought, quite horrid to be so tall. "Perhaps you would prefer to discuss horseflesh?" she suggested. "Or hunting? Do you hunt, Sir Frederick?"

"No." This time he didn't pretend to attend her.

Oh yes you do, she'd thought, half scornful, half amused. *But not the poor fox or other creatures of the wild. And at the moment your prey seems quite happy with another. I hope she's wise and avoids you altogether.* Similar contemptuous thoughts flittered through her mind as she waited.

The music struck up and, her mind on Sir Frederick, Harriet didn't notice she moved with more grace than usual until the movement of the dance separated them and her new partner complimented her on her dancing. She blinked, chuckled, and decided she had discovered the secret of poise: one forgot oneself. When they met again, the forms bringing original partners back together, Harriet ventured another bit of conversation. "Do you think the king will be well enough to open Parliament this year, Sir Frederick? Or will there finally have to be a regency?"

"What?" He frowned, obviously straining to hear what his quarry in the next set said to her partner. A remnant of good manners brought his attention to his own partner. "I'm sorry, Miss, er, Collwood? I didn't catch what you said?"

" 'Twas nothing, Sir Frederick." They swept apart.

When they met again Harriet suggested the moon might rise in the west for a change. Sir Frederick agreed. She thought the steam engine might replace sail upon the sea. Even this ridiculous suggestion brought nothing but preoccupied agreement. The dance ended— and the sport. For once Harriet found herself irritated a set was over.

She allowed Sir Frederick to guide her back to her seat. He bowed over her hand muttering politenesses far too quickly and rose, his eyes meeting hers for the last time. She made no effort to hide her disgust or her scorn, and he blinked, stared at her for a moment. "It's been delightful, Miss, er . . . ," he began, and realized for the first time that he didn't know her name. His brows rose when she chuckled. "Er, I'm sure we'll meet again," he said. Sir Frederick then moved away but looked back once, a perplexed expression drawing his brows together. He was unused to a young lady treating him so cavalierly and— but only for a moment—he wondered at it.

So, thought Harriet, she'd made an impression on him. But obviously, he'd put her quickly from his mind and moved on to the circle surrounding the *ton's* latest beauty. When the ball ended and she returned to her temporary home on Curzon Street, Harriet was unable to sleep. She sat at her desk and drew out writing materials, mending a pen before setting ink to paper:

Dear Papa,

Poor Mama will be so disappointed in her only daughter. I do not take. Ah, the horror of it, the disgrace, the tittle and the tattle as I walk in the park or am announced at a ball. The fear I have that my family will disown me! Oh, Papa, will you, truly, be disappointed if I return to you unwed?

Tonight was the latest of the society functions to which my revered chaperon has begged or borrowed or, for all I know, stolen an invitation. It was, as usual, a very boring evening—except for one incident, which I will relate in detail in a moment. Father, I have reached a decision. I will no longer pretend to be other than I am, despite my chaperon's horror at my normal demeanor. I will enjoy myself in my own way, no longer caring how my behavior reflects upon the poor lady responsible for me. I will, for instance, urge her to get tickets for musical performances and the theater, which is good, when I can hear the actors—which is rarely! We will attend the lectures I enjoy so much and go to exhibits. Please say you will forgive me. Please allow me to return as soon as possible to the happy home from which I was thrust. Please, please, arrange my passage back to you and Mother!

Now let me tell you what happened. I am completely disillusioned, dear Papa, in the set of humanity designated *rake*. It is a hum. It is a bug-a-bear to scare young demoiselles, a story for children! Why the most notorious rake in London is nothing but a court-card . . .

Court-card? Harriet returned to the present, the word jarring her mind from the impassioned letter she'd written that long ago night. She stared blindly around the bedroom in the old inn in Calais. Never in his life, she thought, had Sir Frederick Carrington acted the mincing prattling court-card!

But, however that might be, dear Papa *had* arranged for her to return to Lisbon and, once there, she'd spent hours with her pen writing and polishing her "memoirs." That writing, she thought, her eyes narrowing, had been a ridiculous collection of satires, setting far too many well-known *tonish* figures to ridicule. What had she done with it? She turned her head to where a highly polished wooden chest sat on a table and thought, drowsily, about unlocking it and searching it.

She hadn't thought of those manuscript pages for years. If they still existed amongst the papers she toted wherever she went, they should be destroyed before, somehow, they chanced to fall into the wrong hands. She had not been kind to society in that writing. Perhaps, in her disillusionment and because she'd resented her lack of success, she'd been cruel in order to restore her own self-esteem? Yes, she thought and yawned, she really must look to see if those pages existed and, if they did, burn them. Another yawn and her head nodded. Snuggling into the corner of the high back of the chair, Harriet fell asleep.

Not half an hour later, a key turned softly in the door. A tall figure slipped into the room. The man moved on stealthy feet toward the fire and paused, staring pensively at the peacefully sleeping woman.

Four

Frederick ran his finger across the thin, black, stage-villain's moustache he'd affected when he'd first realized he'd a reputation as a rake. He'd originally grown it while in the mood of thumbing his nose at society; now it was so much a part of him, he'd very likely not recognize himself if it were shaved off.

He certainly didn't think of it as he wondered if he should awaken Harriet. She looked tired. Even in sleep she appeared tense and unhappy. She also looked younger with that strand of softly curling hair loosened from her usually well-disciplined French roll. Such beautiful hair. Such a strong young woman. He'd wondered about her, how she felt, what she was doing, on numerous occasions during their stay in Paris.

Then, when he'd gone out looking for feminine distraction, he could find none among the demimondaine who appealed to his senses. Now, quite suddenly, he understood why. None of them had pale blond hair. None of them were tall and slim and capable of calmly shooting at a villain attempting to ruin a girl in her charge. That Harriet had missed the villain and nicked the horse didn't bother Sir Frederick. Dueling pistols were notoriously badly made and a wise man tested his, knew their every quirk. During their stay in the Swiss château, he'd enjoyed teaching her to handle the set which had belonged to her father.

But that was weeks ago, and the adventure still not finished. Before he could pursue his sudden impulsive decision concerning Miss Cole's future, they must once again outwit the enemy. Carefully, gently, Frederick lay his hand over her mouth and stared into the grey eyes blinking open, widening. He put a finger across his lips, urging her to silence and, when she nodded, released her, seating himself in the chair opposite. He was bemused by the willpower required to move away from her.

"I'm aware it is common practice for you to invade a woman's bedchamber, Sir Frederick," she said keeping her voice low, but nevertheless scathing. "It is not, however, something with which I've had experience. Is there an etiquette of which I should be made aware?"

He smiled at her ice-coated question. "If I were here for the reasons you impute to me, I would gladly teach it to you. Since I've come to thicken the plot for your escape to England and for that only I must deny myself the pleasure. I believe," he teased, his eyes running down her figure, barely hidden by her dishabille, "that I'd enjoy teaching you—"

"Enough!" Harriet blushed. "I well know I'm not the sort you prefer to, er, tutor, Sir Frederick."

Piqued and repiqued! Frederick grinned appreciatively. She was obviously one who woke instantly and completely. Frederick tucked the knowledge away—as he hoarded every tiny clue to who and what she was.

After a moment in which she struggled to regain her dignity, Harriet asked, "In what way may I aid in our escape?"

"You may hold the tickets for your party's embarkation this evening."

Frederick dug the slim bundle from an inside pocket. It was necessary to open his jacket wide to do so, which gave Harriet, if he'd thought of it, a view of a strong broad chest covered by no more than the finest of white shirting. His low-cut silk vest was shaped to his body and didn't interfere with her impromptu study. The sight sent shivers through her, which she controlled with great effort in the short time available while he rebuttoned his coat.

"You purchased them for us?" she asked, needing to say something, anything.

"Yes. On Madame's orders. Yves and I bought them when we went for our own. We believe we've left a misleading trail for the comte. With luck he'll believe you and the others intend to transfer from this hotel to another. You *will* leave here, but will go straight to the quay where the captain will expect you to arrive at the last possible moment. He'll leave port the instant you and your luggage are aboard."

"You've talked to the captain?"

"Not yet. But I will."

"He will cooperate?"

Frederick remembered his first crossing of the Channel nearly a year earlier on this same packet when he'd made an effort to meet the captain. He'd spent a fascinating crossing talking to the greying man, hearing of adventures in the Royal Navy. Later Frederick had listened while the captain complained about the boring but responsible job of crossing and recrossing the Channel. Boring, yes, but the man had collected some hilarious tales about his passengers and had passed those on, too. The man would remember him and would cooperate.

Frederick said, "I know the captain. I'll tell him enough

of the story to gain his assistance. That is not the problem. The hardest part, Miss Cole, will be leaving you behind and boarding early. I must, you see, trust you to arrange things so that you reach the quay at exactly the right moment."

"You do not like leaving control in another's hands, do you Sir Frederick?"

"Not when I deem it important nothing go wrong."

He stood and Harriet rose as well. She pulled her robe around her slim form and, for the first time, remembered how she was dressed. Her cheeks warmed in embarrassment. Frederick tucked the loosened strand of hair back behind her ear. His touch left a trail of heat behind.

"You must go," she whispered, her voice tight.

"Yes. It is highly improper for me to be here, but I cannot leave quite yet. Cob is to give us ten minutes and then, when the time is up, he'll wait until the passage is clear before tapping at the door. If you do not trust me, you may join the others in the next bedroom." Sir Frederick hoped the signal would come soon. He wasn't entirely certain he trusted himself!

Given the opportunity to escape, Harriet found herself, perversely, unwilling to do so. "I do not understand you." The thought had become a litany inside her head. Once again she said it aloud. *Someday,* she thought, *I'll learn to keep my thoughts to myself.*

"You have a distorted view of me, gained I know not where. I'd like to change that once we've reached safety, Miss Cole."

She blinked. "Why?"

"Why?" What reason would she accept? "Not long ago I discovered that a woman can be a man's friend. It was a strange and wondrous revelation which has had months

76

to take root and grow. I find I like the notion. I would like to be your friend, Miss Cole."

She shook her head. "The ultimate rake? The most dangerous man in England for womankind wishes a woman for a *friend?*"

"Yes. I am not such a dangerous man, Miss Cole."

"You have been our friend, more than once, now. I can make sense of it only if I believe you to have designs on Frani."

"But I do not. She is a delightful chit, open and trusting, much like a kitten. But she doesn't interest me in the way you wish to believe." A sharp rap at the door said time was up. Wishing it were not so, Frederick made a movement of dismissal. He sighed as he accepted he must go. "We will continue this conversation another time, Miss Cole. Eventually, perhaps, you *will* understand me."

"I think I wish to do so—I don't know why." The impulsive denial of comprehension brought more color into her pale cheeks.

You don't know why, my love? Oh, but I think you do! Even with that thought ringing in his head, Frederick managed to speak calmly. "Then, with any luck at all, we'll eventually reach an understanding. I'll next see you aboard the packet, Miss Cole."

If all goes well, they each added in the privacy of their thoughts.

Frederick slipped through the door and disappeared. Behind him the tall grey-eyed woman, her mind confused and heart rapidly beating, lifted her fingers and touched her cheek where he had briefly stroked her skin.

Oh no, thought Harriet. *You're not dangerous. No, not at all. Of course not!*

She glared at the closed door. That man was a danger to even so staid and proper a lady as she'd become. In which case he was still more a danger to the young woman she had in her care. *Learn* to understand Sir Frederick Carrington? She understood quite enough, thank you, and would, in future, avoid him to whatever degree she could manage.

Or she would if she could rid herself of this idiotic compulsion consuming her. It *was* idiotic, the fact she wished to get to know his history, his thoughts and beliefs!

Harriet stared down at the tickets clutched in her hand. She counted them, found there were enough for their entire party. Madame, of course, had given him the number.

Whatever chaos ruled her heart, there was still their escape to plan. Harriet stalked to the connecting door, pulling the tie to her robe tighter. As she reached for the latch, she stopped. Madame, at least, would raise eyebrows that she'd received Sir Frederick while dressed thusly—not that he'd given her any choice in the matter, but Madame couldn't know that.

Wondering where her wits had gone, Harriet dressed quickly. Once her hair was smoothed and tightly pinned back, when her neat grey dress rustled around shod feet, and, last but not least, after she'd recreated the poise which was usually so much a part of her—*then* she went into the connecting room, ready to organize her troops.

"Well, Cob, you're looking much more cheerful."

"We be going home, m'lad."

Frederick turned toward the low window looking out over the noisy hotel yard. "Yes. You'll be glad to return, will you not?"

"Well now, *that's* the truth and all." Cob folded another shirt and laid it in the portmanteau, which he filled quickly and neatly. For all the valet looked an ex-bruiser, which he was, he had a deft way with packing and a gentle touch with a razor—on those occasions when Frederick didn't insist on shaving himself.

More than twenty years ago Robert Strong, called Cob for reasons no one but himself might know, had won Sir Frederick's father a packet. He'd beaten his opponent to a bloody pulp in a makeshift ring well hidden from the eyes of disapproving authority, and he hadn't come off unscathed himself.

The old baronet had asked the young man how he might reward him. Cob, hurting badly from two cracked ribs and a ringing head, told the baronet he'd like a change of occupation.

"And what might you be thinking would suit you, lad?" had asked Frederick's father.

"Well, sir, I'd ambitions to be a valet before I got talked into fighting."

"Valet? *Valet?*" The tall dark-haired man with wide white wings of hair drifting back from his temples threw back his head and laughed. "Well, and so it shall be," he said when he'd stopped. He'd taken Cob home, introduced him to his sixteen-year-old son and told Cob to take care of the boy.

It was, mused Cob, one of the few good things the wicked old baronet had ever done. He and young Frederick had hit it off. And they'd been together ever since. He'd gone up to Cambridge with his charge, dragging the lad out of one sort of high jinks after another. And he'd seen the young man turn bitter after a petticoat affair when he'd just turned nineteen. Not that Sir Fred had a very high opinion of women before that contretemps, thought Cob—and with reason when one considered his willful selfish grandmother and cold, self-centered mother—but that ex-

79

perience had soured the lad, changed him into something close to a true woman-hater.

Then there'd been the danger they'd endured during the war—which had been both a good time and a bad. It had certainly been hard keeping his tongue between his teeth when, drinking with his colleagues, they'd sneered at Frederick's self-proclaimed cowardliness!

More recently, there'd been that frisky miss who had, Cob believed, touched Frederick's heart. That minx had almost got him, thought Cob, and wondered what had gone wrong. Something had. That slyboots, Chester, Frederick's young tiger, had gone around smirking for weeks before Sir Frederick left England so precipitously. During those months preceding their flight, Frederick had swung wildly from mood to mood—until, early one morning, that dreadful message arrived from Dover that Cob was to pack for an extended tour of the Continent, that they were off to Paris.

Ol' slyboots had had to find himself a new job, thought Cob, which was the only satisfaction he'd gotten from the move.

So. Now they were going home. Cob glanced to where his master still stared out the window. The mood had changed again, but Cob couldn't yet tell if it were for the better—although, how could it not be? Inheriting all that money from that old bat in Florence had surprised Frederick more than anyone.

Cob recalled the day he'd followed his master to the cemetery where she'd been interred. Cob had waited for nearly an hour as Frederick stood before the ornate tomb complete with marble cherubs and laurel leaf swags. Frederick had stared at it, his body rigid with an emotion Cob had been unable to read.

But the money. The money would come in handy—if

Sir Fred didn't lose it at tables or turf. There had never been enough money—although Frederick had always managed, one way or another, to have the best. What plans had his master laid now that he was rich? He'd mentioned they'd return first to London where he must consult with his man of business—likely to see to the mortgages, thought Cob—and then they'd go on to the old estate where they'd stay awhile, Sir Fred had said.

But that decision was made before Sir Fred had his first run-in with the evil Frenchy, before he'd taken on responsibility for Madame's party. Cob sniffed. The young one was just such a one as Frederick had run after in his search for revenge on fickle petticoats. Was he after this one?

Cob didn't approve of Frederick's long war against womankind and had told him so more than once. Frederick's new behavior while on the continent had led Cob to believe his master had given up his old ways.

Ah well, thought Cob philosophically. One could never say it was boring serving Sir Frederick. He'd watch. And, if necessary, stick his bit in the pot and stir it up to keep his master out of deep trouble. Women. They were, thought Cob, the bane of male existence.

Some hours later Frederick, Yves, and their valets boarded the packet to England. Two entered the skiff that took them out to the anchored ship with a last look at the quay and a long satisfied look at each other. The same dark man who had followed them to the ticket office watched them go. Of the other two men boarding the packet, one, a thin Frenchman dressed in the sober black of the proper valet, entered the boat with trepidation, winning grins from the sailors loading piles of luggage into a second boat. The last, Cob, took his place stoically, not looking forward to the journey over the rough Channel, but longing to reach England and home. Cob had had enough of foreign lands to last him the rest of his life—although if Sir Fred were to say they were off again, then off he'd go.

Back at the inn the three women ordered two long-suffering maids this way and that, changing their minds a dozen times. The day lengthened as the harried servants packed and repacked. Maria mumbled and Petra grumbled at Madame's unusual vacillation.

Finally, late in the afternoon, the maids raised their eyes to heaven in silent thanks, followed their ladies into a hired carriage and looked forward to a good meal at the hostelry to which they were headed. Neither had had time for more than a roll and a bite of cheese at midday and each felt they deserved a rest.

But what was this? There was no hotel in this direction. The maids, Maria and Petra, looked at one another and the brighter of the two suddenly grinned. Both women knew the troubles their youngest lady was having with Monsieur le Comte. A fine trick this. Another thought followed on the first and, the sisters' minds, working alike, formed identical frowns on nearly identical brows. A fine trick *if* it worked.

Three large skiffs and attendant sailors awaited them. The luggage was bundled into two boats in a rather helter-skelter fashion and rowed away. The other waited for the five women.

Harriet was concerned. "Madame, it is not too late for you to change your mind."

"I'll not rest until Frani is under the protection of her grandfather."

"Grand-mère, we are warned, *oui?* We can protect ourselves. You are ill."

"I am not ill. I am merely worried. Come, child. Let

82

the man help you into the boat." Both young women watched as Frani's grandmother was settled on a seat and wrapped warmly. "Well?" Aristocratic always, Madame's arrogance was obvious as she asked the sailors, "For what do we wait?"

Harriet felt a warm pride in the strength and courage of the old woman.

They were transferred to the deck of the packet and, almost before their feet were firmly settled on the well scrubbed planks, the anchor weighed and the boat moved out. Sir Frederick stepped forward, his eyes going to Harriet first, but she dropped her gaze immediately. He turned to Madame. "I have reserved two cabins for your party. Would you care to remove to one now?"

Madame grimaced. "No. I know how I am on water. I learned many years ago I do much better if I stay on deck."

"It will be cold."

"I will be warmly wrapped."

"As you wish." Sir Frederick moved away, found a sheltered corner on the lee side, and had a long deck chair placed there.

Soon Madame settled, her head leaning against the caned back, her eyes closed. Harriet hovered until her mistress opened one eye. "See to Françoise. After all we've endured I do not want the minx lost by falling overboard," finished Madame caustically.

"Sir Frederick thinks we should go to a cabin, but I do not believe that notion will serve. Frani is exploring under Monsieur de Bartigues' careful eye."

"Ah." Harriet noted a speculative gleam in Madame's eyes. "Monsieur de Bartigues. What do you think of the man, Harriet?"

"He seems," said Harriet slowly, "a proper enough

soul—although I doubt that, given he is friends with Sir Frederick."

"You will not give the baronet an inch, will you, even after all he has done for us?"

"I remember being told that he is always in need of money, and Frani is a wealthy young woman."

"When did you hear tales of his need, Harri? You've never explained where you first learned of his reputation."

"It was years ago," said Harriet shortly.

"And—as I have said before to you—times change." The stubborn young woman Madame had hired to help care for Frani pressed her lips together. That had been a lucky day, thought Madame, the day she'd decided to hire Harriet. "Sir Frederick appears to be in funds now," she added to see what reaction that would raise.

"Yes. And if he is, I wonder how he got it," was the caustic response.

Madame chuckled. "Suspicious wench. Ah well, time will tell."

"Will you rest now?" asked Harriet, obviously glad that Madame seemed willing to drop the subject of Frederick Carrington. "You are warm enough?"

"Yes, I'm fine. Best of all, we are safely away. If the comte were aboard, Sir Frederick would know. He'd have told us. We are, for a time, free from the man.

The packet moved out of the harbor, slicing through waves that to Harriet's eyes seemed large and dangerous but the sailors' behavior seemed calm enough. The deck of the ship rose and fell, rose and fell, as it plowed through the huge swells. She saw Madame's hand go to her stomach, her eyes close tightly and a frown appear.

Harriet, worried, asked, "Are you all right?"

"No of course I am not all right. I'll not be right until

we reach Dover," said Madame crossly. "Do go away, Harriet, and let me survive this in my own way. See to the others."

Feeling sympathy for the brave woman, Harriet was, nevertheless, glad she herself did not suffer from *mal de mer*. She started forward, but found the rest of their party approaching. Françoise, she thought, noting the girl's set mouth and trembling limbs, was not to be so lucky. The girl leaned heavily on Yves' arm.

"I will help her to our cabin," said Harriet, perceiving that the crossing was going to be an exceedingly unpleasant experience since she'd spend all her time tending to the sick girl.

"No," contradicted Sir Frederick. "I've asked that another chair be placed near her grandmother's. She will, believe me, do better on deck in the fresh air."

"She will be embarrassed if . . ."

"But far less ill even if she is to, er, shoot the cat," he interrupted before she could find a polite way of finishing her sentence. He added in a soothing tone, "Please, Miss Cole, I know what I say."

Half an hour later Françoise told Harriet in a cross voice to stop hovering. "If Grand-mère can survive without complaint, so may I," she said.

With that the girl closed her eyes tightly, her mouth firmed. She would say no more. Harriet, looking from one sufferer to the other, frowned. She hesitated to leave them and finally moved no farther away than to the nearby ship's rail.

Sir Frederick joined her there. "I have checked on your maids, Miss Cole."

"And?"

"I was told to go away." He grinned. "So far, we have two women under the weather, two very ill, who will not

85

believe they'll be better off on deck, and a valet who, between sieges, swears he'll die—and that if he does *not* he'll believe the good lord is punishing him for sins he cannot remember! The rest of us are managing quite well."

"You neglect another. *Your own* valet is also suffering. He says, however, that he will not succumb." She noted Sir Frederick's swift frowning glance toward Cob. "You were unaware?"

"Cob never complains. Our passage to France was smooth as silk, and I'm sure he had no trouble then. I had not thought—"

"No. Why should you? He is just a servant."

"Scorn? In this case you are very wrong, Miss Cole. Cob is far more than a servant. He is my friend. He has been with me for over twenty years. On more than one occasion we've depended on each other to save our lives." Frederick stared at the water. "He's been more a father to me than my father ever was."

She blinked. "You *are* concerned, are you not?"

"Yes. Perhaps another chair . . ."

"Would he take it?"

Frederick grinned at her sapient question. "We'll have it available just in case he will do so. He'll not remove to a cabin, of that I'm certain." A third chair appeared and was placed a little apart from the others. When Sir Frederick returned to Harriet's side, he leaned against the rail and studied her worried face. "You must not be so concerned. No one dies of *mal de mer*, no matter how much they may wish they might."

"Madame is old. She has been ill."

"Yes. But she is also determined. She will live to place Mademoiselle Françoise in the grandfather's care. She is a strong woman, Miss Cole."

86

"I know." Harriet turned to stare over the rolling waves. The wind caught the scarf she'd tied over her hat and blew the ends wildly. "It is getting worse."

"In its way, it is better. The stronger the wind, the sooner we'll reach Dover. The captain predicts something under four hours."

"There is that." They were quiet for a time.

Sir Frederick broke the long silence. "I've been trying for weeks to remember why your name seems familiar."

Harriet glanced up at him, her eyes flashing daggers before turning away again. She thought of that dance where he'd called her three different names. He'd have no memory of that and couldn't be referring to it. Ah well, she supposed she must attempt to answer as politely as he'd asked.

"Perhaps," she said, "you've heard of my father, Timothy Cole—since he was rarely in England, I'm certain you'd never have met him."

"Timothy Cole . . ." Frederick snapped his fingers. "The embassy staff in Lisbon and later in Vienna. Of course! Tongue Valiant Tim!"

Harriet choked back a laugh and turned wary eyes on him. "He never liked that cognomen."

"But he deserved it." Brown eyes met grey, and grey fled. "An admirable man, your father. With his intelligence he should have risen higher in the diplomatic corps than he, in fact, did. Telling his superiors what he thought of them did him no good. He couldn't keep his tongue between his teeth, could he? I see where you acquired the trick of saying what you think."

Harriet frowned. "You met my father?"

"Twice. Once in Lisbon and once in Vienna. We had, er—" He paused and his eyebrows rose. "—business—"

Again he hesitated, wondering how much she knew of her father's work.

She glanced at him, away quickly, her hands tightening around the rail. "My father was involved in work he found shameful but necessary."

Finding he'd be giving away no secrets, Frederick nodded. "I know. Spying is not a gentlemanly endeavor. Luckily for myself, I was not much of a gentleman to begin with. I was, you see, a counterspy in England for most of the war. Very occasionally I was sent abroad."

Through Sir Frederick's mind passed the cynical thought that it was unusual for him to feel the need to justify his existence in anyone's eyes. It was, he decided, just one more indication Miss Cole meant a great deal to him.

After a moment he continued. "It was a great loss when your father died, Miss Cole. He may not have approved of the coordination efforts he ran so beautifully, but he did it very well, and it was a much needed skill. I know of no one who could keep so many reins running smoothly, keep them untangled and doing their proper work."

Harriet brushed aside her wind-tossed scarf so she could stare at him. "I had not thought you were engaged in the war effort," she said.

"No man . . . or woman . . . is a flat two dimensional animal. We all have many facets to our souls, Miss Cole." Frederick spoke dryly. He stared at her, wondering at her thoughts.

Again she flicked a look his way. "I've painted you all black, have I not?"

"I wish I knew why. I can't have insulted you personally since we hadn't met before this adventure threw us together—" his brows flew together at the wry smile his words induced "—or had we?"

"Once. Long ago."

"Not in Lisbon. Nor in Vienna. I went nowhere where I'd be seen and recognized during either of those brief visits. So where? When?"

"In London," she admitted after a struggle to remain silent. "Nearly eight years ago."

"You'd have been very young."

"I was eighteen and reluctantly enduring a season."

Frederick thought back, but could no longer separate one season from another during that period of his life. "Perhaps I hurt some friend of yours?" he asked cautiously. "Surely I'd recognize you if we had been introduced."

"We *were* introduced," she said, "You, however, were much preoccupied with another young lady and, I think, never heard my name. At least you called me by several different versions before our dance was finished."

"We danced?" He turned to stare at her. "Why don't I remember?"

"As I said, there was another lady, a very beautiful young lady. She was dancing in the next set."

Sir Frederick closed his eyes. He pulled in a long breath and let it go slowly. "I see. You are a woman scorned and not about to give an inch now we've met again."

"No. I've no wish for revenge. I *had* that—although you were unaware." His mobile eyebrow rose, silently asking a question. "I made a May-game of you while we danced," she explained. "It was the most enjoyable set of my whole miserable experience in London. I laughed about it for months." When he asked how she'd done so, a twinkling eye telling her he'd not hold it against her, she described her small revenge. She finished, "Then I suggested the new steam engine might someday replace sail."

"I hope I agreed to *that*. It will, you know."

"Ridiculous."

"No."

Sir Frederick explained why he believed it true. Harriet argued. He responded. Their discussion passed to other things and, slowly, but without their noticing, well over an hour passed. The moon peeked from between scudding clouds and Sir Frederick looked around. Yves lay on still another chair, wrapped tightly in a warm rug. Madame and Françoise slept uneasily. So did Cob.

Farther along the railing stood a scowling stranger who occasionally glanced their way. Sir Frederick eyed him thoughtfully. Then he looked to where a sailor stood, arms folded, one knee bent and his foot steadying his bulky body as he leaned back against the superstructure. The captain had ordered that huge man to guard this party and the man was unquestioningly following orders. Frederick relaxed.

"As much as I'm enjoying our conversation, Miss Cole, I think you should rest. You will be called when we reach Dover. Tomorrow, if Madame is able, we'll travel on to London."

"You've arranged transport?"

"So I hope. I'd no notion I'd have passengers when I first sent a message to my friend, but, if Lord Halford is in London, he will have purchased a team and carriage for me. It will be waiting in Dover. If he has failed me, then I'll hire a post chaise. You ladies may have the coach and Monsieur de Bartigues and I will ride." Frederick frowned. "I still do not like the notion that you'll arrive in London under my care."

90

"Once in London you may leave us. I believe Madame intends hiring a suite at the Pulteney Hotel in Piccadilly. From there she will contact Lord Crawford."

"Who?"

"Lord Crawford."

"Crawford! But he can't be Françoise's grandfather. He *has* no grandchildren."

"There was a family argument when his daughter wished to marry Frani's father. He disinherited her when she eloped."

"Impossible. His daughter drowned nearly twenty years ago. I remember it well. There is a memorial plaque in the castle chapel."

Harriet turned to lean back against the rail, eyed him. "How do you know so much?"

Frederick's grim expression softened. "Because, my suspicious one, she was my favorite cousin, one of the few females in the world I actually liked. I was devastated when she drowned."

"Your cousin? I'm sorry that I must tell you Lord Crawford lied. She died only five years ago."

Sir Frederick fell silent, staring over the phosphorescent tipped waves. "How could he have done such a thing? She was the old man's only offspring. Or she was when I left England last spring." He forced a chuckle. "I've been gone just long enough that it is possible his new wife has given him another. He remarried not long before I left, you see."

"Oh dear. I wonder if his wife will welcome Françoise."

"She will not."

"You sound very sure of that."

"I am. The woman my uncle married is a most vicious woman. She will be jealous of Mademoiselle Françoise's

91

beauty and still more jealous of her youth. Poor Cressida."

"Why do you call her so? She married a rich man by her own choice, I presume."

"And expected to honeymoon in Paris before returning to London where she hoped to live the lifestyle to which she's always aspired. My uncle had concocted quite other plans after delving into her history. He took her to an island off the Scottish coast. A nearly deserted island with an old, uncomfortable and drafty castle. There he meant to keep her until she was pregna—er, I mean to say, increasing."

"Oh, the poor lady."

"She would be given a choice, my uncle informed me: give up society, the balls and whatnot and, I must add, the gaming tables, which she loves well—or agree to bear her new husband an heir. She will have had a hard choice since child-bearing is something she's feared and carefully avoided."

"So, you may have been cut from his will?"

"It is no longer important." Again he felt that uncharacteristic need to explain himself. "Odd as it seems, while in Florence I did an old woman a good turn. She died soon after, and I found she'd left me a fortune I didn't know she possessed." Sir Frederick frowned. This compulsion to explain himself to Miss Cole was ridiculous. He never explained himself to anyone!

"A fairy tale ending," she said lightly.

"So one might say." Sir Frederick turned away.

When he didn't turn back, she said, "Thank you for the conversation and company, Sir Frederick, but I've become a trifle chilled and will go down to my cabin for a time."

"I apologize, Miss Cole," said Frederick, suddenly stiff

and formal, angry with himself for thoughtlessly keeping her out in the wind. "I should not have kept you standing about for so long."

"Don't be ridiculous," Harriet responded crossly, her features showing no expression, her mind a muddle of new impressions. Exasperated with herself, her tone was chilling when she continued, "If I had wished to go sooner I would have gone. It is still several hours until we reach Dover. Until then, Sir Frederick."

She swept away toward the stairs leading to the cabins and disappeared. Sir Frederick, a wary eye occasionally checking the comte's man, found his mind wandering from one thing to another. Why, when he'd fallen in love with a pert minx like Elizabeth only a year earlier, should he so soon find himself far more deeply in love with an utterly different style of woman? Then there were the inconsistencies of women: why, when they'd enjoyed a long, interesting, and non-aggressive discussion, had Miss Cole shifted, there at the end, from newfound friend to the icy shrew she'd shown herself to be from the time of their odd introduction in Switzerland?

Down in her cabin, snuggled under blankets, and finally warm and drowsy, Harriet wondered much the same thing. They'd been getting along so well. Why, when he'd done nothing more than apologize in that ridiculously stiff way for keeping her out in the cold, had she suddenly felt rejected and lonely? Someday, my girl, she told herself, you'll lose your temper in the wrong situation and find yourself well and truly in the basket!

On deck, Sir Frederick scanned the sky. A storm, a bad one according to the captain, was brewing in the North Sea. When it broke, traffic on the Channel would cease, travelers held in port possibly for days. That was well and good, assuming the storm broke before the morning packet left Calais! On the other hand, here and now, he wished to protect the women from the elements, and he hoped the rain held off until he had them settled at the Ship Inn, which should have rooms reserved in his name. He'd give them to the women if Madame had not foreseen the need to reserve rooms and the place was overcrowded, as it often was when careful travelers waited for calm, clear weather.

He frowned toward where Madame lay. Her color was bad and there was a blueness around her mouth he didn't like. She needed rest, but most of all, she needed freedom from worry. Would she find that once she'd handed Françoise into his uncle's protection? Or would she discover that Crawford's new wife was nearly as much a danger as the comte? Frederick sighed, wishing there were a simple answer.

Dover's famous white cliffs were visible now, ghostly pale in the skittish moonlight, the moon showing itself less and less often as the cloud cover worsened. They'd have been within sight of those cliffs some time ago if it were daytime and the sun shone on them. He cast another wary glance toward the billowing clouds whipping across the sky and prayed there would be time to disembark before the heavy-bottomed harbingers of the coming storm opened up and soaked the world.

He looked ahead, his hands on the rail. At least here, in Dover, they would not have to transfer to small boats and be rowed in. There would be a gangplank down which they could walk and a hack or chairs in which the women could ride to the hotel. His grip tightened as he heard soft steps behind him, but he didn't turn his head. Had he, carelessly, at the last moment, given the comte's murderer a chance at him?

"Sir Frederick?"

He relaxed at Harriet's tentative question. "I was about to send for you. Did you rest, Miss Cole?"

"Yes. Will it be long now?"

"I believe something less than half an hour. There," he pointed, "See? England awaits us."

"What a busy port even now, at night."

"Hmmm."

They reached simultaneously for Harriet's scarf which blew across his face. Their hands met. Holding both her fingers and the soft material, Frederick turned. "Are you looking forward to being in London again, Miss Cole?"

Harriet's fingers trembled. His words were courteous, perfectly polite, but the gentle pressure of his hand and the warmth in his eyes were saying something different. She searched his face, barely hearing her own voice respond with a quiet negative. "I was not happy in London. I have no fond memories of my one and only stay there."

"It will be different this time, Miss Cole."

"How will it be different?"

"You are older, for one thing."

She nodded. "And little better than a servant for another."

His hand tightened around hers. "You are much more than a servant!"

Harriet looked away, refused to respond to such a silly comment.

Sir Frederick sighed softly, but changed the subject to one she'd deem less controversial. "I have had an idea I believe will satisfy any fears you have about putting up at another hotel—even one so well run as the Pulteney. It should satisfy Madame as well. It will take time to contact my uncle who rarely visits London and is unlikely to be there when we arrive, and I think it will be best if you visit his new wife's brother. Lord Halford has a moderately large and well-situated London house. He may be told the whole story of the comte's persecution of Mademoiselle with no concern that he'll add the story to the London gossip mill. He will be prepared to protect Mademoiselle Françoise. Most important of all, with the connection through his sister, who is married to Frani's grandfather, no eyebrows will be raised, and we'll avoid scandal."

"You mean we need not be tainted by our association with yourself."

"Exactly."

"A confirmed rake worrying about the reputation of a beautiful young girl! You are a strange man, Sir Frederick."

"Only to a mind as suspicious as your own. Perhaps it is *because* I have led the life of a rake I know the dangers surrounding women such as yourself and wish to circumvent them." He raised an eyebrow, his gaze questioning.

"Oh, not myself," she responded. "I am well and truly on the shelf, a confirmed ape leader. At six and twenty I've given up all hopes of attaining the married state, of course. Furthermore, I am a companion, a servant, as I have said. Again there is no reputation to protect. But, for Françoise, I thank you."

Frederick's lips tightened. "Miss Cole, somewhere deep within that poise and strength and loyalty you exhibit, there is an insecure and unhappy woman. Bid her adieu. On the instant! You are lovely. You are intelligent. And you are *not* on the shelf." He scowled down at her, his fingers tightening around hers and the scarf. "Do not waste your visit to London as if you were a desiccated and torpid old woman."

The color in Harriet's cheeks, already rosy from the wind, deepened. She tugged at the hand she'd forgotten he held. "We are nearly arrived. I must see to our baggage since it will be beyond our poor maids to direct its unloading."

He sighed softly, knowing he'd failed once again to reach the woman inside the lovely creature he would have for his own. "Your maids will not believe it, of course, but tell them their suffering is about to end." He watched as she moved gracefully along the deck which, since they'd entered the harbor as they spoke and into the protection it provided, no longer rose and plunged so dangerously.

Five

When Harriet disappeared, Frederick turned back to the rail. They had approached near enough he could discern individual figures along the torchlit dock. One, a tall man wrapped in a many-caped driving coat, caught his eye and held it. He waited and, assuring himself it was who he'd thought, he grinned widely. Bless friends everywhere!

But, he thought, a small anxiety entering his soul, was Robert Merton, Lord Halford, alone—or had he brought the minx who had been, briefly, between them. Frederick hoped he need not yet face Elizabeth. Not until he had the three women safe. Not until he had nothing on his mind and could put the whole of it to controlling whatever riot Elizabeth might still raise in his heart and soul! He didn't *think* there'd be a problem—not if what he felt for Harriet were real—but if there *were* feelings for the chit, he wanted any such emotion to do no damage to the long friendship between himself and Robert.

Frederick waited impatiently as the sailors warped the packet closer to the dock. He waved to Robert, who waved back, his hand going quickly to the hat nearly blown from his head. The two men grinned at each other.

When the gangplank was in place, Frederick hurried down it and went straight to his friend.

"I'd not expected this," said Frederick. "I only asked that you choose me a team and carriage and have them delivered here."

"You've been gone very nearly a year. Someone should welcome you home. I've been here for the last three packets." The two men clasped hands. "Is all well with you?" asked his lordship.

The question was not, Frederick knew, as innocent as it sounded. He smiled. A hint of nostalgia, perhaps the slightest touch of pain could be read in the quick grimace passing across his features. "All, believe me, is well. Or, actually, it isn't." Frederick grinned, his brows rising in arcs. "You don't know how opportune your arrival is," he said on a wry note. "We've a problem, Robert."

"We've a problem? When *you've* a problem, a woman's mixed up in it somewhere." One brow rose, a grin spreading across the handsome face. "Remember, Fred, I'm a married man now and a reformed character. You mustn't mix me up in anything I'll regret."

"You won't regret it. Besides, I make an exceedingly odd knight-errant. You'll do far better."

"Ah ha! A story."

"Yes. I'll tell it later. It is important to get Madame la Comtesse, her granddaughter, and Miss Cole out of sight. Have you a hack waiting?"

"How about my carriage? It's there."

"Excellent. In fact, it couldn't be better for lots of reasons. Wait here, my friend."

With Yves' help on one side and Frederick's on the other, Madame walked down the plank. She stood straight, if not terribly firm, before Lord Halford, nodding at Frederick's introduction. "We'll go no farther than the

Ship Inn tonight, Madame," he finished gently, "but believe me, Lord Halford will help you and yours as I have done."

Harriet helped Françoise down to the dock. Brief introductions were made but Frani obviously felt too unwell to care. She joined her grandmother in the Halford carriage and Harriet, after one last look at Frederick, a look he couldn't interpret, joined her mistress and her charge.

Too few hours later, after a brief night's sleep, Yves, Frederick, and Robert met in the private parlor the latter had reserved. Another half-hour, breakfast, and good English ale under their vests, Yves inserted a word here and there as Frederick explained their association with the French party.

"We'll be happy to have them as guests, Fred," said Robert. "The young one will be company for Elizabeth, which will give your Miss Cole some freedom from worry."

"Will it? Save her worry, I mean? Or perhaps you are suggesting that marriage has sobered Elizabeth, turning her into a sedate and settled matron?" Frederick was surprised at how easily the teasing words fell from his lips. He was also pleased; surely it meant he need not fear his first meeting with Elizabeth. "Hmm? Has it?"

Robert choked on the last of his brew. He laughed at the dry question. "No. I fear it has done no such thing."

Frederick felt a fleeting sense of jealousy at the satisfaction he heard in his friend's voice and decided he'd congratulated himself too soon. "Then Miss Cole will be more occupied than ever," he said. "She'll feel responsible for twice the trouble, if I know our Miss Cole. Poor Miss Cole," he added.

Robert looked from Frederick to Yves. "The young

one seemed very quiet, almost too quiet. Not the sort to cause anyone concern."

Frederick and Yves turned to look at each other. They grinned. "Mademoiselle Françoise suffered, some, on the crossing. By now she will be returned to normal—"

As if to prove his words, the door burst open and Frani, with Miss Cole following more sedately, entered.

"—As you see," he finished and turned toward the women. "I told you you'd recover once dry land was under your feet, child."

"Mais oui, it was true, what you said, and now, me, I am hungry. Grand-mère had tea and toast, but *I* wish *food,* yes?" Frani strolled to the table and reached under the napkin for a leftover muffin. "Hmmm."

"And you, Miss Cole?"

"I too would feel better for breakfast," she agreed in her usual calm way. Yves rang for a waiter, and the two women were soon served.

"Now," Sir Frederick suggested, "perhaps I should introduce you again to a connection of yours, Mademoiselle de Beaupré." He did, giving Robert his full title and explaining the relationship.

Françoise answered prettily when Lord Halford offered his home, inviting the party to be his guests. "My wife will be glad of company, Mademoiselle," he responded with a smile.

After again saying what was proper, Frani sent a speculative look toward Yves. "Now that I have eaten, I wish exercise. Monsieur de Bartigues? You too would like a stroll, *oui?* Me, I wish to look around now that I feel more up to things."

"I think not, minx," Frederick interrupted. Robert glanced from his friend to Yves but said nothing. "Any moment it will rain—storm, actually. You'll do well to stay inside the inn."

Françoise pouted. She wandered to the window and peered through the thick bluish panes. Harriet joined her there, pointing up at the heavy clouds. The girl's shoulders drooped but, shortly, she recovered her spirits and returned to where the men were gathered around the fire. "You were making plans when we arrived, were you not? For me? My safety?" she asked.

"We were just coming to the point of making plans. We have two carriages and a party of—" Robert turned to Frederick, "—how many, old friend?"

"The women have two maids. I and Yves have valets. That's nine. There is yourself and those you have with you?"

"Just my man, the coachy and a groom."

"We have your carriage, and the one you've purchased for me. We must hire a post chaise for the servants and luggage," Frederick decided.

Words passed back and forth quickly among the men until Miss Cole cleared her throat. "I fear this is premature, my lord," she interrupted. "We cannot remove from here until Madame has recovered."

Frederick sent a sharp look her way. "No. Of course not. Is she in a bad case?"

"No worse than one might expect. But rest, not another long journey in a swaying carriage, is essential. She is very tired. As you know, she never totally recovered from her, er, *illness* in Paris."

"Grand-mère will wish to continue, Harriet. You know she will."

"Yes. She will wish to. She will not rest entirely easy until she has settled your future with your grandfather." Harriet's lips firmed. "But, Frani, she must not attempt

102

it today." Miss Cole stood, nodded to the party. "I must return to her now. Come Françoise."

Françoise shared a pleading glance amongst the men. "Must I?"

Harriet answered before one or another male could give in to that wistful look. "Yes, my dear, you must. England is a new country with different rules of conduct. You will have lost your reputation before ever reaching London if you stay here alone with the men."

"She means, Mademoiselle Françoise, with *me*."

"Quiet, Fred," scolded Robert. "Do not listen to him, my child. Miss Cole meant exactly what she said. If I were a nearer relative than a mere great uncle-in-law—" Françoise giggled at the relationship. "—or if you were affianced to, say, Monsieur de Bartigues—" Her eyes flicked toward the young man indicated and the faintest rosy hue gave her complexion color. "—then, perhaps, you might stay. As it is, I fear you must not." Robert bowed.

No one but Frederick noted the well-covered embarrassment Yves experienced when hypothetically tied to Françoise, and he wondered at it. Had his young friend fallen in love with the minx? An odd emotion, part hope that it was so and part concern filled him. Yves was a younger son, true, but of a fine old family. It would be a good match. The chit, however, was something of a flirt. She'd had no one but Yves on whom she might practice her wiles during their journey from Switzerland. Now, once she was settled in London and there was more game afoot, would she ignore Yves, hurt him?

Once the women had gone, Frederick told Robert about the man on the packet he feared was the comte's spy, if not worse. He'd sent Cob to locate and keep an eye on him. "Something," said Frederick, "must be done about that one. It would be best, I think, if he did not follow us to London."

Robert nodded, and they fell silent, staring into the flames of the neat fire in the grate. Presently, and seemingly at random, Robert mentioned there was a third-rate acting company in town.

"Oh?" Frederick sat up, a slow smile spreading across his face.

"What think you?"

Old friends, their minds working in tandem, eyed each other.

"Oh, Wales, perhaps?" suggested Frederick. "Or, better, west to Wells and down into Cornwall?"

Robert entered a caveat. "Do you think they could get so far?"

Yves cleared his throat, his confusion obvious. "I seem to have lost my place in this discussion."

Robert smiled. "The small acting companies are ever in need of funds."

"And they are well-supplied with actresses and with men who occasionally take petticoat parts," said Frederick. "Fine, tall, raw-boned maids those men would make, I'm sure."

"And," Robert added to Frederick's comment, "because they need money, they are amenable to . . . persuasion." He rubbed his fingers together in a suggestive way.

The sentences flew at Yves from either side, and he turned his head back and forth at each additional bit of information. His eyes widened. A chuckle burst from him. "A ploy to trick the comte's spy!" Another laugh, more robust, filled the room. "Have you," he asked when he could speak again, "always read one another's minds?"

"We had years of experience. It's been essential at times that we follow one another's thoughts."

Yves sobered. "This is the friend you mentioned, Frederick?"

"Yes. We worked together throughout much of the war."

"And now we will work together once more. I think a stroll to the theater and then, if they are not there at this hour, on to whatever boardinghouse the troupe has given its patronage? Some fresh air suits you?"

Thunder rolled and suddenly the windows streamed with water.

"Fresh *air?*" asked Yves.

"Wellington weather," murmured Frederick, his eyes meeting Robert's.

"Hmm. Then we are fated to successfully trick the comte's man, are we not? At least long enough we may get the women safely to London."

"I don't understand," complained Yves, once again.

"It always rained before or during Wellington's greatest victories. It became something of a superstition amongst the foot soldiers. The rain might make the fighting more miserable, but it did great things for their morale nevertheless. That's all."

Nearly an hour later, wet and, he was certain, as miserable as any foot soldier had ever felt himself to be, Yves followed Frederick and Robert into the small parlor of a large ramshackle house situated not far from one of Dover's less well known and, very likely, unlicensed theaters. Water streaming from their cloaks and the brims of their hats, they waited before the hastily built fire on the small hearth. It smoked. Frederick swore fluently in three languages between bouts of coughing.

Breaking off abruptly in mid-oath as the door opened,

he bowed slightly to the tall greying man who entered. Another hour passed in negotiations but, in the end, all were pleased with the results. The money offered was generous, but on top of that, the troupe's leader bargained for an introduction to the owner of one of London's lesser known but well-run theaters. In the long run, that introduction would do the troupe far more good than any amount of money.

That evening the players announced their last performance in Dover.

"Me, I do not see why I must give over a perfectly good gown to a *salope.*" Françoise pouted.

"A more proper French word would be *souillon,*" Harriet scolded when her charge used the extremely vulgar word for trollop. "You've been promised a new wardrobe in London. Why worry about an old cloak and hat? Or the dress which I remember you once swore became you not?"

"But they are—"

"They may, with luck, trick the comte into running quite the wrong direction once he arrives on English soil," said Harriet, still lightly scolding.

Françoise pulled her robe more tightly around her and shivered. "I believed he would not follow us here," she said in a small voice.

"The men believe he will."

"Why will he not give it up? He makes my flesh crawl. I will *not* marry him. I will *not!*"

"No, of course you won't. No one wishes you to do so. Especially your grandmother. Would she have put herself to such exertion, such strain, if she didn't care what

106

happened to you? Remember, she hasn't given in, although she nearly lost her life to the comte's wickedness."

Françoise had the grace to look embarrassed. "I am sorry, Harriet. *Mon Dieu!* I am a terrible hoyden and thoughtless as well, am I not?"

"Yes you are," agreed Harriet in a reasonable tone.

Françoise giggled and threw her arms around Harriet. "I do love you. You keep me sensible."

"You *are* reasonably sensible, but you are very young." Harriet watched the girl, thought she knew what Françoise plotted. Her voice was sharper than she intended when she warned, "You will not meet the troupe, you know. It is impossible."

Frani's eyes widened, her face suddenly blank of all expression. Harriet eyed her doubtfully. Immediately a suspect innocence filled her charge's features, worrying Harriet excessively. Harriet bit her lip. It would be improper for Françoise to converse with actresses. Very improper, but knowing Françoise as she did . . .

"They are to come here tonight, are they not?" Frani played with her hair. "The actresses? So that they may set off tomorrow as if they were us?"

Harriet nodded, eyeing Frani closely. "After the performance, they come here dressed as if they had been patrons of the play. It should answer, I believe."

"And they'll be booked into a room here?" persisted Frani.

"Yes," Harriet again eyed her charge. Françoise smiled, a smug smile which disappeared when she noted Harriet watching her reflection. "Frani, what are you planning?"

"Me? Nothing. What would I plan?"

The girl searched her mind for a change of subject, asked a question about styles and what was proper for a young woman entering the social whirl in London. Harriet answered as best she could though she did not feel she was qualified to deal with the subject. After awhile, Harriet believed she'd been wrong to suspect Françoise's intentions. It seemed the girl had felt only a moment's temptation to meet the actresses but then had perceived how wrong it was and relinquished the notion.

The day, passing slowly, was spent almost entirely in their rooms. The rooms were nice enough in their way, but Françoise grew more and more bored. Harriet, watching Madame carefully, felt the day's rest had done much for the brave invalid. If nothing set her back, they could leave the next morning, early, for London. It was, Harriet remembered, a six to eight hour journey for heavily loaded coaches. If Madame had the strength for the hours of travel, then, once in London, she would have time to recoup and, hopefully, regain the good health she'd lost in the process of saving her granddaughter from a horrid future.

Dinner was a quiet meal. Françoise demanded and got a description of the theatrical company. Yves described the house in which the actors had been found, the badly ventilated parlor and the poor furnishings. Frani was shocked.

"What is the matter, child," asked Frederick, noting her expression.

"They are so very poor, then? Me, I have always envied actresses. All the excitement and the crowds and—" She made an expressive movement with her hands. "—and everything."

"A very few thespians make their fortunes," explained Lord Halford. "The very best are occasionally adopted as pets of society. But the majority? They are, indeed, poor."

Poverty was not something with which Françoise had

experience. Horrified, she secretly decided to add another dress to the portmanteau for the girl who would pretend to be herself. That and the gift of jewelry which she was determined to make the women for their part in her rescue, would, she hoped, express her grateful feelings to them. Frani knew the men had arranged payment, so thanking them personally was the only excuse for meeting the women she'd conjured up. Harriet might think it improper for her to introduce herself to the actresses, but where was the adventure in that? None. She'd take the jewelry along herself and thank the women for what they did for her.

Madame la Comtesse was consulted and announced herself quite ready to proceed to London. It was decided they would leave in the morning. The party, except for Madame, had adjourned to the parlor for dinner. The meal ended when a waiter came to clear away the broken meats and put a decanter of good brandy on the table. Harriet drew a reluctant Françoise away. Encouraged by the men to have an early night, they went to their rooms.

"Frani," coaxed Harriet, once they'd reached their own room, "you aren't thinking of those women, are you?" She'd become suspicious again when she'd overheard her charge asking Monsieur de Bartigues questions concerning the troupe.

"Who?" asked Françoise, pretending innocence. "Oh. The actresses. It is very sad, is it not?"

Harriet knew her charge well. She realized she'd been taken for a flat—as the saying went. "You, my dear, are a basket-scrambler," she said. Françoise had not heard the term and, after warning her it was not a phrase to be added to a young lady's vocabulary, Harriet, glad of the chance to distract Françoise, explained. "It refers to someone who is always on the scramble to make ends meet, having to plot and improvise. It comes from being so poor that, when they travel, they must scramble for a place in the 'basket' at the rear of a stagecoach, exceedingly uncomfortable accommodations, I understand. So perhaps," mused Harriet mischievously, "the term does not apply to you. More likely you are a here-n-therian— literally someone with no settled place of residence, but, by extension, a person of no consistency. One never knows what they will be up to next," she added at Françoise's questioning look.

They laughed and proceeded to while away the time with Harriet distracting Frani with some of the cant she'd learned over the years—the portion which would entertain but not suborn her charge, that is. The candles burned low and, twice, they added coals to the fire.

Harriet suggested they might go to bed but Françoise dawdled, one ear cocked to the comings and goings in the hall and, when, after a long period of silence, a new party arrived, their voices low but penetrating, she knew the time had come. The hall fell silent.

"I will meet them, you know," said Françoise.

"Who?" Harriet responded, her tone sharp. "The actresses? It is not proper."

"Who is to know? Will you come?"

Harriet sighed; she knew that stubborn look and that once it appeared there was nothing she could do—nothing short of chains and a convenient dungeon! "You are determined?" she asked, just to make certain.

"Oui." There was no compromise in Frani's tone. The single word said more than a paragraph.

Aware she should not, Harriet gave in. Françoise *would* go, and it was far better she not go alone—and if they *were* to go, then better to go at once; Harriet wanted to reach the women before they retired. If they were found in dishabille it would be bad enough, but to find the women visiting rooms in which they had no business, would be beyond anything—far worse than merely improper: Knowledge of the arrangements amongst the cast as to who slept in whose bed would be detrimental to the young girl in her charge. Besides, and it was the clinching argument, Harriet had something of a curiosity about the women herself! "Let us go, then."

They were too late, in part. Gowns, ruffled and bowed and rather cheap-looking, decorated the bedpost, the open door to the armoire, and the back of a chair. The three actresses—dressed in diaphanous wraps that brought a flush to Harriet's cheeks and had Françoise goggling—were, respectively, draped across the bed, standing near the mantel, backlit by the fire and, the el-dest of the trio, leaning back against the door, the handle of which she still held, having just closed it.

Françoise recovered first. "I came to thank you for what you do for me," she said prettily.

"Well, miss, now we see you, we can understand why your menfolk are a worryin'," said the ethereal blond on the bed.

"What a Juliet she'd make," said the dark-haired girl by the fire, sighing dramatically.

"A far better one than *you*," retorted the blond who turned sideways and rested her gilt-haired head on one hand. "She, one can see, is properly innocent for the role."

"Hold your tongues," said the middle-aged woman at the door. "It is not proper for you to be here, Miss," she scolded Françoise.

"So Miss Cole has told me, but I could not let you go without thanking you myself. Do be careful. The comte is a wicked man. He will be angry to be tricked so."

111

The women laughed, knowing eyes meeting knowing eyes as they absorbed the girl's warning. "He isn't the first wicked man we've met, dearie," soothed the eldest. "You needn't worry your head about his particular sort of wickedness."

"But this one is truly evil."

"When and if he catches up with us, it will be the fault of the man who follows us, nothing to do with us. We'll know nothing about it, will we? And don't you worry none, dearie. The agent was pointed out to Henry who will keep a good eye out that the man not get too close too soon. We may be nothing more than a third-rate acting company, but we're honest folk, child, and will do the work for which we are paid. We'll give the man a good chase."

"Which will give us time. We do need time. Please, take these as my personal thank you." Françoise unscrewed the earrings she'd put on that evening. "And this," she said and added the fine chain hanging around her neck with its amethyst pendant.

That was two pieces of jewelry, but there were three women. Françoise had, thought Harriet, not planned well. Reluctantly, Harriet stripped off a bracelet, one of the few pieces she'd inherited from her mother. She handed it toward the last of the actresses, but Françoise stopped her.

"No, Harri. Me, I am prepared." Frani reached inside her skirt to the pocket hidden in her petticoat and pulled out another trinket, this time a pearl and diamond chip pendant shaped like a bird.

For a moment there was complete silence in the room. Then the youngest, who was silhouetted by the fire, spoke. "You're a real lady, you are. We don't meet many, but we know one when we do. Believe me, we'll do our best to trick your wicked comte, my lady."

"We ain't actresses for nothin'," said the older woman gruffly, holding up the amethyst.

The third, studying the earrings closely, smiled. "Aye, we'll do our poor best. And good luck to you too, my lady."

Harriet thought it best they disappear at this point, but Françoise asked a question about the lives the women led, then another. Soon the five were settled near the fire on chairs and a collection of stools, and Françoise was receiving an education few well-born young girls were allowed. If Harriet had been able to come up with a polite means of extracting her from the scene, she would have done so. As it was, she soon realized the actresses were trying hard to edit from their speech anything of too shocking a nature and her eyes met those of the eldest, speaking her thanks silently. She got a merry grin in return.

That woman it was who finally rose to her feet. "Well, dearie, you've had a fine adventure this evening, but we all have a long day ahead of us. I think we'd better part company and get ourselves to bed. I'll just check the hall for you."

The hall was not empty. Sir Frederick, a scowl on his face and his arms crossed over his chest, leaned against the wall opposite the door. His eyes, resting on Harriet, held condemnation. His gaze moved to Françoise, his look softening slightly. "Well minx?" he said. "Are you satisfied?"

"It's been a very interesting evening, Sir Frederick."

Harriet noticed the two younger actresses had changed in an unsubtle manner. Each posed in such a way as to catch the eye of the man in the hall. He ignored them.

"I will escort you back to your rooms, where, little cat, you will *stay.*"

"I will?" Françoise's dimples peeped, and Sir Frederick closed his eyes briefly.

"You will," he said with a rather overly done sternness, "if you do not wish to be tipped up and spanked."

Françoise pouted prettily, flirting up at him. "Surely you do not threaten me so."

"Ah! But *I* will not do the spanking." Frederick went on with pretended gravity, "Your new great-uncle will oblige you."

Harriet suppressed the jealousy she felt at this whispered byplay. As she'd believed, Sir Frederick *was* interested in her charge. She sighed. "It is late, Françoise. Let us return to our room."

From behind the partly open door there were whispered invitations of a sort Harriet hoped Françoise would not understand. Again Sir Frederick ignored the actresses. He led Frani and Harriet down the hall, opened the door to their room, and looked in, checking for intruders. When Frani entered, he caught Harriet's arm. "That was not wise, Miss Cole," he said.

"They were careful not to sully her innocent ears too badly, Sir Frederick."

"Yes. Even such as they recognize innocence when they see it. Whose idea was that imprudent visit? Or need I ask?" his eyes swept toward the partly open door behind which, he guessed, Françoise stood listening.

"Françoise wished to thank the women for their part in aiding her escape to London. As a proper chaperon it is my duty to encourage my charge in polite gestures," said Harriet, perjuring her soul—not that she shouldn't encourage *courtesy,* but it certainly wasn't *proper* in this case.

"Oh Harriet," they heard and detected laughter in the young voice.

Sir Frederick winked at Harriet, and she blushed. "You will inform your charge that a polite note would have been sufficient, that in future, she will remember that." This time there were giggles from behind the door. "And, Miss Cole, you will come to Lord Halford or myself if she ever again suggests something so improper. *You,* at least, knew it was against all the conventions of polite society."

There was, again, reprimand in his tone, and Harriet bristled, ready to argue even though, secretly, she agreed with him. Before she could speak the door was jerked open. "You have no right to scold my dear friend." Françoise scowled at Frederick. "Go away," she ordered.

Sir Frederick bowed and Harriet curtsied, suddenly embarrassed by the intimacy of their argument and a realization of the impropriety of discussing anything at all while standing in the dimly lit hall. Neither spoke and Françoise, her nose in the air, waited only long enough for Harriet to sweep into the room before closing the door with a snap.

"How rude he is." Frani bounced onto the bed, and assumed the very improper pose of the actress, her hand holding up her head. "Very rude. How can you like him, Harriet?"

So the rake had not, yet, made a positive impression on her charge. Harriet hid a sigh of profound relief and felt generous. "He has proved our friend, Frani. Thrice. More, if you count the escape plan which got us out of Calais and now this plot involving the acting troupe. Also, Françoise, he was correct. I should *not* have allowed you to visit those women. It was grossly improper."

"How could you have stopped me?"

115

"Perhaps, as suggested, by telling tales to your new uncle?"

Frani, knowing Harriet would never do such a dishonorable thing, giggled. The young women hugged each other, Françoise yawning widely as they came apart. "I think I am going to like England. I didn't think I would, but I have changed my mind."

"I hope you like it very well, Françoise." Thinking of her season, remembering the sort of young lady who was to be found in the midst of a court of adoring young men, Harriet added, "I believe, however you come to feel about England, England will like *you* very well indeed."

A sleepy Françoise wanted to ask what her friend meant by such a strange prediction, but another yawn interfered. By the time she'd controlled it, she'd forgotten she'd had a question in mind.

It was probably just as well she'd forgotten, because Harriet couldn't have explained her impulsive words—or wouldn't have. Her intuition was based in a confusion of impressions, a pastiche of instances: Sir Frederick's teasing the girl; Lord Halford's obvious enjoyment of the chit; their obviously sincere assurance his lordship's wife would love to have Françoise as a guest; her memories of bright young things dancing in candlelit ballrooms, flirting from carriages in the park, from horseback. . . .

Yes, England was in for a treat. Françoise de Beaupré would sparkle and charm and, with any luck at all, fall deeply in love and make a proper match and, once married, be *safe* from the monster attempting to take her—and her fortune—for his own.

"Oh, you poor lady," Elizabeth Merton, Lady Halford, exclaimed when Madame, leaning heavily on Robert's

116

arm, on one side and her cane on the other, entered her host's London foyer. The butler stood to attention. The housekeeper bustled in from the back of the house and two footmen waited nearby to bring in the luggage. "You poor dear lady. Come, John," Elizabeth motioned imperiously, "take our guest up to her room." Rather highhandedly, she added, "Immediately, John!"

A third footman, his existence formerly obscured by the curve of the staircase, sidled forward. Françoise gasped and Harriet had some difficulty not staring. The man was a giant.

"This is John Biggs, known, so one might guess, as Big John." Elizabeth smiled broadly, obviously pleased by their astonishment at John's size. "John, these ladies have come for a visit."

John smiled shyly, ducking his head in an awkward manner in response to the introduction. There was nothing awkward at all, however, in the gentle way he swung Madame up in his arms and started for the stairs.

"Young man, what do you think you are doing?" The only sign the ailing French aristocrat had difficulty maintaining her dignity while held against the huge chest was a slight thickening of accent.

"Taking you to your room, Madame," the giant answered in a deep voice. He smiled down at her.

Françoise hid a giggle behind her hand, but could do nothing about the sparkle in her eyes. Elizabeth, meeting those eyes, lost the newly acquired dignity of her position as Halford's Countess and hid a giggle of her own. Harriet, looking from one to the other, suspected the two together would be a handful. She motioned Madame's maids ahead of her and started up behind the man carrying their mistress.

Madame's bedroom was two flights up, a large, well-proportioned room furnished in the elegantly simple style known as Queen Anne. Still in the arms of the footman Madame gave one piercing look around, nodded and, more tired than she'd ever been, still managed a firm order that she be put on her feet. John obliged, carefully, as if the lady he carried were fragile and important—which she was.

"Merci. Thank you, I mean," said Madame.

She got another of those sweet smiles and the man, using a long outdated custom found now only in the most remote of country regions, tugged at his forelock and, bashful once his job was finished, sidled out the door.

"Well!"

"It *is* well, is it not, Madame?" asked Harriet, looking around in turn.

Madame chuckled. "Yes. I believe it is."

Elizabeth and Françoise arrived. "I have ordered a light meal, Madame, which will arrive directly. Would you prefer to go straight to bed or would you like to bathe first? My husband has fitted a room to the back of the house as a bathing room. I'll have the tub filled for you if you'd like to soak out some of the aches and pains of travel?"

The housekeeper arrived with a tray, the chain and keys at her waist tinkling with her firm stride. She set out the meal on a table near the window and stood aside, her hands folded together, while Madame inspected the offering.

Almost, the comtesse could be heard to sigh. It was a barely delivered sound of satisfaction. She glanced at Harriet and noticed her blush. "Well, Miss?" she asked.

"Lord Halford inquired of me how you like things done, Madame," she explained. "He sent off a messenger immediately."

"It is well. Now I'd like to be alone, thank you." Ma-

118

dame looked at her niece. "You, Françoise, will wish to become acquainted with our hostess." Madame, despite the pain in her old body, bowed her straight back slightly. "I will beg the indulgence of a bath at a later time, my lady. Thank you for your care of us." Elizabeth, nowhere near the society matron, the mannerisms of which she aped when it occurred to her to do so, blushed prettily. The old woman nodded her head as if something she'd believed had been confirmed: Young Lady Halford would be a proper friend to Françoise.

"Now," said Elizabeth, a few minutes later as she seated herself behind a tea tray in the smaller and more intimate of the two salons one flight down, "I want to know *everything*. Oh, it is so exciting."

Harriet accepted the thin cup and saucer handed her by a silent maid and looked around the tastefully decorated room. The walls, covered in a lovely rose damask, beautifully set off the elaborate fireplace with it's carytids holding up the mantel and lovely airy fret-backed chairs ranged beside each of the doors. How strange that the bright bird-like Lady Elizabeth had not immediately replaced it all with something more modern! "What is exciting, my lady?' she asked, remembering her manners.

"Why, finding out who you are, why you've come to us, everything. I want to know it all. Isn't it just like a man to inform one three guests will arrive, do this, do that, but tell one nothing at all about them?"

Harriet blinked, but Françoise smiled. "My lady," said the French girl, "I do not understand you. From the welcome we received, I assumed you had been told our history. Is it not so, my lady?"

"No! Not so at all, my new friends. Not a single word." Elizabeth paused and raised a hand, "And I won't have it! I get so tired of my lady this and my lady that. I am

Elizabeth and you are—Harriet?—and this is Françoise."
Elizabeth, if she hadn't appeared so much the lady, might almost have been said to grin. "That, my new friends, is all I know."

"But . . ." Harriet blinked.

"Oh, my dearly beloved husband sent quite explicit directions for your care and welcome. He said Madame was ill and needed quiet and rest. He said you, Françoise, were French." A gentle shrug and Elizabeth handed a plate of thinly sliced cake, dense with fruit and nuts and well soaked in brandy, to the maid who passed it around. "But that is all he said. It is all very much a mystery. I am very angry with his lordship for not telling me the secret.

"Oh, *secrets!*" she went on before either could respond. "It is nothing but one great huge secret after another. You see," she explained in a confiding tone, "one day a month or so ago a message came for his lordship. He exclaimed upon reading it and promptly disappeared for *hours,* leaving *me*—" Elizabeth pouted. "—in *confusion.*" The pout disappeared in a quick smile. "Ah well, we poor women are often left in confusion, are we not? Then, three days ago, he packed a portmanteau, kissed me, and," she sighed, "told me he'd return soon." She waved her cup, endangering the pale stripe in the satin covering the tête-à-tête on which she sat.

"Men," she said, making no secret of her disgust. "They are so *secretive.* They tell one nothing. For instance, the next thing *I* knew, the messenger arrived warning me of your arrival. Oh, we *have* been busy. Very busy . . ."

Harriet looked from her hostess to the very bright eyes and supressed excitement of her charge. She hid a sigh. It was quite obvious—in fact, had been almost from the moment of their introduction to the vivacious Elizabeth—

that life would very likely become doubly difficult. How in the world, wondered Harriet, was she to keep a tight rein on the two girls while doing nothing which would dim what was equally obvious to become a close friendship between the two!

"I'm so excited by it all," said Elizabeth, interrupting Harriet's thoughts. She looked first at Harriet, then at Françoise, an encouraging light in her eyes. "Do tell," she coaxed.

Six

"Me, I am only half French," began Françoise, happy to oblige her spirited hostess.

"The plot thickens," nodded Elizabeth encouragingly, her eyes sparkling.

Françoise pressed her lips together attempting to control a smile, but *her* eyes flashed with liking for this new acquaintance. Harriet shook her head when offered a macaroon from another plate and their hostess, guessing her guests might be inhibited by the presence of the maid, waved the girl away, telling her they'd wait on themselves now.

"There *is* a plot," said Françoise dramatically once they were alone. "And a wicked comte as well."

"Ooohhhh." Elizabeth shuddered at the delicious revelation.

"Yes, he wishes to marry me, and I do not wish at all to marry him."

"So your grandmother has brought you to England to escape his unwanted attentions."

"Oh, *more*. To escape his firm intention to have me at any cost. Twice he has attempted to abduct me."

"No!" Elizabeth's eyes widened and a trifle of the excitement faded, giving her a more serious expression.

"Mais oui. We have a new English friend because of the dreadful comte. Sir Frederick—" Harriet noted their hostess stiffen at the name. "—saved me. *Twice."*

"He did?" asked Elizabeth, her eyes wide.

Harriet chuckled, keeping embarrassment under strict control. She could not allow this delightful, but occasionally haughty young lady, to denigrate what the baronet had done for them—whatever her own feelings on the subject! "Sir Frederick warned us what the reaction would be if it were known he'd had aught to do with Françoise. Frani, you were warned more than once. How bad of you to mention his name."

"Oh, *I* can believe him a hero," asserted their hostess blithely, startling Harriet anew. "After all, he was instrumental in my marrying my beloved Robert. Sir Frederick is my friend."

"He hasn't, I believe, the reputation of being friends with women."

"It is true." Elizabeth nodded several times to emphasize the point. "But Robert says he has reason. His mother is such a one as no one could like and his grandmother, well! Her reputation is not what one would wish either. There is no bearing either of them, I believe. Then there was, I've heard it said, a young woman who hurt him badly in his salad days. Robert is his very good friend, too, you see. As well as me, I mean. And he *knows.* I believe a very young Sir Frederick vowed revenge on the female gender and yet," Elizabeth tipped her head thoughtfully, "it was only a certain *type* of female he pursued. I have met a few. They are older now, the sort who will grow into selfish bitter old women, nasty women. And *all,* I believe, have a tendre for Sir Frederick even though he pursued them and then taunted them."

"How do you know *that?"* asked Harriet, trying to

remember more about the young woman who had been Frederick's flirt eight years previously, trying to think if *she* had been the sort who would turn into a shrew. "How can you know such for fact?"

Elizabeth smiled slyly. "There are ways. One only needs to cozy up to the old tabbies, the gossips and the matriarchs. I made it my business to find out all about him."

"You have a tendre for him?"

"Oh no." Elizabeth shook her head. "I am the one woman he wished to wed, you see." Harriet felt a band tighten around her heart, told herself not to be a fool. "Sir Fred went off to France when he learned I loved my Robert. I believe he truly loved me, but all I ever wanted was to be his friend. Now we are, I think. Friends, I mean. Of course, he has been gone for months and months. The last I saw him was at my aunt's wedding." She pouted slightly. " 'Tis a bore that I do not know when he will return."

"I believe you'll find he *has* returned." Harriet couldn't help the dry note to her voice.

"What? When?"

"He escorted us to Paris and then to Calais," said Françoise, taking up the story. "After he saved me the second time—that was in Calais—he came up with a plan to trick the comte. He got us all tickets on the packet, but let drop words to make that evil man believe Madame would wait for better sailing weather, that only he and Monsieur de Bartigues—"

"Who is Monsieur de Bartigues?" interrupted Elizabeth.

"Sir Frederick's friend, Yves de Bartigues." Frani continued as if she had not been interrupted: "—would cross that evening and we waited and waited until the very last instant and then, instead of going to a new hotel—Oh, did I say it was part of the plan to leave the hotel in which we were staying because we could not trust the innkeeper? He was a dreadful man. Anyway, we went straight to the quay and boarded the packet at the very last possible instant and—" Frani spread her hands in a typically French gesture, her shoulders shrugging slightly in the process, "—*Voilà*. We are here."

"And the comte?"

Françoise sobered. "Sir Frederick believes there was a man following us, a spy for the comte, you would say. He and Lord Halford and Monsieur de Bartigues arranged for a group of thespians to pretend to be us and go off somewhere else. We hope they will draw the comte's man off on a . . . a—what does one say?—a wild goose chasing. You comprehend?"

"But he will discover his mistake and what then?"

"Then—" again the shrug, this time accompanied by a slight shudder, "—I suppose he will come to London where he will find us, and I will, again, be in terrible danger."

Elizabeth straightened, raising one finger, "We should take you into the country. Immediately."

Harriet shook her head. "I think not. Wouldn't it be more difficult to protect Françoise where there is so much open space and fewer people? It would be much too dangerous."

"But country people know *everybody* and would warn us if strangers appeared in the neighborhood. My husband could set guards as well as ask his people to watch for anyone unknown to them. If such were seen lurking around we would know, you see—although it would be a dreadful shame to miss the season. . . ."

"Perhaps you should suggest it to him." Harriet turned

125

the conversation from Françoise's problems and delved into Elizabeth's history. She learned the girl had been married for only seven months and was ecstatic about the married state, telling her guests they simply had no idea how pleasant it could be. Harriet, thinking of Françoise's naive ears, thanked the powers that be that Elizabeth was discreet as to what, exactly, she meant by *that*.

"I was a terrible child when I first met Halford," their hostess added as she chose another macaroon with care. She bit into the airy morsel, sipped her tea and nodded. "Oh, a veritable brat. Aunt Jo was ready to throw up her hands in disgust and go off and live in a cottage and grow roses. She said so often and often."

"Aunt Jo?"

"Yes, Joanna, Duchess of Stornway. She remarried a month or two before I did. You'll meet them soon enough. The duke is a very close friend of my Robert. At the moment they reside in the country. They spend an inordinate amount of time at one estate or another, or so it seems to me. But the season begins soon, and they will come for a month or so. I, of course, prefer London. Even when the *ton* is elsewhere it is much more interesting than the country."

Yes, thought Harriet, you would prefer it. The hustle and bustle, the shops and theaters, and company every day of your life. Harriet looked at Françoise and noted that, although she was still excited and interested, she was beginning to droop. "My lady, I think we should retire for a rest before dinner. We are not in ill-health as is Madame, but it has been a long and exhausting journey."

"Oh, where are my manners? I should not have kept you talking forever and ever. Come along. I'll take you to your rooms. I hope," she rose to her feet and was already on her way to the door, the skirts of her pale primrose muslin gown billowing behind, "they are to your liking. *I* like them. His lordship told me I could do as I pleased about redecorating, but there was very little *to* do here in our London residence. Oh, curtains which needed replacing and new hangings for some of the beds, that sort of thing, but his lordship's family has collected only the very best for so many generations it leaves nothing for a new bride to do. I can't tell you how disappointed I was even though I'd not change a thing. Truly."

She rambled on as they climbed the stairs and headed down a hall toward the back of the house. "You see? I have given you rooms across from one another so both may have a view over the garden. I put Madame in the most quiet guest room since she's not well even though it is not the best room. Now," Elizabeth glanced around first one room and then the other, checking that the trunks and portmanteaus had been unpacked and removed, "I believe you have everything you need, but if there is anything, anything at all, just ring and ask the maid—

"Oh," she interrupted herself, "would either of *you* wish a bath now? Let me show you the bathing room. It is quite an innovation, instead of those impossible hip baths in one's room. The separate room is small and always has a fire for warmth and a *long* tub Robert designed himself. It is closer to the kitchens too, so the men needn't haul the water so far and don't mind hauling more as a consequence. Robert is designing a pump sort of thing and intends to put a cistern under the roof so the water need not be hauled at all, but it is not finished yet."

Elizabeth chatted on as she led the way down a half flight of stairs to a small room which Harriet thought might have been designed originally as a linen room or perhaps a still-room. She thought she might like to try it but wondered at having to leave one's room in dishabille and travel along the hall, perhaps running into another member of the household on the stairs and suffering all the embarrassment attendant on such an encounter.

Elizabeth giggled, sensing the reserve in Harriet's compliments on the arrangement. "Hip baths are, of course, available for those who prefer them," she soothed. "Now I will leave you or I will never let you rest. The dressing gong rings at six-thirty and we meet in the library before dinner for wine or sherry. A maid will show you the way."

Françoise, alone in her room at last, swung around and around and fell onto the bed. Oh yes, she truly was going to like living in England. A thought gave pause to her excitement. "Will it be so good when my grandfather comes or will he take me away and bury me somewhere in the wilds?" she wondered aloud. "Sir Frederick said he rarely comes to London, and I think I will wish to stay here forever and ever." But, with the optimism of youth, she put the thought aside and lay staring up dreamily at the painted design of cherubs and angels decorating the bed's canopy. Her thoughts skittered and jumped hither and yon, and, gradually, without noticing, she slipped into a deep restful sleep.

Harriet, knowing her charge to be resting and discovering that Madame had no need of her, went to her own room. She removed her dress and hung it with the others already put away in a large wardrobe—and found herself more restless than ever. The discovery their hostess was the woman Sir Frederick had left behind in England, the one he said had changed his life, was upsetting in ways Harriet could not approve. Why should she feel pity for a rake! What if it would be awkward for him, to meet his lost love again? Why should she feel a deep empathic sadness for him—and, perhaps, just a trifle for herself as well, although she wouldn't allow herself to wonder why.

It must, she thought, have been particularly painful for Sir Frederick to have lost the delightful Elizabeth to his closest friend. Her head tipped. Or was it that very friendship which had led Sir Frederick to give the chit up? Oh, it was so confusing!

She pushed Sir Frederick from her mind, her thoughts drifting in another direction. Joanna. It was an unusual name. Surely not the Joanna Wooten Harriet had met in Portugal. What fun if it were. How wonderful if she were to meet again the woman who had been the young bride of one of Wellington's more intrepid scouts. Since Harriet's father had coordinated various levels of espionage, the Wootens had been invited often to the informal parties her mother planned with such panache. The friendship between the young bride and even younger Harriet had made it easy for Lieutenent Wooten to make secret reports with no one the wiser.

Oh, if only her mother hadn't become unwell just when the family began planning for Harriet's season. If only she might have brought Harriet to England herself, how different those weeks would have been. Her mother would not have forced Harriet into the insipid mold thought proper for young misses facing their first season. Nor would she have forbidden Harriet to ride as her aunt, the impoverished widow of one of her father's older cousins, had done.

It had been late in her London visit when Harriet realized her hastily acquired chaperon hated horses, feared them, and had placed the ban on Harriet's riding so that she, the chaperon, need not worry herself sick when her charge was out. Perhaps, if she'd been seen in the park on horseback, where she excelled, her season might have been very different. Harriet sighed and put away thoughts of the past. It was done and over.

But what did the future hold? Madame would send an express by special courier to Françoise's grandfather. She'd request information as to the next step in putting the girl under his protection. Perhaps he would insist they travel north and meet him somewhere up in the wilds of Northumberland where, according to Sir Frederick, he resided most of the year in the most primitive of castles and only rarely entered society. Or perhaps that island off the coast of Scotland which had been mentioned? Even the provincial society prevalent in Edinburgh or, farther south, in York might be forbidden to Frani.

Then there was herself, her future . . . it was all so difficult, not knowing what was to become of one. As a servant—a well paid and well loved servant, but still a servant—one had so little control over one's life. Would she be needed? Would the grandfather continue her generous salary and keep her on as Françoise's companion? There was a new wife, too, Frani's grandmother-in-law, who would have her own ideas which must, surely, be taken into account by a new husband. A new wife might not wish another young and not unattractive lady—even one so tall as Harriet—taking up residence in her husband's home.

Harriet paced and thought, her mind worrying at the alternatives if her position with Madame were lost. She was surprised when a tap at the door announced the maid, an under-footman following with cans of hot water. "Is it so late? I did not hear the dressing bell. . . ."

"It hasn't rung, Miss." The maid drew in a deep breath. "Compliments of his lordship and would you mind very much attending him a wee bit early in the library, Miss," said the maid, clearly parroting a message she'd carefully memorized.

"I will go down as soon as I can dress myself."

Bemused, Harriet washed quickly. Despite her youth, the maid, Annie, had a deft hand with hair and Harriet, looking at her grey gown with the narrow lace outlining the modest neckline, thought she looked very well. Not a la mode, but neat and properly attired for what she was: Françoise's companion. When she was ready, she knocked lightly at Madame's door, asking the maid to wait a moment. When answered from within, she entered. Madame lay against pillows.

"Are you feeling better, Madame?" asked Harriet.

"Much better. Another day or two, and I will be my old self," added the French aristocrat, although both knew it would take much longer. Madame smiled. *"You* will keep your eye on Françoise and see that she not embarrass me, will you not?"

It was less a question than a statement of a belief which soothed Madame's mind. Harriet felt a glow at the confidence placed in her. "I will do my best, Madame, but," Harriet laughed, "I fear Lady Halford will not aid and abet such modest proper behavior. Our hostess, Madame, is a minx."

Madame chuckled. "Two minxes make for multiple mischief." She smiled. "There, I have made a joke in English, have I not? You can only do your best, Harriet. Have no concern for me; I will sleep now. The housekeeper has mixed me a mild dose of laudanum. Go off and enjoy your evening, child."

"You are too generous, Madame."

"No. I sometimes think not generous enough. You were a godsend, Harriet. When my daughter-in-law died, I was already too old to have charge of a wild chit like my granddaughter. You have done our family excellent service. Whatever Frani's grandfather determines to be her

future, what is to be done with her, *you* will not suffer.
I'll see to that."

"Thank you." Harriet felt a flush warming her cheeks
at the compliment, but ignored it. She also ignored the
lifting of a burden of worry. She still had work to do and,
as she'd pointed out, with Elizabeth for friend, Françoise
would be more of a handful than ever. But, even though
she would not think about it now, her concern for her
future was greatly eased by Madame's promise.

Harriet followed the maid down to the ground floor.
The girl tapped at the library door, opening it immediately
after and holding it for Harriet to enter. She thanked the
girl quietly and heard the door close behind her. Her host
stood, his arm on the mantel, his eyes on the fire, but
straightened and turned as she entered. He bowed to her.

"Miss Cole. I hope all is well with your party."

"I've just come from Madame's room. She has eaten
and will sleep soon. You wished to tell me something?"

"I wished information concerning the problem with
my great niece-in-law," Lord Halford smiled and his eyes
twinkled. "Such an awkward relationship, but such a delight to gain a new and formerly unknown relative."

"You are generous, my lord. Not everyone would be
willing to admit such distant connections into the family."

"Were the connectee not so delightful, perhaps it would
be more difficult," admitted his lordship with that smile
Harriet was coming to like. "Sir Frederick tells me you
can give me the history behind the comte's persecution
of the child."

"I can." Harriet folded her hands before her and began.
"They met at a house party where he discovered she is
descended from those who once owned the French estate
his father was given to support his new title. Perhaps I
should tell you that this happened in Italy. Madame retired

132

many years ago to Lake Como since the winter cold of the Swiss Alps, where the family went when it escaped the Terror, is not good for her."

Harriet went on to describe the comte's appearance soon after that party at their door and his impertinent refusal to be put off from attendance on Françoise wherever they met thereafter.

"Madame, you understand, after the first morning call, gave orders he was to be refused further admittance to her home. She didn't like him. When, within three weeks of meeting Françoise, the comte approached Madame with the marriage offer, Madame made enquiries. What she discovered confirmed her dislike of the man. She refused him. He persisted in putting himself forward so Madame passed word amongst her friends he was not to be encouraged.

"It did not answer. The comte intimidated the young men courting Frani into deserting her side. When he still received no acceptance, he became more of a pest than ever and Madame formed the plan to bring her granddaughter to the protection of her English grandfather. . . .

"We left Lake Como secretly—or so we thought and were climbing toward the Simplon Pass when the comte made his first attempt to take Françoise by force. That was when we met Sir Frederick and he and Monsieur de Bartigues became Frani's champions. At Sir Frederick's suggestion, Madame made a thorough investigation amongst her servants and discovered the traitor who had told the comte of our departure," Harriet finished. "We were warned and have taken extra care ever since that awful experience in the mountains."

"But not before *you* took a hand in the game. I understand It was your intrepid behavior which routed the comte on that first occasion."

Harriet blushed, but answered steadily enough. "My father taught me at a young age to handle firearms. Madame refused to see the necessity of armed guards, feeling perhaps they would give away the fact we were not off on a simple visit to friends. I carried along my father's dueling pistols, but I admit freely I had not truly believed they would be needed."

"Guards were supplied when you continued your journey?"

"Yes. Just before we reached Paris Madame was . . . ill. We'd put up, where we could, with old friends and with relatives of her husband's and son's, but of course that was not always possible. She acquired a serious stomach upset at the last inn at which we stayed. For a time we feared for her life. It was a week before she regained enough strength to continue on to Paris where we stayed until we could leave for England—which she was still determined to do. Luckily we were near Paris where she *did* have friends who took us in once we could remove her from that terrible inn."

Lord Halford took a thoughtful pinch of snuff, shook off invisible grains from the lace at his wrists, and returned his box to a small pocket in his plain white waistcoat. "I think Fred mentioned there was evidence of poison?"

"Sir Frederick is certain Madame was poisoned."

"Madame is her granddaughter's only French protection? There is no male guardian or relative from whom Mademoiselle Françoise could expect help?" He took the snuff and sneezed.

"The family has a tragic history as does so much of the French aristocracy. Frani's father and mother died in an accident a few years back and there are only distant cousins remaining."

"So, if Madame were removed from the scene, there would be no one to stop the comte from whatever ploy he might conceive? While you remained in France, I mean?"

"True." Harriet lost color at the memory of those horrid hours when they didn't know if Madame would recover. She reached for the back of a chair to steady herself.

An oath reached her ears faintly, a hand steadied her. "Sit down, Miss Cole. I did not mean to frighten you, merely to get straight in my mind the situation. Françoise has protection now: myself, Sir Frederick, and her grandfather, once he knows of her arrival." He handed Harriet a glass of sherry. "Drink that. All of it. I apologize for shocking you."

"It was only a momentary weakness. It was a terrible time, wondering if Madame would survive. That man is a monster."

"The monster will find himself at a stand if he dares to show his face in London. Word is already being spread he is *persona non grata*. He will not have the entrée and will find no friends amongst the *ton*. This will not cancel the danger to Mademoiselle Françoise when she is abroad in the streets, but Big John goes everywhere my wife goes and is not a man with whom one trifles. He will watch them both. We'll take good care of your charge, Miss Cole."

"You are strangers to us," said Harriet, her voice choked, "but so generous. How will we ever thank you?"

"By enjoying your stay with us," he said promptly. "I hope it will be long." The door opened, and Harriet looked around when he smiled over her shoulder, holding out his hand. "My love. You are looking remarkably

135

lovely this evening. Not that you don't always take my breath away, of course!"

Elizabeth tripped across the carpet, leaning forward to receive a kiss on her cheek. "No, my lord," she straightened away from him, "no more. You will disarrange my coiffure and you have no idea how long it took to achieve just this style. Such sorry things we poor women, Miss Cole," she said with a pert look at her husband. "The hours we waste making ourselves beautiful for our menfolk!"

"And then will not let the menfolk touch for fear of spoiling the effect," said Lord Halford with a dry intonation. "I believe I would prefer less primping and more freedom, my sweeting."

Harriet felt a cold little knot of jealousy for the love so obvious between these two newly met friends. She told herself not to be a fool. She'd had her youthful dreams, but when the required white knight did not appear to carry her away, she'd come to terms with spinsterhood.

She'd been lucky, after all, to acquire the position in Madame's home, where she was given the freedom to be herself and not forced into the role of a drab little woman stuck in the background of life. She must not forget just *how* lucky and she must *not* allow herself to fall into megrims about what might have been . . . might still be . . . ? *No.* She must not dream dreams of might-be.

Françoise herself appeared then, distracting Harriet from the dreams in which she must not indulge. Frani apologized for her lateness, receiving reassurance it was no such thing, but, very shortly, the butler announced dinner was served and they moved on to the dining room.

Lord Halford, a quizzing glass brought into play, inspected the soup ladled into his dish. His wife demanded his attention. "Yes, my love?"

136

"I do not like this room." Elizabeth frowned mightily as she looked around it. "It will not do, Robert."

"Will it not?" Lord Halford, brows raised, also looked around, noting the high wainscotting above which hung several of the scenes painted in his odd style by that new artist, John Constable, the Axminster carpet covering most of the floor, the highly polished table and sideboard loaded with the very best silver and crystal. "What is wrong with it?" asked his lordship.

"It is too big. Even reduced to its smallest, the table is over large for a small party such as this. It is not conducive to conversing or friendly interchange." She waved her spoon in emphasis.

Regrettably, Françoise giggled at Elizabeth's high-handed manner.

"What, my dear, would you suggest?"

Harriet gave their host points for his mild voice and the twinkle in his eyes.

"I think," said his wife, head to one side, "that perhaps, with just a few leettle changes," she wheedled, "the breakfast room might serve for family meals. Do you not agree?"

"Changes?"

"Hmmm. A new table and chairs, perhaps. A new serving board which would do both for breakfast and also for more formal dining?"

"And new drapes and new carpet and—" teased his lordship.

"Oh, may I?" interrupted Elizabeth.

Lord Halford laughed. "Yes, minx, if you will, you may."

"You spoil me, my lord," she said, but dimples peeped at each side of her mouth.

"Yes. Dreadfully."

Elizabeth smiled a cat-in-the-cream smile. "Hmm, I will think of some way to reward you, my lord."

This suggestive remark was going too far for even such an easygoing husband as Lord Halford. He frowned down his wife's high spirits. She blushed delightfully, sent an apologetic glance toward Harriet and bowed her head over her soup until her color cleared. Harriet was relieved the man was not so besotted he'd allow his wife to go her length in everything. The young woman was as hot to handle as Françoise, and Harriet was sure that, by herself, she would find it impossible to keep the two within permissible bounds.

Three more courses followed, each more tempting than the last: the fish was in a delicate sauce; the meats, properly roasted as only the English seemed able to do, were served in their own juice and *not* hidden under one or another sauce; and, finally, the vegetables were cooked to a nicety in the French fashion, while the sweets course tempted one to excess.

Elizabeth looked around the table as the syllabub was passed still again and finally refused by all. "Have we finished?" There were general murmurs of agreement. "We will not leave you alone with your port, my lord. We will stay and keep you company."

Evidently such shocking behavior on the part of their hostess was not uncommon since the butler proceeded, without blinking an eye, to order the covers removed and the table cleared. It was the first time Harriet or Françoise had remained in a dining room while decanters and a silver bowl of nuts were placed ceremoniously on the table. Normally, women removed from the room at this point. His lordship filled a glass from the decanter at his elbow and the butler poured more of the light wine served with the last course for the ladies. The servants retired.

"Now, my lord, you must explain to me all the mysteries which have been plaguing me. First there was the message which came some time ago, and you disappeared immediately for a whole long afternoon with no explanation as to where you were going or why—even though you had promised to drive me in the park. It was not polite of you, Robert." She scowled delightfully and her husband pretended chagrin. Elizabeth drew in a deep breath and went on. "Then, my lord, you left *again* with no explanation and were gone for *three whole days* only to return with our new friends." Elizabeth pouted, but Harriet noted the very different and more determined expression in her eyes. "It was very bad of you, my lord."

Robert sipped, enjoying the brandy's flavor. He swallowed and glanced down the long table. "But it was none of your business, my lady."

"Was it not? Does that mean you will not tell me?"

"Why should I?" Lord Halford raised his glass and studied its color, watching the candlelight glowing through it.

"Because I am your wife. It *is* my business."

"But, my lady . . ."

"My lord?"

Harriet and Françoise watched each as the exchange went on. Françoise stifled giggles behind her napkin, while Harriet wondered if Lord Halford carried his teasing too far. The twinkle had gone completely from Elizabeth's eyes, and the pout was now real.

His lordship seemed able to judge to a nicety just when to give over, however. He sighed lugubriously, which immediately lightened their hostess' countenance. "What it is to live under the paw of the cat," he said, his eyes on his glass.

"A more unlikely mouse I have yet to see," scolded his wife. "Do tell, my lord. Please?" she coaxed prettily.

"Since you ask so nicely, I will." He quoted the message from Frederick, his request that a team and carriage be chosen and sent to Dover to await his arrival. "But, you see, my dear, I could not allow Frederick to arrive back in England with no welcome."

"What I see is that I was left at home, my lord. Might I not also have welcomed him back?" A short silence followed and eyes met eyes down the long table. "I see." Elizabeth frowned in earnest. "You wished to determine Sir Frederick's state of mind."

"Yes. I did."

"You did not trust him. Or me."

Harriet rose hastily. "You will excuse us, my lady, my lord? Our journey was long and arduous. With your permission we will retire."

Elizabeth, too, rose to her feet, obviously contrite. "Oh my unruly tongue. No, please. I will be good. Truly, I will."

The argument, ready to burst into flames, was doused, although Harriet noted one last look between husband and wife. Elizabeth, putting an arm around Françoise's waist, and waving Harriet toward the door had one last comment.

"We will retire to the Green Salon, my lord." The barest hint of wistfulness could be heard when she asked, "You will join us there? Presently?"

"I will."

"Good."

The women were in the hall when Elizabeth turned and ran back into the room. Harriet caught a glimpse of their hostess falling to her knees in a cloud of pale green silk beside her husband, her hands on his arm. She thought

140

she heard Elizabeth tell his lordship she was sorry. Lord Halford touched his wife's hair and raised her to her feet.

Again the tiny hurting cold spot of unwanted jealousy irritated Harriet and again she flung it away as unworthy of a woman of her age and sensible nature. But it was obvious to her that, once she was more rested, she must sit herself down and give herself a stern lecture on just what she could expect from the rest of her life! And those expectations did not include a home filled with the joy and wonder of love and happiness . . . especially not when the male figure in that dream was a confirmed rake and profligate to boot!

Seven

Harriet looked up from the book she was reading to Madame la Comtesse who lay quietly, still very drawn and worn. She looked older than ever before, although, after two full days in bed, she now spent some time each morning and afternoon on the chaise near the fire.

"Yes, James?" asked Harriet of the footman who tapped lightly on the open door, rousing her attention.

"Sir Frederick to see you, miss. He's waiting in the Green Salon."

"To see me?" Harriet's heart beat faster. "Are you certain?"

"Yes miss. He asked for Miss Cole, miss."

"Run along, Harriet. I'm ready for a nap now, anyway."

Harriet rose from the chair's embroidered cushion and moved closer to the chaise. "I wish you'd let Lady Elizabeth send for a doctor, Madame."

"Hush now. There is nothing wrong with me that having fewer years in my dish would not cure." Madame raised crepey lids and her eyes were as sharp as ever. "I think you should see what Sir Frederick has to say, my dear. It is very possible that he may have news for us."

"Oh." Harriet felt herself blush. Why hadn't she

142

thought of that obvious reason for his unexpected arrival? "I'll go immediately and won't be long."

"Take your time. You spend far too much of that valuable commodity pandering to a tired old woman while the young shop and visit." The eyes closed again and, even as Harriet dithered, she noticed her mistress had slipped into the realm of Morpheus in that easy fashion of the invalid. A worried frown refused to fade as she moved quickly down the stairs and went through the door James opened as she approached the salon.

"What is it?" asked a deep voice. A frown matching her own, Sir Frederick approached her as the door closed behind her. He took her hands into his. "Harriet? Miss Cole," he added in a firmer tone as if remembering it was improper to use her name. "If I can help . . ."

"No. No, there is nothing anyone can do, I believe." More flustered than ever she pulled away, walked over to the fireplace. "Is no one else at home?"

"I don't know," said Frederick with an abrupt wave of his hand. "I didn't ask. Please tell me what is worrying you."

He hadn't asked? "Madame does not improve. We've been here very nearly a week now, and I think her very little better. I cannot help worrying about her."

"What has the doctor said?"

"She refuses a doctor." Harriet turned from the fireplace and stared at him. "You have news for us?"

"News? What news would I have? A messenger has not had time, yet, to reach my uncle and return."

"There has been no sign of the comte?"

"I do not expect it until the wind goes down."

"Then why, Sir Frederick, are you here?"

He smiled—a touch ruefully. "Such modesty. I've come to take you for a drive in the park, Miss Cole. I

143

wish company while I show off my brand new curricle."
He took her arm and led her to the window, holding aside
the long drapery. Harriet looked down into the street
where a pair of beautiful roan geldings switched their
tails and stamped a foot now and again. A scowling young
man with a long nose and reddish hair had a hold of them
just above their bits. Just then he glanced up at the house.
"That's my old tiger. I let him go when I left the country,
but, when he learned I'd returned, so did he."

"Such an unpleasant looking lad."

"Hmmm. I think he's finding service with me less interesting than in former times. *Will* you go for a drive?"

"But why me?"

"Why not you, Miss Cole?"

"Don't make a May-game of me, Sir Frederick. I am
not the sort with whom you deal. Shall I see if Frani
would care to take the air?"

"Thus throwing the lamb to the wolf?" Sir Frederick
sighed. "You are a very difficult woman to court, Harriet." This time he made it clear he meant to use her name.
"If I had wished to see Mademoiselle Françoise or Lady
Elizabeth I would have asked for them. Or," he held up
a hand as she opened her mouth, "if I'd wished for
Robert. I didn't. My dear, it is so very simple. I wished
to see you and, for once, without all the distractions of
Mademoiselle or, for that matter, anyone else."

Harriet turned back to the window to hide her reddening cheeks. "This is the most ridiculous conversation."

"What else can one have with a ridiculously insecure
and modest woman?" he asked blandly.

She choked back a laugh at the dry note in his voice.
"Well, thank you, sir, for the offer of a ride in your new
rig, but I fear I must decline the generous invitation. Madame—"

144

"You are pale, Harriet," he interrupted. "It will do you good to go out. The wind will blow away the cobwebs. Only half an hour. Please?"

She was torn. Madame slept. The comtesse would nap for at least an hour, maybe as much as two, as was usual with her. Harriet looked again into the street, admired the well-formed horses and spanking new carriage. "Oh all right. I will have to change, however."

He nodded. "Twenty minutes, Harriet. Dress warmly."

Even tracking down Madame's maids and asking that they sit with Madame, Harriet returned to the salon just under time. A deep rose carriage dress trimmed with fawn-colored braid showed beneath a woolen pelisse in the color of the braid. Her straw bonnet was trimmed with rose ribbons but otherwise plain.

"I fear I will ruin your reputation, Sir Frederick," she teased, once he'd settled her on the high seat.

"How is that? You may wait here, Chester." A puzzled expression on his narrow foxy face, the tiger stared rudely at Harriet. Harriet stared back, which seemed to disconcert the young man. "Chester, I gave you an order." Startled, the tiger released the horses and, one last look at Harriet, moved out of the way.

"That, I think, proves it." Harriet settled herself more comfortably. After watching closely for a few minutes, she hid her satisfaction that her belief that Sir Frederick would prove to be a top-sawyer was correct. His handling of the mettlesome pair of horses was indeed masterful and showed that ease of manner only long familiarity with the ribbons gave one. Sir Frederick was a true whip!

"I've tried to figure out your last cryptic statement, but I can't. I'm in the dark, Harriet. What proves what?"

Harriet had to bring her thoughts back from Frederick's driving to what she'd last said. "Oh. If the reaction of

145

your tiger is any indication, everyone will believe Sir Frederick Carrington lost his wits while traveling on the Continent. They'll shake their heads and go tsk-tsk whenever you pass by."

"I think I understand, but wish you'd be more explicit, my dear."

Harriet debated scolding him for the use of the endearment, then decided she shouldn't draw attention to it. Frederick undoubtedly used such terms automatically without thinking about them. It was bad enough she had not objected to his use of her given name! "What do you find unclear?" she asked in an airy tone. "Sir Frederick appears in public with a woman for the first time . . . ," she paused and turned slightly, "It is the first time?"

He nodded, suppressing a grin at the revealing hint of curiosity in her question.

". . . and he's with a dowdy and unknown spinster of uncertain years. You will be believed to have lost all sense of your former taste."

"No. My taste will be thought to have improved." He turned through the gates into Hyde Park and allowed his team to increase their pace to a trot. "Dowdy?" He glanced at her, beginning with the half boots, the toes of which appeared beneath the edge of her skirt. His gaze moved on up until he reached her flushed face, her eyes seeing nothing, but staring straight ahead. "No, not dowdy. It is true that the fashion is for frills and laces and all sorts of extraneous decoration. You are right to forego all that. The sharp clean lines of that pelisse could have been designed by none but a master cutter and could not be bettered. I believe you will set a new fashion—an improved fashion."

"Such fustian! I wish you would not pitch me such rum tales. You embarrass me, Sir Frederick."

"You embarrass *me,* Miss Cole!" He chuckled when she chanced a quick look his way. "Such language, my dear. How shocking."

"You don't appear shocked."

"Actually, my love, I find you a delight in all ways."

"Sir Frederick . . ."

"I apologize. Old habits die hard. I forgot this was to be a proper courtship and fell in the loose ways of my youth. Forgive me?"

"Courtship?" Harriet blinked in confusion. Hadn't he used that word when she'd come down to the salon?

He glanced her way. "My heart was lost when you held that gun on me in Switzerland, Harriet."

Her heart quickened its pace alarmingly, but, outwardly, she remained serene. "Your heart has been lost many times, Sir Frederick. I'm sure you'll find it again."

He laughed, but wryly. "No, you're well and far off with that thrust. I lost it only once and then it had merely strayed. I find that, now, there is only a warm spot of friendship for that minx of a girl. She taught me that, you know. The emotion of friendship."

"You have many friends. Lord Halford . . ."

"Ah. Men." A sober expression cleared the laughter from Sir Frederick's face, and his tone was serious when he added, "No, Harriet, even that's not true. Even amongst the male sex, I have few I call friend. But I meant, of course, that a woman might be my friend."

"I will readily be your friend, Sir Frederick. I believe you would not hurt one with whom you shared that feeling. And I'm concerned about Françoise. A hurt to her would hurt me, so if you wish to cry friends, then we shall—and I may stop fearing that you will seduce my charge."

"You wound me. I have told you, and more than once, that your charge is safe from my wiles."

"I'm sure you've told many that."

Silence followed and again Harriet chanced a look his way. His jaw was so firm she thought his teeth must be clenched, and his mouth formed a hard straight line. His expression confused her. He looked angry. But why? Because she was cautious and suspicious and watchful, making his pursuit of Frani more difficult of achievement? And now? She mustn't allow his charm to abate her care one jot. No matter how hard it was to disbelieve him. . . .

"One cannot change the past," he said at last. "One can only move on into the future. I never thought to regret anything I'd done in my life. In the last year I've come to regret much of it. And *now*, all the more, if it is to interfere in our relationship."

"Sir Frederick, I cannot understand you. You have inherited—"

"That news is not to be broadcast around the *ton!*"

"Lord Halford warned us you wished it kept secret. Elizabeth and Frani may be skitter-brained, but are not stupid. They will not breathe a word of how you acquired your wealth." She turned a curious look his way. "Have you forgotten that you yourself told me how it came about?"

"I did? Oh. On the packet. Yes. That need I feel to explain myself to you that is so out of character for me." He nodded.

Harriet let that notion percolate for a moment then thrust it aside. Taking a deep breath she went on. "That you *have* acquired it will soon be obvious to the meanest intelligence and rumors will fly as to *how*. Again, I do not understand you. You will not have it reported how you spent the years of war with France, preferring to be

148

considered a coward; you will not have it broadcast how you quite honestly and unexpectedly came by your fortune, knowing the sort of rumors which will be whispered from ear to ear; you publicly and without shame made your reputation as an unrepentant rake. You seem to *enjoy* making the *ton* believe the worst of you." She turned and stared rudely. "You, Sir Frederick, are *perverse.*"

Sir Frederick maneuvered carefully between two carriages, the park more crowded as the popular hour for promenading approached. "Perverse?" he questioned. "I suppose that may be true. You did not grow up in England, Harriet. You knew the very best of the English aristocracy—those who worked abroad, I mean, the diplomats and the military men. So you can have little knowledge or understanding of how shallow much of those making up London society can be. I learned it early, and I refused to conform. So, I suppose it can be admitted. I am as you say: perverse."

It was Harriet's turn to be silent. "Perhaps I do see. In a way. Surface things are all important here in London. Wealth, status, taking care one's reputation remains unblemished while actually indulging in all sorts of unacceptable behavior. Then there are those who, snubbing those below them socially, allow those above to walk all over them. Yes. A young idealistic man would find that disgusting. So, snubbing one and all, you pretended to be otherwise." Again she glanced his way and back to face forward. "And, perhaps, you became the thing you pretended? What now, Sir Frederick?"

"A well-reformed rake, perhaps? I'll be a sober married man. I'll set up my nursery and improve my estate—which needs improving badly. I will eventually run for parliament," he added, thoughtfully. "The country is in a terrible condition, economically, now the war is ended.

Too many manufactures have had to close their doors; the declining market for woolens means the owners of flocks have no markets for their fleece; mines have closed; the—" He looked at her, smiling. "But you do not wish a lecture on such a beautiful day."

"This is a serious side you show to few, is it not?"

"It is a serious side few are interested in seeing," he countered, again with the dry note she'd come to know. "Not many amongst the *ton* care for aught except that *their* world not change. And their world is such a limited one."

"I have noticed that, and we've been here barely a week. Several ladies have made morning calls. I found them unbelievably dull, but I wondered if that was due to the presence of strangers—Françoise and myself—that the conversation seemed to lack depth but," she added, "our presence didn't seem to stop their gossiping!"

"You will find their conversation does not improve as you come to know them. I heard a rumor you answered the question of how you found England with a reference to the poor crowding the streets of London and that you felt deep sadness at the plight of the ragged children you saw. *You,* my dear, will be labeled a bluestocking if you are not careful to avoid such unacceptable topics. You must know they are not considered proper subjects for a lady's drawing room." His scold was only half in jest.

"If I didn't know it, I quickly learned. I'm becoming proficient at the polite platitude, Sir Frederick."

It was his turn to glance at her. "You fear to be called a bluestocking?"

Harriet thought about it. "For myself, no. But that it would reflect on Françoise and my hostess, yes. It would do them no good even if they weren't exactly harmed by the association."

"And if it reflected on no one?"

"Then—" She turned up damp eyes and met his thoughtful gaze, "—oh, Frederick, if only something could be *done*. Look around you. Carriages, fat horses, well-fed people, attire on any back you look at worth more than poor families see in a year—yet just beyond the park gates are children in rags, their stomachs empty. It is not right, Sir Frederick."

"I am a wealthy man now, Harriet. Marry me and spend it as you will," he suggested quietly.

Harriet clutched at the side of the carriage. She swallowed. Hard. Oh, she *must* keep this light, as teasing toward him as he must mean to be with her. "Is that a proposal, Sir Frederick?" she questioned, a lilt forced into her voice and a smile to her lips.

A flush spread across Sir Frederick's cheekbones. "As gauche and awkward a proposal as a woman ever received, I fear, but yes. I'm quite seriously asking you to marry me."

Her hand tightened over the wood at the side of the carriage. He *couldn't* be serious. "I cannot believe this."

"That I wish to wed you?"

"But *why*? Why *me?*"

"I . . ." began Frederick, only to find it impossible to tell Harriet in so many words that he loved her, to reveal himself so completely. "I like you. I like your honesty, your loyalty, your attitudes and intelligence, your looks—especially those magnificent grey eyes—and I think we could deal well together. In fact, I think we've already proved we deal well together."

"It is absurd. With wealth behind you—as you have now—and even with the reputation of being a rake, you may choose from anyone available on the marriage mart! Lovely young women whose family connections and dowry will help you achieve your ambitions. I am a penniless spinster. I am a *servant*. You tease me cruelly, Sir Frederick."

Sir Frederick turned his head, studied her fine profile and sighed. "Not teasing, but premature, I suppose. We will speak of this again when you know me better." He paused, giving her time to regain her countenance.

Harriet worked to control feelings of mortification. How *could* he do this to her? Or had he somehow guessed at those ridiculous emotions she couldn't quite control whenever he was near? Had he decided she'd be easy prey? Did he think to lure her into his web with a pretended engagement? Undoubtedly, for one reason or other, an engagement which was to be kept a secret between themselves? Knowing she wouldn't be easy game, he'd very likely realized he'd need some stratagem to get her into his bed and if she were to succumb? He'd only throw her aside when something better came on the scene . . . Except that, surely, better game *was* available? Oh, if only she understood the man!

When Frederick thought she was more at ease, he introduced an innocuous question. "Are you prepared for the dinner party Elizabeth plans for tomorrow evening?" She didn't respond. "Harriet?"

"I think I should return to the house, Sir Frederick. I've been absent far too long, and Madame will need me."

"I will be very happy when I may remove you from that house, from being at the beck and call of others. You deserve a home of your own, my love. But I said we'd not speak of that until a more propitious time. Come now, Harriet, cheer up. The world will think I've totally lost my touch if you show that Friday face for much longer!"

She chuckled, as he'd wished, but found it difficult to indulge in even such trite conversation as he instigated.

She refused his help down from the carriage, telling him he need not leave his horses. Her back to him, she tripped up the steps and raised the knocker, letting it fall with a loud tap.

Sir Frederick watched Harriet enter the door, then sat quietly, deep in thought. Such an untrusting lady he'd chosen for his own. It would be a long road convincing her he truly wished her for his bride. That had become clear almost as soon as that impulsive proposal had left his mouth.

"You," he told himself, *"have* lost your touch!"

"You have also gone blind as a bat."

Sir Frederick looked at his tiger who glowered at him. "I don't think I asked your opinion," said Frederick.

Uncowed, the tiger asked, "What're we doing with a long meg like that up aside o' you?"

"Dub your mummer, Chester. Show disrespect for that lady and you'll be looking for work elsewhere."

"So I'll be shutting my trap, then, if'n that's the way the wind blows—but I think you left your wits a-wandering over there among the Froggies." Chester folded his arms across his chest in proper fashion for a tiger.

"Perhaps you'll think better of the lady if I tell you she held me at gun point when we first met."

The arms unfolded. "I don't believe it for a minute. Not a gentry mort like her be."

Frederick's voice took on a dangerous note his tiger had heard once or twice in the past. "Do I lie? Ever?"

His tiger wasn't intimidated. "Only when you have to."

Frederick laughed. "All right. I agree. There have been occasions a good lie has saved the day. But," he added sternly, "this isn't one of them. Any sauce from you toward Miss Cole, Chester, and I'll inform the beak how we met."

Chester frowned. "Arrr, you *wouldn't!*" If Sir Frederick informed a magistrate they'd met when the tiger had attempted to prig a meg or two from what he'd thought a flash cove with more hair than wit, then Chester would be, at best, transported. "You wouldn't," he repeated more doubtfully.

"Yes I would. Be warned." His tiger mumbled something unintelligible. "Perhaps you'd prefer to leave my service now?"

"Here now, I didn't say that! But things have changed in a sorry way."

"You just remember to keep your mouth shut."

"Oh, I'll keep my mummer dubbed. But I don't have to *like* it, do I?"

"No. I won't go so far as to say you have to like it."

Frederick pulled up before Gentleman Jackson's Boxing Salon and reached for his watch as Chester hopped down to go to the pair's heads. Fred flipped open the watch and nodded. A few brief moments of waiting and Yves strolled out, settling the new hat he'd acquired at Lock's, when Frederick had gone to order headgear, and pulling on new grey gloves bought to match.

"Right on time, Yves. How did it go?"

" 'Tis a bloodthirsty sport, Frederick. I do not believe I'd enjoy it at all. I will continue fencing lessons under Angelo instead. I picked up a little of the Italian manner of the duello while in Florence and would like to perfect the style. Swordplay is much better exercise to my way of thinking. One need not worry one will end up with a black eye!"

Sir Frederick chuckled. "It has been said we English are a bloodthirsty lot which explains, perhaps, our predilection for prize fighting."

154

"Oh, I don't mind *watching*," said Yves. "Only partici-pating!"

They discussed the gossip Yves had heard in Jackson's, where Frederick had introduced him to several friends before going to see Harriet. Frederick wended a way through Piccadilly's confusing traffic, the vehicles of all types from sporting to heavy carrier carts, all trying to navigate among well-dressed pedestrians who were jos-tled by sellers of everything from hot meat pies to brooms and the latest broad sheets—along with more than a few pickpockets, just to make life interesting. Finally, he pulled up before the Albany where he'd taken rooms.

"Take them away, Chester," he told his now silent tiger. Frederick and Yves strolled inside and up the stairs. They were met in the hall by Frederick's valet who had been hovering as inconspicuously as possible to head them off. "What is it, Cob?"

"Your uncle arrived soon after you left. He's waiting for you."

"Good." Frederick frowned slightly. "But he can't have had that express we sent him and already gotten himself to London. It isn't possible."

"No. He discovered your direction from your man of business." Cob added the doleful warning, "He appears to be in a cheerful mood."

"He does, does he? Then I suspect he thinks he has bad news for me." Frederick chuckled. "Come and meet Mademoiselle Françoise's grandfather, Yves. It sounds very likely he's recently been made the father of a son."

They strolled into the cluttered masculine sitting room, and Frederick continued on to where his uncle slumped into a wide armchair, a bottle of port at his elbow. The good port, thought Frederick, and made a mental note to thank Cob for attempting to turn the old curmudgeon up sweet. Not that it would help, of course, but the thought was well taken!

"Uncle!" said Frederick in a loud voice. "I'm sorry I wasn't at home when you arrived. I hope my man has taken proper care of you?"

"Hurumph?" The startled movement of one rudely awakened from a pleasant nap was replaced by a wide smile. "Ah. Freddy. How are you, m'boy?"

"Fine. And you?" Frederick pretended innocence. "And your bride?"

"Fine. Quite fine. Strong-minded filly, that woman."

"Is she in London?" Frederick did his best to mask his ambivalent feeling about that, but something must have slipped past his guard. His uncle eyed him shrewdly. Frederick laughed. "All right," he said, "I'll admit I'd be better pleased if she were not. There's something you don't yet know, but when you do, you'll understand."

"Something *you* don't know, too. What's your news?"

"Yours first, I think. My guess is that I'm to congratulate you on the birth of an heir, Uncle? I do. Sincerely. The trouble is, you now have two."

"Two?!" The man rose to his feet, eyeing Frederick warily. "What do you mean, *two,* man?"

"No, not a by-blow—not an embarrassment of that sort. You've a granddaughter, however, much in need of your assistance."

"Granddaughter . . . Françoise? *How did you meet my granddaughter?*"

"You *know* of her? And never told me?" Frederick's voice turned to ice. "Quite obviously I didn't learn of her existence through you!" He glowered at Lord Crawford who glowered right back. "How could I have expected to meet up with Mademoiselle de Beaupré when I'd thought her mother dead these twenty years and more?"

"Well," the older man looked a trifle flustered, "having announced her death, I couldn't very well raise her up again, Lazarus-like, could I?"

"Yes you could. Or at least, you might have done so, if you weren't the most pig-headed man alive."

"Well, I didn't," said Crawford with something nearing a pout. "And she *is* dead now. Unless that too is a lie?"

Was there just a gleam of hope in his uncle's eyes? "I'm sorry to disappoint you. Your daughter is indeed dead. But *her* daughter is very much alive. And in danger."

"Danger!" Lord Crawford's worried look changed to one of suspicion. "Danger? Surely she is no longer in danger. I'll admit I worried a bit before, but the war is ended now."

"Not the war. A scalawag of a comte who has his eye on her fortune and wouldn't mind acquiring the lady as well—particularly as marriage to her would be a sideways justification for his continuing to hold the French estates his father acquired along with a brand new title."

"Fortune?" Ignoring the bit about the estate, Crawford glared. "I will leave her nothing. Nothing, do you hear?"

"Why not? No don't answer that. You'll punish the chit because of her mother's fault. Typical. But, since she has no need of your fortune, it makes no odds. Her father left her very well provided for and her grandmother will add more to the pot, making her a very wealthy young lady indeed."

"Rich?" His uncle sat down slowly. "Rich you say?"

"Just who did you think your daughter married?"

"Some jumped up Frenchie who thought to line his pockets at my expense. One of the young emigres living on his wits and smooth tongue."

"You'd have done well to find out the facts, my lord

157

Uncle. This particular emigre was of a family which was canny enough to save its fortune."

The color faded from the high-boned cheeks and the man seemed to become smaller as remembered pain filled him. "I was angry with the chit."

"So you cut off your daughter without a penny, announced her demise to an unsuspecting world and then, later, when you'd come to your senses, could find no way to reverse it all and still save your pride. Perhaps you'll be glad to know she had a happy life from then, so no very great harm was done." The sharp old eyes lifted to pierce Frederick's, but Frederick didn't look away. His uncle's fell. "Will you also let pride deny you a granddaughter?"

The man suddenly looked older, his mop of white hair seeming less alive and his cheeks more hollow. "Tell me the whole, Frederick."

Between them, Frederick and Yves, who Frederick finally had a chance to introduce, did just that.

"What's your interest in this?" asked his uncle when a pause ensued, once again suspicious.

"The interest any gentleman would have," said Sir Frederick, promptly. "I wish to protect her from a villain."

"Villainy such as your own?" sneered Crawford.

Yves bristled, but Frederick laid a hand on his arm and the younger man controlled his ire. "I don't believe," responded Frederick pensively, "I've ever indulged in attempted murder to remove blocks from my path."

His uncle had the grace to look apologetic. "True, there are villains and then there are villains." After a moment's silence he added, "What do you expect *me* to do about it?"

"The girl is your responsibility."

158

"And, you think," his uncle said with a wry look that reminded Yves of Frederick, "my wife's as well?"

"That *has* been worrying me—as I hinted earlier," said Frederick. He flicked open his snuffbox and offered it around. When the others refused he closed it and returned it to his pocket. "She will not like Françoise, I fear. Not at all."

"A little beauty, is she?" For the first time his lordship showed some personal interest in his granddaughter. "Well, well, her mother was easy on the eyes."

"Not a beauty exactly," objected Frederick. "More a minx. A delightful chit."

His uncle's eyes narrowed. "The relationship is too close."

Frederick laughed. "Be easy. I have no interest of that sort in the child."

"Hmmm. I still don't understand why you've bothered your head about her if it *isn't* that."

"Why is irrelevant. I'll take you to meet her tomorrow."

"You say the grandmother is not well?"

"No. She wore herself to a thread bringing the girl to you. I believe, too, she has not recovered from the poison she was given and that will make her convalescence difficult."

"I've no responsibility for an old lady. I won't have it."

"I don't believe you've been asked to take responsibility for Madame la Comtesse. Robert is willing to care for her and Miss Cole will be at hand."

"I thought this Miss Cole was Françoise's companion."

"She is. But Lady Halford and Mademoiselle Françoise have become inseparable and Miss Cole is not the sort to sit and twiddle her thumbs when there is work to do. Besides, Miss Cole is genuinely fond of Madame."

"A pie-faced old twit, I suppose." Those sharp eyes fastened on Yves when Yves choked back a laugh. "Or am I mistaken?"

"Quite mistaken," said Frederick in cool voice. "She is not in her first youth, but she is neither old, nor pie-faced . . . nor a twit." He stood and strolled to look out the window, his gaze suddenly fastening on a thin, darkly clad man. "Yves, come here, but do not allow yourself to be seen. Look at that man. Isn't it the one we sent off after that acting troupe on the wild-goose chase?"

"I believe it is. The angle and the lighting are bad, but as nearly as one can judge, I'd say you're correct."

Frederick pretended to yawn, moved cautiously away from the window. He moved quickly once beyond sight of the comte's spy. "Cob," he called and when the valet appeared, asked that Chester be sent for. Cob looked disapproving. "Don't get up on your high horse. I have need of him."

"As you say, Sir Fred." Cob bowed slightly, but his expression didn't change as he backed out of the room.

"I don't see why you put up with such disrespect in your servants," complained his uncle.

"Cob is more than a servant as you well know. Ah," he added as Chester arrived, his long nose fairly twitching in expectation of just the sort of order he liked to receive, "there you are. Out on the street is a tall man dressed in black. Cob can point him out to you. I want him followed and wish to know whom he contacts and where that contact lives. Don't lose him." Chester quivered in anticipation. "Cob will give you a purse for expenses. The man is very likely dangerous so take a barker. I'd prefer it, however, if you'd avoid the necessity of using it."

"I'll play least in sight."

"You do that. But remember, a man is often like his

160

master. This one's employer has twice tried poison to rid himself of unwanted interference and will stop at nothing to achieve his end which is marriage with my cousin."

Chester's eyes lit up, his satisfaction at a mystery explained obvious. "Ah, that explains the long meg. Cousin, is it?"

"Miss Cole is no relation," said Frederick, his voice chilling. "You will, however, remember to treat her with respect."

Confused again Chester said, "Gor-blimy, Sir Fred, what you be wanting to have anythin' to do with a mort like that if she ain't no relation?"

"I don't believe that is any business of yours. Cob? Prepare Chester and point out his quarry."

His uncle shifted in his chair when the three were again alone. "Where in Hades did you pick up that gallow's bait?"

"Chester has been very useful to me over the years. The game has changed, but his expertise will still come in handy."

"Which does not explain how you came to have him in your employ."

Frederick grinned. "I caught him picking my pocket. How else?"

Yves chuckled. "And hired him on the spot, I suppose."

"Of course."

" 'Taint no of course about it," said Lord Crawford with a glowering look. "Should have turned him over to the nearest Charlie."

Yves looked confused and Frederick explained a Charlie was the nickname for the watchmen, originally employed during the reign of King Charles II for the hours of darkness and, later, also for daytime duty. He turned back to his uncle. "If I'd turned him in, I'd have lost a cunning and skillful servant—and that at a time when cunning was of prime value! Never mind. You will come with me to visit your granddaughter tomorrow?"

"Do I have a choice?"

"You do not."

"Well, at least, this puts *your* nose well and truly out of joint."

"The dibs are in tune," said Frederick carelessly, not ready to reveal his new wealth. "I think we should drink a toast to your son. What did you name him?" He poured drinks, which were eventually followed by a supper served by Cob. More liquor followed and the conversation wandered over a wide variety of subjects.

Once the preliminary shifting and dodging had ended, Yves was surprised to find Crawford very good company indeed. The conversation was excellent and the wine better. All three men were a trifle fuzzy by the time they wandered off to bed.

Lord Crawford freely admitted, "Not drunk as a wheelbarrow, exactly, but definitely above par . . ."

"It isn't that any of us have shot the cat. . . ." agreed Sir Frederick, yawning.

"We are, each of us, simply very well to go," decided Yves, proud of having acquired the proper English cant phrase for the situation. It had been, all in all, a very interesting evening, decided Yves just before he drifted off to sleep.

Eight

Madame glared from Harriet to her granddaughter. "I *will* get up," she insisted.

Harriet and Françoise looked at each other and back to the bed. "Madame—" began Harriet but was interrupted.

"Do not attempt to dissuade me. I will not meet the man who disinherited my son's wife while lying in my bed. It would do nothing but further his wrong-headed opinion the child made a misalliance. I will not have it."

Madame was obviously very near to losing her temper, an energy draining emotion to be avoided at all costs. Harriet pinched Françoise into silence when the girl would have argued and offered a compromise. "If you would lay on the chaise longue—"

Again she was interrupted. *"Mon Dieu!* I will not act the invalid in *that man's* presence. *Mais non!* Never! That gentle giant, John Biggs, may carry me to the salon. *Exactement!"* she said, her French aroused by her determination to have her own way.

Harriet gave it up. "We'll leave you to rest and prepare yourself. He'll not stay beyond the usual half-hour, I think, and you may return to bed immediately."

With her capitulation, Madame was immediately contrite. "You understand, Harriet, why I must do this?"

Harriet smiled. "I understand. You are at least as proud and stubborn as the man in question!"

Madame chuckled. "You *do* understand."

Harriet removed Françoise from the bedroom, leaving Madame to her maids. "I hope it is not too much for her."

"Why are you allowing her to do this?" scolded Madame's granddaughter.

"Frani, do you think I have it in my power to forbid her?"

Françoise giggled. "No. No one does. But I wish—"

"We both wish. I think her a trifle better this morning. Good food, rest, and the prospect of transferring her responsibility for you to other shoulders—she *is* recovering. But this visit from your grandfather will tire her, Françoise. Do not add to her burdens in any way."

Françoise pouted. "I am, it is true, interested in meeting the man, but I cannot *like* him."

"You will treat him with the deference a grandfather deserves." Françoise shrugged. "I know he cast off your mother, but if *she* forgave him, and you know very well she *did*. If that is so *you* have no quarrel with the man. You *must* behave, Frani."

"I'll try." A mulish expression contorted the French girl's features.

Harriet sighed. "Frani, don't make life more difficult for yourself than it already is."

"He will take me north into the wilds of nowhere as he did his new wife and bury me in a moldy castle, and I'll never be happy again," wailed Françoise, her greatest fear finally verbalized.

"Where did you get that notion?"

164

"Elizabeth has been telling me about him." Françoise's eyes widened. "Do you know the awful thing he did to his bride?"

"I have heard *she* believed they would honeymoon in Paris. I have also heard, minx, that he had good reason to treat her as he did."

Françoise giggled. "Yes. Elizabeth does not like her at all. *She* says the woman was once her father's mistre—" Frani clapped her hand over her mouth.

"That gossip should never have reached your ears." Harriet eyed her charge with a cold look that had Frani blushing. "I would suggest you turn yourself out in prime style and act the lady even though we both know *you are not."* Harriet's voice softened. "Off with you, child. I must change as well."

"You *will* wear the new yellow morning dress?"

"I think not. I am, after all, your companion. It will not do to put the old man's back up by dressing like laced mutton."

Françoise laughed merrily. "Harriet, you are a complete hand."

"You'll refrain from using cant language as well, my girl."

"You did."

Harriet thought back and a conscious look filled her eyes with remorse. Put his back up? Laced mutton? How *could* she have allowed herself to *think* let alone *say* such things! "So I did." Harriet took a breath and, adopting a prim manner, said, "I must not dress in a manner unsuited to my age and station in life. I must present a proper facade so as not to upset the old gentleman's sensibilities of what is proper. There." Her eyes twinkled. "Is that better?"

"Oh, Harriet, I *do* love you."

"I love you, too, Françoise. Now off with you."

Harriet closed her door and leaned against it. The note from Sir Frederick which announced the unexpected arrival in London of his uncle had arrived early that morning and had set the whole household into a bustle.

Elizabeth immediately consulted with her housekeeper on the subject of rigidly proper old men and how to turn them up sweet.

Madame immediately insisted that she would not receive his lordship in her bedroom as all urged her to do.

Françoise immediately drooped tragically, fearing instant removal from a situation where she'd begun to feel very much at home.

Harriet immediately began, again, to worry about her future despite Madame's earlier assurances she would see Harriet right and tight.

So, thought Harriet. To dress suitably for a companion. That was the next step. Then to see that Françoise was acceptably turned out. It wouldn't do for her charge to present herself in full evening dress or some other outrageously inappropriate costume simply because the girl wished to make herself as lovely as possible when meeting her grandfather for the first time!

Later, the scene set in the formal drawing room, Elizabeth, Françoise and Harriet awaited the arrival of Madame. The door opened and, appearing as regal as a woman could when carried in the arms of the gigantic footman, Madame was borne into the room. John very gently settled his charge in the armed chair Harriet had thoughtfully arranged near the fire with a footstool before it. He grinned when Madame thanked him, and now, his duty done, he awkwardly removed himself from the

166

scene. No one spoke. In the silence the crackling of the fire and the ticking of the ormolu clock seemed overly loud.

Harriet glanced up toward the mantel to check the time. Two minutes to the hour. Sir Frederick, Monsieur de Bartigues, and Lord Crawford were due at any moment. The silence became oppressive and Françoise, meeting Elizabeth's eye, reprehensibly giggled. The girl bit her lip and conquered her nerves, straightening and composing her features.

The clock intoned its hourly message and, as the second strike reverberated gently through the room, a knock sounded. Given permission the Halford butler opened it, announced the three men and, as they strolled forward, closed the door with himself in the hall—very obviously wishing it were otherwise since *his* curiosity was no less avid than anyone else's.

Madame didn't attempt to stand. She waited, her hands resting on her cane and her back straight. Harriet thought she'd never looked more magnificent, her dress and jewels very slightly overdone for a morning call, perhaps, but her bearing carrying them off.

Sir Frederick introduced his uncle and the man bowed, straightened, and two pairs of dark eyes met, very slight animosity in Madame's and something very close to apology in his lordship's.

"We meet at last," he said.

Madame nodded. "Yes, my lord. We meet at last. Be pleased to know your granddaughter, my lord." Lord Crawford turned, his eyes skimming over Elizabeth whom he recognized, lighting for a moment on Harriet, and dismissing her, and settling on Françoise. The girl rose to her feet and curtsied.

"Granddaughter. I never believed this day would come."

"It is not my fault it has been delayed, my lord grandfather."

"No, m'gel, it isn't." Lord Crawford sighed. "As Frederick has pointed out to me with far more force than I feel necessary, it is, indeed, *not* your fault."

Now what, wondered, Harriet.

Now what became obvious. Her newfound dignity present to such an alarming degree that it made Harriet hard pressed to maintain her composure, Elizabeth asked her guests to be seated. She rang the bell, and the butler entered followed by two footmen carrying trays.

The polite but overly formal process of properly serving the guests drew Harriet's nerves into screaming lines of pain. Why had Elizabeth decided to make this a rigid exercise in propriety? She met Frederick's eyes, slid her gaze on to Madame and back to his. He too looked at the old woman and, setting his cup and saucer on a nearby table, went to her side. He leaned over her, said something which no one else could hear. Madame nodded and allowed him to help her to her feet.

"Nothing need be decided today." The faintly accented words were delivered with the arrogance which had made Madame la Comtesse a Tartar in her younger days. "I believe you will wish to become acquainted with your granddaughter, Lord Crawford, and you should be allowed to do so in private. Harriet?" Harriet rose to her feet so abruptly she spilled a few drops of tea onto her skirt. "Lady Halford?" Françoise, sitting beside Elizabeth, grabbed her new friend's hand, and sent a desperate if silent message to her grandmother. Madame smiled rather sourly. "He will not eat you, my dear. Come, Lady Halford. We will leave them now."

Elizabeth and Yves rose to their feet. Yves stepped toward Françoise who also stood. He took her hand and raised it to his lips, his eyes encouraging her as well as they could. When he turned to follow, he found Elizabeth awaiting him by the door, the others already in the hall. He sent one last look toward Françoise, who was looking very young and a little lost. The door closed behind them and Lord Crawford hurumphed. Françoise's gaze moved to stare at him, a wary expression marring, slightly, her usual attractive looks. She firmed her spine and waited politely for her grandfather to open the conversation.

"Well, granddaughter, have you nothing to say to your grandsire?" At the closely pressed lips and sparkle he noted in her eyes he chuckled. "Yes? You have, perhaps, much to say and have been warned to say none of it? Sit down, my dear."

She hesitated then sat, and he reseated himself. "You are correct," she said. "There is much I would say were it permitted."

"None of which I have not many times said to myself, child. I missed your mother dreadfully. I allowed my temper to rule my good sense and lost years of her company. Although it was difficult to communicate during the war, I managed to apologize to her; now I extend my apologies to you."

Françoise studied him, her eyes not hiding her rebellion. "My mother and father were very happy."

He nodded. "So Frederick tells me. I am glad."

Françoise relaxed slightly. "Now what?"

He laughed. "What am I to do with you?"

"Yes." She pressed her lips tightly together again, as if forcing back more words.

"Very good, my dear. You have been taught the value of making the enemy come to you."

She blushed slightly, her eyes widening. For a moment she tucked her lip between her teeth, thinking. "I do not understand," she said, finally.

"*Not* so good. Never allow your enemy to see a weakness."

Françoise nipped her lip again, her eyes again studying this man who was to have control of her future. "I see."

"Better," he nodded, judiciously, a twinkle in his eyes. Understanding the game he was playing, Françoise remained silent. The silence stretched, but she forced herself not to give in to him. "You are not stupid and have some control. I like that. Stupid women are a bore," said Lord Crawford, nodding. "So. What, I wonder, *are* we to do with you?"

She raised her chin. "I believe, sir, that was my question."

He smiled, a cool smile. "Enough sparring. I will tell you that I have not yet made a decision. The proper course would be for my wife to present you to the *ton* and look around her for a husband for you. However, my wife is not in London and is not expected here this season. Something else will have to be arranged. In the meantime, I understand, you will be welcome to stay here. Lord Halford, is a good man. He will see you are well protected and that becomes more important every day."

Lord Crawford had watched Françoise gradually relax as he'd told her his current thoughts on the subject of her immediate future. He liked the smile she now gave him which reminded him of his daughter, bringing back both good memories of her youth and bad memories of her stubborn insistence on her own way . . . He nodded. "Hmm. Yes. A husband, I think. One who will know how to control the willfulness in you, which has been allowed to grow unchecked. No, don't poker up," he added when

170

a scowl marred her pretty face. "A bit of spirit is to be desired. But not self-centered and uncontrolled flightiness."

Françoise felt ambivalent toward this new relative. She liked the way he made her think, made her react to him. She did not think she would like having to knuckle under to him, and she feared it would come to that if she could not somehow escape a future which fate had handed her in the form of the evil comte, and return with Grand-mère to Lake Como. She would think on it.

Thankfully, the door opened and Yves and Elizabeth returned to the room. Françoise wondered if Sir Frederick had gone and assumed Harriet attended Madame in her room. Or perhaps Sir Frederick had joined Lord Halford in his office? she thought.

But Françoise was wrong. Harriet was *not* with Madame. Nor was Sir Frederick with his friend. They stood together in the breakfast room window overlooking the back garden, but neither saw bright flowers bordering the well-swept gravelled paths.

"Harriet, you are merely stubborn," growled Sir Frederick.

"I am not. You say the comte's man is in London, again tracking us down, and you say we must do nothing, must go on as we have. It will not do. Françoise must be protected."

"Françoise *will* be protected. How may I convince you?"

Harriet turned away, biting her lip. "I think her grandfather should immediately carry her off to his most medieval castle and lock her up in a tower!"

"You think nothing of the sort!"

She chuckled, but it was a weak sound. "It would not do, of course. Françoise, being Françoise, would climb out a window and down the ivy or into the branches of a nearby tree and run away. *She* wouldn't put up with it."

"Her best chance of escaping the comte is to marry someone else."

"Who?" Harriet had a moment's suspicion he meant himself.

Frederick waved a hand. "How should I know? The season is about to begin, in fact, *has* begun. She will be presented. And she will *take,* which means she'll be inundated with suitors. Surely someone amongst them will catch her eye."

The suspicion fading, Harriet remained silent for a moment. "You believe the comte will give up when she weds?" She thought about it. "He has tried poison in the past. And in Italy he frightened the young men into deserting her. Will not any serious suitor for her hand be in danger?"

Frederick blinked. "Good heavens, Harriet, I must admit that thought had not occurred to me!" He took another turn around the room.

"Sir Frederick, I cannot help being a puddin' heart—as your odd tiger might say," she added quickly. "I'm frightened for her. Oh why did that spy have to discover the trick you played on him so quickly!"

"Since he is watching *me,* it means he has not yet discovered where we've placed his quarry."

"But he must have followed you *here.*"

"Ah, but a morning call is nothing to concern him. And once we leave I will lead him a merry chase, I assure you."

"You have a plan?"

"Yes. I think it would do him good to lurk in the damp miasma ever present near the river on the outskirts of

Chelsea. Perhaps it will settle on his lungs and carry him off!" finished Frederick half spitefully and half seriously.

"The damp? Near Chelsea?" Harriet blinked rapidly, trying to think why. "But why would he do *that?*" she asked when she found no answer.

Frederick grinned. "I have friends in the oddest places. A young, hmm, *actress* of my acquaintance lives there. She fell into what she calls the honey pot not long ago—having earned herself a small fortune, you see—and has retired. And," he added when Harriet frowned, "she has the look of your Françoise."

"An *acquaintance,* Sir Frederick?"

"Yes." He kept his voice carefully neutral.

"A friend of a friend, perhaps?"

He smiled. "You are sharp as a tack, Harriet. I'd hoped to rouse the demon jealousy in your breast." He sighed dramatically. "Ah well. Yes, a friend of a friend, one far better heeled than I was at the time. I could never have afforded the, er, lady. He was more than generous when he gave her her congé, giving her a little house and a life annuity and, as I said, she's retired. More or less."

"But won't you put *her* in danger?"

"I think not. The spy will watch her, thinking she is Françoise kept out of the way. I will ask that she have a friend, *a tall blond friend,*" he added, looking up and down Harriet's slim form, "to stay with her. When Cheviot finally arrives, as he will, he will know it is the wrong woman, of course."

"At which point the spy will come back to you as his only lead, and you will know Henri has arrived on the scene."

"What a mind the woman has!"

"Anyone of normal intelligence must think the same," she said defensively, hating it when he teased her.

173

"I think not. Do not try to suppress your intelligence, Harriet. I like it."

"Then I should become as stupid as possible. You would leave me be and find someone else to harass."

"Harass? Harriet, my love, you wound me. I am not harassing you."

She shrugged, then turned away. "Call it what you will. I find you irritating—and cruel."

Frederick turned her, grasped the hands she tried to keep from him and held them tightly. "I wish very much you would not misinterpret everything I say to you, Harriet. If only you would trust me to know what I feel. If only you would trust me, period."

"I dare not trust you," she said, her voice sounding in her own ears as if she were strangling.

"You will. Somehow, someway, I will teach you to trust me."

"Why?"

"Because I have, my sweeting, lost my heart to you. To regain it, I must also gain yours."

Tears moistened her eyes, and she closed them tightly. "Oh, you flirt and tease and are *cruel.*"

"I see there is to be no understanding from you today and, since the time for a polite morning call has gone by, we must leave or perhaps we will rouse the curiosity of the spy. But, remember, Harriet, that I love you and someday you will admit you are not indifferent toward me. When that day comes, I'll be the happiest man alive." He backed off, stared at her for a moment, bowed, and strode from the room.

Harriet collapsed into a convenient chair and allowed the tension to drain from her. Someday she *would* weaken, and the man would break through her control and, indeed, he would be happy. He would have her right where, for reasons she could not fathom, he wanted her. A lady in her situation *must* retain her reputation or find herself in truly desperate straits. Succumbing to Sir Frederick's wiles would be folly. She'd be lost. Oh the man was a monster!

Harriet remembered the warmth of his hands as he'd held hers, the comforting strength of them. *It wouldn't,* thought Harriet, somewhat desperately, *be* quite *so bad, if only she needn't fight* herself *as well as fight him when they were together.*

An old thought entered her rampaging mind, and she pressed a hand to her heart. If she believed his pursuit of herself was merely a ruse to throw the scent away from his true quarry, then who was that quarry? What if it were not Françoise as she'd assumed? Harriet's head tipped to one side, the straight brows very nearly meeting between her eyes. She frowned ferociously. She'd always thought it Frani, but perhaps it was Elizabeth? The scowl deepened still more. She was still scowling when Halford entered the breakfast room.

"What is the matter, Miss Cole? I thought Frederick was to explain to you our newest gambit for misleading the enemy."

"He did." Harriet breathed deeply, forced her hands to lay quietly in her lap. "For the nonce it will give Frani a measure of freedom, since the spy will remain, one hopes, at his post in Chelsea. How long it will answer is moot, of course."

"Is that why you frown so?" Halford's brows formed their own frown. "That it is not a permanent solution, I mean."

"Frown?" Harriet cast about in her mind for an excuse but could find none. Without her being aware, a faint blush rose up her neck and into her cheeks. "Was I frowning?"

"You were. About Fred, I suspect. Frederick tells me you are the most untrusting lady of his acquaintance and, since there have been many such in his past, I find that something of an achievement on your part, Miss Cole. Congratulations on being unique in your ability to disconcert him!"

"You are teasing me. It is not kind of you."

"Frederick has honored me with the information he wishes you for his wife."

The blush reached major proportions. "The man is a monster. How dare he tell you such lies?"

"Frederick does not lie."

Harriet's eyes rose to meet Robert's direct gaze, a pleading look in hers. "I do not understand him."

" 'Tis simple enough, Miss Cole. All you must do is believe him sincere."

"He is a rake."

"Reformed?"

"Oh, it is too absurd. His attentions have always been given lovely and popular young women. Young ladies much given to flirtation. I am a spinster. I am not an antidote, but I'm nothing like those on whom his eye has fallen in the past." She realized her fingers were twisting together painfully and forced them, once again, to relax. "It makes no sense, my lord. None."

"Time will prove him to you, I believe," soothed Robert, realizing the depth of her disturbance. "Perhaps I could turn your thoughts to a happier subject." His tone teased and drew from her another wary look. "I understand an old friend of yours has arrived in town."

Harriet rose to her feet, Robert automatically rising as well, the ways of a gentleman ingrained into him to the

176

point he needn't even think about it. He smiled, and Harriet returned it, pleasure dawning slowly and erasing her former mood.

"Can you guess?" he teased.

"Joanna!"

"Yes," he said, pleased he'd given her thoughts a new and more pleasant direction. "Lady Jo—or, as one should now say, Her Grace. When I informed Pierce and Jo of our guest, Miss Harriet Cole, Jo became excessively excited. She insisted on coming immediately to see you, Miss Cole."

"How delightful."

"She will arrive any moment now. If you go to the library, you will have the privacy old friends long parted desire. I'll tell Marks to show Her Grace in when she arrives."

"I could not deprive you of your library, Lord Halford."

"You will not do so. I am off immediately."

"To one of your clubs, my lord?"

"To Tattersall's. There is a mare at which Sir Frederick has asked me to look and perhaps put a bid in on. He cannot do it himself since he is forced by circumstances to take a drive out to Chelsea."

Harriet's color faded slightly and again a faint wariness entered her eyes. "A mare, my lord?"

"Yes. Fred thinks it will make a spirited lady's mount."

Harriet's eyebrows rose. She pretended indifference. "Then, of course, you must see to its immediate acquisition, my lord. His current ladylove will be impatient to receive the gift."

"So he hopes, but he believes there is little likelihood of her making use of it in the near future. She is stubborn, you see."

At the dry note reminiscent of Sir Frederick, Harriet glanced at her host. "Lord Halford . . ."

"Yes, Miss Cole?" he asked with pretended innocence.

"Ah, no . . . it was nothing."

"I believe you prevaricate and it actually was *something*," he teased. "And the answer to your unasked question is yes. I truly believe my friend has, at last, lost his heart, and I can only wish him well."

Robert bowed and left her. Harriet's agile mind took his last comment and pursued it along the lines suggested. Sir Frederick had loved Elizabeth. Lord Halford was concerned about his friend's feelings for his wife. If Sir Frederick pursued Harriet, *seriously* pursued her, then Lord Halford could believe the old passion dead. And if Sir Frederick still felt deeply for his friend's wife, he would do whatever necessary to mislead his friend, Lord Halford.

Even to the point where he'd marry a tall beanpole of a woman with neither fortune nor status? But someone as unimportant as herself would have no champions on whom she could call if the marriage turned out to be a sham. Her uncles, following the lead of her grandfathers who should have taken her part, had long ago washed their hands of her father and mother and, as a result, of herself. Oh, it was all so dreadful. If only her heart would behave, would stop yearning for the love she *knew* would be denied her.

To the devil with Sir Frederick Carrington anyway. He had no right to be so attractive to her. The emotions making her blood flow faster only confused her and made rational thought next to impossible!

Made it *more* than *impossible*: Unruly thoughts took a far from modest and ladylike turn so that Harriet was actually relieved when Marks announced Joanna and she was forced to stop daydreaming. Harriet rose to her feet, a glad smile lighting her face. "Jo! Oh, you have not changed a jot!"

"Nor you, my dear."

They held hands and closely scrutinized each other. Harriet decided that perhaps her friend *had* changed. The constant tension Joanna had betrayed when Harriet knew her in Portugal had gone. Her features were relaxed and happiness shown from her eyes.

"I was wrong, Jo. You have changed. There's a new composure, a quiet happiness, and I believe you are more lovely than ever."

Jo laughed, squeezing Harriet's hands. "I know what you mean. I loved my Reggie, but one could never relax with him. All that energy! And his constant need for excitement and distraction! My life with Pierce is very different. I *am* happy, Harriet."

"You once mentioned a man named Pierce. I believed you hated him."

"There is an old saying that love and hate are two sides of the same coin. I hated him because I believed he'd betrayed my innocent feelings for him. A woman, pretending to be a friend, told me lies, and I believed them. Pierce and I straightened that out and my old love for him returned stronger than ever."

"So—you are married. And children?"

Jo blushed. "We've been married less than a year, but yes. I believe so. I've told no one else, Harriet."

Harriet squeezed the hands she still held. "Then your suspicions are very new."

"Yes."

"I'll not tell. Oh, Jo, it is so good to see you!"

They talked and talked, telling each other what had happened in their lives. Jo felt guilty at her friend's recent history. "If only I had known! We shouldn't have lost touch when I left Portugal. After Reggie died at Waterloo I returned to chaperon Elizabeth for my brother, and I didn't hear of your parent's deaths. I would have had you come to me, Harri. I was so lonely, and your company would have been a boon."

"I would have liked that, but if I *had* come to you, I would not have met Françoise. She is a delight, Jo. You will meet her tonight at the party, I believe."

Jo glanced at the mantel clock. "Oh dear. It is *late*. I must go immediately if I'm to return, properly gowned, in time for dinner. We'll meet often now that we can, will we not? Isn't it wonderful?" She hugged Harriet, and they smiled at each other.

Harriet walked Her Grace into the foyer and then, the pleasure of meeting Jo past, she felt guilty that she'd forgotten her duties. She lifted her skirts and took the stairs at anything but a ladylike pace, going first to Madame's room, where she found the old woman sleeping peacefully with one of her maids sewing by candlelight in one corner. Then she went to Françoise's room, where she found her charge preparing to go down to the bathing room.

Harriet could not find it in herself to approve the arrangement. It was *not* comfortable, the idea a woman might run into a man while going to or from that bathing room! Only when Françoise had gone down, returned, and shut her door behind her did Harriet close her own door and begin preparing herself for the evening.

The maid came to do her hair and Harriet, her dress laid out on her bed, sat before her mirror, bemused by the softer style the girl achieved. Should she allow it? Françoise came in without asking permission. She glared at the dress on the bed before bundling it up any which-

180

way. The moment the girl finished Harriet's hair she thrust it at the maid. "See this is burned. It is old and, me, I have tired of it many ages ago. I will not have it, Harri. You have all those new things in your wardrobe, the things Elizabeth and I have chosen especially for you, yet you persist in donning the old. We are in England now."

"Yes. Where the strictures of society are more rigid than anywhere else in the world. I must not embarrass you or Madame, Frani."

"You embarrass me when you persist in playing a backward role," scolded the girl. She opened the wardrobe and picked over the three new evening gowns. "This one, I think," she said as she removed a silvery blue slip with an over dress of white lawn decorated with fine embroidery. "Elizabeth swore this would become you, and I believe she is correct. She has wonderful taste, has she not?"

"She forgets I am a companion and servant."

"We'd all forget it, but *you* will not." Françoise pouted. "I wish you will wear it." She eyed Harriet and a sly look appeared. "You must obey me if you are, as you insist, a servant, my dear Harri, and, me, I say you are to wear it so you will, *non?*"

Harriet laughed. "You are a rogue. You cannot have it both ways, Frani. Either you order me around like a servant, which means I play that part, or I am your friend and you accept that I cannot step outside my place in life."

"Wear the dress. Please?" begged Françoise, her eyes big and round and pleading.

Harriet sighed. The maid had obeyed Frani and gone off with her old gown. If she did not wear the dress Françoise had chosen, she must wear an older and rather badly trimmed gown which she detested. "All right," she said slowly, "I believe none but friends will be at tonight's party. Perhaps it will serve—just this once."

The maid returned carrying two delicate bouquets. One she handed to Françoise who reached anxiously for the card. The other the maid took to Harriet who stared from one bouquet to the other.

"Did Lord Halford send them, Frani?"

Her charge blushed rosily, holding a tightly bunched nosegay of bluish-purple petals. "This is from Monsieur de Bartigues. He says he believes the blue of the violets is dimmed by the blue of my eyes. Is that not pretty?"

"How kind of Monsieur de Bartigues. And, as you say, very prettily said. They would look well in your hair, Françoise, if you wish to wear them." She caught and held Françoise's gaze. "Just remember, Frani, that, if you do so, you are encouraging the young man to hope his feelings for you are returned."

Françoise frowned, glancing from Harriet to the bouquet in her hand. She stared at the card, at Harriet and, thoughtfully, left the room. Harriet, wishing the maid had also gone, turned her back and opened her own card.

Firm black script wavered before her eyes as she noted the signature. She moved closer to the lamp and bent her head over the note: *My friend,* he wrote, *I know you too well to believe you will wear any offering of mine for fear I will misinterpret your meaning. Believe me, I will not do so. These poor flowers are only a token of my esteem, and if you will wear them, I will count it no more than an indication that you have accepted my friendship. Your servant in all things, Frederick.*

The scent rising from the white freesia filled her senses. Friendship. Only in friendship. If only she could believe him, could stop worrying about his motives, his

182

secret concerns. She stared at the flowers, stared at the lamp and then walked toward the mirror. Friendship. She had agreed to that, had she not? If she did *not* wear his flowers, would he believe she had changed her mind? And if *she* changed her mind, would he? She *had* to wear them, she decided. While she and Sir Frederick were friends, he would not harm Françoise!

Harriet smiled grimly as she watched the maid set several stems of the flowers into her coiffure. How easily she had managed to rationalize her situation so that she could do as she wished to do! Friendship? Bah. She did not wish to be friends with Sir Frederick. She knew that. *He* knew that. He *must* know it, his long experience with women making it impossible he not read her mind and emotions. If Françoise were not in danger, did not need her, Harriet wondered if she would casually throw her bonnet over the moon and enjoy succumbing to Sir Frederick's charm.

Charm. Yes. He'd make a charming lover. Harriet sighed. She waited until the maid left the room before unlocking the box in which she kept her papers. She read the note again, and quickly thrust it in on top of the rest. It wasn't exactly a love letter, but it was as close as she'd ever received. When she was old and alone she would take it out and read it again . . . and smile over her memories of this period of her life! Ah, if only those memories could include more . . . more intimate . . . Her thoughts were interrupted.

Françoise asked, "Harriet?"

Harriet closed the wooden lid and locked it. She shoved the box back into the corner of the wardrobe before turning to Françoise. "Yes, love?"

"Will this do?" Françoise turned so Harriet could see the back of her head. Nestled into her curls were two white flowers from a bouquet on a table in the girl's room and woven in with them a few tiny bunches of violets.

"You are asking how Monsieur de Bartigues will interpret your use of his offering?" asked Harriet.

"Yes."

"That you don't know your own mind, I suspect," responded Harriet with such promptitude it made Françoise turn toward her.

Frani's face glowed with a smile of amusement. "That is how *you* interpret it. I asked how *he* might do so."

Harriet's smile faded. "I think he will understand, Frani. But do not tease the man. I think he has become seriously enamored of you. It would not be kind to give him hope if there is none."

"I understand. Were your flowers from Sir Frederick?"

"Yes, my innocent, but Sir Frederick is a man of the world. His note makes it possible for me to wear them without giving him one jot of hope."

"Hmm. I think Monsieur de Bartigues should take lessons. Oh, Harriet, I do *not* know what I feel for him. He amuses me and," she turned her eyes sideways to look at Harriet from under her lashes, "he makes my blood beat faster, and when he touches me, my heart thumps. I do not know what that means."

"It means you do not find him unattractive, but that is not love, Françoise. Attraction is important in a marriage, but friendship and companionship are equally as important—perhaps more so." Friendship and companionship . . . which Frederick offered?

"I will think about it."

"Yes, you do that." And so will I, thought Harriet, as she followed her charge into Madame's room. Friendship. It was *important,* but was not *enough.* Not for her. Love. That was what she wanted. What she'd always wanted.

184

She forced her thoughts from Frederick to Madame whom they discovered was awake and looking much more the thing, far better than one might have expected given her exciting and tiring morning.

"You both look charming," said the recuperating woman.

"You look lovely yourself, Madame," said Harriet, smiling at the lacy cap tied in a bow under Madame's chin. An equally lacy bed jacket showed above covers turned neatly over the thin body. "Are you expecting company?"

"No. I merely felt as if much of the weight of my responsibilities had been lifted from my shoulders and therefore felt like clothing them to match my mood. I think, much to my surprise, I will actually like your grandfather, Françoise."

"I have not yet made up my mind."

"That mulish look does not add to your beauty, my child."

Françoise chuckled at her grandmother's sharpness. "He is an odd man, is he not?"

"Odd? Perhaps one might describe him so." Madame added, thoughtfully, "Eccentric is a kinder word, I think."

"I reserve judgment, Grand-mère—if you will allow me to do so?"

"Allow you? He is your grandfather, Françoise. As long as you show him the respect his position deserves you may *feel* for him what you will."

"Oh. *Respect*." Françoise grimaced.

"Yes," laughed Harriet. "Such a dull thing, is it not? We must go, Madame, or be late downstairs."

"Run along and enjoy yourselves." Rings flashed on the gnarled fingers waved them on their way, and Harriet noted the book laid to one side. If Madame felt well

185

enough to read to herself she *was* improving. Harriet moved gracefully to the bedside and leaned down to kiss the wrinkled cheek. Françoise did likewise and the girls, both wondering what their first evening at a London entertainment would bring them, wished Madame good night before going down to join their host and hostess.

Nine

Harriet curtsied deeply to His Grace, Pierce Reston, Duke of Stornway. He reached for her hand and raised her. Lifting her wrist with his own, he bent gracefully to kiss her hand. "Your Grace?" she asked with something between a social smile and a frown of concentration.

"Miss Cole?"

Harriet turned to Joanna who held her husband's free arm. "I think I understand."

"I knew you would." There was a humor-touched aura of smugness about Joanna. "And you, My Lord Duke?"

"I have always believed you an excellent judge of character, Jo. Your Harriet is exactly as you said she'd be."

"A diplomat as well as all else?" Harriet smiled.

The duke smiled. "All else?" he asked.

"Oh no. I will not add to your consequence. You need none of *my* compliments, Your Grace."

"Diplomat," he mused. "Why did she say I am a diplomat?"

Joanna's eyes met Harriet's and the two women chuckled. "You, my beloved, may puzzle that out for yourself," said Joanna. "Go away now."

He bowed and moved to join Robert near the fireplace. Others arrived, several of whom Harriet had not met.

Beginning to worry that she'd chosen wrongly when deciding to wear a new gown, Harriet asked, "I thought this a small dinner for close friends?"

"Elizabeth has already become something of a society hostess, much to everyone's surprise," Jo responded. "Tonight she has leavened friendship with a few oddities to amuse your Mademoiselle Françoise." Joanna nodded toward the grey-haired woman, a shocking turban balanced on her head, sitting stiffly on a straight-backed chair where an equally grey-haired man spoke in eloquently flowing periods. "They are an odd couple indeed. They've been courting, you see, for longer than you and I have been alive!

"Then," Joanna continued softly, "she added a very few who will be useful to our program for introducing Mademoiselle Françoise to the *ton*. Lady Mary is a bore, but her mother is one of the nicest women anywhere. And I hope Elizabeth reminded your charge that Lady Cowper," Joanna discreetly pointed to where that best-loved of the Almacks' patronesses talked to Lord Crawford, "must be pleased. Not," added Joanna when Harriet frowned, "that that will be difficult. Lady Cowper remembers Françoise's mother and will wish to do what she can for the girl."

"How will she overcome the fact Françoise's mother was believed to have died, drowned, I think, it was?"

"That is all arranged. Lord Crawford has just recently discovered," said Joanna with just the proper degree of restrained drama, "that his daughter did *not* die. She did, however, lose her memory. So sad. Only recently, on her deathbed, actually, has the truth been discovered. All these years the poor man has mourned his daughter when he

188

might have been enjoying both her and his granddaughter's existence."

"What an affecting history. Whose idea was that?" asked Harriet innocently.

Joanna chuckled. "Can you not guess?"

Harriet grimaced. "I presume you mean it was Sir Frederick's. That man is the most devious of creatures, Jo," she added and didn't reveal that she herself had concocted that particular story while still in Italy.

"Actually, I believe he and Robert made it up between them. Robert told my Pierce it was just like old times when he and Frederick used their wits to trap a French spy."

"Why does Sir Frederick refuse to allow knowledge of his part in the war to circulate among the *ton?* Oh," she added, hurriedly, "I know what he *says,* but I cannot believe he truly likes his black reputation. However perverse he may pretend to be, that goes too far."

"Whatever his wishes," soothed Jo, "it *is* becoming known, the part he played. Stories get around, you know. The men who were in the government during the war now sit in their clubs drinking and reminiscing and, more than once, Robert or Pierce has been asked if he can verify such and such a tale. The tales are then told to wives. Or mistresses. Servants overhear and word spreads that way. One can keep nothing from the servants, you know. Sir Frederick has not long been back in London, Harriet. He does not know, yet, to what extent his reputation has changed."

"And when he does? When he begins to receive invitations from the matchmaking mamas and the chaperons urge their charges to be polite to him instead of fearing him?" Harriet spoke fiercely, frowning at the thought. "Ah," she added, *"then* we'll see!"

189

When she didn't go on, the duchess frowned. "See what, Harriet?"

Harriet's eyes met her friend's, a startled look in them. "What? Oh." She blushed. "I was thinking out loud. Please ignore me."

Joanna would have probed, but just then Lady Cowper joined them, and the conversation shifted to more general topics, including the Patroness's promise that vouchers for that pinnacle of social acceptability, Almacks, would be sent on the morrow for both Françoise and Harriet. "I remember your mama, Miss Cole. One dislikes speaking ill of the dead, but your grandfathers were fools. Because of the silly feud *their* fathers began, they broke with their own children when the two insisted on wedding. Will you be seeing your uncles while you are in England?"

"My uncles have ignored my existence all my life, Lady Cowper. My preference would be to ignore theirs, but I have sent polite notes of my return to London to those most closely related and, if they deign to acknowledge me, I will not be backward in showing them such respect as they deserve."

Lady Cowper laughed. "I see much of your father in your wording, Miss Cole. He was a brave and charming man, but he had that same tendency to say exactly what he thought." Lady Cowper smiled. "No, don't poker up. I once had a tendre for him, long ago in my salad days. Do not fear to take your proper place in our world, my dear. I will do what I can to smooth the way."

Harriet blushed and thanked Lady Cowper prettily. The lady flicked a finger against the younger woman's cheek, smiled sweetly and moved on to join Elizabeth and the lady in the turban.

Lady Jo had impatiently awaited her moment. "See what?" she hissed, referring back to Harriet's comment about Sir Frederick, but again they were interrupted, this time by Lord Crawford. Crawford had married Joanna's longtime rival and taken the woman away from London. For that the duchess felt she must be polite to the man. "Good evening, my lord," she said. "I hear we are to congratulate you on the birth of a son."

Lord Crawford's eyes narrowed, a sardonic twist to his lips. "Yes. A healthy boy with powerful lungs. I will pass on your words to my wife. Cressida will, of course, be delighted to hear from you."

"Of course." Joanna's tone was colorless. "And how is Cressy?"

"In good health when I left her."

"Will she be coming to London later for part of the season?"

"Probably not. The burden of motherhood . . ." He allowed the words to trail off. "I will write her concerning Françoise. She will, of course, be delighted to discover my daughter did not die as thought but lived many years happily married to de Beaupré."

"Of course she will." Again the colorless tone, but this time Joanna blushed as the sardonic expression on his lordship's face deepened into disbelief. Joanna refused to comment further, however.

Harriet was glad when Marks announced dinner. Then she wished he hadn't. It hadn't occurred to her that Elizabeth, wishing to forward the growing relationship between them, had chosen Sir Frederick as Harriet's dinner partner. Reluctantly, she placed the tips of her fingers on his offered arm and, finding the place toward the end of the procession protocol decreed was theirs, they followed the others. She searched for a conversational gambit to lighten the tension, but could think of nothing which was unprovocative.

"You are in great looks tonight, Harriet."

"Thank you, Sir Frederick."

"Biting your lip, again. Now stop that," he whispered near her ear. "It makes them rosy and inviting, and it is wrong of you to tempt me under these circumstances!"

Harriet choked on a laugh, turned her eyes toward him briefly, but not so briefly she didn't see his teasing look. "You are incorrigible. And wrong. Françoise forced me into this gown, Sir Frederick. I thought it would not be improper because I believed only very close friends were invited this evening. At some point the party grew far beyond Lady Elizabeth's original plans."

"Improper? Harriet, I should spank you. Why do you feel you are improperly dressed? It is perfectly proper for you to wear the clothes chosen for you by your employers. If your employers are generous, then thank them prettily and enjoy what you are given. Will you be equally stubborn about wearing what your husband buys for you?"

"You spoiled it. I was much in charity with your argument until you added that last question."

Frederick had seated her during their whispered conversation and now Harriet turned to her other dinner partner, another of the oddities pointed out by Joanna. If she remembered correctly, this one was called the Nabob. She introduced herself and asked his name since they had not been introduced earlier.

"Timothy Markem, Miss Cole, at your service." The man grimaced. " 'Twould seem I'm your relative, Missy. On your mother's side of the family. Sorry to say I totally lost track of Tim and Trillium years ago. The war, you know. And my years in India."

Harriet searched her memory but could recall no one named Markem. "Our relationship, sir?"

"Cousin of some sort, missy. Taught ol' Timmy to hunt,

192

you know, when I'd be visitin' your mother's family." The man's eyes showed a disturbing tendency to dampen at the memory. "The boy was the only one of that bunch up at the manor worthy of my interest, or so I always thought. And your mother a jewel beyond price, o'course. And here's their little girl. Well, well. The years come and the years go and one never knows just what they'll bring, does one?" He heaved a sigh. But his attention turned to the servant offering the soup and, his spoon in use, his interest in Harriet disappeared.

"Hurumph," said Sir Frederick.

"Hurumph yourself," muttered Harriet as she too pretended great interest in her soup. A soft chuckle from Frederick made her flick her eyes toward him. But he had turned, at a question, to Lady Cowper on his other side.

Course followed course and, finally, Timothy Markem heaved a sigh and patted his mouth. "Now that," he said to Harriet, "is what I call a nice tidy English meal. Not so spicy as I like, o'course. Got used to the foods in India, you know, but find English cooking a nice change—once in awhile, anyway."

Why the man wasn't as fat as a flawn, assuming he ate that way most days, Harriet couldn't imagine. By taking very small portions she'd managed to eat her way through many of the offerings, but she was already feeling over full and there was still the sweet course and the cheese and fruit course. "Lady Elizabeth has a fine cook," she offered.

"So she does. So she does." Mr. Markem stared at her rather rudely she thought. "Ol' Tim leave you well to do, Missy?"

"Why no." Harriet was so startled by the rude question, she answered truthfully. "I thought everyone knew. I am companion to Mademoiselle Françoise."

193

"Dressed up fit to kill, Missy."

Harriet bit her lip, suppressing a desire to tell the man it was none of his business. "Madame la Comtesse is a most generous employer," she said repressively.

"Hmm." He was silent so long Harriet thought he'd finished but, just as she was turning toward Frederick, his hand caught hers, and she glanced from it to him. "Old man now. Not long for this world. Ol' Tim was a good boy, and I liked him. M'godson, y'know. And Trillium. Pretty as a picture, your mother. I'm not a rich man, Missy, but I'll do what I can for you. When I'm done with it all, you know."

"Sir!" Harriet blushed rosily. "I'm not sure I understand you, and this is no place for a conversation like this in any case!"

"Now don't go putting up your back. No one's paying any attention to us. As private a place as one could wish, the dining table. People either intent on stuffing themselves or talking so loud they can't hear anyone else talk anyway." Which was true. The cloud of noise around the table was a loud buzz. "So. I'll be visitin' me solicitor tomorrow. Mind, I don't intend to shuffle off soon jest to oblige you, but thought you might like to know my little bit will come your way when I do put my spoon in the wall. No gambler, me, so I'll not be losin' it at the tables or anything like that. No, you just be patient, missy. Someday you'll be all right and tight."

Markem turned to the footman who stepped up to his elbow just then and glanced over the tray of tarts, pointing to several, which the servant carefully transferred to his plate. For a long moment Harriet watched him, shaking her head when the footman asked if she wished a sweet. "Sir."

"Hummm?" asked her boorish relative, his mouth full.

194

"I don't know what to say to you."

"Don't need to say nothing. It's all said." He patted her hand, and his interest returned to his plate.

"You seemed to be having a disturbing conversation with the Nabob, Harriet," Sir Frederick said.

"Why is he called Nabob?"

"You don't know who he is?"

"We were not introduced earlier, Sir Frederick, and yes, we have just had a very disturbing conversation."

"Care to discuss it?"

She looked at him, met his eyes which watched her kindly. "He tells me he is a relative, but I don't remember my father speaking of him."

"Markem is the last of his particular line and related to your mother's family, I believe. He went off to India at an age when most men are thinking of settling down to a quiet and peaceful middle age. He returned a few years ago, but doesn't much care for society, I understand, and is not well known."

"I wonder how Elizabeth knew of him."

"Not Elizabeth. Robert. I believe they've had some business dealings. You didn't know he was related to you, Harriet?"

"No. Except that he tells me so, I still don't know it!"

"Ah. But you must cozy up to the old gentleman and butter him up and get yourself into his will. Even if he left you only a pittance, a pittance of *his* wealth would be a fortune to those who have none at all."

"Frederick, you are not serious." She stared at him. "I *could* not do as you suggest . . . Ah you are bamming me again. I wish you would not jest so."

He chuckled. "You wish no such thing. But, since I know you could not become a toady and bow and scrape even to win yourself a fortune, I'll admit I was teasing

195

you. You've the least sense of self-interest of any woman I've ever met. Ah. I believe this interminable meal nears its end. Yes. Lady Elizabeth has risen." Frederick, too, rose to his feet, helped Harriet to hers. "We'll not sit long at our port, my dear—or so Robert informed me earlier."

Harriet followed the women, her mind dazed by what had just passed. Markem a relative? Markem a *rich* relative? Would he really leave her something in his will as he'd suggested? Not that she wished him ill, but he was not young. Five years? Ten? Oh, no, she must not think of such things! Besides, perhaps the old man was merely talking and hadn't meant a word of it—or like many older people, meant it when he said it, but would forget before tomorrow came. She must not count her chickens. And *he* said he was not rich—whatever Frederick and the world believed. So, even if he did leave her something, it might not be enough to live on. Harriet pushed the whole disturbing conversation from her mind.

One of the young ladies moved to the pianoforte and Elizabeth spent some moments with her sorting through the music. When the candles had been moved to just the right position and another stool found which pleased the lady better, Elizabeth came to sit beside Harriet. "I can't recall. Were you introduced to Mr. Markem before dinner?"

"No. We introduced ourselves."

"I noticed you had a long conversation with him there at the end," said Elizabeth.

Harriet ignored the question Elizabeth was too polite to ask, and said, merely, "Yes. A most confusing conversation. Shush. Lady Mary is ready to play."

It was torture. Harriet loved music. She'd begun training at her mother's knee, but, when it became obvious she had at least a modicum of talent along with much

196

enthusiasm, the Coles provided her with professional tutelage. Her music was another thing the chaperon, during her one season, had ignored, being totally unmusical herself and preferring to believe young ladies should not be encouraged to make fools of themselves. While in London, Harriet had practiced only when the lady napped or was out.

The men arrived and Lady Mary immediately began a long and painful rendition of a piano adaptation of Handel's *Water Music*. Sir Frederick moved to stand behind Harriet's chair. He leaned down and whispered in her ear, "She should have been drowned at birth. Or a new law should be passed adding the murder of music to the overly long list of offenses punishable by hanging or transportation. I believe there are well over a hundred such on the books so another would surely be a mere bagatelle. The wince I saw you give as we entered, suggests you agree with me."

Harriet stifled a giggle. "Do you enjoy music, Sir Frederick?" she asked once she was sure she could do so without laughing.

"Yes. But *that* is not music. I will get tickets for the opera and we will attend a newly mounted performance of Mozart's *Magic Flute*. Would you like that?"

"Of all things, but I do not think Françoise should be seen in such a public place. Society parties are one thing, but the Opera—oh, *anyone* may go there who has the price of admission."

"I do not believe," said Sir Frederick pensively, "I said anything about inviting Mademoiselle Françoise. I shall make up a party with Pierce and Lady Jo."

Harriet did not know how to answer. "We must be still."

Indeed, several persons had noted the whispered conversation, and Harriet was quite certain rumors would circulate the *ton* at the earliest possible moment: Sir Frederick had new prey in mind which was of a surprising, perhaps one might say, incomprehensible sort. They would be watched wherever they were seen together and gossiped about.

Harriet wondered if perhaps Elizabeth *could* convince her lord to take Françoise out of London as she'd once suggested and away from all the eyes and ears and wagging tongues. The notion that Frederick was making her an object of gossip hurt. But there was nothing she could do. Honesty made her add an unpalatable truth: there was little she wanted to do. Sir Frederick had some magic about him that made fools of the women toward whom he turned his attentions, and she was no exception. She sighed.

Lady Mary was diplomatically forced to give up her place to another and, when that young lady had sung a ballad in a rather shrill voice, Françoise took her place. Frani, knowing her skill was minor, played and sang two charming folk songs, one in Italian and the other in German. Few in the room understood the words, but most enjoyed the light-hearted music—especially after suffering Lady Mary's stilted playing and the attempt at song which had followed. When she finished, Françoise gestured toward Harriet. "If you wish to hear something really special, Miss Cole will oblige you, I'm sure."

Harriet glared at an unrepentant Frani, glanced toward Elizabeth who nodded, toward Joanna who moved to join her and urge her to the instrument. "I remember how well you played in Portugal, Harriet, and I suspect you continued your training in Vienna. Please play for us."

Harriet looked at Sir Frederick and noted the speculative tilt of his head. Suddenly determined to show him she was not totally without the skills thought necessary for young ladies in the *ton,* she rose and went to the keyboard. She thought a moment and then, setting her fingers to the keys, moved into the first movement of one of Herr van Beethoven's newer pieces. The man's work was only beginning to be known in England, but it had been very popular in Vienna. Harriet's skill was such that silence descended around her. Even those who usually forced themselves to politely endure music, found their emotions touched by the power and verve of Harriet's performance.

Hands clapped, bringing Harriet out of the almost trance-like state into which she always passed while playing. She blinked, looked up to see Sir Frederick leaning on the piano and staring at her, his pride in her obvious for all to see. She blushed, dipped her head to stare at her hands.

"Harri, play one of your own. That thing you call *Dance of the Elves,* maybe," suggested Frani.

Harriet sent Françoise a look which would have singed her if the girl had not been armored behind a smug satisfaction at the impression her companion had made on Lady Elizabeth's friends.

"Do play it for us, Harriet." Joanna moved to her side, placing a hand on her shoulder. "I know how modest you are and that you prefer to hide your light under a bushel, but indulge us. Please."

Harriet firmed her lips, looked around the room where—except for Lady Mary who pouted, her nose quite out of joint by the nearly professional performance they'd just heard—the guests nodded encouragement. She looked up at Sir Frederick. He, too, nodded. She sighed and, beginning softly, a few light dancing notes floated into the air. They became the theme underlying the more complicated movements, as she played Françoise's favorite of the pieces she had composed for her own enjoyment. Harriet finished and refused to play any more.

"Wonderful," said Lady Cowper, "It is always most agreeable when a new musician joins the ranks of the *ton*. We will hear you again soon, Miss Cole, if I have anything to say about it."

Harriet did her best to fade into the background during the rest of the evening. She had one more brief conversation with her newfound cousin, but he said no more about adding her to his will and she was glad. She found his references to India interesting and was pleased when he invited her to come see his treasures. He said he would send her an invitation soon and took his leave. Others followed him and soon only the Mertons, the Restons, Yves, and Sir Frederick remained in the drawing room with Françoise and Harriet.

"Well, I think that went off all right. Did you talk to Lady Cowper, Frani?" asked Elizabeth, accepting one last glass of wine from the butler who carried a tray around to the drastically reduced number of people.

"She was very nice. She talked about my mother." Memories were dampening the girl's eyes. "It's good to know someone who remembers her."

"Your grandfather remembers her. *I* remember her." Sir Frederick took snuff, brushed a few minuscule grains from his lapels. "We do not count as her friends?"

"You are not female, Sir Frederick."

"No." He grinned a quick flashing grin. "No, I most definitely am not female. Does that make a difference?"

"Yes," said Françoise, refusing to let his teasing change her mood, "I believe it does."

"I understand you, I think," said Joanna. "Lady Cowper remembers the things important to a daughter, what she wore at her come-out and so on. Do not let the men tease you, Mademoiselle. You are right to appreciate someone who can recall those things your mother would have told you if she were here now and introducing you to the *ton*."

"*Exactement*. She did tell me about my mother's introduction, the ball and what she wore. That sort of thing. Oh, I wish she were here!"

Near tears, Françoise looked at Harriet who went immediately to her side. "Come, love. I believe it is time we retired. We're not used to such late hours. Say good night to the company, Frani, and we'll go up now."

Sir Frederick managed a few more words with his illusive love. "The opera? You will come if I arrange it?"

She hesitated, glanced toward Joanna who was speaking to Robert. "Yes. If Joanna will chaperon me, I would love to hear the opera once again."

"Good." He smiled at her and reached for her hand. "You see, Harriet? We find more and more reasons why we'd make a good couple. A mutual love of music is a lifelong bond, is it not?"

"Do you play, Sir Frederick?"

A flush reddened his cheekbones and he glanced around, bent near to her. "It is my darkest secret. You mustn't tell a soul: I inherited a violin from my grandfather. I manage to squeak out a tune now and then. But do not allow word to get around. It is a strangely unmasculine talent in this modern era."

"You are serious!"

"More or less. I'm not ashamed of it. I merely do not advertise it."

"We will attempt a duet someday soon."

"Yes. I would like that, Harriet."

She studied his bland features, nodded hesitantly, wondering at her impulsive invitation. But music was something which interested her deeply. She'd trained under some of the best European talent during her years on the continent. Music had, often, soothed the pain of the loss of her parents, soothed her when her situation as a servant became personally painful however kind and generous her employer and however much she loved Françoise.

Music. Sir Frederick, the ultimate rake, was musical? Would wonders never cease?

"You wanted to see me, Betty?" said Sir Frederick somewhat later that evening after a fast ride into Chelsea.

"You took your sweet time getting here, Freddy m' boy."

"Betty, I'm tired and it is, as you intimate, late. It is a long ride to Chelsea when I looked forward to my bed. Why the desperate sounding summons I found upon my return to my rooms tonight? Have you encountered problems? Has that Frenchie been bothering you?"

"Not directly." The young woman took a turn around her small parlor, stopped before the fireplace where she knew the light would shine through her peignoir. She pulled a tress of hair forward and played with it. "I suddenly discovered a flaw in our agreement, Freddy. That's all." She looked up at him from under her lashes.

Frederick studied the stance, the beckoning expression, of the former demimondaine. He thought of pretending he didn't understand but decided it wasn't worth it. "I thought you'd retired, my girl," he said.

"Ah. That merely means I can pick and choose. But how can I choose when I must play the part of an innocent young lady?" She pouted. "A houseful of women does not agree with me, m'buck."

"You're being paid well for your part in this game, Betty. And I do not believe it will be for long. The weather has cleared."

"I don't know what the weather has to do with anything." She approached him slowly, her eyes never leaving his. "I'm lonely, Freddy. And I miss . . ." she touched his chest just above where his vest dipped low and wiggled a finger between two tiny buttons to his flesh. *"You* know what I miss."

Frederick found her wrist, pulled her fingers away from his body. "I can't help you, Betty."

She immediately put her arms around his waist and snuggled close. "But such a wonderful lover I'm told you can be, my lord! Even so, I think I can show you things you don't know. Try me, my lord?"

"Don't, Betty. You know very well I'm not of the aristocracy. Calling me my lord is purely toadying."

"Pooh. A baronet is far above *my* station in life. Freddy . . ."

"Betty, you're a fine woman. Under certain circumstances I'd enjoy a liaison with you, but," he sighed deeply, just a touch of regret in his eyes as he looked down into hers, "I cannot oblige you now."

"Why? Oh, *I* know," she smiled and snuggled closer. "You think you cannot afford me. It is not like that any more, Freddy. I no longer need to ask great sums for my favors. You know that."

"If I tell you a secret, will you swear to keep a still tongue?"

"You—" Her eyes widened, and she backed away from him. "—are, er, ill, Freddy?"

He chuckled. "I see I should answer that positively since it cools your hot blood, m'girl, but no, I have not got the pox. No. I have—" He frowned. "You do not swear."

Betty bit her lip. Frederick knew what went through her mind: she'd keep her word if she gave it, but she was reluctant to do so. She wanted him, he knew, and had been celibate much longer than was usual with her. On the other hand she doted on secrets.

"Oh, very well," she pouted. "I'll not tell."

"I have fallen deeply in love, Betty. I could not oblige you if I would. There is no woman alive except the one who holds my heart who effects me that way now."

"I believe I could tempt you, and you gave me leave to do so, Freddy."

Betty approached again, and again found that tempting route to his chest. She opened his shirt, spread her hand fully against his breast. A few moments later she backed away.

"Or perhaps not." She eyed him. "Is she prettier than me?"

"Pretty?" Frederick turned and did up the opening not looking at her. His body, he'd just discovered, was not quite so innocent as his mind and heart! Thankfully she'd given up before he'd given away that interesting fact in obvious fashion. "I think the world will say not. But the world does not know her. She is too tall by society standards and far too intelligent. She hides a masculine sense of loyalty and bravery behind a very ladylike exterior. Tonight I discovered a new side to my lady: she has a magnificent touch on the pianoforte. She is unlike any woman I've ever known—and you'll admit that I've known many."

"Tall." Betty smiled, a speculative look in her eye. "And blond?"

"Perhaps she is blond." Sir Frederick's eyes twinkled. He gave into her obvious curiosity. "Yes. She is currently companion to the endangered young woman you pretend to be."

"Ah well." Betty twisted a strand of her long hair, the dusky coil winding around her wrist. "You say you believe this masquerade will not go on for long?"

"Another day or two at most."

Betty turned away. "Then perhaps I will survive it. But *then,* Sir Frederick, I will present myself in Town to find myself a man."

"Once the crow watching you so closely is gone from his perch you are free to do as you please."

"Will you return, Sir Frederick?"

"Perhaps, but I doubt it. I will send a message when I'm certain your part is played. Do remember the man is dangerous. Do not do anything foolish in the meantime. Stay with others who can protect you."

"I will do so. I have always believed in looking after my neck and so far have not failed to protect it."

Frederick left as he had come, that is, through the back door and down the garden to where he'd left his horse. Soon he cantered toward London, the faintest twinge of regret in his mind that he'd not taken Betty up on her offer. Celibacy had been little problem the long months in Europe, but now, with Harriet near to hand, seeing her every day, he found it more and more difficult to keep his hands off her—and relief from another source might not be a bad idea. And yet . . . no, there was something in what he'd told Betty: she might give him physical relief, but she would not give him the soul deep peace which only his Harriet could provide. His very stubborn Harriet . . .

His gelding dropped back to a walk, slowed more as Frederick mused about his love. *Ah Harriet. Do not,* he thought, *keep me waiting long!* Discovering his horse was chewing on the young spring leaves of a roadside bush, Frederick chuckled. "You'll have oats in your stable, Ranger. Up, boy. I want my bed. My lonely, *oh so lonely, bed!*" The steed's ears laid back, twitched once, and, obediently, he moved on.

Ten

Cob set the second boot aside and removed the soft cotton gloves he wore when handling them. As he picked up Frederick's discarded coat and cravat, his eyes moved around the room, checking the fire, the decanter, the drapes. In the dressing room he held up the coat, searching for dirt or creases. He gave it a shake—and sneezed. Pulling the material close to his face he sniffed. And scowled. He turned his head to look through the open door to where Frederick lounged with a deep scowl of his own, sleeves rolled up and buttons open part way down his chest.

Cob stalked to where he'd left the boots and picked them up, careful to avoid finger prints. He stood looking down at his master almost trembling with suppressed anger.

Frederick glanced up after a time. "All right Cob. What is it?"

"Feeling right proud of yourself, Sir Fred?"

Frederick blinked. "Proud? What are you talking about?"

"Took a little ride out to Chelsea, did you?"

Frederick sighed. "You know I did. You gave me the message."

"Couldn't just find out the problem and ride home, could you, Sir Fred?"

"That's exactly what I did."

Cob hugged the boots. "Didn't think you'd ever start lying to *me*."

Brows climbing toward his scalp, Frederick's mouth thinned. "Of what are you accusing me now?"

Cob's scowl deepened. "Don't think I'll ever get the stink of her perfume out of that coat."

"Then give it away."

"Certainly, Sir Fred. Might be for the best, Sir Fred."

Frederick stared into the fire, and Cob moved slowly toward the dressing room only to stop when Frederick spoke. "Cob."

"Yes, Sir Fred?"

"You can stop Sir Fredding me. I'm innocent."

Cob blinked. "But . . ."

"The, er, lady flung herself on my chest. I couldn't very well let her fall."

Cob heard the dry humor in Frederick's voice and relaxed. "I may *have* to give away the coat. You wouldn't want the reputation of wearing that sort of scent."

"Do what you can, Cob."

Frederick heaved a sigh and wondered how many men went so far as he would go to appease their valets feelings. He grinned to himself: Perhaps if all men had for valet a friend as loyal and valued as Cob, then all would do as he did. He lay his head back and swirled his brandy round and round in his glass, his mind drifting from Cob to his lovely and beloved Miss Cole. Would he ever find a way of gaining her trust? Was music a means to that end? He looked across the room to the tall armoire. Laying, nearly hidden, atop it was the case to his long-ignored violin. Tomorrow he would tune it up and then he must

208

spend his every free hour practicing. . . . If music were the key, then let there be music!

Not many streets away tired horses hung their heads when a much spattered traveling coach pulled to a stop. The guard climbed stiffly off the perch and opened the door. The dark cavern of the interior seemed empty at first. "Lady Crawford?" he questioned the seeming emptiness.

"Knock, you fool. Do you expect me to stand in the street while waiting for the door to open?"

His mouth thinning, Lord Crawford's servant bowed, turned and climbed the short flight of steps to the heavily carved door. The knocker was off which gave him pause, but then, shrugging, he pounded loudly on the thick wood and waited. He tried again and again waited. He was just reaching out for the third time when the sound of bolts and chains being released could be heard on the inside.

"Well?" asked a testy voice. "Who's gettin' me out o' me bed this time o' the night? 'Twill be dawn soon enough."

"Lady Crawford has arrived."

"So? What the bleedin' bones am I to do about it?"

"His lordship will have your head for washing if you don't watch it."

"Since his lordship is nowhere about, he'll not—if you say nothing, that is."

"Lord Crawford is out?"

"Lord Crawford has not been *in,* if you get me meaning. I ain't seen hide or hair o' him since he ordered the house closed the end o' last season."

"Where's the butler?"

"What butler?"

"What do you mean, what butler? Lord Crawford's butler, you doddering old fool!"

"Ain't nobody here but me. And I'm goin' back to bed."

"Allen," said Cressy from the coach, "what is the problem?"

"The house has not been opened, my lady. This man says there is no one here but himself."

"But, then, where is Lord Crawford?"

"I don't know, my lady."

The door closed softly during this exchange. The guard swung around as the first bolt slid closed. He pounded out a loud rat-a-tat-tat on the solid oak. Another bolt slid shut and a chain rattled. "You old villain you! Open this door!"

"Quiet!" hissed Cressy. "Do you wish to rouse the street?"

The guard approached the carriage stiffly, disappointment a tight knot in his chest. He'd thought he could, finally, rid himself of his impossible mistress and, after a warm drink, fall into bed for hours and hours of much needed sleep. "What do you wish to do, my lady?"

"Drive on to the Pulteney."

"A hotel, my lady?"

There was only a suspicion of an insolent taunt in his question, but it made Cressida, Lady Crawford, bite her lip. She'd experienced great embarrassment the evening before when she'd stopped at a posting house. The landlord had not believed her to be Lady Crawford, but a totally different sort of woman—despite her arrival in Lord Crawford's coach. With the crest on the door panel, he couldn't deny that it was owned by his lordship—only that his lordship would allow his lordship's wife to travel without female accompaniment.

"Damn my maid anyway."

It wasn't that poor woman's fault she'd fallen down the stairs while carrying all Cressida's bits and pieces from the posting house, but Cressy felt servants had no right to discommode their betters. The maid had broken her leg and, deciding she'd not be held up, Cressy had left the suffering Abigail behind, telling the landlord to bill Lord Crawford for expenses—including a doctor. That had been two nights ago, and now she was in the same fix as the evening before. No maid. She'd driven on far too many stages this day in order to avoid the embarrassment she'd be made to feel as a woman traveling alone. She couldn't, wouldn't, go to another hotel.

"My lady?"

"Be quiet. I'm thinking."

Where was Lord Crawford if he were not at his own town dwelling? And why was he *not* there? All her careful plotting and planning could still turn to naught if she weren't very careful indeed. Not come to London during the season! How dare his lordship forbid her to come to London?

The guard shifted from one foot to the other and clenched his gloved fists, fighting back a snide comment. He'd wondered about this journey from the start. There was the express letter to his lordship, which her ladyship had opened despite Lord Crawford's agent doing what he could to prevent her. The letter was read, thrown on the fire, and that action followed by the temper tantrum to end all tantrums.

Then the whole household was thrown into a pelter, readying everything so that her ladyship could leave for London first thing the next morning. And now here they were in London and his lordship not at home, the house closed up as it was ninety-nine percent of the time—his

211

lordship not having much liking for London and southerners, or northerners, or *anyone,* for that matter, his lordship keeping himself much to himself most of each year.

"Well?"

"My lady?"

"I gave you an order."

The guard flushed. Deep in his own thoughts, he'd missed something. "Sorry, my lady. I'm that tired I don't know if I'm on my head or my heels. Where do you wish to go?" He gave her an expectant look as false as the smile she turned on him.

"My brother's," she repeated with sickly sweetness. "We will go to Halford House. At once."

"Yes, my lady." The guard closed the carriage door and climbed up on the perch beside the coachman, an old man even more exhausted than himself. Coachy was dozing and Allen, a kind-hearted lad, decided not to wake him. He took the reins from the gnarled hands and flipped them across the backs of the tired horses. On to her brother's. Where he'd have to knock up another sleeping household. Hopefully one where there would be welcome, a long drink of warm punch—but more likely ale, given the hour—and a good warm bed. Any bed actually. He wouldn't even ask that it be warm. Only that he be able to stretch out and sleep and sleep and sleep.

Soon there was another door where he waited and waited and which was, finally, grumpily, opened—this time by a half-dressed butler. "Lady Crawford to visit her brother, sir."

"Lady Crawford?" Marks peered out into the street. "At this hour?" he hissed.

"Shhh."

"Like that is it?" he whispered, "Well, get her in, then. I'll wake Lord Halford. John?" The big man had come

212

up silently behind him and awaited orders. "Help unload the carriage, man, while I rouse his lordship." *And where,* wondered Marks as he stumped up the stairs, *are we to put you, my fine lady, what with the house full of furriners and all.*

Robert and Elizabeth came down the stairs together, looked at the piles of portmanteau and two large trunks and then at each other. "Where have you put my sister, Marks?"

"In the library, my lord. It's the only room still warm, you staying up late as you did."

"Very well."

"Robert," asked Elizabeth as she tugged at his arm, "where am I to put her?"

"In your room. You'll have to come in with me."

"I *was* in with you, but I do not like the whole world to—"

"Shhh. I like it no better, but there is nothing else to do, m'love," Robert assured his wife. He took her arm and led her toward the library, where they would now confront his sister.

The sleepy housekeeper, not much more neatly attired than the butler, already faced Cressy in the library where she was countering demands made by their unexpected guest: "The Violet room is in use, my lady," she said politely.

"The Green room, then."

"It, too, is occupied."

"Insolence! How dare you!"

"The rooms are occupied, my lady," said the housekeeper firmly.

"The Rose room, then," said Cressy sulkily, "although I like it not."

"It, too, is occupied."

213

"Then where am I to lay my head? A servant's room in the attics?"

Lord Halford and Elizabeth entered just in time to hear this last. "I believe," he said, his voice cold, "that they, too, are fully occupied. For this night, Elizabeth will give up her bed to you but some other arrangement will have to be made on the morrow." Turning to the housekeeper, he said, "Marks will help you prepare the room. After a supper, we'll all come up." He moved toward a table where a covered tray sat. Marks had brought it to him some hours earlier, but he'd not been hungry, and he'd not touched it. He looked at the plate of buttered bread, curling slightly as it dried out, the cold meats, the cheese . . . he shrugged. "This will do." He smiled wryly. "Well, Cressy. This is unexpected."

"I thought to stay at Crawford's house."

Was there just a touch of embarrassment under the defiance Elizabeth heard in her sister-in-law's voice? "We will be all right for the nonce, Cressy," she said soothingly, "but, truly, the house is full to the rafters. I'm sorry."

"Lord Crawford? Is *he* here?" Cressy hated asking, but her arrival in London had been so different from what she'd anticipated. For one thing, the battle she'd expected to have with her lord must be postponed and, for another, the necessity of coming to her disapproving brother, was a complete anticlimax. She waved away the offered food and stared at Halford, ignoring the minx who had somehow managed to capture him in her first season. Cressy had never understood it. That the chit was niece to her old enemy, Joanna, only made it more intolerable. "Well? Do you know where he has laid his head?"

"I believe he stays with Sir Frederick, Cressy."

"Frederick! Is he back?"

"Yes."

Cressy's mouth drooped. Here was another reason for resenting Lord Crawford's intolerable decrees: Frederick was back in London and she'd not known. Frederick, the man who had tricked her into marrying his uncle! She hated Frederick very nearly as much as she hated Joanna who was wed to Pierce Reston, Duke of Stornway, the only man Cressy had ever truly wanted. She turned to stare out the windows.

"You are tired, my dear. I believe we can take you up now. But quietly. We've an invalid in the house, and she needs all the rest she can get."

"Invalid?"

Half interested, half bored, Cressy listened with only half an ear—until it was mentioned that one of the visitors was her husband's granddaughter whom the express had mentioned—the letter which had sent her hot-foot to London, despite Lord Crawford's orders she was not to leave home. "Someone has gulled you, brother dear. Crawford has no granddaughter."

"He has acknowledged her."

"A by-blow's by-blow from his salad days? And you house her?"

"It is much too long a story for tonight, Cressy." Robert opened the door to Elizabeth's room and waved her through. "But where is your maid?"

"The clumsy wench fell and broke her leg in Thirsk, and I had to leave her behind at the Golden Fleece."

"Then Mrs. Comfort will maid you tonight. We'll see you in the morning and send for Lord Crawford as early as convenable."

"Good."

The door closed, and Elizabeth allowed Robert to guide

215

her back into his bedroom. "Robert," she said, a dark, pensive look in her eyes.

"Yes love?"

"Will you be insulted if I tell you I do not much like your sister?"

"No. I'll tell you a secret instead." He pulled her close. "I do not much like her myself," he whispered into her ear.

Elizabeth giggled, allowed herself to be lifted and settled on the wide bed. Robert pulled the bedclothes up around his wife's shoulders and leaned to kiss her on the nose. She moved her face a fraction and took his lips with her own. Slowly the kiss deepened, and Robert's arms slid around her, tightened. His long body stretched out at her side. All thought of unlikable sisters and too few guest bedrooms disappeared as the flames of passion kindled between them.

Late the next morning, while discovering Madame's desires for the day, Elizabeth lifted her head and raised one finger, listening. "Madame, I believe I'm needed elsewhere. Please excuse me. She strolled from the bedroom. With Madame's door closed behind her, she raced down the hall to her own room, which she entered abruptly and without formality. She looked toward the dressing table and, stepping between the cowering maid and her unwanted guest, warned, "Don't you dare throw that!"

Cressy gritted her teeth. "That maid's insolence is not to be borne. Get her out of my sight."

"Put down that scent bottle." It had been one of Robert's first gifts to her and Elizabeth, prizing it, was sentimentally attached to it. "I will be very unhappy if it is broken."

Cressy looked at her hand, raised her brows as if she didn't know how the bottle had come to be there and, with elaborate care, set it down.

"Now, what has our maid done to offend you?"

Cressy scowled again. "I merely asked her about your other guests, Elizabeth. She refused to say more than that they arrived some time ago and that the old lady was ill. She *refused* any more information."

A masculine voice answered that. "Good. I am glad to know that my servants obey their orders."

"Robert!" said Elizabeth, glad to have him arrive since she wasn't certain how to handle the situation. She held out her hand to him.

He strolled on into the room. "Elizabeth," he said, mimicking her tone and slipped his arm around her waist. "Do remember, my dear, to put a bonus into that girl's wages next quarter, will you? Such obedience in the face of my sister's determination should be rewarded."

"She might appreciate it more if it were given immediately, my lord," said Elizabeth demurely.

"And, given immediately, it would reinforce her good behavior." Robert nodded. "Excellent, my love." He glanced at his bewildered, but still angry sister. "My servants have been warned they are not to speak of our guests. If you have questions, you'll have to ask me."

"Last night you said my husband's granddaughter was here." Cressy didn't tell them she'd already had the news of the chit's existence from the letter she'd opened, even though it had been addressed to her husband. "I do not believe you."

"I will allow Lord Crawford to explain what he will to you. But hear me, Cressy. There will be no more temper tantrums while you reside under this roof or I will have you, your trunks, and all your bits and pieces out on the street. There will be no polite waiting until you're ready to leave us either. You will *not* disrupt my home."

Cressy turned back to face the mirror. "Oh go away. You are horribly irritating, brother."

"Lord Crawford will be here in half an hour. I suggest you be ready, sister."

"Half an hour?" Cressy's heart beat faster, but she responded languidly. "I cannot possibly be dressed in half an hour. Wherever did you get such a notion? You may send his lordship up here."

"That I will not. You are building to a rousing good fight, are you not? Even though you've been made aware there is an invalid in the house and that such disturbance would not be in order. Well, I'll not have Madame disturbed. You, Cressida, will take yourself down to the library from which I've had all breakables removed." The last was said with a touch of rue. Robert's eyes met his sister's in the mirror and, for a moment, an emotion approaching understanding passed between them.

Cressy smiled sourly. "You know me well, brother."

"As you know yourself, my dear. Have you never heard the phrase, one collects more flies with honey than with vinegar?"

"Often. Ever since the nursery." She again met his eyes. "I suspect I do not like flies, Robert."

"Your saving grace, Cressy, is the fact you know your failings and can occasionally laugh at yourself. Control your temper if you can, m'dear. You'll not get away with your starts in this house, as you well know."

" 'Twas once my home, too, Robert."

"A woman's home is with her husband, Cressida. That is the way of things."

218

"Oh go away. I will come down as soon as I may."

"Soon" stretched to well over an hour and, when Cressida finally showed her face there was a combination of emotions not quite hidden from those who received her in the library. Robert saw respect for Crawford, which he hadn't expected. He also noted defiance and determination. He sighed.

"Well, lady wife?"

Not, thought Robert, *a hopeful sign.* Lord Crawford was as ready for battle as was Cressy.

"Well, my lord husband?"

"It is *not* well. You lied to my servants."

"You left me no choice."

"And our son, madam?"

"I presume our son goes on as always." Cressy shrugged. But somewhere deep inside, she, too, wondered if the boy fared well. It hadn't occurred to her when she left Northumberland that she might worry about her child. She had disliked children all her life and that her own might somehow be a different matter had not occurred to her.

"He needs his mother."

"Your heir has Nanny, a wet nurse, two nursery maids, and a footman. He is well served, my lord."

"Luckily for you I trust Nanny completely or you would feel my whip on your ribs, lady wife."

"Oh, come now!" Cressida's eyes widened. "You would not beat a woman?"

"Would I not? Believe what you will, m'dear, but go too far, and you'll find out. The hard way."

"Robert!"

"No, this is not my argument. Do not call on me, Cressy."

"You would let him beat me?"

Lord Halford nodded. "As our father should have done."

Cressy, her eyes holding his, had to believe he'd not aid her. She bit her lip.

Robert turned to Lord Crawford. "What would you now, my lord?"

"I would order her back at once, but she has exhausted my servants, to say nothing of the horses, and they are in no fit state to take her."

"So?"

"So, perhaps . . ." Crawford scowled. He walked toward Cressy and took her chin roughly between his fingers. "If you promise to behave, you may stay for two weeks."

"Only two weeks?"

"Two weeks. You may spend my money on fashions and fribbly things. You may visit friends and acquaintances. You will attend the theater and the opera, I presume, and you may go to *tonish* parties. But, on one condition, Cressida." He caught her eyes and held them, his stare fierce. *"You will not gamble."*

Her cheeks whitened. "Not play?"

"No. Not at all." His fingers tightened until Cressy feared bruises would result. "I will not be ruined by my wife's gambling. I will set you aside and divorce you if I find you have not obeyed."

"You would not!"

"I would."

"I . . . do not believe you."

"I think you do."

"But . . ."

"You will promise or I will send you home post with especially hired guards to see that that is where you go."

Cressy blinked rapidly, thinking furiously. Could she

pass up the temptation to sit at the tables? "Even silver loo, my lord?" she pressed, hoping for she knew not what.

"Even that. *No gambling.* It is a sickness with you, my lady wife, and I will cure you of it or deny you my name."

Divorce. The thought frightened Cressy far more than the thought of a beating did. Bruises healed, if her husband actually went so far as to inflict them, which she doubted. Yes, bruises healed, but the disgrace of being a divorced woman—which she *could* believe he'd do, would follow her throughout the rest of her miserable life. "I hate you, I think."

"Hate me with a passion, m'dear. I care not."

"No. I am nothing now. Now I have produced for you the heir you desired."

"You are my wife and the mother of my son. Let that be enough for you, Cressy."

Again silence stretched, and Robert, pitying his sister, cleared his throat.

Ignoring the sound, Lord Crawford prompted his wife. "You do not promise."

"I promise to try." He shook his head at her response. "Please, my lord. I cannot do better than that."

A touch of desperation colored her tone, but Lord Crawford didn't relax a jot. "It will not do. I will organize your journey home."

"No!"

"Then you must promise."

"And if I cannot keep it?"

"I suggest that you do."

Cressy took a turn around the library. She could feel the fever in her blood to join a card game—or hazard . . . she could almost feel the dice between her fingers. It had been months and months. How could she keep a promise not to gamble?

"Well?"

"Oh, the devil take it, *I promise*. I cannot go back to the country without new gowns. What I have are rags and lack style." She shrugged, but it was obvious she only pretended indifference.

"Two weeks, m'dear. You *can* keep that promise, believe me. It can be done."

"You will open Crawford house?"

"For a mere two weeks? Ridiculous. No, I think the Pulteney, a suite of rooms."

Robert again entered the conversation. "Elizabeth has been busy this morning, my lord. If you can accept the rather crowded conditions, we can arrange accommodation here. Miss Cole and your granddaughter will share the room Madame la Comtesse occupies. Madame will take Elizabeth's room, and you and my sister may have the back rooms over-looking the garden."

"We do not wish to impose."

"Look at Cressy and think if you'd like to rephrase that, my lord," said Robert with a laugh.

Cressida did indeed look as if she preferred the idea. "I cannot like living in a hotel, Crawford." She was also mulling over the problem of the granddaughter. "I would prefer to stay with my brother, sirrah."

"But I'm not certain I wish you that close to my Françoise. You have a well-deserved reputation, m'dear, for an uncontrolled temper. It might lead you into doing or saying that which I would not wish done or said."

"How dare you!" Cressy looked about for something to throw but, as warned, there was nothing. She stamped her foot. "Oh, how dare you say such a thing to me!"

"Leave us Halford," ordered Crawford.

He did, but removed only so far as the room across the hall. From there he listened, without shame, to the argument which followed Lord Crawford's public version of Françoise's history. He was not surprised Lord Crawford did not trust Cressida with the *true* version. It would be ammunition for her if Cressy were to lose her temper—which she undoubtedly would. Over an hour later Cressida, exhausted by emotions which swung widely, opened the library door. "It's decided then. You'll inform my brother of your decision?"

"I will. Go to your room, lady wife, and show no one that stormy face."

Cressida laughed, a sound rapidly approaching hysterics. "But my lord, I no longer know what room is mine!"

For just a moment Lord Crawford looked as disconcerted as he ever could. His eyes met Cressida's and the humor of the situation rose between them. He held out his arms, and she walked into them. He drew her to his chest. For a long moment his exhausted wife rested there.

"Feeling more the thing, m'dear?" he asked softly.

"I'm calm now. Do I look a hag?"

"You are as lovely as ever, m'dear, but a hairbrush and a wet rag for your face might not come amiss. Wait here while I discover where you may retire."

Once Cressida was settled, Halford invited Lord Crawford back to the library where he poured Madeira into a pair of stemmed glasses—which had reappeared with Cressy's absence. "Were you not a little hard on her, my lord?" He stared into his glass, raised his eyes to stare at his elderly brother-in-law. "Do you wish you had not married her?"

"That is a very personal question, my lord."

"I *am* her brother."

"Do you wish that that were not so?"

Halford laughed at how neatly the tables had been turned. "I'm perfectly willing to admit, here in this room and only to you, that there have been many times in my life I have wished it were not so."

"Then you'll be surprised, I think, to learn that I've no regrets concerning my marriage. I like your sister."

Halford blinked, the glass he'd been raising to his lips stalled as he stared over its rim at his guest. "You *like* her?"

"I like her spirit. I understand her frustration with the way her life has gone." He held up a hand as Halford would have spoken. "No. Do not argue. She is to blame for much of her own misery, that is undeniable, but it hasn't always been easy for her; and, yet, that has not broken her. She needs a firm hand on the reins, however. My family is long lived, so that even though I can give her thirty years, I am unlikely to die any time soon. I will not out-live her, but, with luck, I will have broken her of most of her bad habits before my life ends and she is free, again, to go her own way."

"You *like* her?" repeated Halford.

Lord Crawford chuckled. "Do not, I pray, let that information come to my wife's pretty little ears. I will lose what authority I have over her if she comes to believe she may wind me around her fingers. This is a fine vintage, my lord."

Halford, his mind shuffling the unbelievable information he'd just been given around in his mind, nodded. He followed Lord Crawford's lead and changed the conversation to non-personal subjects. Soon Lord Crawford rose from his chair, and Halford followed him to the door.

"If I am to remove to this house, I must make arrangements. I am not certain it is wise having Cressida stay here, but I am pleased for myself to be given the opportunity to be closer to my granddaughter. Thank you, my lord, for the invitation." Lord Crawford accepted his hat from Marks and strolled into the street.

Halford stared for a long blank moment at the door Marks closed on their guest. Then he threw back his head and laughed. When she'd married Lord Crawford, his sister had done a far better day's work then *she'd* ever admit. But what a joke it was! Poor Cressy wouldn't see the humor, however. In fact it was a joke he must enjoy alone, since it would not do to spread word of the armed camp in which the couple lived. He chuckled again, accepted hat and gloves from Marks, and he, too, left Halford house for a time.

Eleven

Françoise watched her companion dress for the opera, which Harriet was to attend with Sir Frederick and the duke and duchess. "I cannot like her, Harriet." Cressy had been at Halford House for only two days but had made her presence felt.

"You are not alone, Frani. Elizabeth tells me Lady Crawford's reaction to you was not unexpected, the jealousy and general nastiness, I mean. Your grandfather has shielded you as much as he can, but he cannot be here at all times. My friend, Joanna, says Lady Crawford has always been difficult. It may help if you remember it is not just you who draws her fire, my dear."

Harriet didn't repeat Joanna's story of how Cressy had lied in an attempt to come between His Grace, the Duke of Stornway, and Joanna during Joanna's first season and how that interference had been so successful that Joanna had married Lieutenant Wooten instead. Then, when she was widowed, Pierce had courted Joanna again, and again Cressy had tried to interfere, but, this time, she'd not succeeded. That was no story for an innocent girl!

"I like that gown, Harri," said Frani, drawing her companion from her thoughts.

"I do, too. I must show it to your grandmother before I go down and must not forget to thank her for it."

"Are you excited that you are to attend the opera, Harriet?"

"I am."

And she was. Not only was it opera, a form of entertainment for which she had a passion, but Sir Frederick would be her escort. At some point in the past few days, Harriet had decided that she would enjoy his company whenever she could, even though she could not bring herself to trust that he truly loved her. Her reputation could go hang while she made memories on which she could draw in the dull days of the future!

Harriet stood before the cheval-glass and checked that all was right with the full concert dress she believed a totally unwarranted expense on the part of Madame la Contesse—which thought might imply she was ungrateful. Not true. She was exceedingly grateful because she'd not embarrass Sir Frederick by improper attire. Or perhaps just a trifle improper? Her hand went to her throat which rose above an excessive expanse of chest. Surreptitiously, she attempted to pull the bodice a trifle higher. Françoise, noticing, giggled.

"May I borrow that zephyr shawl you bought a day or so ago?" Harriet asked with as much indifference as she could manage.

"I think not."

Harriet turned, noted the twinkle in Françoise's eyes. "Why not?"

"Don't sound so suspicious. Simply, I think the color very wrong with that gown. Now my long shawl, the French silk, which you drape over your elbows . . ."

"No." Harriet sighed. "That will not do the trick. You know why I wished the other."

"Yes, so you could cover up your shoulders and bosom! Don't do it, Harri. You've lovely shoulders."

"I notice you say nothing of the bosom. But then," she turned back to the mirror, "what could one say? I wonder if I should have spent some of my savings on wax bust improvers."

"You are teasing! You would not."

Harriet laughed, but wondered if she *had* jested—entirely. "No. I would not. Oh," she said glancing at the clock on the mantel, "look at the time. Come. We will visit your grandmother together."

"I wish I were going out."

"Do you? But you turned down the invitation to Carlton House."

"I've no wish to be introduced to the Regent. I have heard many horrid stories about the crush and the heat, and I cannot like the prince's extravagance. *Mon dieu,* I am not English, me, so I need not bend the knee to him, which is just as well, I think."

"Frani, you must not say such things. Besides, you are half English."

"I know." Harriet was disturbed by an unusually serious expression deep in Françoise's eyes when the girl went on thoughtfully. "I do not *feel* English, Harri. I *like* London, and I am enjoying our visit here, but to live in England always? *Non.* I think not."

Harriet studied her charge, a new worry in her mind. She chided herself for being too wrapped up in her own emotions to have a care for Frani's. "What is this? Have you been unhappy, and I not know it?"

"Not unhappy. Just . . . out of place? Not quite comfortable, perhaps?"

"Lord and Lady Halford have been so kind."

"Very kind. Also the others we have met. But—oh, I

228

do not quite know how to phrase it. . . . Harriet," she added in a rush, "do you not miss Italy? The lake and the warmth and the sun and our friends and flowers everywhere." A startled look settled on Frani's face. "Perhaps it is maybe that I am homesick?" she suggested.

"I'll stay home this evening."

"No." Françoise took her hand and led her to the door. "That you will not. You will come and let Grand-mère see how well you look, and you will go down and await your Sir Frederick, and you will enjoy the opera. That is an order, Miss Cole! I'm sorry, Harriet. I should not have said anything to spoil this special evening. Forget it, please?"

"Forget what?" asked the imperious woman resting on a chaise longue set near the fireplace as they walked into her room.

"That I have been silly. I should not have told her, for now she will fuss."

"How have you been silly?" There was a harsh tone underlying Madame's demand for information.

"She has admitted to a little homesickness, that is all," soothed Harriet. "And she has asked that I not let it worry me."

Madame shrugged. "If *that* is all! Of course you yearn for home, you silly child. So do I. But we are here, and here we will stay until something is settled about that dratted comte."

"And then, Grand-mère?"

Madame held out her hand, and her granddaughter slipped to a position on the rug beside the chaise longue. Frani rubbed the heavily-veined hand against her cheek. Madame looked at Harriet who hovered nearby. "Leave her with me, Harriet. Go now and enjoy yourself." The old woman smiled and nodded. "You, my dear, deserve to enjoy yourself."

Harriet bit her lip. Both women, young and old, had given her leave to forget her position. She would not allow it to go to her head, but she would take all the pleasure she could from the treat. "I will not be late."

"You will be as late as you please," contradicted Françoise with a nice pertness, and went on with an arrogance reminiscent of her grandmother. *"Allez!"* Frani pointed toward the door.

Harriet went. She joined the others in the formal drawing room, where only Cressy had not yet appeared. She was complimented on her looks and blushed at the attention both Halford and Crawford paid her. "Please, you will turn my head. Save my blushes, I pray you!"

"Elizabeth," said Lord Halford, musingly, "would not that sapphire set you inherited from your grandmother go well with that dress?"

"It would indeed," agreed his wife. "Pull the bell, Robert, and I will send for it."

"No. Please." Harriet continued her protest as Robert obeyed. "I could not borrow anything so valuable."

The argument went on for a few minutes, Elizabeth quietly, somewhere in the middle of it, ordering Marks to ask her dresser to bring down the required jewels. When they arrived Robert opened the case and went to stand behind Harriet. He lifted the necklace around her neck and, bending, fastened the tiny clasp.

Cressida swept in as he worked at it. She'd left her room in an excellent mood but seeing that the despised Harriet was receiving yet another mark of favor, her good humor evaporated. "Do you think it wise, loaning a servant valuables?" She frowned as Harriet was handed a matching bracelet.

"Very wise when the so-called servant is Miss Cole. How lovely you look, Cressy," added her brother, knowing compliments would ease his sister's mood.

Cressida turned her back on Harriet, for which act Harriet was thankful. There had been one barb after another ever since Cressida discovered that not only was Frederick paying court to Harriet, but that the hated Joanna was an old friend of the companion. Harriet knew the reasons for falling under Cressy's disfavor and ruefully tried to avoid confrontation, but it was difficult.

The door opened again, and Marks announced the duke and duchess and Sir Frederick. Cressida turned. Her eyes met Joanna's and, for a moment, the two women stared blankly at each other.

"My dear, how lovely you look." Frederick strolled over to Harriet's side and raised her hand to his lips. The room faded as she stared into his eyes. The overly polite exchange of greetings going on around them was irrelevant. Frederick put her hand on his arm and held it, covered by his other hand. "Are you ready? A cape or shawl?"

"I've a cloak. Marks is keeping it ready for me."

"Then I believe we should go."

"Rather early, is it not?" drawled Cressida on Frederick's other side. "Or will you sneak in so the *ton* will not see the young person on your arm?"

Lord Crawford joined them before Sir Frederick could indulge Cressida in the row for which she obviously wished. Otherwise, she'd not have used a pejorative term when referring to Harriet. His lordship's hand on his wife's wrist was not gentle. "You will apologize, my dear."

Reluctantly, Cressy did so. It did not improve her temper, but, by then, Frederick had realized the impropriety of quarreling.

"We wish to hear the whole opera, Cressy," said Joanna, soothingly. "We are going for the music, not the usual reasons."

"To see and be seen? But you *will* be seen, Frederick. How the *ton* will talk!"

"Cressida."

She turned to look up at her husband, bit her lip and, for just a moment, her eyes flitted around the room before she looked at him again. "Yes, Crawford?"

"Come here, m'dear."

Her face hardened. Then his eyes went cold as ice in a certain way they had. It was an expression she'd learned meant she'd better obey. "My lord?" she asked, leaning near.

He spoke to her so quietly no one could hear and, as they spoke together, Robert motioned the others to leave, following them from the room.

"Do not, Miss Cole, allow my sister to upset you," said Robert. "She will if she can."

"I believe my common sense will carry me through, Lord Halford."

"I believe it will, too. Enjoy yourselves," he said.

Frederick settled Harriet's cloak around her shoulders, the deeply tanned hands lingering there for an extra moment. Startled she looked up and their gaze met for a long moment. Frederick felt a moment's exultation when she dropped her eyes in confusion. That she did not frown, nor rebuke him for his temerity surely boded well for the rest of the evening. He followed her out and gently helped her into the waiting carriage.

"Did you visit the opera when you were in London

before?" he asked her once the four were settled, the men facing back.

"Oh yes. It was one of the few occasions I remember with some fondness—not the intervals, which were all that interested my chaperon, but the music! As much as I love Françoise, you cannot know how much I miss opportunities such as this to listen to the great musicians of our age. Sometimes I have missed Vienna's music nearly as much as I miss my parents—which must sound a cold, cruel thing," she added, blushing.

"I think we can understand, Miss Cole," said the duke. "For someone in whom music is very much part of their soul, to be deprived of it leaves one as if lost in a desert."

"You do understand."

"Did you think we would not?" asked Frederick, a trifle put out his friend had spoken before he himself could do so. Harriet didn't look at him, and he sighed. He very much feared she had thought exactly that—at least where he was concerned. Would he never find a way through that protective shell she wore like armor?

He looked out the window at the ancient buildings that had once been the homes of great Elizabethans. In these streets and byways Shakespeare had walked. Did Harriet think him so insensitive to his surroundings he didn't know that? Or did she think he saw only the poverty, the beggers and prostitutes, the latter's garish dress a contrast to the rich gowns of the *tonish* woman exiting coaches near the steps to Covent Garden's main entrance. He glanced at Harriet. Forgetting his irritation as he noted her rising excitement, he felt at peace again: He had found one way of giving pleasure to his Harriet. He would gradually discover others. And someday she would come to him free of fears, free to love him as he loved her. He smiled into her eyes as he helped her from the coach and

233

gently placed her hand on his arm. They followed the duke and duchess into the opera house and through the crowds, up the stairs, and finally, into the crimson-draped box.

The duke's box was situated near the stage but not quite directly across from the royal box. His Grace commented on the fact that they would not have the privilege of seeing royalty that night, given the gala the prince was holding at Carlton House.

"Did you not receive an invitation, Your Grace?" asked Harriet. Only as the words left her mouth did she realize how rude they were. "Oh dear. My unruly tongue!"

Pierce chuckled, stretching out one leg, his hand sliding into that pocket. He leaned back in his chair. "Well, dear?" he asked Joanna. "Did we receive a card?"

"I cannot recall." Jo put a finger to her forehead and pretended to frown. "Now did we or did we not?"

Sir Frederick laughed. "Don't roast my poor innocent so. She'll die of blushing if you keep on in such a way."

Pierce smiled. "We did indeed receive an invitation, Miss Cole. I, however, had an unexceptionable excuse to avoid the affair."

"You did, Your Grace?"

"Joanna has told you she is increasing?"

"Yes." Harriet felt her cheeks warm at the reference. That a woman was with child was rarely, if ever, discussed between the sexes.

"And you'll also be aware the prince has an almost superstitious dread of illness?"

Harriet frowned. "But what, Your Grace, has one to do with the other?"

"I informed our prince of our expectations and said that I feared for Jo's good health. Perhaps, I said, a damp stranger, standing too near, might infect her. Our prinny was most understanding."

Harriet blinked. "But, you do not fear a crowded opera house?"

"Oh, we arrived early, did we not?" He waved a hand. "We'll either leave early or wait until all is clear. Our box, itself, is quite exclusive, of course."

Harriet looked from one to the other, letting her eyes rest longest on the laughing countenance of her friend Jo. "You, Your Grace," she scolded Pierce, "are a complete hand." A conscious look entered her eyes. "I mean, Your Grace, that you are a joke-smith of the first order. You *did not wish* to go to Carlton House this evening!" she accused.

"You have found me out. I trust you will not be so poor-spirited as to spread the tale of my perfidy abroad?"

Harriet chuckled. "I see I am to keep on my toes in your company, Your Grace, or be taken for a flat!"

Frederick said, "I know you will never be that, m'girl. You've too much in your cockloft to ever be taken for a flat."

"Oh no. Oh, Joanna, will you pinch me when my tongue runs on? I *must* break myself of the habit of using such language."

"I don't believe I've heard you do so quite so freely before this evening," said Frederick thoughtfully. "Why tonight?"

Harriet's eyes dropped to her hands. Collecting such words and phrases had been a hobby with her for years. She enjoyed them, but she did not use them—except in a joking way with Madame, who also enjoyed them. So why, now, had she dropped the guard on her tongue? Only occasionally did she slip as she'd done tonight. But twice in as many minutes? Perhaps because she liked these people, felt relaxed with them? Was the reason that simple?

"Harriet?"

She looked up at Frederick, met his gaze and once again felt drawn into his soul through his eyes. "I believe I forgot, for a moment, my place in life, Sir Frederick—not that I should speak such words even if I were not a mere companion to dear Françoise."

"You felt you were among friends," he interpreted. "Which you are." She blushed slightly, but held his look steadily enough. He went on softly, "Cannot you bring yourself to call me Frederick? My friends do, you know."

That was too much. She looked over the railing toward the orchestra, as the musicians' random twitterings and trills fell away into silence. Saved, she thought, by the curtain!

The first interval brought curious acquaintances to the box. Conscious of how the *ton* would look upon her, a mere companion, intruding into such exulted society as that of the duke and duchess, Harriet tried to keep quietly in the background. Then Lord and Lady Cowper appeared. Joanna and Frederick had made it difficult to stay retired, but, when she was asked to sit beside Lady Cowper in the front of the box, it became impossible.

"Are you enjoying the opera, Miss Cole?"

"Very much, my lady. I have missed hearing it regularly since leaving Vienna. I became quite spoiled there, I fear."

"Yes, it must have been delightful during the Congress of Vienna." Startled, Harriet stared. Lady Cowper chuckled. "Oh, not the dreadful diplomatic business of sorting out the problems caused by Napoleon's ambition—but the music. I've heard wonderful tales of Viennese music." Lady Cowper glanced around the boxes, waved to one lady, smiled at several more. "Well, I believe that will do. Miss Cole, I am hosting a musical evening next week. I wish you will indulge my guests with a piece or two?"

"I . . ." Harriet, flustered by the sudden awareness Lady Cowper had been assuring Harriet's success in the *ton*, didn't quite know how to reply. It would be terribly rude to say no, but she never played in public!

"I will send a note to Lady Halford tomorrow, of course, although I did mention the possibility the other evening when you played for us. Please do not say no, Miss Cole. It would be an excellent opportunity for you to meet a portion of London society which you'll like. My guests will be chosen from among those who truly love and understand music, you see!"

"You are too kind, my lady. I must consult with Madame, of course."

"I see the interval is about to end." Lady Cowper rose to her feet and, with a mischievous look, said, "Believe me, Miss Cole, London will accept you with open arms."

"Thank you, my lady." Harriet blushed and, rising, curtsied as Lord Cowper came forward to offer his wife his arm. The door closed behind the last of the intruders, and Harriet dropped into a seat. "She is so kind!"

"It is very easy to be kind to you, Harriet," said Frederick, "but to what, specifically, do you refer?"

She couldn't voice her suspicion that Lady Cowper had come to their box for no other purpose than that the *ton* would see a patroness of Almack's talking with an unknown young woman! So what *could* she say? "She has invited me to play at a musical evening next week."

"Excellent. I will beg, borrow or steal an invitation. To miss hearing you play would be more than I could bear," said Sir Frederick.

"Oh, *flattery.* I wish you will not."

He touched her hand, waited until she looked up at him. "Will you ever believe in me, Harriet?"

She was surprised at the wistful note she thought she detected in his voice, more surprised to find the same emotion in his eyes as well. Her blood flowed faster. Again the music saved her from the necessity of forming a suitably polite reply. She shushed him, heard him sigh, and was relieved when he accepted they must be still.

A few moment's later, startled, she glanced down at his hand, long fingered, strong, and so warm and comforting as it clasped the slender bones of her own slim fingers, but then, when she tugged, he released them instantly—which, she found, didn't make her happy, either! If only she *could* allow herself to believe him!

"Lady wife," said Crawford to Cressy that same evening when he found her in the palace's card room, "we've been asked to present ourselves in the new throne room."

Cressida looked up, guiltily, from where she watched a game of whist. "I am not playing!"

"No," Lord Crawford's eyes twinkled, "but removing you from temptation is the way of a wise man, m'dear."

Cressida bit her lip, but, meeting the humor in his gaze, she laughed. "I believe you are correct." She placed her fingers on Lord Crawford's arm and let him lead her from the card room to which she'd drifted almost as if her feet had a will of their own. She had refused a seat at one of the tables, but it had been hard—very nearly impossible. She'd known she should leave and, in a way, she was relieved her husband had come to find her. "Who, my lord, has asked for us? Or was that a polite ruse?"

"No ruse my dear. And who else, my lady? The prince himself."

"Really?" Her eyes widened.

"Really. He wishes to congratulate us on the birth of our son."

"Have you . . ."

When she stopped speaking, he halted their slow pace toward the designated audience chamber and looked down at her. "Have I what, Cressy?"

"Oh," she tossed her head, "I just wondered if you had had word as to how the boy goes on."

"Nanny writes with an impossible hand, but if I deciphered it properly he goes on famously. I will be glad to return to him, however."

"Two weeks." Cressy clutched his arm. "You promised me two full weeks!"

"Yes. You will have your treat, Cressy—if you will behave."

Cressida thought back over the last few days and knew she had *not* behaved. But it was so hard. Some demon drove her and he could not possibly understand. She didn't really understand herself. Right now, at this moment, she hated her behavior, hated herself—but she knew it would not last. Oh, why was she so horrible?

"Come along now, my lady wife."

The next day, standing at the top of the front stairs, Harriet pulled on gloves, preparatory for a walk to Hatchard and Son's Bookstore where she hoped to find something in French which might interest Madame. The knocker clanked and, stepping back, she paused, waiting to see who arrived. Sir Frederick stepped in and spoke too softly for her to hear. Marks took the hat and gloves handed him, passed them to a footman and, with them, a message. The footman disappeared toward the back of the house and, after another word or two, Marks followed, leaving Frederick alone in the hall.

This was such odd behavior that Harriet remained absolutely still, not certain she wished to encounter Sir Frederick so soon after their evening at the opera. Something in her vacillated wildly every time she saw him and every time it only got worse. Then Big John walked quietly toward Sir Frederick who drew him off to one side. She watched the expression on the big man's face, the thinning of his mouth, the furrowing of his brow. His body stiffened at one point, then relaxed and he nodded as Frederick pursued the topic, speaking quickly but firmly.

Harriet swallowed. She didn't need to be told what subject was under discussion, she *knew*. The comte had come to London. He was here. Her heart pounded at the thought. When John, with one last firm nod of his head turned and strode away, she set her foot on the step and started down.

"Harriet, love!"

"Don't. Not now. Not when *he's* come again to plague us. The comte? He has arrived, has he not?"

"Yes. But you mustn't worry." She stopped on the bottom step and glowered at him, causing him to chuckle. "Telling you that is like telling the tides to turn before time, is it not?" He strolled toward her as he spoke, taking her hand and lifting it. He turned it and opened the buttons at her wrist, bringing her hand to his mouth. His breath tickled. Worse, his tongue, trailing across her pulse, made deep slow shivers sweep through her body. His voice had a throaty note when he said, softly, "Ah, my dear, how I long to make you mine."

"As you have many before me."

"You wound me to my soul, Harriet."

240

"Do you have one?"

"So I hope. This is not the same as in the past, my Harri." He put her hand, the palm flat, against his chest. "Don't you feel it?"

"Lust, Sir Frederick?"

"Love. I can admit it now I'm certain. The two are quite different."

"Elizabeth . . ." Harriet almost choked on the name, and he touched her cheek with his free hand. "You wish to throw dust in the eyes of your friend," she persisted. "While you pursue me, Lord Halford will believe you no longer feel anything for her."

"Harriet," he said quietly, "I'll not deny that Elizabeth changed my life. It would be both ungenerous and unfair to deny it. Because of her, my eyes are opened. I no longer seek to wound and take revenge, believing women a lesser and more despicable species. I know now that women, like men, come in all shapes and sizes, that some are good and some bad. Most are neither particularly good *or* bad. Because I now see clearly, I am free to love as others do. And I love you."

She could not, after that, doubt his sincerity, but she could doubt that his flattering observance would continue. This whim of his that he truly loved her would pass, and he'd go on to another love and another. She sighed, wishing she felt free to follow her heart and to the devil with the future.

"You are dressed to go out," he said when she didn't respond. She explained her errand. "You would not go alone!" he said, his tone sharp.

"No. I will ask John to attend me. Elizabeth says she'll not need him until this afternoon."

He smiled. "Let us not bother Big John. I will escort you."

She hesitated and, then, giving in to the need to enjoy what she could of his company, nodded. He looked around, frowned slightly as he noticed a partly opened door a few feet down the hall. Had it been ajar earlier? He could not recall. And what did it matter? He called for Marks who appeared with his hat and gloves and, taking Harriet's arm, smiled down at her.

Oh such warmth in that look! If only she could trust in it, she thought, trust he'd not become bored with her as he had with so many in the past, trust that the love he professed to feel would last a lifetime. Their lifetime. *Together*.

The front door closed behind them, and Marks returned to his pantry where he supervised the regular silver polishing. All was quiet in the hall and the partially open door, which had caught Frederick's momentary attention, opened further. Cressida entered the foyer, her mouth set in a cold hard line. Her eyes, below hooded lids, burned with anger.

How dare that woman—a servant—pretend to be indifferent to Frederick? No woman was indifferent to him. Cressida hated Frederick, but even she was not unmoved by his charm. Perhaps she could put a stick in the spokes by warning Harriet of his rakish background? Cressida tipped her head. No. The woman seemed aware of the danger and was holding herself separate from him—yet she had gone out with him for escort! Yes, she would definitely have a little talk with that cosseted and petted and overindulged companion to her unexpected and unwanted granddaughter.

But what was that bit about Frederick and Elizabeth? Cressy's smile was unpleasant. Perhaps she might have a talk with her brother as well. She yearned for revenge on the beastly baronet—and causing a break between Sir

242

Frederick and Robert would certainly be that. Frederick would be hurt if Robert drew away from him. So, yes, she would have a little talk with Robert about dear Freddy and the much despised Elizabeth.

Then there was that French girl. The idea of playing grandmother to a chit only ten years younger than herself was ridiculous, and she would not do it. Well, twelve years—if she were to be completely honest at least with herself, but a *grandmother!* A woman of her years! It was a ramshackle situation. Perhaps if the girl were an antidote or stupid or . . .

Cressida reran those thoughts and bit her lip. Was she really such a self-centered and envy-filled creature? Oh well, there *was* nothing she could do to hurt Françoise, nothing she really *wished* to do. But Frederick. That was another matter entirely. Frederick deserved anything which would wound him!

Cressida, thinking furiously, climbed the stairs and strolled down the hall to her bedroom. She opened the door and found a maid polishing the table in the window, the scent of lemon oil heavy in the room. "Haven't you finished? You're behind time."

The maid glanced guiltily at the clock, took a second look. She was not slow in her duties. Her ladyship was merely cross as a bear. As usual. The girl curtsied, gave the table one last swipe and, gathering up her basket of cleaning equipment, silently left the room.

Cressy locked the door behind the maid and turned to stare at the huge armoire, which took up much of one wall. Ever since the guests had been shuffled and a maid had filled that monster with her clothes, Cressy's mind had played with a memory from her girlhood. Now, with memory, came temptation. There once was a sliding panel at the back of that armoire which opened into the armoire in the room next door. Dear detested Harriet's room. Supposing it still worked . . .

When very young she'd wondered at the existence of such a contrivance, having accidentally discovered it. Now, knowing the family history and being old enough to understand such arrangements, she knew the panel had been her grandfather's route to his sister-in-law. He'd had the room which was now Madame's. That room had, then, had a dressing room which also opened into Françoise and the despised Harriet's room. In her grandfather's time it was a rarely used guest room. *This* room had been her great-aunt's. It was a disgusting arrangement, that the old man, marrying one sister, had kept the other as his paramour, the secret panel his clandestine way of reaching her.

Cressy opened the armoire and shoving, compressed her dresses into one end. Leaning in, she pushed sideways on the back. The panel moved a few inches, caught and held firm. She jiggled it, pushed again. Nothing happened. Something held it from opening further. She knelt on the floor and put an arm through the opening. It was an awkward position, but she found a polished wooden box shoved to the back of the matching armoire and pushed it aside. The panel slid open easily.

Cressy hesitated. Miss Cole was out, but Françoise was not. Or what if the maids hadn't finished in their room? She touched the box. A jewel box? Her hand slid around it, testing its size. Surely not. Neither girl had jewels to fill something that size. Cressy, letting curiosity get the better of her, pulled the box through the open panel and into her room. She set it on the table where she could study it and found brass initials, HMC, set into the side. Harriet something Cole. She attempted to lift the lid and found the chest locked. Blast. Again she studied the box.

It was solidly made but it could be forced—and thereby reveal someone had been into it, of course. Or perhaps she could pick the lock?

Cressy tried the keys she had to her trunks and jewel box. None worked. Then she tried various other things: a file, the points of her scissors—which slipped and left a scrape along the wood—a long stiff hairpin twisted into a semblance of a key shape . . . and the lock clicked over.

Her heart beating fast, Cressy lifted the lid. The first item was the card from Frederick and her anger, which had dissipated in the effort to open the case, returned.

Friend, he had written! Frederick was friend to no woman. It was a new device in his war on her sex, that was all. Yet Cressy could feel the sincerity in the words, the firm strokes of his pen. She raged inwardly. What if Frederick truly loved Harriet?

Love! Why should he be allowed that felicity when she had missed out on it all her life? Not, of course, that anything could come of it even if Harriet returned his love. Frederick's pockets were always to let. Frederick could not afford to marry Harriet even if the two wished to do so because, with the birth of her son, Frederick's pockets would remain empty. It had become necessary for Frederick to marry an heiress. For a moment Cressida gloated at the thought, but her curiosity took over and she dug more deeply, encountering hand-written music and then more of it. Was there nothing else?

Near the bottom she found a packet of letters tied in ribbon and sighed with relief. *Here* she would find what she needed. Love letters. Cressy opened one. The pure and honest Harriet would be found to be no better than . . . Her mother? thought Cressida in disgust. Harriet's mother had signed each and every letter. Cressy threw down the packet in disgust and paced her room. Nothing.

There was nothing she could use to discredit Harriet. The upstart was more sly than Cressy had thought. She looked at the clock on the mantel, shocked by how much time had passed. Returning to the table, she reached for the music, intending to stuff the box and return it to its place when her eye was caught by a sheaf of paper revealed by those she'd removed. She caught a name, that of an eccentric man around town, and, trembling, she reached for the packet. Greedily she read down the page, lifted it, read the next. A chuckle of real amusement escaped her, and she read on. A noise in the hall and a tap at the door swung her around, the papers guiltily if inadequately hidden behind her back.

"What is it?" she called.

"A luncheon is laid in the morning room, my lady."

"Thank you. I'll be down in a few minutes."

The sound of receding steps allowed Cressy to breathe freely again. She laid aside her find, replaced everything else and closed the lid. Damn. It had been locked. Oh well, Miss Cole could just wonder about it and would probably assume she'd forgotten to lock it. Cressy's thumb ran along the scrape and she decided she'd better hide that. She had an oil she used as a base for a mixture for when her skin was chapped. A bit of that perhaps? It helped, darkening the scraped place.

Very soon she slid the case back through the panel, set it where she'd discovered it and, a smile playing around her lips, closed the panel. As she straightened her clothes along the rod she wondered where to hide the papers she'd kept. She looked around her room and shrugged. Under the mattress would do for now.

Remembering the vignette she'd read, Cressida chuckled all over again as she left her room. The piece was really very well written, very witty. Harriet, it seemed

246

had all sorts of talents—at which thought Cressida scowled again, but it faded as she remembered this particular talent provided her with the ammunition needed to ruin the woman and, thereby, any hopes Frederick might have in that direction.

"Well, my dear. You seem particularly happy." Lord Crawford eyed his wife through his quizzing glass, speculatively.

"My lord!"

Lord Crawford's eyes narrowed. "I think you must tell me what has pleased you so?"

" 'Twas something quite ridiculous, my lord," improvised his wife quickly. She used the satiric vignette Harriet had written. "I was merely thinking of Poodle Bing and trying to decide which was the better groomed, his lordship or his ever present poodle." A flush darkened her cheekbones, but she held his thoughtful gaze. "Think, my lord, which, for instance, would you judge to have the better coiffure?" She forced a disarming grin.

"Hmm." Lord Crawford smiled but still eyed her. "It is a problem, deciding between the man and his dog, is it not? I am on my way downstairs. Will you allow me to escort you, my dear?"

Cressy, relieved she'd not given herself away, nodded and placed her hand on his arm. "Do you join us for luncheon, my lord?"

"No. I've an appointment to see my solicitor. You have plans for this afternoon?"

"Hmm, I thought I'd make a couple of calls, ladies I've not seen for some months, you know," said Cressida vaguely.

"Would I know the ladies perhaps?"

"I believe not." They had reached the foyer and Cressy, not wishing to tell him just whom she'd visit since she was not yet sure herself, turned away. "Have a good day, my lord." She walked down the hall and entered the morning room which was in temporary use for informal meals while Elizabeth's plans went forward for the breakfast room's renewal.

Lord Crawford stared after his wife, his fingers sliding up and down his jaw. Such pleased ebullience as she'd exhibited as she left her room was most unusual. He didn't trust it. Or her. On the other hand, at the moment, he was too pressed for time to delve into new devilment on his wife's part.

Marks approached, and Lord Crawford forced his curiosity to the back of his mind. The appointment with his solicitor was important. A codicil must be added to his will concerning Françoise. Although he had no reason to believe he'd not live for many years, at his age such things were too important to delay.

The girl would *need* nothing from him, but he wished to do something nevertheless. So, he would leave her her mother's portion, which he'd withheld when his daughter had married in such a ramshackle way. Then, as well, he'd determined on an immediate gift, a life interest in a pleasant little estate situated on the Thames not too far from London. His observations had led him to believe Françoise would not settle in England, and he disliked the thought of losing her once she was freed from the danger the comte represented. He hoped the estate might draw her back for visits and, when visiting London, she might visit him as well.

Lord Crawford had, as he knew all too well, ruined his relationship with his daughter. It was his goal, now, to find a place in his granddaughter's affections. If it could be avoided, he'd not lose Françoise as well!

Twelve

The stroll to Hatchard's was made enjoyable for Harriet by Sir Frederick's light-hearted banter which he carefully kept away from the personal. At one point, he even had her giggling very like a girl still in the schoolroom—much to her disgust. How did he do it? What magic was there in him that he could turn a respectable, not to say staid and proper, spinster into an irresponsible child?

Not that she felt like a child. Far from it. She felt more alert, far more alive, far *far* more the woman, than she ever did when he was not by. Again it was magic—some trick of voice or smile which kept her eternally teetering on the edge of the precipice leading to her own ruin. Just thinking of her weakness for the man brought to mind all her fears for the future. The joy faded. So did the day which, she was surprised to find, was overcast when she'd thought it bright and sunny. She sighed.

"What is it, love?" he asked.

"You shouldn't call me that."

"I never do where strangers might overhear. I've sensibility enough to know how you'd dislike that. Do not refuse me the right to use endearments when alone with you, for I do not know what I should do if I must forever watch my tongue. But you do not answer me. Why do you sigh like Juliet at the moon?"

"Perhaps for much the same reason?" she responded and then wished she'd not said something so very particular to their situation. "Please—do not put me to the blush. I cannot like it, this flirting. . . ."

Sir Frederick sighed in turn, but much more quietly than the wrenched breath about which he'd asked. "So," he said and paused to think. "What may one safely discuss?" Again he searched his mind. "Hmm. We go to Hatchard's. Is it possible you are unaware, my dear Miss Cole, that Hatchard's is a meeting place for the more conservative element among intellectuals? One might even go so far as to say it is a hot-bed of Toryism."

Harriet thanked him with her eyes for changing the subject. "Be it stronghold for Tory or for Whig—or, for that matter," she added, "a safe-house for Jacobites!—I would go there. I've never been in a better run bookstore or one in which the choice ranged so widely."

"Hatchard's has been excellently run since it opened in 1787—or was it '88 . . . ? I remember going with my grandfather when it was still quite new. He died not long after, but I've never forgotten that day in London tagging along with him when he went first to order a book and then to his solicitor's in the city. We ate in a coffeehouse, a high treat for a lad my age! Later we rode in the park in what would now be considered an old-fashioned landau, but at the time it was quite slap up to the echo with the top folded down and his coachman up before. He was special, the old gentleman."

"You loved him, did you not?"

He glanced down at her, his expression warm with remembered affection. "It doesn't surprise me you've guessed. I've not thought of him for years now. I wonder what brought him to mind . . ."

"You were telling me of coming to Hatchard's when it first opened and now we've arrived at their door again." She paused to look in the nearest of the windows. "Do you know if they've anything in the French tongue?" she asked quickly, wishing to keep the subject to the impersonal. She should not have asked that question about his affection for his progenitor. It had been a mistake, but how could she not hear his love, hear it in his voice . . . ?

"Now the war has ended, Hatchard's begun bringing selected books over from the Paris publishers. I think you'll find something to your taste."

"To Madame's taste," she corrected.

Sir Frederick asked a clerk to show Harriet what they had and moved off to join acquaintances who were happily occupied in disparaging the latest Whig effort to reform the government. Frederick found the topic of interest but, since his sentiments leaned away from the Tory position, he didn't attempt to enter the discussion: A lone voice among a multitude of Tory arguments would be lost—especially since Sir Frederick would have come down on the side of moderation which would have pleased no one—Tory *or* Whig.

More acquaintances entered, one of whom seemed entirely out of place. That man, a gentleman Sir Frederick had never particularly liked, approached him as the only other sporting soul available. Frederick looked toward Harriet, discovered she was still turning over books, and set himself to be polite to the boor at his side. The conversation followed expected lines: a recent race, an upcoming pugilistic battle, the purlieus of which was still in doubt and, inevitably, the man's latest mistress. Worst of all, the man went on to mention Harriet—whose presence he'd obviously not observed—in an insulting manner.

"Such a long meg she is," he sneered and added, slyly, "And beyond her first youth, I believe? But there must be some reason you've taken such an interest in her. Mind you, there's something about her looks which grows on one . . . still, one assumes there is something not obvious to the casual glance—Perhaps you'll give me the nod when you've finished with her?" The man gifted Frederick with a leer appropriate to his insinuation.

Frederick stared at him, the stare verging on a glare. "I'll thank you to speak with respect of the woman I hope to make my wife."

"Wife!" The man hooted, drawing eyes. He lowered his voice, but the tone of his conversation didn't shift. "You? If you were to wed, it would never be to a chit so colorless and drab as *that one*—although, as I said, she grows on one . . . But, married? The rake reformed! I wish I may live to see the day! No, no, you can't pull the wool over *my* eyes.

The chill surrounding Frederick deepened. "I've no wish to do so."

A wary man would have backed down at Frederick's tone. This one was too obtuse and merely leered knowingly.

Frederick added, his voice dangerously soft: "I'll only add that if I hear such views spreading around the *ton,* I'll send you a message via my seconds, and we'll meet."

"Meet?" The ice in Frederick's eyes finally registered as the words had not. The man goggled. "A duel? Over *her?*"

"You do not know her. Since I do not like you, you'll have no chance to know her and will have to take my word that she's a very special lady."

The boor backed down, retracting his words with alacrity, and, when Harriet approached a few minutes later, he was very nearly obsequious—which confused her no end. "What an oddity, that creature," she said once she'd paid for the books and they'd left the shop.

"No one to worry you."

"You do not like him."

"You can tell?"

"It is in your eyes, in the set of your feature. . . . I don't know. Something . . ."

"If you can read that, why can you not read my love for you?" He laughed when Harriet quickly looked away, but there was a bitter note to it. "Suddenly, I understand. It is because you dare not look me in the face when I say such things. Are you afraid you will see that I do—or that I do not?"

Harriet could not answer him. How could she when it was not so much what she might see *now* as what she'd see a year from now—months from now—weeks . . . even *days,* if he were to meet his next love so soon.

"I did not mean to lower your spirits, my dear," he said softly. "Why will you not trust me?"

"Because I'm a coward?" she asked after a moment when his waiting silence grew unendurable.

He chuckled. "No. I think I can attest to the fact that you are no coward. Whatever is wrong between us, my love, it is not that."

But it *was*. Harriet was relieved to discover she'd arrived at the Halfords' front door and appreciative that it was opened immediately by the watchful Marks. She thanked Sir Frederick for his escort, thanked her lucky stars she'd been saved from attempting an answer to his last comment, and entered the house—where she changed from her walking dress and took the books to Madame.

Madame was pleased to receive them and, one being an old favorite, immediately began reading bits to Harriet who was thankful for the distraction.

The diversion didn't last long. A footman arrived with a salver on which rested an old, rather grimy, calling card. The corner was turned down to indicate its owner had come in person and waited below.

"Now who is this?" asked Madame. She peered at the ornate and spidery writing, deciphering it with difficulty. "Marie de Daunay. Can it possibly be she still lives? I've not thought of her for years. Still unmarried I see and no surprise, that. A tiresome girl and very likely a tiresome old woman." She nodded. "I'll see her. Bring her up."

"Madame, do you think you should?"

"You fear she will bore me? Perhaps she will, Harriet, but she will be welcome even so. We will talk of our youth and when she leaves I will exult at how much better my life has been and how much wiser and full of fine happenings and everything else which is good." Madame chuckled at Harriet's bland look of disbelief. "But, Harriet," she coaxed, "think what few pleasures are left to such an old woman as myself. You wait, my girl. You'll grow old yourself one day! You'll see! Leave me, Harriet, and, once you've ordered up refreshment appropriate to a morning call, you may have the afternoon to yourself. Go. Enjoy. Make memories so that someday you too may gloat over the good days of your past!"

Harriet wondered how she would fill the unwanted hours, but she soon seated herself at the pianoforte in the music room. As was usual with her, Harriet was so lost in her music all her cares and worries flew away, and she was, for the moment, at peace.

* * *

Not many streets away, Cressida was shown into the boudoir of a woman she knew more by reputation than otherwise, a woman carefully chosen from among half a dozen options.

"Thank you for receiving me with no more notice than I've given you," said Cressida carefully.

Lady Munson's eyes narrowed. "I've little time to give you since I am preparing to go out almost immediately. I'll be frank. I receive you only because I know my abominable curiosity will allow me no rest if I do not discover what the notorious Cressida Merton wishes of me."

"You are, as I'd heard, frank to a fault—that is not an insult, my lady," Cressy added when the woman's chin rose an inch. "It is exactly as I wish it. I am, by the way, Lady Crawford now. We married at the end of last season, but perhaps you missed the announcement?"

"I remember. It's more that I can never think of you as married."

Cressy's eyebrows arced.

"You wish to know why? It is because I perceive marriage as the blending of minds and souls . . . and cannot believe you capable of it. You are far too selfish, my dear," explained her ladyship with just that touch of condescension certain to have Cressy gritting her teeth. "But no more sparring, my dear, enjoyable as such exchange may be. Cut line and speak. Why have you come to me? What is it that you wish of me?"

Cressy drew in a deep breath, taking great care that her temper didn't get out of hand. "I have discovered a viper worming its way into the bosom of the *ton*. I believe it must be defanged and removed from where it may very well do damage to one and all."

"Who is this woman you've taken in such dislike?" asked Cressida's hostess shrewdly.

"Did I say a woman?" Cressy shrugged. Since Lady Munson would have to know Miss Cole's name there was no reason to play games. "You are correct, of course. It is a woman. And one I dislike. Which is why I've come to you. You see, whether I like her or not is irrelevant, but that would not be understood if I were to attempt her unmasking."

"You'll have to explain that."

"Perhaps you can accept that, whatever my faults, I believe in protecting our own against the sort of poison she feeds onto paper with an inimitable style." Cressy removed from an oversized reticule the pages she'd purloined from Harriet. She sorted through, looking for the one about Lady Munson. "Perhaps you'd care to read this?"

Cressy's acquaintance gave her a sharp look before accepting the vignette. Cressy watched her closely and was not in the least surprised when the woman's eyes lit with amusement and, a few lines later, her ladyship actually chuckled.

"You see how well the author catches one's foibles, do you not? *You* are amused. But do try this one. Do you think *Brummell* would laugh? It is his privilege to stick pins into others, is it not? I cannot think he'd like the favor returned."

Lady Munson accepted the page eagerly. Again she chuckled. More than once. When she finished, she met Cressy's gaze squarely. "You are aware, of course, that the author has a touch of genius. What is it you wish done?"

Again Cressy swallowed unpalatable words. Why did everyone dote so on Harriet Cole! "I wish done whatever you think should be done. *I* can do nothing for a variety of reasons—not least, as I've said, that anyone who knows me would assume I'm acting from mere spite. So I've come to you. You have a reputation for sound judgment with regard to the written word. I'll give you the work, and you will do with it what you think best." Cressy held out the rest of the thin manuscript.

"Perhaps I'll decide to destroy it. This is the original, is it not? You've made no copies?"

"So far as I know those pages are the original and only copy."

Rather warily Lady Munson eyed her guest, while thinking deeply. "I will read them, of course." She chuckled. "I do not believe I could *resist* reading them, but I cannot think the author particularly vicious—and from these examples don't understand your assurance that she is. Nor do I perceive where you see the venom."

"You are amused reading about yourself here in the privacy of your salon and with the knowledge that you hold the only manuscript. But would you care to see her words in print in a small leather bound volume with gold lettering? Perhaps launched with the publicity given Lady Caro's *roman à clef, Glenarvon?* Or, since the author may not have access to a good publisher, she may decide to write a weekly column in one of the less discerning periodicals, a scandal sheet which *enjoys* stirring the pot now and again."

"Have you reason to believe she'll publish?"

"The creature in question has lived most of her life abroad. I cannot say what she's done in the past—but if you had such talent, could you bear to have it hidden away where no one would ever read your words?"

Lady Munson flushed hotly. It was well known she was a mediocre writer. True, she'd had an occasional essay published, but always it was through the influence of some particular friend who had taken a hand in editing it. Her own talent was small, and she knew it.

In a related arena, however, she'd succeeded. Her expertise as a literary hostess was without limits, and invitations to her salon were coveted. In the last few years, she'd concentrated her special powers on discovering new talent and giving it a boost by introducing it to the old. However that might be, Cressy's gibe hit home. It was very true that she could not have borne to hide away a gift such as the unknown authoress enjoyed.

"I'm sorry," apologized, Cressy—not sorry at all. "I should not have said such a thing."

Lady Munson gathered her dignity around her. "I will read what you've given me, and I'll decide what is to be done with it. If I think best, I will burn it. You can accept that?"

"I can because I don't believe you will. You, too, will see the danger and will wish to ostracize the perpetrator of such malicious nonsense."

"Malicious perhaps. That remains to be seen. But what I have read so far is not nonsense. I repeat. My decision may very well be to burn the lot." She narrowed her eyes and studied the woman sitting across from her and was obviously surprised when Cressy merely nodded. "I must know the name of the authoress—in case," she added reluctantly, "I conclude I agree with you."

Lady Munson's obvious distaste for the notion they might think alike on any subject whatsoever was another insult Cressy forced herself to swallow. "Have I not said?" Cressy gathered up her belongings, preparatory to leaving. "It is my granddaughter's companion, Miss Cole. Miss Harriet Cole."

Cressy kept her satisfaction well hidden. Lady Munson

had taken the bait and, whatever was threatened about burning it, the woman would not. She could never bear to destroy anything so well written. She would be driven by the need to share the pages with one or another particular friend, a friend who would pass the vignettes on to another. The pages would circulate slowly, but *they would circulate*.

The business would take far longer than Cressy liked—in fact, she might have left London before Harriet found herself a pariah among her own kind. It might take weeks, but, at some point, Miss Cole's satire would find its way to someone who would *not* read merely for amusement, someone who would find the writing biting and vicious and would act! Oh yes. And then the uppity Miss Cole would find herself ostracized. . . .

Poor Fred, thought Cressy, a smile hovering around her lips. "Poor dear man—how he'll dislike it all," she muttered aloud. The smile faltered, disappeared, as Cressy regretted her absence from the scene of Miss Cole's downfall. Second thoughts, however, recalled her husband's dislike of such pettiness. *Perhaps,* she decided, *it is better that we'll be gone.*

Harriet stood in the entrance hall and once again perused the note Elizabeth's butler had brought to her moments earlier. It had been delivered by an oddly-dressed footman in a mismatched and ill-fitting uniform. "Mr. Markem wishes me to come today?" she asked him after reading the bluntly worded note for the third time. "Now?"

"Yes, miss," said the footman, his eyes twinkling. "I'm to escort you and, later, return you home."

"It is very short notice."

The footman's ears reddened, but he grinned roguishly. "My master has spent many years in the East. Too many perhaps? One wonders if he has forgotten one does not order up visitors as one does one's tea, for instance?" The footman, after a look at Marks' outraged features, took care to repress a chuckle.

"Yes," said Harriet, "I think perhaps he has. On the other hand, I would enjoy a visit with my relative. Marks, give this young man an ale while I prepare myself for going out."

Quite obviously Marks would much rather have thrown the impertinent servant out on his ear, but Miss Cole did not often give orders which it was beneath one's dignity to obey. He nodded agreement in a regal manner and, with an equally appropriate but far more snooty expression, ordered the messenger to follow him.

The Nabob lived somewhat out of the way in an area of town which had been pretty much deserted by the aristocracy. The growth of the new Squares and Terraces between Oxford and Piccadilly had led to the *ton's* removal westward, leaving many old-fashioned mansions to be converted into tenements. Markem's house was very nearly Elizabethan, the ceilings low and the rooms dark; the entry hall was stuffed with oddities acquired in his travels. The footman opened a door onto the dimmest room Harriet had entered for some years. An odd odor wafted toward her, and she sneezed. Then she peered into the gloom.

"I have been too long in the East and have forgotten the British climate does not give one an aversion to the sun," said a soft apologetic voice from deep within the room. "Hopstead, open the drapes. We will have light."

"You forget, sir," responded Harriet, "that I too have lived where the sun can be one's enemy. Hopstead, we

260

will have just a very little light, and it please you, my cousin."

The old man chuckled. "I knew I'd like you. Tim and Trillium's girl. Couldn't help but like you, could I? Come in. Come in. Don't dawdle about. I'm too ancient to wish to waste time on fiddle-faddle."

Harriet wended a careful way toward the voice between low tables, both carved teak and heavy brass, the large cushions strewn seemingly at random and, in odd contrast, very comfortable-looking leather-covered chairs. As she maneuvered around a particularly awkward combination of furniture, the footman—who must have had cat eyes, she thought—reached the drapes and opened them a few inches. Harriet stopped short, her heart thumping.

Straight before her, looming over her and startling her, was a more than life-size statue of a woman. It had been carved from an artist's lewd nightmare—or so she assumed. The undraped figure had a waist of unbelievable smallness combined with large hips and pear-shaped breasts, which Harriet was certain could nowhere be found duplicated in living flesh. The figure's stance was contorted into what must have been an exceedingly uncomfortable position. The half squat with the statue balanced on the ball of one bare foot, was, she decided a dance position.

That, however, was not what appalled Harriet. It was the necklace of human skulls around the goddess' neck and her eyes, which seemed to glow, and the six or eight arms, forming a spider work frame around the body, each holding some attribute of the goddess' powers, and, not least, the incense burning in a holder before her which had a shocked Harriet wondering if her relative had become a pagan during his years abroad . . . .

"Don't like my Kali, hmm? I've Hindu servants who

would be very unhappy were I to be rid of her, you know. They visit her early each morning—as you can see."

Harriet understood from this that Markem had *not* become a pagan.

"Well, well, sit yourself with your back to the lady, if you will. We'll be cozy enough and get to know one another."

"If you've no objections, I'll sit sideways to her. I don't quite trust her not to spring at me and would prefer to keep an eye on her! Tell me about her," Harriet suggested.

The old man did so with gusto and, finishing with Kali, he handed Harriet small carvings, some ivory and some gold, from the table beside him. Each was another Hindu god or goddess and, for each, he had a story.

"It is a rich and complex culture, my dear," he said at last, "and one an incomer may never truly fathom. As soon as one thinks one has a handle on some aspect of it, one learns something new which contravenes the theory one has constructed. It was a fascinating study, which I never ceased to wonder at, during all my years out there."

Silent, Mr. Markem pondered those complexities until, with a start, he returned to the present. He smiled a smile which, in some subtle way, reminded Harriet of her mother. For the first time she saw a family resemblance. Perhaps she wasn't quite alone after all?

"Now," he said, "you must tell me something of *your* life, my child. Begin with Trillium and Timothy's marriage. I encouraged them, you know, but I'd left England before they actually got up the nerve to go against their respective family's wishes. We wrote for a while, but we rather quickly lost track of each other," said the old man sadly.

"They were disinherited."

"Oh, of course. It was to be expected, and I did warn them."

"I don't think either cared a straw. We were a happy family. I'm glad I was allowed to grow up on the continent with my mother to teach me and my father to guide me. It was an unusual life, but far more enjoyable than that which girls my age here in England were forced to endure."

"I'm sure it was. When did they die, your parents?"

Harriet spoke briefly of the carriage accident, describing the sudden storm which had led to it. She said no more.

Mr. Markem smiled. "I like that. You do not whine that you were left alone or that your relatives did not come to your rescue."

"I am not such a paragon. I have resented that my uncles ignored me. I am not so perfect, you see, that I didn't wish for the opportunity to throw back in their faces any offer of help they might make me!"

He chuckled. "Oh yes. I do like you. Then you found means of supporting yourself with no difficulty?"

"I was excessively lucky that Madame la Comtesse needed me just when I needed a position."

"She has treated you well?"

"Very well."

The door opened and an odd spicy odor wafted in from the platters held by servants Harriet's cousin had brought with him from the East. The dark men padded on slippered feet to where a table sat to one side, and they began unloading a meal onto it.

"Is it so late as all that?" asked Markem. "My dear, I would invite you to dine with me, but I think you would find my food difficult. Me, I am used to it and find English food excessively bland." Harriet gathered up her

263

reticule and gloves. "Cousin, before you go, I will inform you that I've made a new will. You need have no fear for your future." He reached for the hand she held out to him and held it between both his own. "Nor need you fear fortune hunters will be after your money, child. The man you marry will only have charge of the interest, and that *after* you've been paid a considerable allowance. Of course there are also dress allowances and living allowances. You will have any bills of that order sent to the trustees. No, no, do not pucker up. And you need feel no obligation to visit an old man. I'll not be changing my mind since I do it for Tim and Trillium."

"Thank you, sir," she said pertly, "for relieving me of what might have been a terrible burden—assuming I'd felt a need to toady to you! As it is I've enjoyed our visit very much. When I return it will not be because I fear for my future but because I wish to. I *will* return—if you do not forbid it."

"Whenever you've a free hour or two and happen to think of me, feel free to come. I'm very much at home these days."

Even as dark as the room was, Harriet thought she detected a faint ruddiness in his cheeks.

"I'm writing my memoirs," he added as if it were a dark secret. "Nothing important, you know. Just a little something to keep me occupied when I've no business dealings. Even retired, one must watch one's investments, so I am not bored or without occupation. Still, I like a pretty woman as much as anyone so you must come when you will."

Since the two Indian servants seemed a trifle edgy and kept stirring this or looking under the cover of that, Harriet decided she must take her leave or spoil her cousin's dinner. She was bowed out by the oddly-dressed footman who followed her. She decided that her cousin could not be nearly so wealthy as was suggested by the title Nabob. If he were, surely he could afford a new uniform for his footman! Once home, she spent half an hour describing the visit to Françoise and Elizabeth—both of whom begged her to take them with her the next time she visited.

"For where else could one see a six-armed woman and now you have described her I am longing to see her. Tell us, what other treasures did you see?" asked Elizabeth.

The conversation continued until it was time to go upstairs and dress. Only Lord and Lady Crawford were going out—which was felt to be an advantage since the rest could enjoy a quiet evening *en famille,* unbothered by Cressy's poisoned tongue.

Cressy's good mood of the afternoon lasted on into the evening. She and her husband enjoyed the opera, and she didn't feel one pang of regret that it was an evening in which she'd couldn't even watch others at *their* gambling. All in all, it had been a very good day.

Had it been a good day for her son . . . ?

Where had that thought come from? Cressy tripped on the stairs and grabbed for the bannister to save herself from a bad fall. Crawford's hand was firm on her elbow as they continued down and out of the Opera House.

"You nearly fell," said Lord Crawford as they left the brilliantly lit building. "Are you all right?"

She cast him a startled glance. "It was nothing. I just wondered . . ."

"Wondered?"

Cressy drew in a deep breath. Staring straight ahead she asked, "Have you had more news from Nanny?"

"The boy has had a slight cold."

"Cold? *He has a cold?*"

Lord Crawford looked speculatively at his wife. "I

don't feel it is anything about which we need worry. If I'd felt otherwise, I would have told you, my dear."

"But . . ." She bit her lip, ducked her head and turned it slightly away from him.

"But you *are* worried, are you not?" He silently helped her into their carriage and followed her in although it had been his intention to go on to his club. "It is not something of which you need be ashamed, you know," he teased. She didn't respond. "How worried are you?" he asked when the coachman started forward.

A mild frown creased her brow. "My lord, are you certain . . ."

His eyes narrowed. "How can one be certain, my dear? Childhood is a chancy thing. One can but do one's best and pray."

"Pray . . ."

Another silence stretched. Finally, quietly, he asked, "You are my son's mother, Cressida. What is it that you wish?"

"I . . ." The boy's mother. *I am his mother,* she thought and remembered how sweet the baby had smelled when brought to her by the hovering and suspicious nanny who trusted no one but herself with the boy. She remembered how the infant had snuggled warmly against her, his tiny hand, a starfish shape against her gown. "His mother . . ."

"Shall we go home, Cressy?" asked Crawford softly.

Home. Home to the child who might love her . . . if she were very careful. Might. Love. Her.

"Oh God yes, please let my child love me," she whispered so softly his lordship strained to hear.

Crawford had realized early in their relationship that Cressy was starved for love, but he'd also realized she'd so little experience of it she wouldn't recognize it if it were offered to her. A wise man, he'd planned his assault

266

on her emotions carefully. His combination of firm control and an even-handed justice along with humor where appropriate and the occasional show of mild affection had seemed to be succeeding with her. Now, at this moment when she appeared vulnerable and appealing, he must be very careful indeed. He must not allow her sudden softening to lead him into error.

"Shall we go home, Cressy?" he repeated.

"Home?"

What is home, she wondered. *Where my son is,* answered something deep in her mind. She mulled that over before responding.

"Yes," she said. "I would, I think, like to go home . . ."

"Then, as soon as I finish my business in town, we will go."

Crawford hid his satisfaction with her response. The idiotic woman would, if she thought she were pleasing him, very likely change her mind and refuse to go. Perverse woman!

Thirteen

"What would you think of taking a picnic to Richmond," asked Elizabeth the morning after Harriet had been a great success at Lady Cowper's musical.

It had been an emotionally exhausting performance for the pianist and now she sat at the breakfast table, a trifle bleary-eyed, with Françoise and Elizabeth. Frani immediately and enthusiastically endorsed the notion.

"You do not say anything, Harriet. Do you not think a picnic in Richmond park a delightful notion?"

Before Harriet could form a response, Robert, who had just entered the room did so. "Delightful," he agreed with a touch of sarcasm. "Just the place for a lovely little kidnapping, think you not? Don't be foolish, my love. Jauntings of that nature where one is in the open in a public place where anyone might go are not to be thought of."

Harriet nodded. "I was about to say much the same thing, Elizabeth. Françoise, do not pout. It makes you look the very infant that you insisted to me only last evening you are not."

Frani's frown disappeared with a chuckle. "You! You always make me laugh. It is not fair, I think, that you can do that and I cannot."

"It was such a good notion," said Elizabeth, a speculative look warning her husband to pay attention, "I suppose that an evening at Vauxhall is not to be thought of for much the same reason?"

"For exactly the same reason," he said, his voice stern.

"Even if we were to attend one of the masquerades, which is what I had in mind, and all were to go masked?"

"When have you ever attended a masquerade and not guessed immediately those who are your particular friends?" he promptly asked.

"But the comte is no one's friend!"

"No, and I don't doubt he'd have difficulty discovering which minx was which. So," he added when Elizabeth would have interrupted, "very likely he'd run off with the both of you."

Elizabeth looked disconcerted. "Oh dear."

"Mais non! It must not be. You must not find yourself in danger because of me. Me, I say it is so," insisted Françoise.

"Well, I agree it is very uncomfortable to be kidnapped," said Elizabeth, "and I do not think I would care for it to happen again, so perhaps we'll postpone plans to go to Vauxhall."

Françoise immediately demanded to know when her hostess had found herself the captive of another and listened avidly to the whole story of how Elizabeth had wished to befriend Sir Frederick, and Sir Frederick had determined to marry her. "But now we are all very good friends just as I wished," Elizabeth finished. She turned to Robert. "But, my lord, if we may not ride out to Richmond and may not go to Vauxhall, what may we do?"

Lord Crawford strolled in in time to hear that last. "I must assume you object to Richmond because it is open to the public?" he asked Robert. "I have a small property not far from London on the banks of the Thames. Perhaps a party might go there. It is not public, and my people may be warned to watch for strangers. It has very nice gardens and a strawberry patch famous throughout the region that should be coming into fruit about now. Would that be an acceptable substitute for Richmond, my lady?" he asked turning to Elizabeth.

"I think it sounds unexceptional." She looked to Robert, a wide-eyed hopeful look that had him chuckling as he gave permission.

"I fear I cannot join you on this expedition," Crawford continued. "Cressida and I will be returning home tomorrow—which means you and I must have a discussion concerning my granddaughter, Lord Halford." Robert agreed, gravely, that such was indeed necessary. Lord Crawford went on to Elizabeth, "I will send a letter to the house steward at River Castle that he is to be prepared for you whenever you may wish to come." He bent a thoughtful look on Françoise. "I shall tell him to hire extra groundsmen as added protection." Then he spoke directly to his granddaughter. "My child, this isn't how I'd planned to tell you, but you might like to pay the property special attention. I've given you a life interest in it, you see."

Françoise stammered thank-yous at the same time Elizabeth questioned why her company was leaving so suddenly.

"Elizabeth!" scolded her husband. "It is rude to ask!"

She blushed when everyone chuckled. "But I don't understand, and I wish to do so. I thought it was decided they'd stay until the beginning of next week."

"Cressida made the decision last night . . . I think you'll find she's content to go." When Lord Crawford noted Robert's eyebrows rising he added, "We miss our son and wish to see for ourselves how he goes on."

A sardonic look crossed Robert's features, but he held his tongue. Elizabeth was not so well-schooled in properly reticent behavior and words spewed from her. "Content? To leave London in the middle of the season? Because she wishes to see her son? Cressy? I don't believe you!"

Crawford laughed. "It does sound a trifle havey-cavey, does it not? But you will see."

They did see and were bemused by the interesting fact that it was true. Cressy *was* content to leave for the north at her husband's side! But before they left, Lord Crawford had a long discussion with both Sir Frederick and his brother-in-law concerning Françoise. The girl would not be safe until the comte's pursuit of her had come to an end, but they were agreed that the girl should remain in London for the season. If nothing were settled by its end, then she, her grandmother, and her companion were to be escorted under heavy guard to Crawford's home in the north and new plans would be laid.

At some point something must be done about the comte. Sir Frederick suggested he be forced into a duel which would put period to his ambitions once and for all.

"I won't say the notion has no merit, nephew," said Lord Crawford, "But, for the moment, things can be allowed to drift as they are in the hopes the man will either give it up and go home or, alternately, put himself into a position from which he can be permanently but *legally* removed from my granddaughter's life. We all wish her safe and secure, but a duel must be a last resort." He glared at the other two and, reluctantly, they agreed. "Good," said Lord Crawford and added unexpectedly, "Now that you are no longer my heir, Frederick, I find I like you very well. I've no desire to lose you to that man's random but lucky shot—I am not wrong, am I, in assuming it would be you who would challenge him?"

The picnic at River Castle was postponed twice. Once it rained and then Harriet came down with what she considered a stupid chill. She suggested they go without her, but no one would have it so. Then, in a cross and invalidish way, she worried that no one could properly watch out for Françoise while she was confined to her room.

"Nonsense," said Madame, who visited Harriet toward the end of her convalescence. "I myself have enjoyed going out among the English *ton* again. Imagine! There are still men and women whom I met at Versailles when I was only a girl. And," she added a trifle tartly, "they talk of something other than the past, unlike Marie de Daunay! Me! I have had a very interesting time chaperoning our little package of trouble." Her eyes twinkled. "I think it might be generous of you to remain ill for another day or two. The Dowager Lady Porrison holds a Venetian breakfast, and I wish to attend. She, too, visited France when we were young, and I believe she was enamored of the man I eventually married. At the time, I was most upset whenever he was polite to her."

"And now you wish to gloat."

"Would I do such a thing?" Harriet just looked at her mistress who chuckled. "You must remember, my dear, that when one reaches my age, there are not all that many pleasures left to one. If I gloat a trifle that I won the prize . . . well!" She shrugged, an exceedingly graceful Gallic movement.

"Can you not go if I've left my chamber?"

"Of course, I may. I am teasing you, my child. And I

272

can tell you one gentleman who will be exceedingly perturbed if you are to remain much longer above stairs. I would not put it past him to come up and see for himself that you are recovering."

Harriet blushed. "If you refer to Sir Frederick, I could believe anything of that man."

"Why will you not agree to marry him?" asked Madame curiously. "Do not answer," she added, gently, "if you would rather not, but the marriage would be an excellent solution to your future since he assures me he is able to maintain you in a life of luxury and wishes to spend his life making you happy."

"That," said Harriet, "is the trouble right there. Happy. I am so happy when I am with him. I cannot believe how I feel, how wonderfully content to be in his company. And then," she said, staring into the corner of the room, "I wonder how soon it will end. When will some other woman catch his eye, and when will he stray from my side to pursue her? I don't think I could bear it, Madame," she finished, her eyes filled with a pain caused by the mere anticipation of pain.

"My dear, are you not a trifle idealistic? Men stray. Even the very best of them will look and *wish* they were free to do more. Heavens, child, women do the same, do they not?" she asked rhetorically—which was just as well since Harriet could not have answered, such a notion never having occurred to her. "Your Frederick, of course, is of the breed who may or may not do more than look and wish, but if he strays, then I think you'll never know of it."

"Is that not worse? Never knowing? To never be certain? To always wonder . . . won't such constant suspicion come between us and cause unhappiness?"

Madame stood up and looked down her nose at her

granddaughter's companion. "You must come to your own conclusions, child. I think you do the man an injustice with your suspicions and your fears and your lack of trust in him, but I am not the one he wishes to wed so perhaps it is easier for me to look at the man with clear eyes." She went to the door, and her hand on it, turned for a last word. "I will not drive out to this River Castle, so you will oblige me by regaining your usual good health by Friday. You may then join the party. Françoise is very excited at the thought of owning property—even if it is no more than a life interest. There is no keeping her back, I'm certain, no matter how much I'll worry while you are all off on this injudicious jaunt."

"You do not approve? It is to be, I believe, a rather large party."

"A large party does not necessarily mean security." Madame's brows rose in polite arcs. "Can you promise me, for instance, that Frani will not take it into her head to indulge in an impromptu race which will carry her far from the main group of riders?"

Harriet bit her lip. "No. I can only promise that some of us will ride like the wind after her."

"The men will watch her. You must not put *yourself* in danger, Harri. Frani will, if she so indulges, be chagrined she has broken all her promises to behave; if you were hurt because she's done so, she would be heartbroken, so leave it to your escorts, my dear."

"Perhaps we are making mountains, Madame," suggested Harriet. "Perhaps she *will* behave."

She did. Françoise rode sedately with the rest of the party out to River Castle. At last the group rode in between wrought-iron gates set into posts built like mini-

ature, stylized, towers with crenelated tops. Tall rhodo-
dendrons lined the drive, which curved along the inside
of the fence for a distance and then, turning, opened onto
broad gardens which, from this point, went straight down
to the river. Off to the side was the house. Everyone
pulled up, leaving Françoise somewhat apart so that she
had a good view.

The girl's eyes widened. "But it is not a castle at all!
It is . . . I do not know what it is!"

"What it is," said Robert, Lord Halford, in a bemused
tone, "is a veritable jewel of a Gothic cottage! You are
to be congratulated, Mademoiselle Françoise. Lord Crawford has given you one of the most perfect examples of
the cottage *orné* I've been privileged to see."

"It is so strange," said a confused Frani.

Robert chuckled. "So it is. But that is exactly as it
should be. The philosophy of such a cottage was that it
intrigue and bemuse. Do you wish to explore?"

Françoise kicked the side of her mare and moved forward. "Oh yes. Do let us explore!"

As Frederick passed him, an erstwhile groundskeeper
came out from the bushes and asked for a moment of the
gentleman's time. Frederick recognized the guard from
when he and Robert had reconnoitered some days previously. He reined in and pulled over. "What is it, man?
Has someone attempted to gain entry who is not on the
list?"

"Your party is the first to arrive although I understand
there are carriages to follow. My work would be easier
if you were to go over this list here and tell me who has
come. You all rode by so fast I couldn't very well ask for
names, now could I?"

"I'll check the list." Frederick scanned it. "I believe
only two carriages follow. One carries these three

women," he said and pointed where he meant; "and the other Her Grace, Joanna, Duchess of Stornway. Both will have attendant riders, but the duchess knows the problem. If she does not object to the riders, you may safely allow them entry."

"Very good, sir." The man slid back into the shrubbery and disappeared while Sir Frederick, impatient to rejoin Harriet, rode on.

He found her seated on a bench in the shade of a rose-covered rustic and staring at the thatched-roof house. "Do you find it too grotesque?" he asked, making her jump. "I'm sorry if I startled you," he added contritely.

"I didn't see you and, yes, you startled me, but that's all right," babbled Harriet, flustered at his sudden appearance. She gathered her poise and added, "Grotesque? I think I do, but Françoise will love it. She and Monsieur de Bartigues have already had a quick tour with the others trailing behind. Now I believe she is exploring the gardens—also fully chaperoned by a large group."

"Do you think I'm scolding you for leaving her alone? I am not. She knows her danger but, here, within the walls, she should be safe enough. You cannot be at her beck and call every moment, Harriet. Nor should you be. She cannot grow and mature if she is never allowed to err."

"Ah. But to err at this particular moment might be to ruin her whole life!"

"Yes. But as you say, she is with a large group. Even if it disperses—as it will, the grounds are not so large that she will ever be out of view of one or two—" He chuckled softly. "—over and beyond Yves, of course, who will not leave her side."

Harriet nodded. "That's what I thought," she said, keeping her features sober with an effort.

He smiled down at her. "You can be very nearly the minx your charge so often is, can you not? You were not worried for a moment for her safety. Are you tired?"

"The ride was, perhaps, a bit more than I should have attempted so soon after leaving my room. So, yes. I'm tired. But I'll be fine after our peaceful hours of pleasure here. Don't worry about me."

"I cannot help but worry. Did Madame tell you I was near to breaking every rule of proper behavior and coming up to see for myself how you did?" He grinned, his teeth a white flash in bronze skin. "Ah. You blush." He seated himself and reached for her hand. "Do you think I would not?"

"I know very well you would if you decided it was the thing to do—and bedamned to convention."

"Tut tut. Such language."

"I fear I've more of my tongue-valiant father in me than is sometimes quite comfortable . . . Sir Frederick," she added, "did it seem to you there were some in today's party who avoided me?"

"What?" Frederick, who had been playing with her fingers, stilled. "What are you talking about?"

"I wished to speak with Lady Massingham and she made a ridiculous excuse not to ride by me. Then there is another side to it. In the past Lord Ashford has paid me no particular attention, yet today he seemed to positively haunt me, laughing at the oddest moments. I understand neither of them."

"I didn't observe what happened because I was on the watch for ambush," said Frederick slowly, resuming his distracting touches on her fingers. "About what did Ashford wish to talk?"

"He asked my opinion of various people in the *ton,*

how I saw them." Harriet's eyes widened. She clenched her free hand into a fist. "Surely not!"

"Surely not what?"

She looked up, having, in her consternation, forgotten he was there. "What? Nothing. Never mind . . ." She freed herself from his grip, turned slightly away from him.

"Something agitates you to the point where you become incomprehensible, and I'm not to mind?" Before she could respond he went on. "I *do* mind. Very much. What is it, Harri?"

His obvious concern touched something in her, and she was tempted to tell him—but her better judgment restrained her. "Perhaps it is nothing. I truly don't wish to discuss it. At least not now. Not until I may see if . . ."

"If . . . ?"

"Sir Frederick, please. Until I return to London, I cannot confirm a suspicion which, if true . . . well, I do not see how it *can* be true. Have you explored the cottage yet?" she asked, deliberately attempting to force the change of subject for which she'd asked.

"No." He spoke curtly. "Harriet, at the very least, I thought we were friends. Friends share their troubles."

She faced him, reached toward him, and he gripped her hands tightly. "I promise I will tell you if what I suspect is true. If it is not . . . then I wish never to speak of it. Please."

Frederick scraped the fingers of one hand back through the hair at his temple. He glowered. Then he softened. "So be it. Come, Harri, my love," he said with sudden gentleness. "Let us go exploring."

She went gladly. Twice she caught a glimpse of small groups of people who were, it seemed, talking about her. Because she was so foolish as to go about on Sir

Frederick's arm? She thought not. Once, as she and Sir Frederick approached the woman who had snubbed Harriet while riding, the lady turned on her heel and hurried off at an angle, obviously avoiding meeting them.

"I see what you mean about Lady Massingham. Do you know her well?"

"I remember her from when I was in London before. She always had a dirty neck," said Harriet dryly. "In fact, that hasn't changed."

Sir Frederick chuckled. "Yes, but given the bathing habits—or should one say the lack thereof—prevalent in society, she is not the only one, surely."

"The only one to call attention to the fact by the jewels she wears."

"Don't most women wear jewels? Assuming they have them?"

"But Lady Massingham always wears that same collar of diamonds. Above the necklace she is clean. Below it . . ." Harriet shrugged.

Sir Frederick barked a laugh. "I never noticed. She isn't wearing diamonds today, surely?"

"Her riding dress is high necked. Besides, it would be inappropriate for an entertainment such as this."

"Has that stopped her in the past?" He strolled on before she could answer. Her hand held in the crook of his arm, there was nothing for Harriet to do but walk on as well. They came to the strawberry patch, which had been invaded by others as well. Sir Frederick released her and bent to search under leaves until he found a large sunwarmed berry which he held until she opened her mouth. He popped it in and searched for another.

A servant appeared with a stack of small baskets, and they accepted one, soon filling it and carrying it off to a shady spot where Joanna sat on a rug. She was, she said, like a princess—or an invalid—awaiting the duke's return with her berries. "I feel such a fool sitting here in this indolent way," said Jo, her eyes flashing. "I wish I could convince Pierce I am in perfect health and must not be coddled and petted and wrapped in cotton wool. He will drive me mad, Harriet!"

"Next time you'll know better than to tell him until there is no avoiding the question!"

"Not tell me what? That she is increasing? If she does not, I will wait until the child is born and beat her for keeping such a secret!"

The duke looked large and intimidating, and Harriet would have been a trifle afraid of him, but Jo just grinned. "Beat me, Your Grace? Hmm. I wonder what I would do in a case like that . . ."

He dropped down beside her and handed her the tiny basket which had looked odd in his large hand. "I would not. You know I would not . . . but I would not like it, your keeping secrets from me. You know that, too." The basket tipped, spilling berries in all directions, but they ignored it.

"Then you must stop behaving as if I've turned into a piece of prized china and I'll promise not to keep such secrets from you."

"That is a difficult promise to make, my love."

Sir Frederick offered a hand to Harriet and, since she was feeling embarrassed by the conversation between the duke and his duchess, she took it gladly. They strolled toward the river. Out in the middle, a barge, at anchor, held a large number of rough-looking fishermen. Seeing it, Sir Frederick's eyes narrowed. He glanced around and saw that most of the guests were drifting toward the tables set out on the terrace near the house. Word had been passed by roaming footmen that a luncheon was available for those who wished it and most, after the ride out from London, were hungry enough to hurry toward the waiting feast.

Frederick looked down at the woman on his arm. "Harriet, will you do something for me?"

"If I can. What do you wish?"

"What I *wish* to do, I may *not* do."

She arched her brows at his teasing reference to making love to her. "Then what is it I *may* do for you?" she asked sternly.

He turned them away from the water, steered her toward the steps up into the rose garden which occupied the level just above the one on which they strolled. "I want you to pretend to become very angry with me. I want you to stalk off and go to the house. I want you to find the steward and tell him to send at least ten men down to the river. Once you've done that, I want you to tell Robert and Pierce to join me here and tell Yves to take your minx into the house and into an upstairs room— with a chaperon, of course—and make her stay there until I think it safe she leave it."

"Frederick?"

"I've no way of knowing if I'm right, but I don't like the looks of the men fishing on the river. No, do not turn. Stop and glare at me. Say something. Raise your voice and show anger. And do it quickly, love. One man has his hands on the rope to one of the small boats tied to the barge."

The show Harriet put on was classic and, his back to the river, Frederick whispered, "Bravo, love. If I didn't know you were not truly angry I'd be wondering what I'd done to deserve your ire. Now get help, Harriet. Quickly."

Harriet stomped away. She shook her head when Frederick called in a pleading tone that she return. Once at the second pair of steps, she lifted her skirts and hurried faster. Frederick should not have remained in the lower garden, she thought, half frantic. He was alone. He could not fight so many men. They'd be on him and might even kill him.

Oh lord, she thought, nearly panicking, *they very well might kill him!* The comte hated Sir Frederick for his part in spoiling past plans! Could it possibly be true that those men had come for Françoise? Out of breath, Harriet rushed across the terrace to where the steward was overseeing the buffet. She pulled at his arm and drew them a little apart.

"Men on the river," said Harriet, panting. "Sir Frederick says to send at least ten men immediately. Please hurry. He's alone there." She turned on her heel, seeking out Robert or Pierce and found them at the same table. She gave them Frederick's message and, ignoring Elizabeth's shocked face and Jo's stony look, searched for Françoise . . . and couldn't find her. "Where is she?" Harriet asked Elizabeth.

"Where . . . ?" began Elizabeth, but went on quickly, "Oh, Harri, how could you? How could you send our men into danger that way?"

Jo rose and strolled toward the low stone barrier that edged the terrace. Elizabeth, her face white, joined her. Harriet, tugging at their sleeves, demanded their attention. "We, too, have work to do. *Where is Françoise?*" she asked, separating each word from the next and emphasizing it.

Joanna came to Harriet's conclusion. "She isn't here."

"She didn't say anything to either of you? A stroll somewhere? An exploration of something?" Harriet felt a touch of panic. "Where is she?"

"I do not see Monsieur de Bartigues, either," said Jo.

282

"One must assume that they are together, so she isn't without protection." Joanna, her hands clenched lightly, looked back down toward the river. Three boatloads of rough men had left the barge. They rowed toward three widely-spaced points on the riverbank, separating their forces, and making it harder for a few men to stop them all. Joanna swore softly and glanced back to the guests. There were some men she thought might join the coming fray and quickly approached one after another.

"A fight? What fun! Where?" asked one young gentleman overly loudly, alerting everyone—the duchess had hoped might remain in ignorance—that there was trouble.

Before Joanna could prevent him, he jumped the low wall and took off, several young men following after him. Chaos erupted among the women. Shrieks and mild hysteria and, in one case, a dead faint, were enough to make Elizabeth lose control and burst into tears herself.

Harriet went inside and made a quick search for Françoise. She came down from the upstairs to find the parlor full of women, Joanna soothed where she could and scolded elsewhere: Joanna no longer had time to worry about Pierce. Harriet discovered that Elizabeth was so afraid for Robert she'd stayed on the terrace to watch— although she could not distinguish him from the others who had joined to repel the invaders.

But where was Françoise? Harriet hadn't listened closely to the steward's description of the property and its various points of interest, but she seemed to remember something about a man-made Gothic ruin, a picturesque note common to such properties—but where was it? After briefly searching for a servant to give her information, she stopped to think. She'd arrived on the west side of the property. She'd wandered around the south half and down near the river with Frederick. She'd searched the house. The only place she had *not* been was to the east side of the house. Just then a footman entered the hall. She called to him.

He hesitated but came a few steps closer and bowed. "I am to join the fighting, madam. I must go at once."

"Many men are already fighting. I must find the young woman they defend, and I fear she may have gone to explore the Gothic ruin. Guide me to it at once."

"But . . ." He looked longingly in the other direction, sighed, and led her to a side door. They exited and hurried down a path between tall hedges. "There, madam," said the footman. "It isn't really much of a ruin . . ."

His words were cut off by a scream. One quick look at Harriet, and an expression of sudden anticipation crossed his face. He was off at a run, Harriet after him.

"Non, but *non,* you will not! You will not kill him," screamed Françoise.

Her voice came from the far side of the moss-covered stones tumbling from a half-destroyed wall, which had been carefully made to look as if it would fall in the next wind. Harriet noted a stake as big around as two thumbs which had been driven into the ground to support a young tree. After pulling it out, she lifted her skirts and raced toward the end of the folly nearest the road.

As Harriet rounded the ruin's end, she found, immediately in front of her, a struggling Françoise held high in the arms of the comte. Without thinking, she raised the stake and swung it, hard, at the comte's legs. He dropped Françoise, who crawled away, climbed to her feet and, without looking to see how Harriet fared, ran back the way she'd come. The comte had fallen to one knee. He rose, a vicious, hateful look contorting his face, and reached toward Harriet's throat. She pulled the stake back, preparing to swing again, and he turned, limping away into the shrubbery.

For a long moment she listened, heard snapping twigs and swishing branches and, finally, silence. Slowly she let go of the stake, one finger loosening at a time. Slowly, she allowed herself to slide down the side of the folly until she was sitting on the ground, her head bowed over her knees, her hands holding her bent legs close to her body.

So it was that Françoise and Yves found her some minutes later. Yves had a blood-stained handkerchief wound around his forehead, and Françoise was chiding him for insisting they find Harriet, convinced he should rest, should take care of himself . . .

"But, oh, Harri," she said when they came upon her. "I didn't *think*. You! Are you hurt, too? Are you dead, maybe?" Françoise asked the last in a small voice as she dropped to her knees. She put her hand tentatively on Harriet's shoulder. "Oh, surely you are not dead!"

"Not dead. I can't quit shaking," murmured Harriet, her voice so low Françoise had to bend to hear her.

"You were so brave," said Frani.

"I did what I had to do." Harriet straightened, laid her head back against the sun-warmed wall. "Where's the footman? Was he of no use?"

"I sent him back for help," said Yves, a trifle ruefully. "I didn't know you'd sent the oh-so-dear comte off all by yourself with his tail between his legs."

"I couldn't have done it, if he hadn't been so surprised by my sudden appearance." She described what had happened from her point of view. Yves, recovering consciousness, had immediately had the presence of mind to ask Françoise how she'd escaped the comte's trap and had heard the younger girl's story then.

285

Just then Joanna, a gun in her hand, arrived, guided by the footman, who was looking young and excited and obviously feeling important to have had a hand in rescuing the pretty young miss, even if it hadn't been a very heroic one. Françoise and Harriet had to explain all over again. "Then," said Joanna, "the fight by the river was merely a diversion to draw the men away."

"And he was lucky, the comte, that I had decided to explore instead of eat luncheon. Poor Monsieur de Bartigues is not so lucky. His poor head," said Frani, looking sad. "It is broken."

"Merely scratched. Don't make so much of it, mademoiselle."

"The last I looked," said Jo, "the fight was about over. The men will return to the terrace with what captives they've taken and will want to know where we are. Especially, mademoiselle, they will wish to know that *you* are safe. We must return, if it is not too much for you, monsieur—or for you, Harri?"

"I'll make it back to the house, but if you don't mind, I think I'll lie down for a bit."

"When we leave, you must come with me in my carriage," said Joanna soothingly. "I will like to have the company," she added, knowing how excellent a horsewoman Harriet was and fearing she might feel insulted by the offer.

"I'll gladly join you," was the quiet response. "I was tired before from the ride, but now I feel utterly exhausted. Françoise," added Harriet in a stronger tone, "I swear if something like this happens again, I'll leave you to your fate. I don't think I could survive, again, the horror I felt when I rounded that corner and saw you in that evil man's arms!"

They arrived at the side door through which Harriet

286

had come a surprisingly few minutes earlier and found Sir Frederick just inside, a black eye coming up nicely and a frown of major proportions drawing his brows together. Pierce followed on his heels, a bruised jaw and scraped knuckles indicating his part in the recent melee. Behind *him* were Elizabeth and Robert. Robert, except for an open shoulder seam, looked unmarked, but Elizabeth was hanging on him as if she'd never let him out of her sight again.

Sir Frederick glowered. "So," he said. "We cannot leave you for more than a moment, and you find mischief to make us prematurely grey! How dare you all disappear like that. A gun, Your Grace?" he asked, seeing it for the first time.

Françoise and Yves appeared from between the hedges, and the bloodstained bandage brought more words of concern. Finally the men quieted down enough to hear the tale and, with no thought to whom might be watching, Frederick pulled Harriet into his arms and held her close. "Don't you ever do anything so foolish ever again, do you hear me?"

"I am not allowed to be foolish, but it is quite all right for you to remain alone, where more than a dozen men intend to start a fight? Men who are the henchmen of a man who wishes you dead?"

"Men are born with the right to be foolish," soothed Frederick, but he was not unhappy with her sharp comment because of the caring he heard behind her words. "Women are supposed to have more sense!" When he thought again of what might have happened to her, he pushed her away enough to look into her eyes. "Harri, love, you *are* all right? He didn't hurt you?"

"He didn't have time. I came upon him so suddenly we were neither prepared for it. But he had his arms full of Françoise and could do little. I, on the other hand, had a weapon and used it." She shuddered again as, in memory, she felt the heavy stick thud against human flesh. It was a moment she'd long remember, very likely in nightmares. It had been awful, the sound and feel of it.

Pierce, who had been quietly talking to Joanna, broke in on them. "No one will be satisfied with a rural idyll after all the excitement so I fear the day is ruined. Robert and I will organize the homeward trek. I think we should return now to the parlor where some sort of explanation must be made, and then the horses must be brought around. Harriet, do you think you can put a good face on things for just a little longer? Joanna and I have come up with a tale we think will cover everything and not result in scandal for Mademoiselle Françoise."

"I've been unable to see how we may avoid scandal, so if you've a notion, do let us hear it," said Frederick.

"If we suggest those men were a rabble roused by the high cost of bread and upset by our romping, we may assert that they wished to make a statement of sorts and may convince everyone it was merely an accident of time and place that they chose our particular party to attack. We'll say nothing of you women and your *trifling* adventure, of course," he added on a dry note, "but I don't know where we can say Monsieur de Bartigues was fighting, because no one will have seen him by the river. Perhaps no one will think to ask, but, if they do, we must say something which will explain his bruised head."

"They will soon notice it was caused by a knife and not by fists," said Françoise, clutching at Yves' arm.

"A knife? That leaves a distinctive scar. Blast. Some of those men carried bludgeons, but none were armed otherwise so far as I know."

288

"Perhaps a small mob arrived from the front? Perhaps I and a few footmen managed to run them off?"

"Yes. We can say one of them pulled a knife on you. Good. Shall we join the rest?"

The rest had lost the edge of hysteria, but were babbling about what had happened and were drinking more than might have been expected at a garden party. Any man who had been hurt in the fighting was basking in the attention of some young woman—except for those few with more serious hurts. These were dealt with by more practical older women, who allowed a younger female the important role of soothing the wounded male by holding his hand and telling him how wonderful he was.

The duke soon took control of the noisy throng. He called for quiet, told the story they'd concocted for public consumption, and suggested that, since the day had been spoiled, perhaps they should leave as soon as horses and carriages could be brought around. They'd plan another party when there was no more danger of the sort that had ruined this one.

Not, of course, that most of the adventurous young men felt it had been ruined! They, much to their womenfolk's disgust, had enjoyed themselves hugely and said so.

"Men," decided Françoise, "are exceedingly strange creatures indeed, are they not?"

Harriet was prone to agree.

Fourteen

When Madame was told of the latest attempt to take her granddaughter, she went off into a long tirade in such rapid French that even Harriet could not follow her thoughts. Everyone listened in awed silence. Françoise, who did understand, was the most silent of all until at last, agitated, she exclaimed, "No no, Grand-mère. *Mais non!* It is impossible that you do as you say!"

"What is it?" asked a bewildered Elizabeth. "What *did* she say?"

Ignoring her hostess, Françoise continued. "You cannot take a sword and run him through and through and through!" She put her arm around her grandmother and leaned her head into the old woman's rigid shoulder. "Nor, I think, can you shoot him and shoot him or give him over to be guillotined! Me, I think the English do not have Madame Guillotine, is that not so? So it would be best," she finished with a certain insouciance, "if you were to have him arrested. They could just hang him until he was dead."

The tension broke and everyone, including Madame la Comtesse, laughed. "An excellent notion, little one," said His Grace, Pierce Reston, grinning broadly. "Unfortu-

290

nately, under English law, that would require a trial, and you and Miss Cole would have to give evidence before the court. I think you'd not enjoy that, my child, so, although it is a very good idea, arresting the comte, I think we must come up with another." The duke looked around the group. "Robert? Frederick?"

Both men sighed and shook their heads. Robert spoke slowly. "All we can do is as we've been doing. The women must go nowhere without protection. Big John will be warned the comte is now hiring bravos to aid him; and he must, therefore, have assistance as well. Are you listening, Elizabeth? You are to go nowhere unprotected. Françoise?"

"I do not wish the evil comte to have me. I will be good," promised Françoise. Then she shuddered. "I am afraid of him. He makes my flesh crawl, and when he touched me today, picked me up, I thought I would faint it was so awful—but I was worried about poor Yves so I didn't. Is it so very bad, Monsieur de Bartigues' head?" she asked with a pretty hesitancy.

Yves had developed a very slight fever by the time they approached London and had been sent on, under protest, to Frederick's rooms. Françoise was not easy to reassure, but a promise that the young man would visit her the next morning finally did the trick.

Harriet had only just arisen from her sickbed, had ridden out to the party and there she'd undergone emotional ups and downs which had worn her to a thread. Frederick noticed how she drooped and went to her side. "You mustn't worry about the minx, my dear. We'll see your charge comes to no harm. You must trust us."

"I know you'll do your best, but today proved one cannot foresee everything. If I had been only a few moment's later, he'd have been gone and Françoise as well." She trembled much as Françoise had done. "Frederick, it was awful, finding her in his arms, that way!"

"At least you gave him something by which to remember his failure." Frederick tipped up her chin, stared seriously into her eyes. "From what you said, he'll be limping for several days! It was very well done of you!"

Harriet shuddered. "I will never forget how it felt to hit him that way. It was terrible, Sir Frederick."

Since his joshing didn't ease her, Frederick suggested she retire to her room and ask the housekeeper give her a mild dose of laudanum which would compose her for sleep. She must not make herself ill again. Harriet, agreeing her bed would be welcome, excused herself. The party broke up soon after and, after sending off a note of regret to the hostess to whom they were promised, the household had a quiet night.

Frederick, on the other hand, strolled first to his rooms and then, once he knew Yves was sleeping under Cob's watchful eye, on to White's. The porter at the door stared at his black eye but asked no questions. Members of the club were not so polite. The story of the fight by the river was already making the rounds. It had grown to a tale of a veritable riot, but Frederick laughed that to scorn. A handful of bully boys out on a spree, he insisted.

"A handful?" asked Cleary. "I heard boat's full—three, at least."

"Yes, but such very small boats," said Frederick, not looking at the speaker but scanning the room as if for someone special. "Veritable teacups of the boat family."

"Life is always so interesting wherever you are, Sir Frederick," said the man, an oily note Frederick didn't like in his voice.

"You think it interesting to find yourself sporting this?" Frederick pointed to his face. "I can think of many far more interesting ways to spend an afternoon than fighting with river rats. They weren't even *clean*," he added on a pensive note.

"I wasn't thinking of the fight. I was thinking of your latest, er, lady. Quite a talented piece of work, is she not?"

The tone had changed from oily to biting and Cleary now had Frederick's full attention. "She plays far better than one's average amateur, as she proved at Lady Cowper's not long ago, but she has had the benefit of tutoring by some of the best musicians of our time, and she loves her music."

"There's that *as well*," agreed his tormentor, nodding judiciously. "Perhaps the lady is a trifle *too* talented. Tell me, has she published her satires on the continent? Were they well-received? When does she intend to publish here?"

"So far as I know, she has no such plans and has never had an ambition to earn a living by her pen," said Frederick, wishing he had at least a glimmering of what was in the wind.

"Tom Moore says she could," said a kinder voice, chuckling. "Quite a way with words, he says."

Sir Frederick looked around to see who spoke. He immediately pulled himself together. This man was not one he could fob off. "Moore was so complimentary?" he asked, feeling his way. Then he remembered Harriet's story about the woman who had snubbed her, the biting wit when she'd described the role of the diamond necklace that defined where cleanliness stopped. Surely Harriet hadn't been so foolish as to write up bits and pieces describing important members of the *ton!*

"Moore laughed himself silly," said Lord Winthrop, an

amateur poet of some status and an aristocratic light in London's literary circles. "Said he couldn't wait to meet the author."

Oh, Lord, she's done it now. She must actually have written about the ton! thought Frederick ruefully. "I see no reason why he may not—assuming he's sober at the time!" he said, and the group's laughter at the caveat broke the tension. Most drifted off to games of chance or to other conversations, but not Winthrop and not Frederick's tormentor, Cleary.

"Don't think everyone's so tolerant," said the latter suggestively.

"No, there are some," said Winthrop, "who feel she went too far when she said the Regent's generation was too fond of Maraschino and tended to creak when they bowed. It is felt to be too clearly a dig at Prinny himself." Winthrop met Frederick's eyes. It was a warning.

"I can see where some might think that, particularly those who found themselves showing to a disadvantage elsewhere in her words, perhaps?" asked Frederick with still more caution.

Winthrop's eyes twinkled. "You have never been a stupid man. I've always wanted an opportunity to tell you how much I admired the facility with which you pulled the wool over most everyone's eyes during the war."

Frederick glanced at Cleary, who listened avidly. "Not yours?" he asked.

"No," said Winthrop gently. "You see, I remember how you jumped into a fight to trounce that Gooderson bully at Eton when he was determined to bring one of the new boys to heel. Gooderson weighed a good twenty pounds more than you did and must have been three inches taller."

Frederick looked sharply at Winthrop. "I'd forgotten that . . . was that *you?*"

"Yes. I was very nearly ready to give in to the bully's demands when you took over. Thank you. I've been meaning to say that for years."

Frederick's ears felt hot. "Forget it. It was nothing, a trifle."

"It wasn't a trifle to a very young boy who was homesick and very much out of place amongst such very male society." Winthrop grimaced. "You see, my father died when I was but a babe. I was raised by my mother, my aunt, my grandmother, and four older sisters. Needless to say, I'd not had much contact with the rougher side of life."

"It was a very long time ago."

"What did he mean, you pulled the wool over our eyes during the war?" asked Cleary belligerently.

Frederick had been ignoring the man who hovered near. "Nothing. Nothing at all," he insisted, holding Winthrop's eyes and silently insisting the subject be dropped. After a moment Winthrop shrugged.

When Cleary got no response to his demand for information, he suggested, "Still think you should do something about your latest lady. Drop her, maybe?" Again he got no verbal response to a suggestion, but Winthrop looked at him as if he were a toad. Cleary, his ears burning, stalked off.

"Don't think you have a friend there," said Winthrop thoughtfully.

"No, he's never been a friend. I don't know why he'd change at this late date. Winthrop," added Frederick, "will you do what you can if you hear more talk of her writing?"

"I'll help gladly," said the younger man warmly. "You haven't seen it?"

"No. I suspect, from what I know of Miss Cole, it wasn't supposed to have been seen by anyone. I'll find out tomorrow."

He joined a table and played late. Because of that he slept in, so that Joanna was the first visitor to enter Halford House the next morning and inquire about Harriet's health. "So she spent a good night and is feeling more the thing? In that case, please announce me," she said.

Harriet was not only up but had eaten and was now in the music room. ". . . with as many servants as can manage to find jobs nearby, doing more listening than working," added the butler a trifle acidly.

Joanna gave him a commiserating smile and suggested gently that if she were to be announced, perhaps Harriet would stop practicing and perhaps the servants would return to the work for which they were hired. She was announced with alacrity.

"Joanna, you should not be out and about so early!"

"I, too, went to sleep at a ridiculous hour last night and couldn't lay abed this morning." Joanna fiddled with the slim roll of paper. "Besides, I had an early morning caller."

"It must have been a true early bird."

"No," chuckled Jo, "merely a bluestocking who actually believes that proverb about early to bed. She's already wealthy enough to suit her and has her health, I'm sure, but she has a great desire to be wise . . . which, come to think of it, she may very well be. Harriet, do you think the adage may have something to recommend it? Ah, but forget that nonsense. Were you aware some of your scribbles have become all the rage—except where you are being taken to task by people who feel the pinch of your words?"

Harriet paled to an ashy tint. She dropped into the chair behind her, staring at her old friend from painfully wide eyes. "My . . . scribbles . . . ?"

"You didn't know. I thought as much."

"I wondered yesterday, and then forgot when . . . but surely not . . ."

"I tell you they have spread far and wide." Jo handed Harriet the pages. "See for yourself, my friend. These are copies, of course, but I recognize the style from the letters we've exchanged. You give yourself away in every line."

Harriet was afraid to unroll the stiff paper. She didn't want to find her own words staring at her from the sheets. Jo took them back, untied the ribbon, and spread out the top one.

"Well?" she asked.

Harriet read a handful of words, turned her head. "Mine."

"How did they come to circulate in the *ton?*"

"If you think . . . !"

"Relax, Harriet. I know very well you'd not do it yourself. Who knew of them?"

"So far as I know, no one."

"Where did you keep them?"

"In a wooden chest I've carried with me everywhere for many years now. It's upstairs in the back of my armoire."

"Shall we go see if your work is still there?"

Harriet, reluctantly, led the way. They found the chest unlocked, and Harriet noticed the scar running off at an angle from the keyhole. She ran her finger along it. "Someone forced this."

297

"But who would do such a thing?"

Harriet began emptying the case. She reached the bottom and hadn't found the satire. "Could the comte have had my papers searched and those vignettes stolen in order to discredit me? Maybe to force Madame to rid herself of my contaminating presence?" she asked.

"How could he guess there would be something so damaging? You appear to the world as an intelligent and perfectly respectable female—except, of course, for your predilection for Frederick's company!"

Harriet blushed. "Don't. Please. Jo, what am I to do?"

"You'll stare blankly at anyone who asks about your writing and change the subject."

"I'm afraid that won't do," said Frederick from the doorway. "The word is too firmly established that Harriet is the author."

Harriet, involuntarily, took a step toward him. Then she remembered herself, remembered she had no right to ask for his comfort or his care—in fact, had forbidden him the right to offer such. Frederick, however, had no scruples. At the hint she wished it, he came to her and drew her into his embrace, pressing her head against his shoulder.

"It'll be all right, Harriet," he whispered into her hair.

"How can it be?" she mumbled into his coat.

Joanna, guessing at the half-heard exchange, said, "Frederick is correct. A nine day wonder at most, Harriet."

"But what am I to *do?*"

"I still think she gives a questioner a look of blank incomprehension," said Jo.

Frederick grimaced. "Do you think she'll get away with that when she meets Tom Moore or Lord Winthrop?"

"When would she ever meet Moore?" For the moment, Joanna ignored Frederick's reference to the poet.

"I had a note from him this morning. He requests an introduction—and promises he'll not have drunk a drop. Last night, you see, I was told he wished to meet Harriet. I said I saw no reason why he should not—assuming he was sober. Word must have traveled like the wind to have reached him so quickly."

"And Winthrop?"

"He was Moore's petitioner. He, too, wishes to meet the new rising star upon London's literary firmament."

"He can't have said that!" said Harriet, raising her head to look up at Frederick.

He smiled at her, glad to see she wasn't totally downcast. "He said exactly that. It's the way he always talks about literature, you see."

"Surely not."

"Oh," said Joanna, "but he does. What a delightful subject for your viciously wicked pen, love."

Harriet stiffened. "I'll never write anything like that ever again," she insisted.

"Have you seen them?" Jo asked Frederick.

"Not yet."

Jo shuffled through the pages and found the one describing Frederick. With a grin, she handed it to him. He skimmed it, his cheeks reddening, looked down at Harriet's pale gold head with a rueful expression in his dark eyes and handed the page back to Jo. "Something else, perhaps? I don't think I quite properly appreciate that one!"

Harriet pulled away, startled from her preoccupation by his tone. She looked up at him, looked at Jo, looked at the thin sheaf of pages her friend held. She extended a hand. "Give those to me!"

"So that you can burn them? It will do no good. There are a dozen copies, at least, floating about London—and perhaps still more, moving, via the Royal Mails, to every corner of the land."

"That need not be another. Give it to me, Jo."

"No, Your Grace" said Frederick, "give it to *me*. I don't wish to be put to the bother of tracking down another copy so that I may see if there is anything of too damaging a nature. If there is, then we'll have to think of some means of defusing it."

Jo handed them over, and Frederick slipped the roll into a pocket in his coattails. Harriet watched them disappear, still wistfully wishing she might burn them. She remembered what had been written about Frederick. It was the least accurate portrait of them all. Her hurt that he hadn't bothered to hear her name properly, complicated by her infatuation, had colored her words, distorting reality far beyond what was allowed a proper satirist.

Jo broke the silence, asking quietly, "Can anything be done if she's libelled someone?"

"Oh dear. Perhaps someone will sue!" suggested Harriet, a new fear rearing up to plague her.

"I doubt anyone would go so far. It would only make more of what is surely only a tempest in a teapot," soothed Jo.

"Only time will tell, but I, too, doubt anyone would be so foolish as to draw attention to what they must hope may soon be forgotten. Harriet, you are still tired, are you not? I think perhaps you should rest again today."

"Perhaps I will." Harriet looked longingly at her bed. To cower down under the covers seemed a delightful escape from her problems. It had been one thing after another for months now. Firstly, Françoise's irritating suitor had become an acute problem and, because of him, Madame was made ill. Then, her stupid feelings for Sir Frederick had settled into a constant nagging ache to plague her. Her playing in public had become an issue, one she'd lost, and, now, her ridiculous scribbles had come to light to haunt her. She wondered what would happen next to bedevil her.

Harriet returned to invalid status and had two full days of peace. She rose early the third morning feeling very much more herself and wondered why she had played the fool for so long.

"It is merely that when one is not feeling well, things are blown all out of proportion," said Madame as she and Harriet drank their morning coffee together. "Now you are well again, and I am thankful. I should not have asked that you accompany Françoise out to that river cottage place. I should not have done so because you had been so recently ill, but I am very glad I did, if you had not been there, Harriet, Françoise would have been lost to us."

"I think I had a relapse that day—and then that stupid satire." Harriet shook her head. "Who can have found it and why?"

"Do you truly not know?" asked Madame, and Harriet met her gaze, her look questioning. "But that has been obvious from the beginning, *that*. Her precious ladyship, Françoise's new grandmother, dislikes the both of you intensely. She dared do nothing to harm Frani. Therefore, she did what she could to harm you. I suspect she searched your box to find love letters or some incriminating document of that ilk. What she found was—or so she thought—much much better."

"Joanna tells me it will be nothing but a nine days wonder. Three of those nine have passed," said Harriet with a certain dryness. "Do you think I might remain ill for another six? Just think, it would all be forgotten, and I might forget it as well."

"I believe the nine must be passed where the *ton* may at least see you if not speak with you. They will only postpone their curiosity until you do appear, so playing least-in-sight is not the answer." Madame straightened. "Today I would enjoy a ride in the Park. Her Grace will join us, of course, and, I think, Lady Cowper? She is very grateful that you played for her musical, and she owes you a service in return, does she not? I will write her a note requesting her company."

"You think to surround me with respectable women and hope that will take the sharp edges off the curiosity?"

"Something of the sort," admitted Madame la Comtesse. "It will not hurt you to be seen with one of the patronesses, and you did not say anything about Lady Cowper so she'll wish you no harm."

"It would be better if I could be seen in the company of one I *had* harmed," murmured Harriet.

"What? One you've harmed? But you've harmed no one. Me, I have read your words, you see. They are quite humorous, I think."

"I should never have written any of it. When we were in Calais I thought of them for the first time in years. I remember thinking that I should find and destroy them—and then I went to sleep and forgot them again. How much trouble could have been saved if I had not!"

"What is done is done. Bring me my traveling writing desk, my dear. I must write notes to Her Grace and to Lady Cowper."

"And then you must convince me that it is truly best for me to be seen in public. I've thought that perhaps I should return to the continent. I am certain that among your acquaintances there is *one* whom you might convince that, if they would only hire me, I would become an indispensable member of their staff."

"Nonsense. You are an indispensable member of *my* staff, and I cannot part with you. Instead, we must see this threat of scandal is scotched—is that correct, scotched?"

"Yes. I cannot think where the expression comes from, though. I wonder . . . from scorched, perhaps? Or scratched? Or the mixing of both?"

"While you wonder, Harriet, retrieve for me my desk!"

The carriage ride was difficult for Harriet, but Madame had been correct that she must be seen. To be seen in such company did her no harm, of course. No one spoke to Harriet about her writing except for Lady Cowper—who made one pouting comment that she felt slighted: *she* was not included among those about whom Harriet had written! No one *spoke,* but, again and again, Harriet felt the speculative looks turned her way. She flushed so often she was certain her cheeks would be permanently reddened.

Frederick drove in the park that day, warned by Jo that Harriet would be making an appearance. He'd debated whether it would do Harriet harm or good to be seen driving with him. Associating with him might cause worse gossip, thereby driving out the old, or it might rouse simple curiosity which would either dilute the tattle about her scribbling or stir it higher. Either seemed desirable to him.

Chester was the first to sight the barouche in which

the women rode. "There's that long meg you favor so much," he grumbled.

"Where?" Frederick craned his neck.

"Just turning down by the Serpentine. And there's that man in black you had me followin'." Chester said the last in tones of deep disgust. "I still don't see how that jessamy slipped my leash."

"You've seen the man I set you onto? The one you lost?"

"Don't go rubbin' my nose in it, gov. Don't know how the cove came to lose me that way. Haven't felt the same since," added Chester. "Must be losin' me touch. Gettin' old, maybe . . ."

Since Chester was very likely barely into his twenties, Frederick ignored his tiger's grumbles. "I'd still like to know where he reports and where the man to whom he reports lives!"

Chester's head came up, his long nose twitching. "I'll try again."

"No, you must have been spotted—no matter how difficult that is to believe." Chester immediately preened at the compliment. "Find a boy to follow him," suggested Frederick after a moment's thought, "because, if he *has* noticed you once, he'll have an eye out for you. So just follow him out whatever gate he leaves by and then set a likely looking lad on his tail."

"Right you are, gov." Chester dropped off the back of Frederick's rig, moving off in the opposite direction from where the comte's man stood.

Frederick put Chester and the enemy from his mind. Using all his skill to guide his team through the press of traffic, he came up with Madame and her party. Once there, he realized he should have ridden, that without Chester, he had no way of leaving his team so that he

304

night join the women in their carriage. Sighing, he set his horses to pace alongside Madame's, and for a few moments made light conversation with the ladies. When one of the *ton's* more notorious gossips rode up to greet Lady Cowper, Frederick spoke a trifle loudly. "Miss Cole? I'd hoped you might come driving with me today but reached Halford House only to discover you'd already gone. May I have the pleasure tomorrow—assuming the weather continues good?"

Harriet looked first to Madame, then to Jo, and finally at Lady Cowper, who smiled at her. She looked back to Frederick and nodded.

He too smiled. "I shall look forward to it," he said gently, nodded to the others and drove off.

So the next day Harriet rode with Sir Frederick. Some of the riders who approached his phaeton were not so reticent as had been the case the day before, and Harriet relied a great deal on Frederick to see her through the ordeal. She sighed in relief when he said it was time they return to Halford House—but the relief instantly turned to horror when he added, "After all, Harriet, you'll need time to prepare for Major Morningside's ball this evening, will you not?"

At breakfast Harriet had told everyone she was *not* going to the ball. She repeated her determination to remain at home to Frederick.

"Nonsense. Things are going very well as you would know if you had more experience. You must be seen, my love. Hold up your head, and all will go well. Hide or show fear, and the vultures will peck out your eyes. I'll come early and escort you ladies."

"I believe Lord Halford attends with Elizabeth."

"Very good. I'll have company, then, while propping up the walls, will I not?"

"Why should you prop the walls," she asked suspiciously.

"Because you will be besieged with requests for dances and I've no desire to stand up with anyone but you." Her cheeks glowed. He flicked one with a finger. "I like it when I achieve a blush in your cheek. I don't think many can achieve such a coup, and it gives me hope you feel more for me than you'll allow yourself to admit." Again he touched her cheek in that especially tender way he had. "Perhaps one of these days, I'll simply buy a special license and abduct you. That should solve all problems quite neatly."

"As it did when you abducted Elizabeth?" asked Harriet with sudden sweetness.

Frederick flicked a look sideways. It was his turn to feel his ears heat and a flush redden his cheekbones. "That turned the tables quite neatly, did it not?" he asked.

"If you mean I managed to embarrass you for a change instead of you embarrassing me, then I suppose it did."

"You are correct, of course, that it did not answer with Elizabeth—for which I thank my lucky stars. Besides, one should not repeat oneself. Repetition makes of one a bore. So I guess it will have to be Saint George, Hanover Square, after all. Now there's an interesting social problem: living right there on the square, as you do, will you, my bride, call out a carriage to carry you to church, or will you walk the few yards required to reach its portals?"

She stared straight ahead. "Since the problem does not arise, I'll not worry about it."

Sir Frederick said, his tone thoughtful, "Then I see no choice but to become a bore."

It took Harriet a moment to work out his meaning, but when she realized he referred again to kidnapping her and marrying her out of hand, she gasped. "You wouldn't!"

"Not yet, anyway. You see, I've not given up hope I'll bring you to admitting you love me as much as I love you and, once you've done so, I don't think you'll argue that an early marriage is much to be desired. So, as I see it, my problem is that I must discover a way to make you admit it."

"This is a nonsensical discussion and, anyway, there comes Lord Winthrop. Please do not embarrass me before him."

"Have I ever embarrassed you before strangers?"

Harriet frowned slightly. She thought back over their relationship. "If I cannot think of an occasion, it is surely only because I have managed to put it from my mind with true Christian generosity."

"Vixen," he whispered and pulled up to introduce her to Lord Winthrop.

That night on the way home from one of the more frustrating evenings she had ever experienced, Harriet was a trifle irked to discover Frederick was not interested in discussing how difficult it had been for her. Why, he didn't seem to care she'd had to face down the whole of the *ton!* Instead he and Robert avidly discussed an imminent prizefight between the current champion and an up-and-coming young bruiser. The meeting was planned for two days hence, and Robert was not about to miss it. From his suppressed excitement, neither would Frederick.

Nor, it was discovered the next day, were Monsieur de Bartigues or Pierce Reston willing to be absent from what was touted as the fight of the decade. All, it seemed, had heavy wagers on the outcome and each was determined

to see every left cross and cross buttock and knockdow
and every drop of blood.

The women shuddered and frowned and expresse
their disgust with the whole thing, but it did no good
The men were going. That fact was quite clear. The sit
was near enough to London they could ride out in th
morning and return immediately following the bout. The
would not dawdle afterward, but they *would* attend. It wa
quite decided.

The morning on which they left for the fight saw th
arrival of a message from Madame's French acquain
tance, Marie de Daunay. Madame la Comtesse grimace
and frowned.

"What is it, Madame?" asked Harriet, seating hersel
at the breakfast table. "Surely not more trouble?"

"Not trouble," said Madame, holding the folded invi
tation at arm's length and squinting very slightly as she
reread the spidery writing. "Not that. Only a minor irri
tation, really." Madame sighed. "I will go, of course, but
it will be a dead bore—as Elizabeth would say." The slight
frown, which had called Harriet's attention to her troubled
mind, deepened.

"I don't think I should if it is bound to be a bore,"
teased Harriet.

Madame smiled. "Yes you would. It's Madame de Daunay."

"The lady who came to see you a week or two ago?"

"Yes. A very old acquaintance, one I knew in my
youth."

"I seem to remember you spent the afternoon reminiscing."

The frown returned. "And that is the problem, Harri.
Remembering the days which once were is all very well
in its way, but she *lives* in what she believes was a glo-

ious past. She will not think of the realities of today. She can talk and talk and talk about a ball at Versailles forty years ago but doesn't know Napoleon did the unspeakable and divorced his first wife, or that Fat Louis was chased from Paris when the monster returned from Elba for the Hundred Days!" Madame lowered her voice. "One understands, of course . . . *Her gloves were darned,*" she explained in almost sepulchral tones.

"I see," said Harriet and did. Madame de Daunay lived in the past for the simple reason that poverty made the present too terrible to admit to. She sighed. "When is the invitation for?"

"This afternoon. It is such short notice I wonder if she thought perhaps I'd not accept?"

"More likely her life is so restricted she doesn't think in terms of having a score of invitations from which to choose. Not that we do today, but that is unusual, is it not? A visit won't tire you too much, will it? You've only begun to go out again."

"I've quite recovered myself, Harriet. Don't hover. I cannot bear to feel smothered."

Harriet studied her mistress surreptitiously. She decided the lady would do—assuming nothing new happened to overset her. A quiet afternoon with an old friend might actually do her good.

Madame wrote a note of polite acceptance. Then, too late, she discovered the town carriage had been ordered by Lady Halford and her granddaughter for a trip to the shops in the Royal Opera Arcade where, they had heard, one could find the most marvelous silks and, if one were careful, bargains in the way of gloves and stockings, as well as elegant trifles such as fans and feathers and music boxes. They'd left half an hour earlier.

For a time the problem seemed unsolvable, but Madame, having made up her mind to go, was not to be thwarted. "Marks may send a footman to find me a hac which is not too dirty and with a horse which is not to decrepit and a driver whom he believes may be truste to take me where I wish to go. I will then make my wa by hired carriage. It will be a little adventure, you see."

And so it was arranged.

Fifteen

Madame la Comtesse's quiet afternoon began that way: she rode to her appointment in a hired hack as planned and found it uncomfortable but not so much so as she'd expected. As a result she cheerfully overpaid the driver, although she chided him for requesting such a sum. He gave her a cheeky grin and drove off happily pocketing the outrageous amount for which he'd asked—and gotten.

Madame entered the small house, finding much what she expected: well-worn drugget on the hall floor and, glimpsed through a door, carefully repaired upholstery on the chairs and settees in the small sitting room in which the drapes had been pulled nearly closed—very likely in the hopes it would make the room too dim for the visitor to see how badly in need of replacement most everything was.

Madame entered the room at Marie de Daunay's invitation—and peace and quiet were abruptly at an end.

"You!" said Madame, an expression of distaste crossing her face.

"You know each other?" asked Madame de Daunay brightly. "How very nice."

"Be quiet," said de Cheviot to the spinster in sneering tones. "You've played your part. It is done now."

Madame de Daunay looked from one to the other. "But I don't understand. What is this?" Her voice rose, shrilling. "Why do you have that gun?" Still shriller: "What game is this you play with us?"

"I said for you to be quiet! Well, Madame? It has taken many months but I have won, have I not?"

"I doubt it." Hortense de St. Onge, Comtesse de Beaupré raised a hand and yawned.

Vauton-Cheviot stamped his foot. "You will not sneer at me. You will admit I have tricked you finely."

Madame la Comtesse eyed him much as she'd study a bug. "A coward's trick, of course, to use an unsuspecting old woman."

Vauton-Cheviot struck her and then looked appalled. "I didn't do that." His voice rose. *"I didn't do that."*

"Then why do I feel as if the last of my teeth had been loosened?" asked Madame, touching her jaw gently.

"What is this? What is happening?" whispered her hostess. She looked from one to the other, her eyes huge in her thin old face. She clutched a hand to her throat, fear of the comte and dismay that her old friend should be so badly treated warring within her.

"You have been tricked by this evil man," said Madame kindly, "You have helped him to trap my granddaughter, you see. For so very long now, he has tried to achieve his goal of a marriage to her . . . I wonder what will happen to foil him this time?" she said, watching him thoughtfully and forced a chuckle.

"You are a fool. *Nothing* can interfere. *Nothing.* I will succeed. I will have her!"

"I doubt it," said Madame once again. She glanced around. "Are we to await her here?"

"No. Never." Vauton-Cheviot motioned with the gun. "Forward. Up the stairs with you. With *both* of you!"

"But we have not had our tea," wailed the confused old woman. "I do not understand why you behave in this so odd fashion, Comte. It is rude. And . . ."

"You will be still!" screamed the harassed comte. "Up the stairs."

Regally, as if climbing the steps in her own home, Madame swept upward and up again. At the very top of the house, built under the roof, was a small room, obviously meant for a maidservant. Madame dipped her head under the low lintel and entered it. She looked around: a narrow bed covered by a dust sheet; a chest of drawers; a small table on which a cracked washbowl sat—and nothing else. There wasn't even a curtain at the small dormer window set high where the roof slanted down and made much of the room too low to be used. There wasn't even a small rug by the bed.

"You will not succeed, Comte," said Madame, turning to stare at him. "You should stop this before you find yourself in the hands of the English law. Your rank, such as it is, will not help you, I believe. Nor, I think, will the French Embassy, which would find you something of an embarrassment just at this time, would it not?"

The comte blanched. "No. It will not happen. You will be quiet. And you," he said turning on his landlady and raising his voice, "you may stop that whining and sniveling. It will do you no good." The comte recovered his high hopes when he saw how cowed the one woman was. "All will go as I wish. There is nothing which can stop me this time. I know, you see, that your host and his friends have gone to Croydon to a prizefight. Men excited by watching the violence of a fight have a need to relieve

313

their high spirits. They will not return until late, and I will be long gone. *With Mademoiselle Françoise!*

"Nor will it do to follow me," he said with an evil look. "I will long since have made sure of the mademoiselle, you see." His eyes were hot and his hands perspiring at the thought, so much so he had to change the gun from one hand to the other as he wiped his damp palms along his trousers. "Oh yes. I'll make quite sure of her. I do not wish to force *ma petite,* but I will. Oh yes. I will if I must to be certain she is mine."

"It will not happen," said Madame serenely although inside she quailed. "You should have learned by now that my granddaughter is not for you."

"It will come to pass. It *will.* Just as I have planned!" Cheviot's eyes narrowed and a sinister little smile played around his mouth. "You may relieve your boredom, Madame, by imagining what comes to *you.* I'll not leave before achieving some small revenge for your slights to me, I assure you."

With a laugh which sent shivers up Madame's spine, he shut the door and locked it. When the sound of his steps receded to the lower floor, Madame la Comtesse rose from the bed on which she'd seated herself and tried the door. It was solid and far too heavy for two old women to break open. She turned to the window.

Pulling the bed away from the wall and into position, she climbed onto it and peered through the grimy pane. The window looked out over a narrow yard, across the neighboring yard, and on to a row of houses which had been abandoned. The windows had been boarded up, several displaying charred wood from the fire which had swept along from one house to the next some weeks earlier. Also, the window through which Madame peered was

314

far too small to climb through even if it would open—which it would not.

Having made her survey, Madame decided there was nothing to do but await rescue. She seated herself. "My old friend," she said kindly to the poor woman who had thought to be her hostess, "as the dreadful comte has said, it will do no good to snivel and weep. Sit down now and quiet yourself. Please do."

But the de Daunay woman would not be soothed and Madame la Comtesse resigned herself to the unpleasant company of a woman permanently on the verge of hysterics.

Françoise followed Elizabeth into the elegant, chandelier-lit passage along which lighted shop windows stretched on and on to the far end. Among such wonderful temptations, it would be simple to amuse oneself for an hour or two. A perfumery immediately caught Elizabeth's eye just as Françoise saw a window draped with a rainbow of ribbons. They separated without a thought in their heads regarding all the lectures given them concerning Françoise's safety.

The young French woman was debating between two blue ribbons of almost, but not quite, the same shade when she heard, just behind her, a softly feminine, lilting voice speaking in French. "Mademoiselle, I have a message for you. No, do not turn," insisted the hidden woman. Françoise froze, clutching the ribbons in her hand. "I will slip a note into your reticule, chére," said the soft voice. "You will look at those oh-so-beautiful ribbons for several minutes more before you read the note. Do not look for me. I am nothing more than a message carrier in any case and quite unimportant."

Françoise shivered. "Who—"

"Remember," cautioned the woman. "Wait some minutes . . ."

"Who are you?"

There was no response. For a long moment Françoise didn't dare to move. Then she turned and scanned the small shop, struggling against other patrons who crowded her close to the table. No one paid the least attention to her. No one looked as if they'd had a thing to do with her—but someone had recognized her, had accosted her, had given her a note. Someone, Françoise knew instinctively, who meant her no good.

Her hands shaking, she searched her reticule and found the folded bit of paper. The message was short and to the point: *Come without delay to the address below if you wish to see your grandmother alive. Tell no one. You are watched, and it will go badly with your friend if you do not obey.* Françoise shuddered. Again, still more surreptitiously, she looked around. Still she saw no one with any obvious interest in her. What could she do? *What could she do?*

Françoise scrambled through her mind for a way out of the trap which had been sprung. Oh, it was so terrible she could barely think. But, first, she must do nothing which would harm Elizabeth. That was very important. So how? Perhaps if she were to pretend to be ill, and they were to go home—perhaps she could find help there? Harriet? Harriet would know what to do.

Françoise pushed away from the table, wanting a bit of room where she would not be jostled from all sides, somewhere where she could *think*, but the Arcade was overly full that day, and there was no room to be had. Home. She pushed through the crowd until she reached the shop door. She had to go home. Frantic, Frani searched faces for Elizabeth's. She saw Big John, whose tall frame stood head and shoulders above everyone else. She threaded a way toward him, scattering apologies here and there as she stepped on a toe here or stumbled against someone there. She reached her quarry and, her eyes big with fright, stared up at him.

"John?" she said. "Where is Lady Halford, John? I do not feel well. I must go. At once, John."

The gentle servant frowned down at her, saw how white and pulled about she looked and then, raising his gaze, scanned the shoppers. He peered through the window of the shop his mistress had entered. She wasn't there. He looked into the next. "She is here, Mam'zelle, looking at silk stockings, I think. Follow me, little one."

Thankfully Françoise dropped in behind Big John and was swept along in his wake. "Elizabeth . . ." she began upon reaching her.

"Françoise? Do look. I cannot believe the price! They seem first quality, do they not?" She turned. "I think I'll have a dozen pair—Françoise? What . . . ?"

"I do not feel well. I am sorry, but may we go home? Now?"

"Of course, we may. Why did you not tell me? We should never have come if you were not well."

Françoise allowed herself to be scolded and petted and herded back to the carriage which awaited them near the entrance. She was silent on the drive back to Halford House and, after an attempt or two to find out what was wrong with her guest, Elizabeth, too fell silent.

I will have gotten Elizabeth out of it. She'll be safe at home, thought Françoise frantically. *But what next? Oh, if only the men had not gone away today. Why today of all days? Or,* she wondered, not being exactly stupid, *is that why today was chosen? Because, with them away, it*

*was a good day in which to abduct me again? I get so
tired of abductions. They are such a bore.* She closed her
eyes and turned her head against the squabs first one way
and then the other. *No. They are not a bore. They frighten
me, I think. Oh Harriet what must I do? Grand-mère . . .
Dear God nothing must happen to Grand-mère. . . .*

The carriage pulled up in front of the house. As Big
John opened the low door and put down the steps, it occurred to Françoise that the friend mentioned in the note
might mean Harriet and not Elizabeth as she'd first assumed. She opened her eyes wide, her flesh losing still
more color. She mustn't, couldn't, ask Harriet for help.
She mustn't endanger Harriet. The evil comte would kill
without compunction as he'd once tried to kill Grand-
mère with his poisons. It must not happen. Françoise
shuddered and reached for Big John as her knees buckled.

The huge man caught her, picked her up and, at a nod
from Elizabeth, carried his slight burden into the house
and straight up to the bedroom she still shared with Harriet.
Harriet was there and, taking one look at her charge's white
pinched features said Françoise must go to bed. Frani,
thinking of the order that she come immediately, grew very
nearly hysterical, accusing Harri of smothering her, moth-
ering her—demanded that she be left alone, that all she
needed was to sleep and not be disturbed. *Not at all.*

"Go away, Harri. Just go away and leave me alone,"
she wailed, deeply worried as it became obvious Harriet
meant to stay with her. "I don't want anybody. I don't
want *you.*"

That's true enough, thought Françoise, *but I don't mean
it as an insult, Harri—don't take it that way. Please don't
look so cold. Oh, Harri, if only I could tell you, could
explain . . .*

Huge tears dripped down Françoise's face as her beloved Harri turned away. Hungrily, Frani's huge eyes devoured the tall slim form of the woman she loved and admired so much. They'd never again see each other, and Harriet would never understand why she'd had to be so nasty, why she'd tricked her so . . .

Françoise's mind raced, but she turned her face away when Harriet looked back from the doorway. With a chilly reminder that she would stop in later, Harriet finally left, and Frani was alone. All alone.

There would be no rescue, no one coming at the last moment to prevent the evil comte from doing as he willed with her. But Grand-mère . . .

Whatever happened to herself, she must not fail her beloved grandmother. Nothing must happen to the valiant old lady simply because Françoise was too much a coward to face a future of utter misery with the comte as husband. A very brief picture of Monsieur de Bartigues flickered in and out of the girl's mind. She pushed it away, clamped down on even the possibility of ever knowing the joy of Yves' love, a possibility she'd recently begun to think very important indeed.

The house was quiet. Harriet had picked up a pile of books from the lending library before she'd left the room, quite obviously intending to return them. She was gone. Elizabeth had muttered it was just as well they'd come home because she'd too long avoided a discussion with the housekeeper concerning the inadequacies of the second housemaid. Elizabeth would be occupied in the small office near the housekeeper's rooms for some time if the situation were only half so dire as Elizabeth had suggested. Françoise tried to think where the servants would be at this hour, what they'd be doing. Enjoying their rest period, she decided, but it would not do for one of them to catch her sneaking out as she must now do and do quickly. She must be careful. *Nothing must happen to Grand-mère!*

Françoise opened the door to the hall. No one. Good. Quietly she opened the door to the backstairs and listened intently. Again no one. She slipped down the steps and crossed the hall into the little salon at the back of the house, where she looked around fearfully. Still no one.

Frani breathed in a huge breath and breathed it out again slowly. So far, so good. Crossing to the French doors at the back of the house, she peeked into the garden. Again no one.

Drawing in another big breath, Françoise opened the doors and slipped along the balcony to the stairs which would take her down into the garden. Once on the garden path, she stopped again, her whole body trembling. What if Elizabeth saw her from a window? A servant? What could she say? How could she convince someone, anyone, she'd no choice? She *must* do as ordered?

Calming herself, Françoise stared down the long beautifully planted garden toward the back gate. The bright flowers mocked her even as the gate beckoned. That was it. If she could reach that gate and slip through it, she'd be safe . . . or rather, she'd never be safe again. She'd be in the comte's hands. Françoise shuddered once again, gritted her teeth and moved swiftly down the gently curving path.

The gate. Her hands were on the latch. She lifted it. She slipped through the narrowest possible opening and closed it behind her.

Françoise leaned against the gate and allowed a few tears to slip down her cheeks. Had she truly hoped she'd be seen, be stopped? How foolish she was to hope for rescue when Grand-mère's very life depended on her.

With renewed determination, the girl walked down the

lley and along the street to where several hansom cabs
vaited in a row to be hired. Minutes later she was on her
vay to her fate. Frani stared blindly through the dirty
vindows not even noticing the smelly straw on the floor
or the musty odor coming from the squabs. Such things
didn't matter. Nothing mattered. Nothing would matter
ever again.

Far too soon they reached the address, and the driver
pulled his tired horse to a stop. "Here ye be, missy. Can't
hink why you'd want to come to a place like this, but
hat'll be five shillings, luv, there's a dear."

Françoise paid without arguing the outrageous amount.
She was doomed and the sooner she faced her doom, the
better it would be. There. The door to number thirty-five.
Climbing the steps, Françoise raised the knocker, allowed
it to fall.

Instantly the door opened. Wiry fingers grasped her
wrist. She was yanked into the hall, and the door
slammed.

It was done. Françoise was in the hands of the comte.

Across the street from number thirty-five two women
stared. They looked at each other and then strolled on.
"It was. I know it was," said the actress who had laid on
the bed and received Frani's earrings.

"What's that sweet minx doing here?"

"Ye don't think it was that man we were hired to fool,
do you?"

"Whatever one thinks about *that* sly business, she's no
call to be visiting someone who'd treat her like *that,* do
she now?"

The cab, which had gone on to the corner to find room
to turn, returned the way it had come. The actresses, act-

ing as one, waved it down. They haggled with the driver before climbing in. The journey seemed to the worried young persons to take forever, but soon enough they pounded on the Halford House door.

Marks opened it, took one look, and attempted to slam it shut. The blond actress put herself into the opening and would not move no matter what names Marks called her. "We have ta see someone," she insisted. "We have ta tell 'em what we seed. Now you slumguzzling ol' fool, you let us in or you'll be sorry, I tell you."

"The likes of you don't come to the front door and don't go around back because we don't want the likes o' you here at all." Marks again tried to push the door closed, pressing it into the woman.

"You stop that, you fat-bottomed, clapperdogeon, ol' jack pudding. You'll see . . ."

The argument concerning the butler's looks and ante-cedents might have gone on forever if Harriet hadn't chosen that moment to return from the lending library. Marks had to open the door for her and the women slipped in before her. "What is the problem, Marks?"

"These . . . *young persons* . . . insist they got news and must tell someone but it's an old trick, Miss Cole. They'll put their glims on what we got and where it is, then tonight or tomorrow night someone on the dub-lay— I mean *housebreakers*—will . . ."

But Harriet had had time to look the women over and held up her hand. "I believe we met in Dover," she said, quietly to the blond.

"Yes'm, miss. That we did. You tell that cod's head, here, we're honest, we are."

"Yes, I agree you are honest. Certainly you did your work well for us. Now, tell me why you've come. Please?"

"Rather tell one of the gentlemen," said the spokeswoman, looking away and back. "Might not be proper for a lady's ears."

Harriet frowned, looked at Marks who had *his* ears on the prick. She said, "Perhaps we should go into the back salon. Marks, please bring tea." Once she'd closed the door on the curious butler, Harriet continued, "I fear you'll have to reveal your secret to me. Lord Halford and his friends are gone for the day and although they've promised not to be late, I believe it will be sometime yet before they arrive."

The blond shook her head. "That's a shocker, that is." The woman sighed. "Rather tell a man which would be more proper-like, but since I can't and the little lady may h'got herself into hotter water than she knows, here's the way of it. . . ."

She described what they'd seen and Harriet glanced up at the ceiling, back to the women. "But that can't be. Frani came home from shopping quite done up. She insisted she only needed to sleep, that I was to go away—that no one was to bother her . . . !"

Harriet rose to her feet and lifted her skirts to an indecorous height. She raced from the room and up the stairs. For half a moment she hesitated to open the bedroom door. Then she did. She looked in. Empty. The dratted girl was gone!

Fool. Idiot.

Harriet didn't know if she referred to Françoise or to herself for not guessing something had happened to push her charge into such shocking and uncharacteristic incivility. Instead, she'd allowed herself to feel hurt that Frani could accuse her of smothering her when it had only been love and a care for the danger the girl was in that had made Harriet perhaps a trifle more careful, more watchful

323

than most chaperons. And then, because she'd allowe
those few hasty words to overset her, she'd failed in he
duty to protect Françoise when real danger appeared. B
she mustn't fail. She must go immediately to the rescue

Harriet opened a drawer in the dressing table and gen
tly removed one of her father's pistols. She checked
and put it in her reticule. When she looked into the mirro
she saw only a mental vision of Françoise. "I'm coming
child," she said softly. "I'm coming, Frani." Returnin
quickly to the salon, she asked the women to tell her hov
to find the house into which the French girl had bee
forced.

The two looked at each other, shook their heads. "Can'
tell you the number, but it's on Becclesway Street. Abou
half way down, I'd guess."

"*About* that. Maybe a little closer to the High than otherwise?" said the darker actress doubtfully, speaking fo
the first time.

"I could *show* you . . ." said the first.

Harriet frowned, deciding what was for the best. "
think you must come with me," she said, finally. "Then
perhaps you'd be kind enough to return and wait to show
the men where to come—just in case I have trouble. Le
me think. Ah. I'll leave a letter. Marks will let you in and
feed you . . . Can you think of anything else?" She looked
from one to the other.

"Sounds like you done thought of just about everything, it do," said the younger woman admiringly.

Harriet scribbled a quick letter to Lord Halford and
rang for Marks. She gave him directions concerning the
women's return and asked that a hack be called.

"You mean the carriage," he said, much on his dignity.

"If I'd meant a carriage I'd have said so. Marks, do not
argue with me. Time is important. I don't know quite . . ."

When she trailed off he said, "Perhaps I should call er ladyship—"

"Perhaps you should do as you are told!" snapped Harriet.

Harriet was usually the kindest of mistresses, never raising her voice and, as a result, she was well-liked by those serving the Halford household. Marks flushed royal purple at her reprimand, knowing he must have overstepped badly if Miss Harriet were so angry that she'd not only raise her voice but be scathing about it as well. He bowed and left the room. Harriet and the women followed. Soon they were on their way.

When they reached Becclesway, the jarvey pulled up and demanded his five shillings, not that he expected such luck as he'd had before with the dreamy little miss he'd brought earlier. A good thing he'd no such expectations. Harriet knew a point or two more than the devil, and even if the actresses hadn't gasped, warning her she was being cheated, she'd not have paid so much. She pressed what money she had in her reticule onto the actresses and told them to pay the man what was owed once they'd returned to the Halfords.

"I don't think the men will be late. They are to come straight back and not go on to one of the suppers so common after such affairs." She looked from one to the other. "Whatever happens, thank you. You've done well."

"Oh, well." The actresses looked to each other. "Only did what was right, you know."

They watched as Harriet approached number thirty-five. No one answered, and they watched her try the door which was, it turned out, on the latch. They saw her push it open and look into a dark hallway.

Waving the cabby to go on, Harriet entered the house, her fingers working at a knot to her reticule wishing she had the gun in her hand. Quietly, she moved toward the stairs. She was just beyond the sitting room door when with a rush, the comte came up behind her and pulled her back against him, his arms squeezing her tightly.

"How did you know where to come?" he growled in her ear.

"How could I not know where to come?" she asked irritated she'd been tricked so easily.

"She left the note behind her, did she? Stupid chi Hand it over."

Harriet immediately responded, "You think I've brought it with me?"

"The devil take it. You've been a plague, a bane, thorn in my flesh. I hate you."

"Thank you."

"Thank you? You thank me that I cannot stand the sigh of you?"

"Of course. For someone like yourself to *like* me would be the insult."

The comte stiffened, his arms squeezing her closer and beginning to pain her rather badly. Harriet wondered i she'd have a broken rib or two before he let her go. He upper arms were tight against her sides, but her lowe arms were free. Steadily she worked at the knot in he reticule ribbons. If only she'd not been in such a hurry to approach the house that she'd done them up badly after giving the actresses her money.

Suddenly, the comte released her, grabbed her by one elbow and swung her around. "Careful. You'll upset me," she said crossly.

"Upset you. I'll upset you." He yanked the reticule from her hands, ripped it open and dumped its contents on the floor. "Ah. I thought you'd have it. Fool. You

hould have had it in your hand when you entered. Twice
fool for coming at all."

"Someone had to come. The men were away." She
hrugged, eyeing his shaking hand which now pointed her
wn gun at her chest. "You might remember that gun has
hair trigger. Unless you wish to shoot me out of hand,
f course. But even if my friends allowed you to escape
ustice, which I don't believe for a minute, I don't think
he English authorities would care for it, do you? For
murder? So. What will you do now?" she finished as if
t weren't at all important.

"I'm going to think. But first I'm going to put you
vith the others. Up the stairs."

Hiding her relief the word "others" gave her—imply-
ng as it did that they were still alive and well—Harriet
urned. He hadn't killed Madame or her hostess. And
Françoise was, very likely, with the others. At the comte's
nsistence, she climbed. She didn't drag her feet, but she
lidn't hurry. At the top she saw the key in the door and
urned to look at the man.

"Open it," he ordered.

She did and looked around the small room. "Hello,"
she said brightly.

"Oh, Harri, not you, too!" Frani turned into Madame's
shoulder and began to cry.

"Come, Françoise," scolded Madame. "That is no way
to greet a friend, is it now?"

Frani raised a tear-wet face, straightened her shoulders.
"I'll be good," she said, setting her jaw.

"Excellent," praised her grandmother, patting her
granddaughter's shoulder gently while her eyes exchanged silent messages with Harriet's.

"Fools!" screamed the comte "Are you all fools that
you don't know what comes to you?"

327

"What comes to us comes," said Madame quietly. "W
will not rant and rave and cry and weep. We are not wea
females," she said ignoring the fact the old woman wa
quietly having still another fit of hysterics in her corn
of the cot. "We are of the de Beaupré family, you see.
she finished in a kind voice as if that explained the
behavior.

"*She* isn't. She's a doxy and a . . ." The comte slowl
grinned, his stained and rotting teeth not a pleasant sigh
"So, Mademoiselle Marplot! I have decided what I wi
do. What a revenge it will be! What sweet revenge!"

"I thought you said you would be leaving quite soon,
said Madame, thinking he meant to ravish Miss Cole an
leave her debauched. Setting that notion against he
granddaughter's needs left her in a quandary indeed.

"I will leave once I've destroyed that woman who ha
destroyed my plans twice now," he said and pointed
shaking finger at Harriet. "Destroying her, I will hav
revenge on the man who loves her, the man who has als
foiled me more than once. They will soon see they canno
sneer at the Comte de Cheviot. They will see. All of th
fools who pretend I am a no one will see."

"What will you do?" asked Madame.

"You will not have heard the name Ma Cooper?" H
looked at the bemused faces. "No? I will tell you. Sh
owns a bordello. A very special bordello that caters t
the very special tastes of men who have not quite th
normal sorts of desires. She supplies what is needed—fo
a price, of course. Comprehend?"

Madame paled and reached for Harriet's hand. Harrie
tossed her head, pretending not to care. Françoise stil
looked confused which, thought Harriet, was just as well

"I'll return. Far too soon for your peace of mind, I'l
return. Think what comes to you, vixen. Dream night

328

mares, the very worst you can think up! But you are too innocent, and they will not come close to the fate which will be yours once I've sold you to Ma Cooper!"

His evil laugh was muffled as the door was once again slammed and locked. The sound of his steps disappeared.

Sixteen

Françoise clutched at her grandmother's hand. "Grand-mère, what did he mean?"

"What he meant will remain incomprehensible to you, child. One hopes *forever* incomprehensible. He is not a good man."

"We *know* he's an evil man, but what would he do with Harriet?" Françoise looked from her grandmother to her friend and then, puzzled, forgot her question—much to the relief of her grandmother who hadn't a notion of how to explain the comte's threats. "Harri, what *are* you doing?" asked Frani.

"You can't think I wish to remain here to discover what plans our vicious comte has for me, do you?"

"No, of course not, but there is no way out. Truly."

"We'll see." Harriet had tested the door and discovered as Madame had before her its quality. She, too, looked out the small window, and wondered if she could squeeze through if she were to break out the frame . . .

"It's too small," said Françoise. "Even I could not get out of it could we get it open," added the girl, reading Harriet's mind. "We talked about that earlier." Her eyes followed Harriet's as her companion studied the small room. A few moment's later, she asked, sharply, "Why did you climb on that dresser? What are you doing?" asked Frani.

"What does it look like?"

"But there is nothing above the ceiling, surely . . . Harriet, did that corner give a little?"

"I think it did. Climb up here and help me push."

"But what good will it do?"

"I don't know, but if you've another suggestion, make it!" said Harriet a trifle crossly.

Françoise climbed up beside Harriet on the wobbly chest of drawers. She put her back against her friend's, and they pushed up, grunted, pushed again . . .

"Frani, I don't think we're working quite together. Now when I say three, *push,* all right?"

"Oui."

"One . . . two . . . *three . . ."*

"I believe," said Madame judiciously, "the edge bulged a trifle. Do try again."

"One . . . two . . . *three . . ."*

This time they felt the corner of the thin ceiling give and lift away from the wall. Twice more, and they'd pushed it as high as they could, leaving a ragged opening into a dark cavity only a few feet high. Dirt sifted down and, when Harriet pushed her head up into the opening, she came back down swearing softly and brushing furiously at the cobwebs covering her face.

"Oh dear. You cannot go up there, Harri," said Françoise with great seriousness.

"My child, of course I must go up there. I should have seen a wall within arms reach, you know. One built between this house and the next. But there was none. I can climb across to another house and come down into another room such as this and get help. Madame," she said, turning to their hysterical hostess, "have you a friend along the row of houses here? Someone who would help us?"

But nothing could make Madame de Daunay speak sensibly. She wailed and moaned and cried that they would all be killed and how could she have known? The man was a gentleman. He was a comte. How could she have known he was a murderer and would leave them all to die here alone and afraid and . . . ?

Harriet gave it up and turned back to the job at hand. "Frani, push up as hard as you can so that I may squeeze through more easily."

"But, truly, you mustn't."

"Of course I must. It is our only hope, my dear."

"No." Frani eyes widened painfully. "Spiders, Harri. Great fat spiders." She shuddered and actually looked ill.

Harriet put a hand on Françoise's shoulder, squeezed gently. "I must chance them," she said quietly. She'd forgotten Frani's one fear, a fear no one who knew her took lightly. "I'm sorry, child, but what may come to us if I do *not* go would be even worse than spiders. Believe me."

"Worse?"

"Far worse." The two young women stared at each other for a moment.

Françoise gulped. "All right, Harri. I'll be good."

"Yes, of course you will. Now, push!"

Harriet took a deep breath and pulled herself up into the dark cavity, which stretched ahead of her into black nothingness. She wished there'd been a lantern or even a candle to light her way, but, after a soft word to the women below, she started crawling along from rafter to rafter, carefully feeling her way and, under her breath, swearing at the clinging cobwebs and dust and dirt.

A ghostly vision of a smiling Sir Frederick floated before her eyes encouraging her. For a long moment she stared at the vision, swearing an oath that if she managed to come out of this adventure with her honor intact, she would go gladly to her love in whatever capacity he wished of her. . . . She'd even marry him, no matter what pain might come of it, because there would also be joy . . . great joy.

It seemed she'd moved slowly and carefully for hours, balancing from rafter to rafter, although it could not have been anything like so long. She put her hand out to find the next—and hit a brick wall, knocking herself off balance so that she fell against the thin ceiling of the house she was currently above. Her hand pushed right on down through the thin slats and plaster, her shoulder following.

A sudden shriek told her the room beneath her was not unoccupied. "Good," she said softly and, turning, put her feet through the hole she'd made. She enlarged it, sending plaster and dirt down onto the frightened little maid's bed, which only increased the child's screams. Once the hole was enlarged Harriet dropped into the room below. She picked herself up, turned—and faced an old-fashioned blunderbuss held in the shaking hands of an elderly man.

"Don't move an inch!" he ordered.

"I won't," she soothed. "But," she added, "you must help us."

The man wasn't listening, was obviously very nearly as frightened as his maidservant. "Don't move," he repeated. "I've sent for a runner, I have. He'll clap you in irons, housebreaking being an o-fense against the crown, it is. Don't you move now. Dangerous, you are, but don't you move, because I . . . Why are you grinning like a fool?"

"You've already sent for a runner? Wonderful. You are just wonderful," said Harriet, wishing she dared throw her arms around the man's neck. Then, remembering how dirty she was, she reconsidered. Surely no one would appreciate a hug, given her present condition! "Thank you," she said fervently.

"You think it a good thing? You're crazy." The old man set his jaw, scowled and resettled the gun, some of his fear fading. "Bedlam. You've escaped from Bedlam, 'tain't no tother explanation. Good thing," he muttered, "that I sent for a runner. A good thing, she says." He shook his head. "What is the world a coming to, that's what I want to know when a housebreaker wants the runners sent for! Says thank you and grins like a fool she does!"

He muttered some more while the poor maid cowered in a corner. Harriet lifted a hand to wipe away some of the cobwebs tickling her face, but thought better of it when the gun was raised an inch. She sighed. How long, she wondered, before the runner arrived? How long did they have before the comte returned and found her gone? What would he do?

Harriet had decided the Frenchman was not quite sane, that his long pursuit of Françoise had, at some point, turned an already weak mind. The insane did not behave as others, and she feared that if he returned before she could bring help, he might kill the others out of hand— except for poor Françoise, of course!

"How long will it take your runner to arrive?" she asked politely, her heart beating fiercely in anticipation.

"Too soon for you, you pretty felon. He'll take you off in chains to Newgate, he will. You'll like that?"

"He'll listen to my story and help us."

"Story! He'll listen to my story. Just look at that ceiling. Look at the damage you've done to my ceiling. Oh, yes. He'll listen, he will. He'll listen to me lay charges!"

Luckily for Harriet, one of the more intelligent of the Bow Street Runners arrived. He looked at Harriet, obviously a young woman with money behind her, if the value of her clothing and her poise meant anything, and he looked at the ceiling about which the irate homeowner continued to rant.

"Now," he said, in a slow country voice, "we'll just sort this all out. You've a story, you say?"

"I was held with three other women in a room much like this by an evil man who would marry one of us. We managed to push up the ceiling, and I crawled through under the roof. I came this far before I came down through that hole. Send to Lord Halford's residence if you require proof of what I say and who we are, but hurry. The man will return and when he does—well, I fear he may kill the others if he finds me gone. Won't you please help us?"

"Well, now. Evil abductors and heroines. Good as a play this is," said the runner, his gaze speculative.

"You must believe me." Harriet thought furiously, trying to come up with a means of convincing him. "I know. Come back with me to where they are held. Madame la Comtesse and Mademoiselle Françoise and the house owner, Madame de Daunay are locked in that room. That would be proof, would it not?"

The runner pursed his lips. "I think maybe it would," he agreed, ignoring the old man's pleas.

"Here now, ain't you going to arrest the jade? Ain't you going to carry her off in chains to Newgate?"

"Not until I find out the truth of her tale. Don't worry, she won't escape me," the runner soothed the old man. "Now, miss, up with you. Can you make it?"

Scratching her arms rather badly, and almost sick with fear for the safety of those she'd left behind for what seemed far too long a time, Harriet, helped by the runner, forced a way back up under the roof. She made her way carefully along the rafters, but this time had, so faint it was barely visible, a triangle of dim light ahead of her where the ceiling had been forced up. Keeping her eyes on it, she made better time and soon looked down into the room.

"Has he come back?" she whispered.

"Harriet! *Mon Dieu,* we thought you'd never come," said Françoise fervently. "Did you bring help?"

"Yes. A runner. Sir, if you'll back up a bit, I'll turn and get back down with my friends." Again it took careful maneuvering, but Harriet managed to lower herself to the chest and from there to the floor. "Sir?" she called.

"I see you. Look out below," he said and, making far less work of it than Harriet had done, soon stood before them. His first action was to try the door and discover that it was, indeed, locked. His next was to bow to Madame who nodded her head in such a regal manner he'd not have been surprised to discover she were royalty rather than mere aristocracy—and French at that! He soon had the whole story of the comte's persecution of Françoise, of how he had been foiled in the past and how, this time, he'd so very nearly succeeded.

"So he's gone to collect Ma Cooper, has he? Maybe he doesn't know this is her day for driving in the park. That's why he's not back yet, you see. I wonder if he'll wait for her. We've been looking for a way of shutting up that house of hers for a long time now. If she's really coming to buy you, miss, then you'll have done a prime service to your countrymen—or rather to the women she uses—if you'll just cooperate with me. Ah, but we must be sure she actually pays your comte to take you away or we've got no case, you see." He grinned. "Course,

336

what might make you happy, if you think on it, if we get a case against Ma that way, we got a case against your comte, too, you know—because if she's a buying, then he must be a selling. . . ." He eyed Harriet. "Can you trust me to see you safe? You'll have to play a part, you see, and you'll have to wait for the very last minute before rescue."

"But what of Madame? What if he . . ." Harriet couldn't finish.

"You fear he may come up here and put a bullet through the old women before taking you down to Ma Cooper?" The runner rubbed his chin. "I guess I'd better call for help. Someone can wait up in that space with a gun." He gestured to the ceiling. "We won't let your villain harm any one of you. So, *can* you play the part?" he asked sternly, staring at Harriet.

She bit her lip, looking at Madame for advice. Madame said, "I think you must, Harriet. Do not worry for us. The man says we will be safe."

Harriet shook her head. "I cannot help but worry, Madame, but I'll do my part," she said.

"Then I'd best go arrange things. Now, you all don't worry. I won't be gone from the street. If the villain arrives, and I'm not ready, I won't try to play the game all by myself." He smiled at the women, swung up on the chest, and moments later, disappeared into the dark.

"Well," said Madame.

"Is it well? I can't believe he'll have time to arrange what must be arranged."

"He said he'd not let any of us be hurt," said Françoise, hesitantly. "Does that mean I won't have to go with the comte?"

"Yes. You've been saved again, Frani. I think you must have a guardian angel who works all the hours there are in order to protect you." Harriet chuckled, the relief of it all making her a trifle light-headed.

"It is not to be laughed about, that guardian angel," said Madame fiercely. "I have often prayed to that angel that it come to Françoise's aid, and I have always been answered. Today I have been answered still again, although not in the way I had thought to ask! It was not *you* who were to come to our rescue, Harriet, but Sir Frederick and his friends. I cannot think how my prayers could have been misheard this way," she said a trifle peevishly. "They never have in the past."

"I wouldn't concern myself, Madame. The ways of Heaven are ever mysterious," said Harriet.

"So they are. Now, Marie, haven't you understood? We are to be rescued. Help is at hand. Cease your crying and remember you are a lady!" Madame shook her old friend. When that didn't help, she slapped her lightly on one cheek and then the other. "At once! Stop this. *We will be rescued.*"

"But my ceiling! My important boarder! My tea is ruined! My life . . ."

"Nonsense. I will see that your ceiling is mended."

"You will?" Madame de Daunay began to calm.

"We can brew fresh tea," suggested Harriet.

The formerly hysterical woman looked surprised and then muttered, "I never thought of that."

"You will find yourself another important boarder," said Madame. Here her old acquaintance looked skeptical, but Madame went on without allowing her to deny the possibility. "Your life is *not* ruined, but think how terrible life would be for my precious Françoise if the comte had his way. *Her* life would truly be in shreds if he had taken her away."

The old woman's eyes widened, her returning confusion obvious. "But why do you say so? He wishes to marry her, does he not? I do not see why you have not arranged the match with all possible speed. When I was young, my father would have been delighted in such a match."

"He's a terrible creature. You believe I should give my granddaughter into the hands of one such as *he?*"

"He is a comte," said the old lady stubbornly.

"Bah. He is of the new aristocracy and is nothing. *Nothing.* Never shall my Françoise wed such a one."

Madame de Daunay blinked. "But—"

"Never."

While the two old women argued, the runner returned to the house at the end of the street. He finally convinced the old man that four women were truly being held prisoner, and, once that was accomplished, he sent his servant off to Bow Street for yet another runner, a note from the first explaining what was wanted held tightly in the boy's fist.

Once that was in motion, the runner went outside to reconnoiter. He was in time to see three men, none of whom looked like the women's description of the comte, pounding on number thirty-five's door. He strolled down the street and, approaching the arguing men, he eavesdropped shamelessly.

"I still say," insisted Halford, "that we can't just go haring off without some notion of what has happened."

"You don't know the comte," said Yves desperately. "We must follow at once if we are to save my poor Fra . . . I mean, mademoiselle from his clutches. He will . . ." He couldn't finish the terrible thought of what de Vauton-Cheviot would do to Françoise the instant he felt himself safe to ravish her, stopping at an inn . . . or perhaps even in the carriage . . . !

"Calm down. We do not know that they've left yet, o—
if they have, how they travel. For instance he may b—
inside and not wish to answer the door, knowing we'—
thwart his plans. The best thing is to knock up the neigh—
bors and see if anyone has heard or seen anything. Surel—
if a traveling coach loaded with baggage left this stree—
today, someone will have noticed it and can describe it—
Come now. You, Yves, cross the street and ask there—
Robert, you take the houses on that side, and I'll go thi—
way . . . excuse me," he added, turning and bumping int—
the runner.

"Don't think I will, not if you're going to be a marplo—
just when I'm about to lay a real villainess by the heels—
Jeremy Wickens, Bow Street," he added, showing his ba—
ton of office, which he'd had hidden under his coat.

"Villainess? What villainess?" asked Yves. "We'r—
here to stop a *villain.*"

"A very brave lady inside has agreed to help bring ar—
evil woman to justice, she has, and I don't think she'd b—
too happy with you if you interfere with our plans. O—
the other hand, if you've a mind to, you can help th—
course of justice," Jeremy finished, looking from one t—
the other.

"As Yves said, we've a villain to catch."

"Hmm." Jeremy nodded. "That'd be your comte. —
heard all about the comte from the little mam'selle. Sill—
man, I think. But if he takes money from Ma, which —
think he'll do, mind, he'll be im-pli-cated in selling —
woman into slavery, won't he? And *that's* against Englisł—
law. So. We can take the man when we take the woman—
Howsoever that may be, it's Ma Cooper I'm after, now—
and you just remember that, hmm?"

"Slavery?" asked Halford, curiously.

"Ma Cooper!" said Frederick, horrified.

340

"What are you talking about? Françoise is in there and frightened and we must rescue her. At *once*," said Yves, his mind capable of only the one thought as long as his love was in danger.

"Ma Cooper," repeated Sir Frederick. "de Vauton-Cheviot intends to sell my Harriet to that woman? Does Harriet have any notion what that means?"

"I think you'll find she has a fair idea," said Jeremy calmly. "She wants to cooperate," he added warningly when Sir Frederick seemed about to charge the closed and locked door and batter it down with his bare fists.

The men argued, Frederick insisting the runner must not put Harriet into danger, that there was no telling the many ways things might go wrong. Finally the runner convinced him that Harriet truly wished to help put the vicious Ma Cooper in prison.

"Yves," said Frederick, sighing, "stop sputtering. Do you think I'm any less worried about my Harriet than you are about Mademoiselle Françoise? They are safe enough for the moment, at least. Much as I dislike the idea, we'll have to wait to rescue them until the time is right. You've a plan?" asked Frederick, turning back to the runner.

"I do. And, since you're here and my colleague is not, then you'll have to follow orders, you hear that, good-fellow-my-lad?" he asked, turning on Yves.

"But Frani—she must be terror-stricken . . ."

"That the little dark-haired one?"

"Yes. Beautiful dark hair . . ."

"Well, last time I saw the chit, she didn't look affeared to me. Her back was straight and she stood beside her grandmama and looked as if threats of that French invention of the devil, Madame Guillotine, wouldn't make her turn a hair. She'll do," he added, high praise indeed from a man who'd always considered women more a nuisance than a help. "They'll *all* do except maybe that watering pot what owns this ken—er, house, I mean." He shook his head at his lapse into thieves' cant. "Now then, I' tell you my plan. . . ."

The men put their heads together, and soon Yves was sent to take his place above the women's prison room where he could spy on the comte's entrance there. Also while waiting, he could talk to his Françoise and reassure her. Moreover, he swore he'd shoot without compunction if it looked as if the comte meant to kill the older women before taking away the younger—but only if it came t that. Lord Halford hid behind his carriage a bit down the street. Sir Frederick, removing his jacket, hat, and crava rolled up his sleeves and squatted with the runner an dice in the area next door to number thirty-five. The waited. And waited. The runner began to wonder if th comte had gotten cold feet and decided to leave th women locked up while he made a run for the coast.

Just as everyone was about to give up in disgust, seedy carriage pulled up in front of the watched house An irate comte jumped down, handed the jarvey a coi and turned to help an exceedingly fat woman to th ground. "I tell you time is of the essence. We must hurr if all is not to be lost!"

"Hold your bonebox. At my age you don't hurry fo any reason at all." Ma stood there getting her breath whil the comte went to the door and unlocked it. "Now, yo say she's a real lady, do you? Don't know as I believ you. No real lady would be caught dead in this stree Not a coming here all by herself, she wouldn't."

"Come and see for yourself." The comte did everythin, but jump up and down in his nervous desire to be gone

342

You can judge if I'm telling the truth or not. One look at her will tell you."

"Proud as the devil himself, you said," said the woman, a speculative note to her voice.

"Prime goods, I tell you. Chaste and proud and not easily broken. I promise." The comte hopped from one foot to the other. "Come. Do come."

The two entered the house conveniently forgetting to close the door. The runner and Sir Frederick immediately took up positions on either side of it, their ears cocked to what was going on inside.

"Well, now. Where is the goods, hmm?"

"Upstairs. I've locked her in with the others at the top of the house."

"Then get her, fool. Don't think I'll climb myself up all those steps do you? Not when I've the girth on me *I've* got. Foolish man. Get her now if you're in such a hank."

"Such a what?" asked the confused comte, his foot on the bottom step, but half turned to question her.

The woman sighed. "Hank. A hurry. You are the one to insist time is of prime importance. Get her."

"All right. All right. I'll get her."

The fat woman whistled softly through her teeth while she waited. It wasn't long. Within minutes the comte returned, Harriet ahead of him, her arm forced into an uncomfortable position behind her back. She stared at the fat woman who stared back, still whistling.

"Did I lie? Did I? Is she gentry or is she not?"

"You didn't lie about that, now did you? But she's older than I like. Can't offer more'n a monkey for one so long in the tooth as that. Even that's too much."

"A monkey! Only five hundred? You'll make twice that on her first time out!"

343

"Yes, but then I won't make much beyond it. Only virgin goods is worth so much. Those old goats who think virgin blood'll cure 'em of what ails 'em are fools, that they are." She laughed vilely. "And you know what's said about fools, now."

"Hand over the money. I haven't all day. I must be on my way with the other one."

"Other one?" The fat woman ceased to dig through the slits in her many petticoats, hunting for the one in which she'd put the roll of soft with which she'd pay for her new girl. "Maybe I'd pay better for the other one." She pulled out the money at last, counted it quickly and handed it over.

The comte grabbed it. "You can't have the other one. She's mine. I'll marry her as soon as we reach France and I'll never have to worry ever again . . ." Suddenly the comte's eyes goggled, widening until the whites showed all around. *"You! You're at a prizefight!"* he screamed as Sir Frederick entered the house right behind the runner.

"It only lasted four rounds, but really, Cheviot, this is becoming tedious," said Frederick softly. "But this time you've gone too far. *This* time English law will put you away where you can harm no one for many a long year. Perhaps for the rest of your miserable life. Still better perhaps you'll hang, Cheviot. I hope so. Once too often you've terrified the innocent. You must pay, Comte, and pay you will."

"Hear now? What's this?" The fat woman had backed into a corner. Now she turned and waddled down the short hall toward the back of the house, where she hoped to find an escape route . . . but, of course, she didn't reach it. The runner was onto her and, shrugging, she returned to the others. "So, now what?" she grumbled, a sour look at the comte who had finally, after much talk, tempted her to come for Harriet. "What happens now?"

"Now I take you and the Frenchie to Bow Street where you'll be charged with the buying and selling of human flesh. Slaves can't be bought and sold in England, you know."

"Who said anything about slavery?" asked the woman. "Don't know what you're thinking, dearie, but nothing like that going on here. No, no. Nothing like that," said the fat woman, her eyes wide open with obviously pretended innocence.

"You just come along, Ma, and no arguments. This time we've got you and no mistake."

"Now, you don't want to bring that poor, sweet innocent into court, do you?" asked the woman, her tone wheedling. The runner refused to answer, and she turned to Sir Frederick whom, she assumed, would be easier to convince. "You won't want the world to know how near your lady, there, came to becoming dirty goods, do you?"

"Won't need to, Ma," interrupted the runner. "Sir Frederick and I'll be witness enough you gave money to the comte. He was selling her, and you was buying her. And that ain't allowed, Ma. Her name never need come into it."

The woman slumped, and she didn't try anything else. She was an evil woman, but she was a realist. She knew when she was beaten. The comte was a different matter. He ranted and raved until the runner was tired of it. When a second runner appeared at the doorway, the two were put in his charge and carted off to Bow Street where they would disappear from society's eyes forever.

Jeremy saw them off and returned to find that Sir Frederick had taken Harriet into his embrace and held her close. The runner shrugged and started up the stairs

345

to release the other women. He returned with the others behind him and found that Lord Halford was leaning in the doorway, his eyes on his friend, and a smile on his face.

Sir Frederick's murmurs could be heard by all. "My dearest love. My precious love. Don't ever frighten me like that again, do you hear me? I'm getting too old for this sort of adventure. Oh, my dear heart, my girl, my Harriet . . . Marry me? Please? I can't stand this . . . not ever again, Harriet. I must have you close. You don't know how I feared for you. You must never leave my sight again. Harriet?"

Harriet turned up her face, looked at him. He looked at her. Then the two were reaching, clutching, their lips meeting in something very close to desperation. Frederick's arms moved, his hands molding her into him as if he wished right then to make the two of them one flesh. Slowly the desperation turned to a gentler passion and then, slowly to love and affection. Finally, he lifted his face to look deep into her eyes. "Marry me?"

Harriet's head cleared enough to look around. She blushed as she found Françoise cuddled next to Yves and smiling at her, a frowning Madame seated in regal dignity on a straight-backed chair someone had found for her, and Marie de Daunay with her mouth agape, obviously shocked nearly out of her wits by such goings on. The runner, Halford and Monsieur de Bartigues merely grinned.

"Now I've compromised you utterly, and you must marry me," Sir Frederick whispered dramatically into one dust covered ear. Gently he brushed a cobweb from Harriet's hair.

"Utterly compromised?" she returned, smiling mistily.

"Well, not quite, but it can be arranged if you wish it,"

he answered. *"I* would prefer an outrageously extravagant wedding at Saint George's, Hanover Square."

Tears of happiness glistened in Harriet's eyes. Somehow during her adventure, all her fears for their future had vanished. Now, in his arms, all was right with her world. "How amazingly conventional of you," she teased.

"But how publicly I would proclaim to the world that, in the hands of the right woman, even the boldest of rakes may be reformed!"

"I think, Sir Frederick," interrupted Madame, "that, given your current behavior, *reformed* may not be quite the correct word. You will unhand my servant at once—"

Sir Frederick glowered, holding Harriet closer.

"—until I myself may see to the immediate arrangement of a wedding." Sir Frederick raised a brow, but Madame hadn't finished. *"Disgraceful,* Harriet," she scolded, her twinkling eyes contradicting her tone. "How could you lend yourself to such terrible impropriety in front of Françoise? My granddaughter, as well you know, has far too many rash notions in her head as it is. She is not in need of further instruction in improper behavior!"

Françoise, flirting up at Yves, confirmed she did, indeed, have rash notions of her own. There was a distinctly speculative look in her eye, one returned by the young Frenchman holding her so comfortingly close.

Madame, observing this, modified her plan. There will be, she instantly decided, *two* weddings to celebrate—and then, with Françoise married and the comte at long last no more danger to anyone, she could retire to her beloved home on the banks of Lake Como and live out the rest of her life in splendid peace and quiet. Madame eyed Harriet and decided she'd have only one regret: she'd be unable to take the young English woman home with her.

Where, after all, wondered Madame la Comtesse, could she find another companion with a knowledge of English cant!

Dear Reader,

So! Sir Frederick turned out to be less of a villain than might have been expected when one finished Lady Jo's story, *The Widow And The Rake* (Zebra, November, 1993 [ISBN, 0-8217-4382-1])!

My next book will be a Christmas Regency, available in November 1994: Ernestine Matthewson is sent to Portugal, charged with convincing her widowed sister to return to her father's house in England, where she belongs. But Ernie's older sister, Lenore Lockwood, insists that her missing-in-action, believed-dead husband still lives. Ernie is appalled to discover how the denial of grief has affected Lenore. She vows that *she'll* never chance such misery by marrying a soldier—a vow which makes falling in love with Colonel Lord Summerton a serious error!

Happy reading!
Jeanne Savery

P.S. Letters sent to *Jeanne Savery, P.O. Box 1771, Rochester, MI 48308* will reach me. I would enjoy hearing from my readers; if you wish a response, please enclose a stamped, self-addressed envelope!

A Memorable Collection of Regency Romances

BY ANTHEA MALCOLM AND VALERIE KING

THE COUNTERFEIT HEART　　　　　　(3425, $3.95/$4.95)
by Anthea Malcolm

Nicola Crawford was hardly surprised when her cousin's betrothed disappeared on some mysterious quest. Anyone engaged to such an unromantic, but handsome man was bound to run off sooner or later. Nicola could never entrust her heart to such a conventional, but so deucedly handsome man. . . .

THE COURTING OF PHILIPPA　　　　　(2714, $3.95/$4.95)
by Anthea Malcolm

Miss Philippa was a very successful author of romantic novels. Thus she was chagrined to be snubbed by the handsome writer Henry Ashton whose own books she admired. And when she learned he considered love stories completely beneath his notice, she vowed to teach him a thing or two about the subject of love. . . .

THE WIDOW'S GAMBIT　　　　　　　(2357, $3.50/$4.50)
by Anthea Malcolm

The eldest of the orphaned Neville sisters needed a chaperone for a London season. So the ever-resourceful Livia added several years to her age, invented a deceased husband, and became the respectable Widow Royce. She was certain she'd never regret abandoning her girlhood until she met dashing Nicholas Warwick. . . .

A DARING WAGER　　　　　　　　　(2558, $3.95/$4.95)
by Valerie King

Ellie Dearborne's penchant for gaming had finally led her to ruin. It seemed like such a lark, wagering her devious cousin George that she would obtain the snuffboxes of three of society's most dashing peers in one month's time. She could easily succeed, too, were it not for that exasperating Lord Ravenworth. . . .

THE WILLFUL WIDOW　　　　　　　(3323, $3.95/$4.95)
by Valerie King

The lovely young widow, Mrs. Henrietta Harte, was not all inclined to pursue the sort of romantic folly the persistent King Brandish had in mind. She had to concentrate on marrying off her penniless sisters and managing her spendthrift mama. Surely Mr. Brandish could fit in with her plans somehow . . .

Available wherever paperbacks are sold, or order direct from the Publisher. Send cover price plus 50¢ per copy for mailing and handling to Penguin USA, P.O. Box 999, c/o Dept. 17109, Bergenfield, NJ 07621. Residents of New York and Tennessee must include sales tax. DO NOT SEND CASH.